I0585320

RACING THE SUN

J. R. Koop

ABRECAN BOOKS

ADELAIDE, SA

Racing
the
Sun

J.R. KOOP

ABRECAN BOOKS

Adelaide, South Australia 5000

Publisher's Note: This is a work of fiction. Names, characters, places, and incidents are a product of the author's imagination. Locales and public names are sometimes used for atmospheric purposes. Any resemblance to actual people, living or dead, or to businesses, companies, events, institutions, or locales is completely coincidental.

Book Layout © 2017 BookDesignTemplates.com

Cover Art & Illustrations © Sylvia Bi

Map © Jasmine Rose Koop

Racing the Sun/ J.R. Koop -- 1st ed.

Print Edition: ISBN-13: 978-0-6485244-0-3

E-book Edition: ISBN-13: 978-0-6485244-1-0

AUTHOR'S NOTE

This book is for anyone who has had to fight to be who they are, like my future wife: a Bangladeshi Muslim who immigrated to Australia at 10. She showed me what the Summer Lands could be, a home of her own invention. A new home for us. Working on this book together helped us through losing her parents in coming out. Much of this story is inspired by our own. I hope it may help others like us.

For the years spent daydreaming

The Neverworlds swirl in her sight. After the feasts, she will depart for Ajrapur, following her family who left days ago. She had lied to stay behind; told them that she needed to lead the prayers and give thanks to her patron, the goddess Kaiduko. Really, she can't stand to see the love of her life marry her brother for the sake of peace.

Pain sparks through her ribcage as she returns to the mortal plane. Kneeling before the low altars of the dream goddess' temple, Iliyah Tyrikaara whips back the golden veil from her ebony hair. The marble floor beneath them thrums with power, with wrongness.

But this cannot be. Her vision must not become truth.

'Send for a messenger,' barks the Praitosí princess, rising to her feet. The candles at the altar sputter out, the oxygen snuffed from the room. Iliyah turns on her fellow dream weavers gathered on the wide steps behind her. As the future High Priestess, they look to her with wide, expectant eyes. So, they have not seen what the Neverworlds showed her.

'Someone find my brother,' she demands, gathering her skirts in her hands as she descends the dais. Saadi will need to know of this news. For if their aunt Nisha is coming for them, then they must fortify the wards of the palace. Even Ajrapur across the border will not be safe.

One of the younger priestesses rises from her knees. She's so young she has barely a freckle of the gift. But she is skilled with the tapestries of time. 'My lady,' she breathes, her urgent voice echoing off the domed ceiling of the ancient temple.

But Iliyah's eyes find the threat before it can be spoken.

The woman in black stands at the open doors of the inner-temple. A dark aura ripples off of her, clouding the room. The priestesses unfortunate enough to be nearest her are frozen in time, their forms unflinching as the banished sorceress strolls further into the temple.

If the wards were new, she would not be able to enter.

'I assume you have seen what is to come,' purrs the sorceress, her pointed teeth glinting in the candlelight. There's the silver glow of madness in her eyes.

Iliyah flicks her hand at an armoured guard by the side entrance. 'Fetch the Crown Prince,' she orders again, knowing that it is already too late. 'Tell him I am dead.'

The shocked silence of her followers echoes in the silent dome.

'A shame,' drawls Nisha, running her hands over the shoulders of kneeling priestesses who tense beneath her touch. Iliyah lifts her chin in defiance as her aunt approaches, the darkness rippling behind her. 'Rahat will be so broken.'

Iliyah releases the folds of her gown; the muslin whispers as it falls against her dark skin. 'Leave her out of this,' she growls, hands balling at her sides. Her fingertips grow warm, but her magic does not come. Could her aunt be blocking her gift?

Nisha eyes her niece's throat and the gems that rest there. 'I don't think that's possible.'

Taking a step back up the stairs to the altar, Iliyah throws up a hand for the others. 'Close the doors; mark the gates! No matter what you must do, keep her contained!'

But Nisha moves so quickly, Iliyah does not catch her movements until she feels the hand in her chest. With her claws wrapped around her heart, the sorceress grins. The world about them stills, the warmth banished from this cold temple. Iliyah feels the arctic arching through her torso.

'At last,' the sorceress sighs, bringing Iliyah to her knees, soul in hand.

Delorran will have to find itself another hero. For Rahat is no saviour. How can she save them when all she dreams of is running?

'Rahat!'

The *rajkumari* leaps out of her skin—seconds before her brother Karnan brings his scimitar down hard on her sabre. The blades scream. This blow is harder than the last, throwing her off-balance. Any harder and he'll have her backed into a corner.

They've been at this for hours now; waiting, dreading the moment that this all becomes real. It won't ever feel real. The red *mehendi* lacing her hands peels against the sword's hilt. Deep red, those strokes are laced across her hands as final as a death warrant.

'Is that all you got?' sniggers her brother as he spins the grip on his scimitar. The ruby in its hilt glints, sparking in the sunlight whilst she hides in the shade.

With a growl ripped from her lips, she lunges, forcing Karnan back. The ill-aimed lunge forces her against the nearest pillar, the sandstone catching at her trousers. Not missing a beat, Karnan raises his blade to his sister's throat with a grin. She gulps.

And just like that, she knows she's lost. Her mind has gotten the better of her. Time is laughing, denouncing her for the fool she is. For each breath brings her closer to that moment. That *moment*. It may have been her idea, but it doesn't make this any easier. Everything is going to change. And soon, she'll have to leave her brothers behind.

'Where is your *head* today?' demands their brother Ashrit from the garden steps. The Crown *Rajkumar* of Delorran paces, wringing his hands behind his back. In the glaring sunlight, his features are harsh, his raven hair mussed, unruly. The polar opposite of Karnan, younger by only two years. 'Honestly, Rahat,' he huffs. Mere days ago, his world was torn apart. 'You know his moves—how are you *losing*?'

The *Rajkumari* Rahat Brijesh turns away, wishing more than anything to curl in on herself and be left alone. They cannot save her from this, though she can save them. She will save them all.

If only.

Her painted hands take better grip on the sabre, but they don't feel like her own. Their laced lines serve a reminder that there's no way out of this mess. Rahat will end the war. The Praitosí Empire will recede; they'll leave Delorran and return its lands to its people. And her people will thrive once more—because of her.

Too bad she can't do it.

Enslaved by the Empire for ten years, and *she* is meant to save them?

They chose the wrong hero.

Karnan's sword blocks her blow. The reverberations are painful sparks up her arm, bringing her back to the present. She's only nineteen; she's rarely left the palace —how can she save an entire country, an entire culture, by herself?

'Dammit, Karnan!' she gasps out, pressing him back with a playful swat of her blade against his.

'Pay attention!' orders their brother, irate in the heat. His *kurta* hugs him tight, the cotton stuck to his skin with water from one of the hundreds of fountains scattered throughout the palace grounds. The water's sprinkling touch is gentle and cool against their flushed skin.

Beside him stands their uncle Badal, brother to the Maharaja, his bird's eyes glaring with unwavering intensity. Sheltered beneath the palace balconies, his dusky features are hidden in shadow. At his brow sits a bright *tilak*, a blessing marked by a priestess that morning. A religious man, Badal keeps his hand over his heart as he watches his niece. For not even he can keep his mind from the coming storm.

Turquoise trousers swim about her legs in gleaming layers as Rahat spins, raising her sabre over her head and lunging with calculated movements as if this were her ceremonial dance. She's been practicing these steps her whole life.

Music trails down from a balcony overhead. Inside, her sisters and fellow dancers are practicing for tonight. The reminder is an unpleasant shudder down her spine. She should be up there with them, practising.

Karnan gives his sister a sideways glance as that sleek grin crosses his features.

Light on her feet, she keeps herself from slipping into the performance, instead becoming one with her weapon as she breathes in the sizzling heat. It's no mere coincidence that her dance simulates battle. Her hair mats at her nape as she leaps, bringing down her sword on her brother's. Over the weapons, the music trailing from above engulfs them.

It sounds like freedom.

Elaborate moves soon have Karnan captivated. As his sister dances back, brandishing her sword as if it were an extension of herself, he ties his crimson sash about his waist. It appears like they're about to dance the Khumaani to the beat, when Ashrit halts in his pacing. The Crown *Rajkumar* sighs as he unsheathes his scimitar with a hiss of metal. Rolling his shoulders, he brushes Karnan aside with a single wave.

'Rahat,' he breathes, the name hardly heard to her ears as she stills her turn. The beat of the dhol drums rain down on them. '*Rahat.*'

She still itches to dance—to lift her hands together and toss up her skirts with high kicks. But she can see the people watching from the palace windows. Young, old, they all stop to witness the bride before her wedding day.

Down another level of the courtyard, foreigners watch the celebrated princess. She's a wonder whispered across the continents. They all wait for her to dance.

Yet she brings herself to a pause. Her silks shimmer with motion.

The windows empty of her audiences.

Her eldest brother stands before her, sword in hand.

She flashes that grin, and without warning, he lunges. The blow's aimed at her side, but she quickly deflects. The swords collide almost clumsily. The scream of steel makes her wince as she retreats. Ashrit's brows are knit, his eyes soldering as he stares her down. 'You don't understand,' he growls under his breath as he throws another blow, using both hands as he swings his blade.

Dropping the sabre to her side, she narrowly misses the bite of his sword. It scrapes the stone ground.

'Ashrit—'

Badal shoots his nephew a glance as Karnan strips himself of his sash. The swath of red falls to his feet as he takes ahold of the twin daggers at his belt. His sister is struggling and the strain is showing. Each block comes with a scream, making Karnan itch to intervene. But they move so quickly he fears he'll harm them both.

'Ash!' he screams.

His brother doesn't deign a response. For days this has been building. The fury radiating from his brother is enough to make Karnan feel sick. He's been waiting for this—waiting for the moment when Ashrit would finally snap.

Guess he couldn't hide the truth for long.

Karnan screams again, 'Ashrit!'

This time their uncle steps forward, holding his hands out in suppliance. Rahat is no more than a swirl of ebony hair and turquoise and gold as she parries their brother, her movements and footwork perfect—just the way her uncle taught her.

A hissed intake of breath makes Ashrit pause, his muscles locking as he watches his sister. Sweat coats her face in a thin sheen, though he tells himself it's the shine of the fountain's spray. Again he attacks, leaping forward with scimitar raised. This time Rahat screams, throwing up her hands without thinking.

The sabre clatters at her feet.

And, captured in the second of a gasp, Ashrit stops himself.

The blade stops short of Rahat's face, making her yelp when she at last opens her eyes. It's as if Ashrit's frozen time. Around him even the air is still. As Rahat sucks in a shaking breath, she stills her hammering heart. He could have killed her.

For too long, they stand frozen in time, feeling the stares of those observing just beyond the courtyard. Rahat watches the regret sinking into her brother's features as he comes to his senses.

Gingerly, he lowers his blade.

The *clang* of the scimitar against the stone makes Rahat flinch. She takes a further step back like he might rush her, but his feet are firmly planted in the earth. He doesn't know what to say. His mouth opens and closes as he tries to force something out, but...

Her hands smooth over her shoulders as she wraps her arms around herself. 'I wasn't ready,' she demurs.

He doesn't look up from wiping his fingers of sweat on his white *kurta*. The fabric of his shirt has ripped in places, though they were too distracted to notice. 'An opponent won't wait for you to be *ready*,' he says, unable to look at her. He can't even look at his brother.

The courtyard suddenly feels too open. Standing before them clad in nothing but cotton and silks, Rahat can't deny that this is something they cannot help. The pressure has been high for them all. Ashrit hasn't been himself in days, but for him to... She doesn't want to entertain what might have happened. 'I'm sorry he left you, Ash,' she says, at last finding the words she should have said days ago.

The *rajkumar* bites his lip. 'I heard she's ugly,' he mutters.

Glancing to Rahat, Karnan comes to the rescue. Sweeping the discarded weapons into his hands, he brandishes the blades like batons. 'Ugliest woman Sā-Mares has to offer,' he says with mock horror. 'I hear she has horns like one of their gods.'

At last, Ashrit looks up. The look in his eyes almost kills them as he cracks a grin, releasing the breath he was holding. 'Horns,' he half-laughs as he rubs his chin, the day-old stubble so unlike him, 'that's a good one.'

A few feet away, Badal keeps his eyes on Rahat. Her hands won't keep still as they pick at the flaking layer of *mehendi*.

She glances up, her gaze flitting to the now-silent balconies above before coming to rest on her uncle. Though he knows it won't help, he offers a reassuring grin. But her face remains void of emotion. From above, she can feel her mother's judging stare, heavy as the seas.

'We all have the same gods, you goat,' Rahat murmurs. Turning her back on them, she brushes them off when they attempt to follow.

Fighting is un-ladylike, purrs her mother's voice in her mind. Rahat swats it away. Dancing the Khumaani has been the only chance she's had to take a sword in hand. All because of her mother. Her mother, the Maharanee, who freely forgets that her homeland, the Asthore Isles, have produced some of the fiercest female warriors in history.

A calloused hand at her arm makes Rahat pull away. Above them, she can feel visitors watching from the backs of elephants along the strips of lush grass level with the lower levels of the palace. Huge stair-platforms separate them, but their gaze feels intimate. She can't shake the feeling that they're strangling her.

'I don't need your sympathy, Karnan,' she rasps over her shoulder. The moment she left the courtyard, her mother disappeared from her balcony; she expects to see her any moment, and when she does, she refuses to cry.

Her brother's sigh is quickly followed by the shuffling of his slippered feet growing quiet. She thought she'd wanted to be alone, but the silence is stifling. Passing through the gates, the gardens spread out before her like flowering blooms. She can hear the birds from the menagerie, the women singing as they work, the visitors having their fun with what they call *exotic* animals, and her sisters preparing themselves for the welcoming dances tonight. Exhausted, she can't imagine having again to dance—*And before so many people?* The thought is terrifying.

Passing a fountain makes her pause. A peacock sings as it passes, feathers fanning before the bird skitters off at noticing the *rajkumari* near.

Along her left side, the outer walls of the palace are open to the gardens and the summer heat. In ornate latticed carvings, they cast delicate shadows upon the steps leading inside. The whooping of a langur monkey not too far away makes her smile as she looks to the fountain. Water falls in sparks against her skin like a thousand tiny kisses.

In the middle of the fountain stands the dreaded creature on her mind: the Naj, a snake-like creature with powerful legs, a whip-like tail, and nightmarish claws. Its bite is deadly, its jaw hinged back as if ready to devour a tiger. Dagger-like fangs protrude from its mouth, and from that mouth emerges a thin trail of crystalline water. Thankfully, this Naj is alabaster. Rahat doesn't know what she'd do if she encountered the true monster.

The touch is cool as she kneels by the pool, washing its icy waters over her hands.

'There you are.' Her mother's lilting accent floats down on her from the stairs to her left. Scooping her hands up under the canary yellow falls of her *saree* dotted with hundreds of bells, the Maharanee joins her daughter by the pool.

'I can't do this, Ma,' whispers Rahat.

Beside her, the Maharanee dips her pale hands into the pure water. It washes over her skin with an almost-purple glow.

Rahat can see the effort it takes for her mother to ignore her words. 'I was hoping you might be rehearsing for tonight,' she says, eyes downcast on the pool, 'or at least making your way to the fitting.' Long lashes brush her mother's freckled cheeks. Her blonde hair is so out of place in this feast of colour that is Delorran. 'We have two days, if I might remind you, and much more than two days' worth to do. There's no time for you not to be taking this seriously.'

Rahat pauses in washing the *mehendi* from her shaking hands.

Without another word, the Maharanee Odelia Feiersinger turns on her heel as she rises gracefully, expecting her umber-skinned daughter to follow.

She hasn't a choice. The air about them grows hot as Rahat lays a hand over her heart. It's hammering, pounding, racing as she tries to stand. The breath catches in the back of her throat. Looking at her mother the Maharanee, she knows that she will never be like that. That she *can't* be like that. Every fibre of her refuses to be. 'Ma—'

'You were meant to be where I left you,' her mother scolds, continuing inside.

'Ma, I can't breathe.'

The Maharanee pauses. She becomes a blur of yellow and gold then suddenly her hands are cupping her daughter's cheeks. Those foreign eyes stare back at her; their bright green like the ocean. Blue flecks encircle the hazel rim of her pupils, the green fading out to the sea; they focus so hard it's like she's staring into Rahat's soul.

'Do you need a rest?' She asks in a whisper, pulling her daughter to her feet.

Rahat isn't sure why she's whispering until she spots several of her younger siblings from the Maharaja's harem milling about the open doors. With them are visitors with varying shades of skin, laughing as they are shown the palace grounds. Many of the younger children have spilled out into the gardens, throwing themselves into the water at Rahat's feet to find shelter from the heat.

Wet trousers sticking to her legs, Rahat takes a step back from the small children frolicking in the icy pool. Slowly, she shakes her head no. 'I just need to calm down,' she says.

Her mother drops her hands at the speed of a glacier. They brush against her sides with the clatter of bells—adorning her from head to toe today, from her ears and bangles to the anklets hidden beneath the sweeps of her *saree*. This might have been what her mother had felt at her age, about to be married off to some exotic Maharaja for the sake of alliances. The similarities form a tight ball in her chest.

'I'm sorry, my darling,' Odelia says, linking her arm with her daughter's. Tactfully, she leads them away from the gathered visitors and tiny children.

Through the doors, down the cavernous corridors, and into the inner workings of the palace they go. The closer they come to the centre of the colossal structure, the quieter the corridors become. Soon they are alone, their words like whispers bouncing off of the ancient carved ceiling stones. Their slippers hiss softly as they graze the floor, reminding Rahat of the sounds of the fields past the palace gates. Light flickers off the walls and their towering pillars, decorated in elaborate patterns and mosaics of legends long past.

'I know too well what you are feeling,' says the Maharanee at last. They've been silent for so long Rahat feared her mother would become her unfeeling self that she's been of late. Ever since Ashrit's lover deserted him for a prestigious heteronormative marriage, she's been on edge. She refuses to let any of her children be hurt so. 'Take deep breaths when it becomes too much,' she tells her, patting her daughter's hand gently. 'Think of what's around you; list them, count them, and keep breathing. Ground yourself in what is reality.'

A man emerges from around the bend in the corridor. At spotting the Maharanee and *rajkumari*, he brings himself to a halt. His arms are laden with beads and furs, ready to be taken to the people he is representing. His swirling facial tattoos claim him as an ambassador from the south of Sā-Mares. Rahat has to tear her eyes away—it's the brother of Ashrit's former lover. They have the same nose, the same knowing grin, though their tattoos differ.

The man averts his gaze as he passes the two women who do not move for him. He passes without a word, not even a brush of his fingers to his forehead in a sign of respect. The Maharanee's eyes do not leave his face until he has disappeared down the corridor, leaving them once again in silence.

'Ashrit must not see him,' growls the Maharanee. 'Your brother's under enough stress as it is; seeing that man would destroy him.'

Rahat ducks her head. If she only dares to speak up, all of this might be over. She can imagine it now: leading everyone into the Hall of Mirrors and parading about as she tells them all, *It's okay everyone, no need to unpack. In fact, we're sending you back to your lands in style! There will be no wedding after all...*

Blocking out the thought, she grips her mother's arm tighter until Odelia deigns to look at her.

'Mind your brother, Rahat,' she says suddenly. 'He's been aggressive with his servants, and I saw what he almost did to you.' A quick look up and down, and her eyes feel like scourers, peeling her daughter's skin away to glimpse what lies beneath. It doesn't take her long to find what she's looking for. 'He scared you, and I'm sorry for that. But he's angry. You must understand, he's going through a lot. That man—that—'

'Ahomana,' Rahat corrects, and her mother turns on her.

'Don't speak his name.' Her expression is deadly. 'We don't speak his name on these grounds.' Swallowing her disgust, the Maharanee shakes out her hair, as if that will help rid the thoughts of him from her mind. 'I would not have minded, if he had wanted both your brother and that horned woman—'

'You know she doesn't actually *have* horns, yes?'

Her mother ignores her. '—had they all worked something out and had a child. But to *choose* her over my son?' The rage seeping into Rahat from her mother is almost unbearable. It squeezes her heart as they round the curved corridors entering the bedchambers of the royal family. Dozens of rooms, dozens of halls all interconnected like a spider's web. 'No,' she says, stern as she snaps the word with her hands for emphasis. 'No. I don't care that he likes men, but to be unable to have children?'

'Ma,' says Rahat, at last drawing her mother's attention. She sighs, not really knowing what to say. Because what in Hadria's Halls can you say? 'Never mind.'

The salmon pink halls fade, changing colour in swift brushstrokes like thousands of chameleons coating the walls. From pink to the purple of dusk, the midnight sky, and brightening to the gleaming turquoise of the *rajkumari*'s silks.

'Do you know how hard it is to find queer princes?' asks her mother, and Rahat almost balks. The laugh that builds in her mother's throat makes her want to scream. 'No, it's true, *schätzchen*. You have no idea how relieved I am that I don't have to scour all of Abrecan for a princess for you—not only would I have no idea where to start on contrasting your *sarees*, but I find I have a little more trouble picking the women out.'

Like the chime of a bell, Rahat goes still.

'Not that you're that way, my darling.'

'Ma—'

'Because if you were, I would be so very ashamed that you couldn't tell me. It would... *kill* me.' A sigh rolls through her, heavy with relief. 'But you're marrying Tahir, so you're not. So thank the gods for that. Because if you were, well... I don't know what we'd do.' Turning to her daughter, her bright eyes go soft. She brushes a hand over Rahat's rosy cheek. 'You're going to save us all, my beautiful girl.'

The pain of tears pricks behind her eyes. Rahat clears her throat, seamlessly shoving her mother away as they continue down the hall. 'You were saying?' she prompts

—anything to get the subject away from what's about to happen.

The Maharanee's eyes go wide for an instant before she grins, revealing the gossip she truly is. 'Ah, yes! I approved of...' She waves her hand in a circular motion, coaxing the name from her daughter's mouth.

'Ahomana.'

'Yes, him. I approved. Noble family, agreeable temperament, he was a good partner for your brother. *Strong*. And then he—' Her hold on Rahat's hand soon becomes a death-grip, till she notices her daughter's pinched expression. 'Deep breaths, Rahat,' says her mother again, though her voice is strained through gritted teeth, 'remember that.'

*

The *lehenga choli* wrapped around Rahat is like something out of a dream. The silken blouse of gold, cream, and scarlet is open at her back, revealing patterns of *mehendi* that trail from her shoulder blades to her coccyx. Two tiny bells jangle at the end of beaded tassels which fasten the blouse at her nape. The front of the blouse is cut low enough to allow room for the elaborate work of gold that fastens her spidersilk mantle over her collarbones. Strings of beads trail about her bare waist, *mehendi* swirling over her stomach. She won't be able to dance much in how heavy a garment this is. The seamstresses have already had to assure her that her dancing *lehenga* will be prepared for when she performs the traditional Khumaani after the ceremony, where she will execute the dance of her ancient people for the last time. Where she will announce that the war is over, and they will be free.

The pressure alone is enough to make her feel faint.

The deep scarlet of the skirt is made brighter by its golden details. Layers and layers of patterns and flowers bedeck her, blurring into one as she spins. The heavy sash gets in the way when she lifts her arms, and the seamstress stands to adjust its folds. Draping it over Rahat's head, she fastens the gossamer in place with a small clip at her crown, hidden away under a circlet of gold. A ruby the size of her thumb rests against her forehead, held in place by the golden band.

'It's perfect,' says the Maharanee to the seamstresses.

Rahat glances down at her feet, hidden beneath the voluminous skirts. Her feet are covered in patterns of lace and flowers. In two days time, they will be adorned with real blooms and bells and gold, making each step toward her husband sacred. It makes her flesh crawl. She can't bear to look at her mother and the women who have worked so hard to turn her into this creature of glittering silks. They know not that they work to beautify a liar.

In the corner of the open room stand the younger seamstresses and servants.

The open window tosses its white curtains lazily, the cloth twirling and dancing with feather-like touches as it brushes against Rahat's cousin's shoulders. The pale girl makes her way from the windows to stand beside her aunt, the fair-skinned Maharanee.

The fifteen-year-old glances up at the Maharanee, who gives her a proud grin and clasps her hand. 'What do you think, my Hazel?' she asks.

The freckled girl finally lets her eyes rest on her best friend, and Rahat does her best not to make a face that will land them both in trouble. Rahat's shoulders twitch when she tries to smile. 'Well?' she says.

Hazel gives her aunt's hand a squeeze. Her freckles seem to flit across her nose and cheeks as her expression shifts. 'I wouldn't think it's you,' she jokes, earning her a pinch to the ribs from the Maharanee. The Asthori girl only grins, taking a step from her aunt and her painful pinches. Rahat doesn't miss noticing her hands massaging her fleshy side. 'You look beautiful.'

As the shame washes over her, Rahat ducks her head. 'Thank you.'

The Maharanee has to stop herself from crying as she watches her daughter twirl for them, the skirts fanning out like blooms in the dawn's light. She turns her eyes on the seamstresses. 'I want this lehenga to *glow*,' she tells them.

Standing before the open windows, Hazel is hardly more than a silhouette as she moves away from the gauzy curtains. The midday sun sparks her auburn tresses, braided about her crown in the Asthori fashion. The girl is virtually invisible to the handmaidens along the wall, though the servants smile her way as she summons one close for a glass of water.

Rahat knows her mother's still talking when she gazes back into the mirrors arranged in a half-circle before her. The candles' reflections are almost blinding, but she is even more so. The seamstress moves to allow her a clear view, and what she sees almost breaks her heart. The *lehenga choli* is too ornate, too perfect. And, as her mother had hoped, it glows like a thousand lanterns. Tiny circular mirrors in the beads of her necklace, and stitched along the folds of her skirt, capture every fractal of light in the darkened room.

'Her shoulders will be brushed with flakes of gold, of course,' purrs one of the women—she doesn't know which one in this light.

Silent, Hazel brings Rahat her glass of water, though the *rajkumari* might have preferred wine with how she's shaking. Hazel winks, her smile so kind that it makes Rahat want to cry.

The ruby feels too large against her forehead. The ring looping gracefully through her nose feels too heavy. A small pearl sits against her nostril, linked to a chain that leads to her left earlobe. Two chains rest against her cheek; one a simple cord, the other tiny intricate loops.

In two days time, she will be a great bride. A great bride with a heavy duty.

The seamstresses speak amongst themselves when the Maharanee slips her daughter a look. Hazel's too busy sliding her fingers over some of the finer details of her cousin's skirts to notice. Catching her mother's gaze, Rahat returns the water to Hazel, not having taken a sip and knowing she won't be able to keep it down with nerves like this. Her shaking hands betray her; Hazel grips one tight when the others aren't looking.

The sudden swell of trumpets from outside saves Rahat from having to answer a question she didn't hear. Almost immediately, dhol drums take up the call.

They're here.

It feels all the oxygen's been sucked out of the room.

Yet the seamstresses ignore the disruption, instead deciding to talk louder about which sash and mantle would look *truly* best with the *lehenga*. All varying designs, their colours make them look the same in the shadows. And Rahat couldn't care less—the sash will be worn for an hour at most, before she strips off all these heavy layers to dance the Khumaani for hours and hours. For the last time dancing the dance named for the country her Delorran was before it was broken apart into the Summer Lands.

The look Hazel gives her distracts her from this fact for only a second.

'Auntie Odie?' asks Hazel over her shoulder, keeping her eyes on Rahat.

The Maharanee pauses in her conversation with the seamstresses. Hands looped under a stunning sash threaded with both gold and crimson detailing, she glances their way. 'I think this one,' she tells them, before nodding. 'Yes, girls, you may go. Enjoy the music.'

'Thank you,' Rahat breathes, feeling as though she's about to fall off her pedestal. A single movement of her arm has the unoccupied servants rushing forward to undress her. The seamstresses stand well out of the way, gathering the rest of their fabrics into their arms. 'I cannot wait to see Iliyah,' whispers Rahat over the women's heads, coaxing a kind smile from her mother.

It takes a while to untangle her from the fine clothes before Rahat and Hazel are able to bundle her up in a *dhoti saree*—a shock to the elder women, who might have preferred to see her in fresh clothes to see her guests.

Meanwhile outside, the trumpets still sing their calls of welcome.

The palace is so full they can hardly breathe. Staircases are strewn with foreign dignitaries all conversing, speaking the layered speech of those avoiding war. Vicious whispers of hatred slither through the crowds amongst the calls of the trumpets. The Praitosí Empire is here. The Praitosí Empire—which is ruled by three.

'Unnatural,' whispers a woman from behind her fan, 'to have three people in a marriage on the throne? No, couldn't trust it.'

Rahat glares at them over her shoulder as they pass, but Hazel lingers long enough to knock the woman's fan from her hand, sending it a-clattering down the stairs. The woman *hmph*'s, but there isn't time.

'Hazel,' Rahat growls, taking her cousin by the hand.

The drumming dies down, becoming quieter as they approach, and Rahat feels like screaming. Too many people block their way.

Ever since she was a child, she's always enjoyed the welcoming dance performances. Music and lanterns in the middle of the day, with drinks and wonderfully delicious spiced treats.

Her stomach rumbles. If only this dreaded day were over already.

Servants rush by them with plates of steaming food, some carrying trays of gilded tea glasses full to the brim with cardamon or sugarcane tea. One rushes by with chai, the scent lingering in the air even after they've disappeared from sight.

'Looks like we missed the chai,' laments Rahat.

She doesn't even need to look to Hazel to know she's pouting like a child. 'But I love chai,' she whines in a small voice, quickly adjusting her expression at spotting an Ellasían ambassador looking her way.

'How's the trade in the northern isles these days?' asks a bronze-tanned seafarer as they pass in one of the lower corridors. The glaring light bounces off his sandy blonde hair.

The girl raises her hand in mock manner as she breezes by. 'I haven't been to the Isles in years, but I assume it's fine,' she calls out.

'Hazel,' Rahat growls, grabbing a tighter hold of her hand and drawing her around the corner. 'Be polite— you know some of the trade-ways have been cut off. And some of these people don't even know you live here.'

'Then why—'

She cuts the girl off when they reach the bottom of the stairs outside, weaving around people gathered in the gardens by the glittering pools as they listen to the swelling music. None are allowed to watch the arrival of the Praitosí Empire, save those welcoming them.

'Because you still look like an Asthori,' Rahat hisses in reply.

She stops mid-step. 'And what does that mean?'

The *rajkumari* sighs, tugging at her cousin's chubby hand. 'Well, just look at your hair and what you're wearing,' she tells her. 'The Asthori ambassador may have ignored you when they arrived but that doesn't mean you're not one of them.'

The sounds of the gardens become too much all at once. Hazel takes her hand from Rahat's, slowly turning her back on her as Rahat grapples for something to say.

'Hey, no—you know that's not true. You're Delorrene, you're one of us, you goat-head, hey, no, please—Hazel, look at me.'

All her begging doesn't feel like enough. Coy, Hazel looks back at her cousin clad in the Brijesh family turquoise instead of the Delorrene red that she *should* be wearing. Pouting, the girl looks her up and down. 'Say it again,' she says.

Rahat holds her gaze, only too aware of how people are actively trying to look like they're ignoring their spat. She can't help her mouth as it's tugged into a grin which mashes her lips together. *You're Delorrene.* Come on, we all know you wouldn't be this mental if it weren't for my brothers.' Brows knit, she hopes she doesn't look like the tiny monkeys Hazel always rushes to in the menagerie. 'Please?'

'Ugh, fine,' she groans, covering her ears and slapping Rahat's arms, 'I forgive you, let's just keep going. You've dragged me all this way out into the heat already.'

Just over the garden hedges, they at last lay eyes upon the giant creature that's making enough noise to compete with the trumpets and drums. Rahat can't hold in her excitement. It's not every day that you see an elephant leading a royal train.

Hazel pauses, eyes wide with amazement. 'Is that a black Praitosí elephant?'

Rahat can't help her eyebrows from dancing. 'Sure is.'

Without catching a breath, Hazel snatches Rahat's hand and pulls her through the crowds which part for them. People of all colours and cultures flit by as they dart through the gardens. The courtyards remain open, everyone from cooler countries choosing to remain in the shade. Only those with night-dark or mottled skin dare to sit out in the middle of the yards, spreading themselves out by the singing fountains.

The palest remain inside on the staircases, their skin almost translucent. Ghostly, despite the light. Rahat swears she can see the snow in their blood, in their muted eyes.

A shiver rolls down her spine. The Lyran people have always haunted her a little. So pale, so statuesque, her mother had once successfully convinced her that they were animated snowmen. Somehow, she'd believed it.

Across the courtyard Hazel races. By the towering vines, half-hidden from sight, stands a bench free of visitors. She climbs up onto the closest step before glancing back at her cousin. The flush of her cheeks betrays her embarrassment. 'Are you sure we should be out here?' she asks, making Rahat laugh.

'Look at you, playing like you're not *dying* to see a certain someone.'

Hazel scrunches her nose, but Rahat follows her up onto the bench to dig her hands into the lush vines.

'You're too cautious,' she goads.

'And you're not nearly cautious enough,' counters the Asthori.

Rahat can't argue with that. Peering over the green wall to the palace gates, she spies the Praitosí Empire. Before them traipse her father's viziers, guiding the giant creature.

Hazel's eyes go wide at seeing the black elephant. Painted with hundreds of colours and patterns, it's a walking mosaic. Matte charcoal skin covered in vibrant pinks, purples, oranges, and blues. Upon the elephant's back is the Emperor's royal box. The King of Kings.

Rahat's always thought Iliyah's father a little full of himself.

Still, the trumpets are roaring.

Tassels of colour cover the elephant's face, blowing gently in the breeze as the Emperor dismounts the giant animal. Emperor Bashshar Tyrikaara-al-Hiraj has always been an intimidating man. The white in his beard is almost undetectable by how precisely it has been trimmed. For as long as she can remember, Rahat has seen something strange in that man's eyes and how they seem to stare for just a little too long. Like a tiger's—they're the same caramel shade.

Rahat reaches back for her friend's hand, trying to think of the last time she had seen this man in her homeland... And she can't quite place it, now.

Dark brows furrow over those deep-set eyes, casting a shadow over the Emperor's face. The noise from the adjacent gardens is enough to make him anxious. Despite being the ruler of an Empire, Bashshar has never enjoyed a crowd. Surveying the courtyard, those palace gates casting great shadows behind him, he notices that while the royal family has not come to greet them, a collection of dancers is makings their way across the wide palace steps.

The dancers twirl in their pluming skirts, spinning in time to find their place though they amount fifteen. Wild untamed hair billows about them as they break into their performance. With soft voices they sing, raising their hands to the sky as they trill praises of the Empire. Yet with each clap of their hands, each stamp of a foot, Rahat can see through their smiles. There is no Delorrene in this world that does not despise the Praitosí for what they have done to their people, all in the name of claiming land.

They spin and twirl like darts, deadly as cobras, with bangles and bells chiming at their wrists, their ankles. Hazel sucks in a breath as she watches the dancers move in their circle, keeping time like an undulating mandala.

Behind the Emperor, his family emerges from their carriages; only the Emperor may ride an elephant. The rosewood carriage doors open slowly, the footmen standing guard with vigilant eyes as their masters emerge. *This is it.*

Rahat holds her breath, unable to help it, as she keeps a close watch—not on the dancers, but on who she's waiting to see. She'll know simply by her slippers.

As expected, the first to emerge is Empress Safia Hiraj, a dark-haired Praitosí, followed by Empress Mahala Tyrikaara, a native Delorrene and Iliyah's mother. Arms linked, the two women are day and night: the first of slick raven hair and almond skin, the second an image of darkness: cinnamon-brown with large russet eyes.

As their husband waves them closer, they move in brilliant bursts of colour: Safia in a *kameez* of periwinkle with *sirwal* pants of peach, and Mahala in an *anakarli* dress of sunset hues. Their gold glimmers as the rubies on their hands catch the sunlight, red as blood.

Bashshar kisses them both on the forehead, his beard smearing the blessings marked on Mahala's brow. As he again turns to the dancers, wiping the red from his face, the Empresses entwine their hands and lean into each other, making Rahat's cheeks flush.

Hazel turns to her subtly. 'You okay?' she whispers.

Rahat does her best to ignore her. 'Yeah, I'm fine.' So why does she feel like a hot tangled mess inside?

Following them from the carriage are Tahir and Zehran, Safia's children. Rahat's throat contracts at spotting Tahir, his hair hidden by his turban as he squints up into the sky. Chiselled features; a pointed chin with slight stubble. A little gangly. He's Rahat's future husband.

Behind him is his younger brother, a man made of muscle. The way he stands is that of a soldier; shoulders pulled rigid as he stands tall. As the third brother, Zehran will never rule. Rahat half-expects to see their eldest brother Saadi with them, but as heir to the Empire, he never travels where there might be danger.

Hazel whispers out the corner of her mouth, 'Do you see her?'

But the royal carriage is now empty. The footman closes the rosewood door and proceeds to that which follows.

Rahat frowns. Iliyah should be in the carriage with her family; her letters had told her so. For weeks, both of them have been waiting to see each other, their letters sometimes no more than exclamations of excitement.

'No,' says Rahat, keeping her head below the vines, 'not yet.'

From the following carriages come the courtiers. The all-black Qadira dismounts from the back of the royal carriage, where she had kept watch throughout their journey. The Rehmayan with her cheetah's eyes surveys the area. Rahat feels her stomach drop when those eyes spot her across the courtyards. They zero in, keeping her pinned. Just like the cheetah, her eyes are bright carnelian rimmed in black to reflect the sun. She's one of the last remaining faerie races—perhaps one of the last of all faeries to survive after the Rapture. The light fabric of her garb keeps her figure hidden away, including the stems that had once belonged to wings down her back. Against all that black, the heavy silver-and-leather braided whip is a threat at her side. The travel scarf keeping the sun off her ebony hair hides her pointed ears. It swims about her face as it's tossed by the breeze, caressing those high cheekbones and flat features. With skin as dark as her garb, she is invisible in the night.

Those animals' eyes do not leave her until Rahat ducks below the vines.

She doesn't pay attention to who comes after that. After the faerie, she knows none of them will be Iliyah.

Yet as the courtyard fills with explosions of colour, bright *sarees* and *qamis* decorating them all, she can feel her heart sinking. The dancing comes to an end, the women ending their performance by sweeping to the ground, their skirts fanning out around them.

Carefully, the Praitosí weave their way between the dancers to seek shelter from the blistering sun. The Delorrene viziers stand aside, ushering them into the shade of the promenade and through to the palace. With a look cast toward the gardens, the princes follow.

An odd sound comes from Hazel's throat before she slams a hand down on Rahat's shoulder.

'Wha—'

'Zehran,' pants the Asthori, her face flooding red.

Rahat hangs her head. Not this again.

'Is it possible that he could *be* any more attractive?' The girl squeals, and Rahat has to drag her below the vines to remain unseen. A strangled gasp is stolen from her lips, but Rahat throws up an arm to keep her from talking.

'Are you an idiot?' she hisses. 'Do you want us to get caught? You know what my *Abba* would say if he knew we were spying on them before they'd been properly welcomed.'

Hazel raises a brow with that challenging grin. 'So you mean he'd be okay with it if we spied on them *after* we'd welcomed them?'

Chuckling, Rahat almost pushes her off the stones. The girl flashes her that smile, turning her attention back to what lays over the vines as she slowly rises to her feet. Careful on the aging bench.

'Oh, what will I do with you...' sighs the *rajkumari*.

'Well, for one,' starts Hazel, and Rahat's laugh almost has them discovered now that the music has died. When the Emperor snaps a look in their direction like a falcon, they shoot back below the vines.

'Did you see that?' the girl pants.

'The way he looked like he'd behead us if he knew? Yah.'

Hazel shakes her head, her eyes glazing over. 'Zehran looked at me,' she says.

A jolt runs down Rahat's spine. The force almost makes her stand upright, but she remembers at the last second to keep low. It's one thing to be seen by Qadira; she has the tact to mention it later. But by Zehran? She's just waiting for him to blurt it out, landing them all in trouble.

Not taking any more risks, she climbs down into the safety of their alcove hidden from the crowded gardens by the thick vines. Those nearby linger close to listen, though pretend to pay them no heed. 'Did he see you?' she asks.

'That's generally implied by *he looked at me*, yes.'

'No,' Rahat shakes her head and guides Hazel down from where she could be seen. 'I meant if he'd realised it was you.'

'Oh.' The girl pauses for a moment, keeping her eyes on the rings decorating her hands. Rings from her mother, her sisters. Her breath becomes shallow when she finally raises her eyes to Rahat's. 'I'm not sure.'

Through the garden wall separating them from being very much in trouble, they listen as the servants lead the elephant away to the menagerie. The chattering of courtiers fills Rahat's ears.

'Who do you think they brought with them?' asks Hazel tentatively.

Rahat bites her lip to suppress a grin. 'Thought you wouldn't be interested in anyone but Zehran, *little commander*.'

The girl frowns at the literal translation of her name. 'I never should have told you that,' she pouts, eliciting a mockingly haughty laugh from her cousin.

Linking her arm through Hazel's, she brings her down from the marble bench. The scent of the sugar vines is sickly-sweet, like honey left out in the sun. It makes her hungry as she thinks back on the chai and braised figs they'd missed earlier. The sun against her skin is a warm embrace, blushing over her arms. The calls of birds make the courtyard feel larger. Yet when she turns to see the dignitaries and children scattered about the courtyards, she has to hold back a groan.

'I didn't catch a glance,' Rahat says suddenly, explaining before Hazel can ask. As she leads her back inside, she feels guilty somehow. The saliva sticks in the back of her throat. The air feels thinner. The way Hazel's looking at her doesn't make this revelation any easier, either. 'Did Iliyah look all right? I didn't spot her, but—her last letter made me worry.'

Hazel's eyes remain on her cousin's face for a touch too long. 'I didn't see her,' she says quietly as they pass by a towering waterfall. A sculpture of a tiger lingers beneath the falls, its front submerged as if it's about to dive under and gobble up the fishes swimming lazily about the cerulean pool. 'You saw as much as I did that she didn't ride with her family. Maybe she sat with her friends,' she says, not quite able to look her in the eye. She knows how much the Praitosí shehzadi means to her. 'I'm sure it's nothing to worry about—and she'd feel awful if she knew you were worrying over nothing.'

'Yeah,' sighs Rahat, 'you're right.'

'Now let's get you bathed and ready for the welcoming ceremony tonight.'

Rahat purses her lips. 'I bathed just this morning,' she reminds her.

The girl squeezes her arm, pulling Rahat into the shade of the palace with a gentle laugh, ignoring the looks of those around them. 'If I hadn't've been there myself, I wouldn't believe it.'

Rahat laughs accusingly, unable to keep the smile from her face when Hazel abruptly spins on her heel and bolts down the hall. Not missing a beat, Rahat follows at full speed, weaving between visitors. Their laughter echoes through the east wing, dancing off the high domed ceilings.

The *rajkumari* sprints along the half-open walls of arched windows overlooking the gardens. Handfuls of half-siblings look up as the girls pass, their joy infectious as they race to the inner chambers.

Hazel disappears around a bend and Rahat doesn't hesitate to follow. This part of the corridor is empty, free of voices. Yet as soon as she banks the bend, she spots her uncle staring at them with wide eyes. Rahat's *mojari* slip on the polished floors to the point that Hazel, standing in the alcove of a doorway, reaches out for her. Hazel's hand steadies her for the second she needs, before she looks up into the face of her uncle Badal.

'Uncle,' Rahat pants.

Badal looks between them, an unsure look upon his scarred face. 'You shouldn't be running like this through the halls with so many people about—what if you'd knocked an old aunty over?'

'We apologise, uncle,' says Rahat, bowing her head. 'We hadn't thought of that.'

Once again, he sweeps his beady eyes over the pair. 'No,' he agrees slowly. 'No, I don't think you did.'

2

The Hall of Mirrors is the oldest mecca of the palace of Ajrapur. Thousands of mirrors decorate the walls, the floor, the domed ceiling. Great pillars stand in circular formation, raising overhead the balconies, set into the ceiling like niches. Beneath these balconies is seating, up a step or two from the main floor decorated with a mandala of gold, marble, and those brilliant shades in-between. From the ceiling hangs a tiered chandelier, its candles flickering against the mirrors surrounding. The room glows as Rahat watches people finding their places. There are faces from all across this world. They gather in the seats of the circular hall, leaving the floor clear for the performance they know will soon come.

Above in the balconies is the Maharaja's harem with their children, gathered in their best. *Sarees* of brilliant shades—greens and ice blues being preferred over yellows and reds—light the golden room with vibrant blooms of colour. From the stands of these balconies hang stretches of flowers from all over the Summer Lands, beautiful blossoms of every colour imaginable. And their perfume? Divine.

In one of the balconies are trumpeters, harpists, and various musicians tuning their instruments. Their all-white uniforms make them invisible within their marble alcove.

Raised a dozen steps above his guests sits the Maharaja Ram Brijesh on his cushioned throne. Sitting cross-legged beside his Maharanee, he overseas as dignitaries gather into the Hall, taking note of those who sit closest. Cultures from all over the world are gathered at his feet; he cannot deny that it makes him a little giddy. It had been his idea to sit and view his audience as they arrived. To remind the people that he is not a true part of the Empire, perhaps, though Rahat has a feeling it's for other reasons. Her father has always been an anxious man.

Great swirling patterns become blurred as she tries to spot the woman she desperately wishes to see. Amongst the chaos, she spots Hazel in her favourite *dirndl*. Worn over a frilled short-sleeve blouse, embroidered black silk gives way to damask pleats that fall to the knee. Thick braids cover her crown, woven through with tiny blooms and crystal beads. All eyes are on her plump figure as she makes her way not toward the Asthori ambassadors gathered, but to the Maharaja's dais. A small bow to her uncle and aunt, and she takes her place beside the royal family at their right.

Sitting beside her is Karnan, who leans over to smile. Warmth floods through Rahat as she watches Hazel fix Karnan's collar, patting down his shoulders with a frown to fix what his fidgeting had undone while waiting. The *rajkumar's* eyes gleam as he looks over his cousin in her new dress. Rahat knows the exact moment he gives her a compliment—Hazel's cheeks flood a red bright enough to rival the *sarees* of those gathered about them.

By their side, Ashrit lifts his head from where he sits with his hands folded in his lap. The golden shoulders of his black *sherwani* glint in the fractals of light reflected throughout the mirrored hall. A scarf of red hangs lazily over his shoulders, so long it gathers in his lap. Loose golden-threaded *sirwal* pants finished with black sandals make him look his part as the Crowned Prince. Vermillion lines his forehead in blessing. His buoyant hair sits untamed about his shoulders. Determined, he keeps his eyes firmly away from where the Sā-Marish representatives are seated. It's with a sinking heart that Rahat realises their mother has told him of Ahomana's brother.

'*Didi*,' whispers one of Rahat's younger half-sisters.

The *rajkumari* glances to the girl, who's taller than her though only sixteen. Her arms are long, elegant and graceful as she reaches up to fix the draping of Rahat's hair.

They wait anxiously for the moment that the Praitosí train enters. Almost everyone has found their seats when the rulers of the Summer Lands finally join them.

All life feels sucked from the room as the Tyrikaara-al-Hiraj family enters, led by their Emperor and Empresses. Everyone holds a breath. Rahat spots the woman with the fan from earlier, curling her nose in disgust as she watches the polyamorous trio crossing the room. Some watch in horror, while others avert their eyes. Rahat catches the outraged whispers from some of her sisters but hisses them into silence. *How dare they judge.*

Zehran and Tahir follow behind, the rear brought up by courtiers in *kurtas*, *qamis*, and *salwars* of greens, purples, and pinks. The only one not bearing any colour is Qadira, still with her whip at her side, in her sleeveless all-black ensemble revealing her toned arms. Though this is perhaps the first time Rahat has seen the *kehrasa* without her headscarf. Her sleek woven braids of raven hair are as long as the whip at her belt. Those calculating eyes pass over all seated, challenging them to speak. Pointed ears mark her as undeniably different. Never mind the fact that she's over three hundred years older than anyone else here.

Still, Rahat cannot see Iliyah with her mess of free-flowing tresses. Rahat searches desperately for the dusky shade between pink and purple that she always wears, but it cannot be seen. Iliyah Ameha isn't here.

Yet the thought dies away as, from behind the curtain backing the dais, Rahat can't keep her eyes from Tahir. His turban is red—a colour of Delorran. There's a slight smile playing at his chiselled features when he spots Rahat peeking through the golden gossamer curtains.

She instantly drops the curtain, letting it fall in soft waves.

Crowding her are her younger sisters, all of them dancers. Dressed in identical mirrored *lehenga*, their skirts are crimson red adorned in gold, their *choli* blouses the same shade. Only Rahat wears a *dupatta*, the sash black against her ensemble, marking her as the *rajkumari* amongst the chaos that will be their dance. Amongst them, Rahat is perhaps the shortest. Standing on her tip-toes, her anklets jingle as she looks for one dancer in particular.

Her cousin Satiyavati Naidu had said she would be here for the dances. Coming from the northern city of Mirahta, it is a fair distance to travel. And she would be travelling on foot, for the jungles are dense and perilous to the north. *She'll be here*, Rahat tells herself as she stands flat on her bare feet, willing her nerves still. She has been performing for years, but that doesn't make it any easier.

Twenty girls, all dancing in time. Each move must be perfect.

'*Didi*,' whispers the closest sister again.

Rahat looks her square in the face as she girl again makes fluttering motions with her hands. She frowns, making the girl sigh, adjusting her earrings which have tangled in her hair. 'There,' smiles the half-Tehrarsi when she's finished. 'Are you nervous?' Her dark slanted eyes pinch at their corners.

Unable to deny it, she gives a tight-lipped grin. 'Always am.'

The girl takes another deep shaking breath. This is her first performance before so many people, but she's Rahat's perfect match in skill. '*Didi?*' she says again. Rahat grips her hand and gives it a squeeze, the curtains standing before her starting to feel invisible. 'Good luck,' she says, returning the hand-squeeze.

She can't help the smile that curls in the crease of her mouth. 'Thank you.'

She tries not to think too hard about not finding Iliyah in the crowd.

Outside beyond the curtain, there's the quiet testing of the musicians before the trumpeter blows a short tune to call for silence. At once, quiet descends, and the Maharaja stands. The servants bearing orbs of light grow still along the walls.

Draped in amber scarves, the Maharaja's ensemble of black, red and gold is threatening. A turban of red sits heavily on his head. A man with a brooding face, the Maharaja Ram Brijesh has not been known to smile since the invasion of the Praitosí Empire. Ten years of being pressed under the thumb of the Emperor has changed him.

Beside Rahat, some of the girls stir. Somewhere in their formation, Rahat hears them whisper, 'But where is the *shehzadi*?' Rahat blocks them out, instead focussing her mind on what must be done.

This will be a performance to remember.

The Maharaja casts his eyes upon the royals, ambassadors, dignitaries, and guests gathered before him. By his side, his son keeps his eyes downcast, not trusting himself not to look up at Ahomana's brother. Beside Karnan in his white *sherwani*, Hazel looks for Iliyah. Her eyes linger on the curtain behind the dais where the dancers wait. Nothing about this feels right.

'Royal House of Praitos,' begins the Maharaja, spreading his arms wide in welcome. 'Bashshar, Mahala, Safia, it is a pleasure to have you and your children with us this night. I welcome you again to Delorran, having missed you for some time.' The laugh that rumbles up his throat is insincere, and Rahat's stomach drops.

The Emperor's face flushes as his courtiers flutter with anxiety.

Yet that laugh continues. 'What an honour to house you as we wed our children at long last,' he says, concealing from his words the bitterness written across his face. He has not been waiting years. He has been fighting, at each step battling to recover his land from the Empire. And he has finally achieved his wish; his daughter in return was the only price. 'But I must ask of you,' he says, bringing his hands together as he surveys them. 'Where is your *shehzadi*?'

A thread of suspicion weaves its way through the courtiers beneath the balconies, hidden from sight in the half-darkness. Behind them stand servants bearing orbs, casting shadows across those gathered. Rahat wishes they'd leave, though they might be the only thing keeping the Empire from considering any further threat or insult.

The smile that stretches across Empress Mahala's face is sweet as she sweeps the great skirt of her *anakarli* dress behind her to stand. 'You must excuse our daughter; as priestess, she has remained in Rahala to lead the morning prayers of Kaiduko's holy feast day, only yesterday.' Those dark glittering eyes glide to the curtains behind the Maharaja. Even without having been told, she knows that the *rajkumari* will perform for them this night. For was it not Mahala Tyrikaara who had first told the Maharanee of the talent her daughter possesses?

'I expect she will arrive the morning of the wedding.'

Joining her husband, the Maharanee stands. A sight in her turquoise and gold *anakarli* dress, her shoulders are draped with scarves of all designs, tassels and pompoms making her feel vibrant and youthful. Those green eyes glitter against her freckled cheeks in the mirrored light. Yet her yellow hair remains twisted about her crown in the style of her homelands.

Saliva sticks in the back of Rahat's throat when she realises what her mother's about to do to defuse the tension. If Iliyah were here she'd laugh and give her a kiss for luck. *A kiss...* She takes a deep breath as her mother raises her hands—visible through the curtains with how they glimmer with dozens of bangles—to strike up the music.

Dhol drums give their first strikes. Men take up the call to sing, their voices rising and falling as the curtains are pulled back, and the dancers emerge. The Maharaja and Maharanee stand between them as the dancers fan out on either side, descending to the mandala-painted floor.

Seamless, they move like ink in water. All at once, Rahat is calm as the music weaves its way through her. This is it. This is where she belongs. Skirts become fans as the dancers twirl, kicking up their legs and spinning, raising their bangled arms to the sky. The lights reflect off of their skirts, sparking to life like thousands of tiny stars. Keeping time with the drums, they are in perfect formation, and amongst her sisters, Rahat is the centre.

This is not the Khumaani—Rahat had been clear that she would not dance her specialty for this occasion. The Khumaani is a noble dance, one that should be concealed from the prying eyes of those outside the Summer Lands.

Here, clothed in the gods' chosen red of her people, she dances a mixture of the tribes' dances scattered across her country. As the beats of the drums slow, she comes to a pause, her eyes meeting Tahir's. And it is as if she's stopped breathing. The moment soon passes, the drums strike, and she falls into groove with her sisters, her body knowing the movements even as her mind falters.

Above on the balconies, her brothers and sisters sing their praises. This is about Rahat, after all. And she shall be their salvation.

The dance comes to an end all too soon. As the music dies about them, Rahat forces herself to take deep breaths. Religious women toss colour down upon them, blessing the *rajkumari* as her skirts come to a still.

She's standing before the Praitosí. They watch their future princess with analysing eyes as she drops her head, brushing her forehead with three fingers in a sign of respect. It smears the red across her brow. A slow smile spreads over her face as, at last, she looks again to Tahir.

His intense coal-dark eyes keep her pinned as he emerges from his seat to join her on the dance floor. White sandals absorb the colour of the dyed powder with each step. The black of his *sherwani* is slimming, threatening, attractive. Tahir has always been frustratingly handsome. A ribbon of turquoise is twisted through the wraps of his turban—a flourish, Rahat knows, for her benefit. So when she smiles, she's surprised by the truth of it.

'Rahat,' breathes her future husband, as he dips at the waist to brush a hand over her painted feet. A shiver rolls through her, from her shoulders to her pelvis. *Gods be damned.* She knows it's nerves. She feels sick.

They haven't seen each other in three years. Her breath catches when he stands, only to bend to press his forehead to hers, in the way couples do. The red blessings stain his face. Rahat feels the heavy stares of her brothers on her back as she relaxes into him. His warm breath caresses her cheeks as he grins, mirroring her radiant smile.

'Hello,' he whispers, quiet enough that only she can hear.

She feels like laughing as the word slips from her lips: 'Hi.'

The other dancers flit to their places, taking silver platters laden with blessings of fruit and flowers to the realms gathered before them. Each speaks the welcoming words of their corresponding countries. The Hall of Mirrors fills with language—

Íla arannai t'dír.

Amongst the voices, it is the ancient Lyran tongue that makes everyone pause. The Lyran words have been imbued with magic for generations. It is the lost language of the faeries. Yet their ambassadors simply smile, bowing their heads without saying a word to prove whether this myth may be true.

Rahat and Tahir remain entwined, sharing breath between lungs as around them, the realms are blessed with welcome. The Praitosí's hand finds hers, hidden within the folds of her skirts, before she pulls away at the sound of her mother's voice.

'I cannot speak of the honour I feel at bringing you all here for this occasion,' she says, again rising to her feet. Focussed eyes keep her at their centre. 'I thank you all for making the long journey to be here to witness the freeing of our people.'

Tahir goes rigid, pulling Rahat's attention from her family. A slight frown plays at her brow, but he shakes his head, dismissing her worry.

Everything about this is so fragile. Their peace resides on the fracturing of a breath. If she thinks about it, it's too much. *So don't think about it.*

The Maharanee claps her hands, bringing the musicians to play once more. The tune is softer, more inviting for those who cannot dance their ways. Rahat's dancers leave the floor, weaving back through the curtain behind the Maharaja's dais.

Slowly and unsure, the courtiers rise from their seats. Chatter fills the hall, filling every nook and curve as the world mixes before them. Voices echo, cry out, rise in falsetto, and Rahat rubs her temples in a failed attempt to block it out. The dozen or so rings on her fingers scratch at her skin.

Where's Hazel? Glancing up, she finds her gone. Only her brothers remain where they're seated, Karnan speaking with Ashrit in soft tones. Something is wrong.

The man at her side remains still, waiting for her to take his extended hand. Tahir is doing everything right. The glimmer in his eyes makes her want him—but want him how? It's not that normal want, not that sizzling of lust that she's so often felt at looking upon Iliyah.

A smile, and she departs.

Make of that what he will.

She needs to find Hazel.

The Maharanee lifts her arms into a welcoming beckon as she descends the dais to join Safia and Mahala. Although their husbands' relationship is tense, Odelia has always had an affinity for the ruling women of Praitos.

'Rahat—' Hazel's call is choked off when she almost walks right into the Maharaja. Her uncle laughs, rubbing the girl's shoulder before he joins his wife with the Empire. Hazel's ears flood red. 'You need some fresh air,' the girl says through her blush, and Rahat couldn't be any more thankful.

Hazel glances at Karnan over her shoulder. One look to Ashrit, and Karnan follows—not onto the floor, as he might have thought, but to the outer balconies, exposed to the night sky and the warm, calming air. They hadn't realised how cramped they'd felt amongst all that pomp and propaganda.

Trailing behind as they disappear behind the dais and up the stairs to their left, Karnan pinches two drinks from a waiting servant wandering past on their way to his father's harem. As soon as he realises, he ducks his shoulders with a wince, before brushing the feeling away. Two missing drinks aren't the end of the world.

As soon as Rahat steps out into the caressing night, she rolls her head back to revel in it. This is her second-last night as a free woman. If you could call what she is free. Running her hands through her hair, she pushes away those evil thoughts. Tahir will be her husband; it's inevitable. No longer is she allowed to dream of Iliyah.

Iliyah, who's not here. Why?

When Karnan hands her the drink, scented strongly with that alcohol tang, she raises a brow. He only shrugs. 'You look like you could need it,' he says by way of explanation, and she downs the drink in one gulp. He laughs, really *laughs*. The sound explodes around them, lighting Rahat up like the very stars themselves. 'Should I get you another?' he offers, only half-serious.

A cool shake of her head is all he needs. That drowsy half-smile lingers upon her lips. 'No,' she says quietly, her voice almost lost to the wind, 'not tonight.'

Karnan offers the drink to Hazel, who shakes her head. 'Can't stand the stuff.'

With a shrug, he takes a sip, spluttering upon the first mouthful. 'Great Serpent, Rahat,' he gasps, balking, 'how did you drink this?'

She only flashes that knowing grin, the one that's always infuriated him. He takes it as a challenge, as she knew he would. Downing it in another gulp, he thrusts his tongue out as if he could sever it afterward.

'Good?' she mocks.

He glares. 'That was foul.'

But the laugh that bubbles out of his sister almost makes it worth it. If he can just keep her smiling, keep her happy for two more days, then maybe she'll be able to survive this. Maybe she won't feel like she's being thrown to the Naj.

The silence stretches out between them, engulfing them. The next two days will be torture for them all, and they know it. Two days, and then to say goodbye. But Karnan will never be able to say goodbye to his sister; she's too important to him to just let her go without—

But he has no say in this. None of them do.

And no matter how much Rahat prides herself on having decided that she'll marry Tahir, Karnan can't help but think that she shouldn't be sacrificing herself for their people. Not her. Not her alone. He can't stomach it.

'So...' Karnan turns to their city, his eyes searching blindly for something beautiful. With Ajrapur as his home, he has always found beauty. With his sister by his side, he has found it in her smile too. 'How are you feeling?'

A clipped snort is her only response.

'Ah.' Clasping his hands, he furrows his brow. It's foolish to think too hard on it, but how can he not? A glance to Hazel, but the girl's avoiding his eyes. She knows something's up. This isn't like them. 'Rahat.'

The pain in his voice is what makes her look up through her curls.

'It's hard for me to see you like this,' he says, and it breaks her heart. 'I know how you feel for Iliyah.'

Her knuckles *crack*, she grips the balcony rail so hard. Clenching her jaw, she can't even bring herself to look at him. How could he know? She's never said anything. When he at last looks at her, she nods, unable to think of what to say.

'You've loved her your whole life,' he goes on. Each breath shudders. 'And having to marry her brother is tearing you apart. I know you think this is noble, that Ma will be happy, that it's your duty as *rajkumari*—'

'Because it *is* my duty, *bhai.*'

'It doesn't mean you always have to follow through.'

In the silence, the city of Ajrapur twinkles. Lanterns strung between hundreds of buildings glimmer in the starless night. The centre of the ancient city at its peak, Ajrapur was constructed upon one of the many mountains of Delorran. Perhaps the tallest in the south. From the middle of the city, people claim to spy the Shallow Sea on one side, and the Sacred Opaline River on the other. Even now, hundreds of people below rejoice the coming marriage of their princess. No longer do they prepare for their freedom in the darkness, but can bask in the glow that is each growing dawn, brighter than the last.

'This is something I must do,' Rahat says quietly, reaching out to rest her hand over her brother's. Those painted fingers are clammy against his skin. 'For the sake of our people, and for our family.' The pain grows in her skull as she feels the tears building, brimming over. Tears streak lines down her rouged cheeks. 'And that is something you must understand,' she gasps out. 'This is my only choice.'

He shakes his head. 'It isn't—'

Her nails become claws digging into his skin. Eyes wide like the moon, she beseeches him, 'Why are you trying to talk me out of this?'

'I just—'

'No, Karnan.' Her panicked hands shake as she turns to him, desperate and unable to explain it. 'Day by day, we are losing our culture. We are becoming something we are *not* and we cannot—'

Behind her, Hazel clears her throat the exact moment the guard stomps his spear. Fear breaks her. Duty makes her stand straighter.

As Karnan turns to those announced, Rahat wipes the tears from her eyes. Hazel wraps an arm around her cousin's middle, calming her and searching her face for any clear sign that she'd been crying. A light nod.

Rahat turns around.

And finds Zehran Hiraj standing in the doorway, Qadira by his side. To keep the *kehrasa* woman from delving through her mind, she focuses on Zehran. On the flowers around his neck. A frown works its way onto her brow, making the Praitosí flash that awkward, half-shrugging grin.

'I had to escape,' he says by way of explanation.

The argument with Karnan is almost forgotten at seeing how at-odds those flowers are to the look on

Zehran's face. Three flower wreaths... 'Three women asked to marry you?' Rahat giggles. 'You were alone for, what, a minute?'

Zehran takes a step back in mock offence. 'You act like I'd say yes.'

Only Karnan keeps a grin from his face. Even the age-old faerie woman cracks a smile, her teeth pearly and sharp like fangs. Yet even through the smile, those feline eyes stare them down, amber-bright and focussed in the darkness. Her silhouette against the glowing lights of the Hall seems to waver, smoke rippling off of her in waves.

Karnan shifts awkwardly as Zehran approaches, leaving the festivities of inside behind him. 'I don't think I've ever felt so out of my depth,' he says with a laugh. At his side, Qadira frowns. Or that could just be her face. 'So many people from lands unconquered! I've never even dreamed of seeing all their worlds—And they all want to talk to me, of course, and—' A look at Rahat's face, and he cuts himself off. 'Is everything okay?'

'Why wouldn't it be?' retorts Karnan from her side.

Zehran raises his hands in surrender. 'Just a question.'

He shifts uncomfortably when he catches Hazel's eyes on him. Or rather, glued to him. In fact, the girl hasn't looked away since he joined them. 'Hello, Hazel,' he says, making the young girl blush. Her only response is an inhaled giggle that makes him feel sorry for her. 'It's lovely to see you again. You certainly are...' He looks her up and down, grasping for a compliment, '*curvaceous.*'

Excuse me? The echo in her mind is visible on her features. It would be less conspicuous if someone had stamped it on her forehead. Crinkling her nose and turning away, she casts her eyes out over the city that raised her. It's perhaps the only time Rahat has seen Hazel react like that to Zehran. Perhaps because she sometimes forgets he's seven years her senior, more suitable for any of Hazel's older sisters, had they come to Delorran.

Rocking back on his heels, it's obvious Zehran can't stand the silence. Not with all of them looking at him. It's a staring contest between he and Rahat, between Karnan and Qadira, and none of them can look away. The *kehrasa* is still as stone, her features controlled as Karnan glares at her with a hatred he does not care to disguise.

Burying his hands in his pockets, Zehran sighs. 'Well. I'll leave you all to... whatever I interrupted.'

He turns, but Rahat lunges to catch him by the arm. There are so many questions she's been dying to ask him. All such embarrassing questions. But there won't be another time like this. *It's now or never.*

His eyes slide over her, analysing the strained look on her face. 'What is it, Rahat?' he asks slowly. The concern is palpable, even as Qadira purses her lips.

She can feel the words on her tongue, working their way up and out. Yet not a sound emerges. For how can she ask, when it reveals everything? It's one thing for her brother to know, but for Zehran—brother of both the man she's marrying and the woman she's in love with? *Gods.* That's the first time she's admitted it.

A frown flits through his features. 'Rahat?'

She swallows her fear to demand, 'Why isn't Iliyah here, *really?*'

And she could kick herself for how she's concealed her feelings—which is to say, *not at all.* In a matter of seconds, she's spilled her heart at the feet of a man who could destroy her future.

Yet the Praitosí hesitates, knowing he's speaking of things he shouldn't. Qadira's hand shifts to the handle of her silver-braided whip, though as to who she's warning, they can't be sure.

'Tahir asked her to stay behind.'

Each word is one more second she feels waiting for the axe to drop. And there it is: Tahir knows. Her future husband knows that a woman could come between their getting married. The future suddenly feels so much more real.

'And what did you say to that decision?'

Her brother's hand at the small of her back offers little support. It feels like the world is slipping, spiralling out from under her. *Tahir knows.*

Zehran leans a little too close for comfort. His breath caresses her neck as he smiles an unwelcome grin. Cruelty flickers in those dreamy eyes. 'I told him it was a good idea.'

With that, he turns on his heel and leaves them out on the balcony. Qadira follows like a shadow, her all-black ensemble hugging her lithe form. If ordered, she could kill them in a second. Rahat almost wishes she would.

At the doorway, Zehran collides with another woman in black. The woman laughs, waving the Praitosí on with a pointed arch of her brow, before turning to her family.

'Well,' says Satiyavati Naidu with a strained smile on her face. Nostrils flared wide, her grin is frightening. 'That was *awkward.*'

Rahat's shoulders relax when she feels she can finally breathe. 'Sati.'

The gentle sway of her hips makes her *saree* glimmer in the light cast by the luminous orbs. The black makes her look more waif than Rahat remembered. But then it has been months, and that smile is so welcome she could cry.

'I was hoping to see you on a happier occasion,' says the northerner, her eyes lingering upon her cousin, their delicate faces so similar. Sati grins like a cat, darkness crawling through her features as she turns her eyes on Karnan. 'How could you not try to talk her out of this madness?'

Instead of yelling, Karnan offers a nod. 'Always a pleasure, cousin.'

She rolls her eyes. 'Isn't it just.' When she turns her sight on Hazel leaning against the balcony, those dark eyes go wide. 'Hazel, *schatzi*! Look at you growing into those curves.' It's the proud look on her face that makes Hazel giggle as she's swept into the older cousin's arms. 'My goodness, you've grown into a looker.'

Karnan tries again to make his sister look at him, but she refuses. Now that Sati's here, she'll be able to get through all of this mess.

Releasing Hazel, Sati moves to Rahat's embrace. Rahat's head rests in the crook of her cousin's neck, making her chuckle at feeling the light brush of breath at her collarbone. 'I am sorry,' Sati sighs into the *rajkumari*'s hair, their jewellery singing upon contact. 'I wish you didn't have to go through all this,' she says, loud enough that Karnan overhears.

'It's okay,' says Rahat, but Sati shakes her head.

'No,' she says, squeezing her harder. 'No, it's really not. You shouldn't have to be doing this.'

'*Sati*,' warns Karnan, and she finally turns her attention on him. Those feline eyes crinkle with laughter, shining black in the absence of light. The shadows make her light northern-Delorrene skin the same shade as Hazel's out here under the sky.

'It's not the end of the world,' sighs Rahat.

Sati purses her lips. 'It'll be the end of your world, though.'

'That doesn't matter. My people are *suffering*. It doesn't matter if I'm happy.'

Karnan and Sati exchange a look. Hazel's almost too scared to move.

Inside, the music is cut off as if strangled. The drums are off-kilter as their beats reverberate through the Hall of Mirrors.

Rahat lifts her head, unsure. There is nothing that should stop the music tonight. And yet here they are, standing in the silence, confused and concerned. For what could be more important than this night?

Slow footsteps echo through the Hall, so loud they make Rahat dash inside. The floor below is crowded as they rush into the alcove above the dais, to spy a man in all-white bearing a glider at his shoulder. The sparkling blue messenger bird is blindfolded to keep it from disrupting the peace and freezing the room, but the man is panting. Flushed cheeks, sweat at his brow.

He's been running.

The messenger holds everyone's gaze as he approaches the dais from the towering doors. No one dares move. It's as if they can sense the news in the letter borne in his hand. The paper's faded, yellowed. News from a day ago. What could have happened? Rahat's grip on the alcove's balustrade is white-knuckled. Her painted hands itch.

Read the damned letter, she wills the messenger when he stands before her father. Dipping his head in respect, the messenger is taking too long.

Sweat drips down her spine, raising goosebumps with its passage. *Read it.*

Those on the dance floor gather again, families and friends rejoining after parting. The messenger's eyes alight on the Emperor, but he cannot hold his gaze for more than a second.

Rahat's hands flash numb. *What's in the damned letter?*

The glider remains poised at the messenger's leather-capped shoulder. Shimmering cobalt blue tail feathers trail down his back. 'Your Majesties,' he breathes, breathless. 'I bear news from Rahala.'

The silence starts to hum.

The messenger hesitates. Takes a breath.

At Rahat's side, her brother runs a hand over her back, coaxing her calm. She hasn't moved from the moment her eyes landed on the white-clad messenger.

'Well?' the Emperor presses, when not a sound is uttered.

Hands shaking, he unravels the scroll in his hand—his actions say he's already read it. His shallow breath rattles in his chest, making Rahat gulp down a deep one of her own. Karnan places a hand over hers at the rail; she doesn't notice the touch. She's lost all feeling already.

'Upon the feast day of the dream goddess Kaiduko,' begins the messenger, reading clearly as the room hangs on his every word, '*Shehzadi* Iliyah Ameha Tyrikaara was visited upon by her aunt, the exiled sorceress Nisha—'

The silence becomes all-consuming. That ache builds in Rahat's head. Nisha, the Emperor's elder sister. Everyone grows still.

'—who is said to have stolen the *shehzadi*'s soul. The *shehzadi*, although left further untouched by the sorceress, has not been sighted since, and has thus been pronounced dead by the seers who can no longer find her on this plane. She is murdered.'

That last word hangs in the air as if it had been screamed. *Murdered*. A groan of pain escapes Rahat as she takes a step back from the railing. The sound echoes across the domes.

This can't be. Iliyah can't be dead. Of all the things that are possible, this is the most outlandish. No. 'Check it again—check it agai—'

Karnan stops his sister from exploding by slapping a hand over her mouth. She yelps, half-shocked back into the present as her mind reels, and her brother wraps her in his arms.

'Take her outside,' Sati orders frantically, casting her eyes over the Hall.

Though a muscle feathers in his jaw, Karnan obeys, practically having to drag Rahat out under the open sky. When he releases her, she throws herself from him, needing to get away from that claw-like stronghold. A glance to the city, to the sky above. Her face is already streaming with tears having run silent. 'I—'

'I know.' Not an attempt at sympathy: just grim understanding.

'But she—'

'Breathe.'

She does as ordered, feeling that knot burning in her chest. This can't be right. *No*. It's all just some sick dream. *It has to be*. But a pinch to her upper-arm confirms it: the night she is breathing, the brother she's gaping at... it's all real. 'No.' It's drawn out, heaved from her as she sinks to her knees. 'She can't be, I—' The words are cut off when she hides her face in her hands, unable to face him. That hurt makes it way up her throat in bone-breaking sobs. 'Iya,' she whispers, her brother not hearing through the smother of her hair.

The guard standing at the balcony entrance turns his back on them, allowing the siblings privacy. Allowing Karnan to comfort his sister in peace. 'Rahat,' he begins, but finds that he doesn't have the words. He won't ever have the words.

She doesn't know what's happening inside as the silence continues. All hell could be breaking loose, but she can't find it in her to care. Iliyah is dead. Gone.

—How?

Karnan shuffles awkwardly by her as she voices the question. 'How?' It's a rasp as she raises her head. It's the sound of a blade upon the whetstone. Gazing up at him through that tangle of hair, her face is contorted with grief. 'How could she be—?' The word won't even touch her tongue. Because Iliyah can't be gone; she refuses for it to be true. *A sick joke, it's just a sick—*

'... and the seers can't see her, Rahat,' her brother says, and she realises he'd been speaking as she'd been pulling at the rings weighing down her hands. 'Her own magic must have died when her soul was taken. If they can't see her, then I doubt even oracles can. And I,' the heavy sigh that slumps his shoulders makes her look him in the eye, 'I don't think anyone's survived facing Nisha before. There's a reason she was exiled. I'm sorry, Rahat, but I don't think there's any chance of her being alive.' As he speaks, he doesn't make to comfort her. He doesn't know how, when she's giving him that stare.

Eyes glazed over, she kneels hunched over the stones. Cast in shadow, she slowly rises to her feet, thinking over her brother's words. The soul—they'd mentioned her soul being stolen. 'This has happened before,' she breathes, throwing her sight out over Ajrapur. Bright lights twinkle in the distance, bright lights symbolising hope. Her city needs her. But Iliyah needs her more. And if she's right about this—if there's any semblance that she could be right—she's going to take that chance. Taeng can see the realms scattered as if on a game-board; Taeng can search for her magic. For the story of the Lord Maris and his Lady Vanja is fable; she knows it is, but there's that glimmer of hope that it *just might be true*. And she can't let that go.

Without a word, she gets to her feet and storms past her brother, refusing to wipe away her tears. The red powder's smeared across her face, but she doesn't care.

Karnan calls after her, but the chaos that has become the Hall of Mirrors is deaf to her ears.

'Cousin.' Sati reaches out a hand for her as she passes, her touch just grazing Rahat as she moves quickly by. Hazel stares wide-eyed and crying. The shock written across her face makes Rahat's heart break.

She sprints down the steps. Nothing reaches her through the menagerie of sound as they call for her, bolting down the steps to breeze past the gathered Praitosí. Ashrit remains seated by the dais, resting back against the wall with his eyes closed in exhaustion. The faces all blur into one.

She needs to find Taeng.

'Rahat.' The voice catches her off-guard. A glance over her shoulder reveals Tahir grasping her *dupatta*. 'Rahat,' he says again, the pain in his voice palpable, but she shakes her head.

His hurt arcs through her. So when she turns to him, she curses herself. 'I'm sorry,' she says, gripping the back of his neck to plant her lips on his cheek. She feels his shock as he quickly recovers, reaching to kiss her mouth—just as she pulls away. 'I'll find you later,' she tells him in a whisper. The man simply nods, swallowing back his pain as he allows the *dupatta*'s shining thread to pass through his fingers.

The Maharaja calls for silence, his voice booming through the Hall of Mirrors. He catches his daughter's eye just as she turns her back on him. 'RAHAT!' he booms, bringing the room's attention down on her.

Hand at the doors, she halts. Everyone is staring, eyes wide in hundreds of faces. They all rely on her. This peace is needed; now more than ever. A sigh leaving her lips, she leans against the door and slips through the small gap, leaving them all staring after her.

3

The smell of damp stone weaves through the innermost parts of the palace thinly veiled by cedar-wood and myrrh. There is no denying what lies beneath these scents so soft on the nose.

Sprinting through towering halls, almost stumbling down spiral staircases of slippery old stone, Rahat cannot calm the thunder in her heart. Intimidating arches give way to latticed walls casting shadows over vast corridors. Scents change, becoming heavier the further she traverses the palace's many houses. From the inner walls surrounding the Hall of Mirrors, to outer buildings and their towering carved pillars, the palace wraps itself around the *rajkumari*. She and the palace are one and the same, the very heart of Delorran.

The thunder grows louder, reverberating through her as she reaches the courtyards. Staircases lead her down as she passes servants and gardeners, animal handlers, and the small children who work within the palace walls. Their eyes follow her as she scoops her skirts into her arms, revealing legs banded with anklets that sing with each movement. But the bells feel like they're screaming.

At last finding the hedges concealed by the menagerie wall, she releases the breath she's been holding. The air rushes into her lungs all at once, making her splutter. The yipping of zebras brings her back to the present. There isn't time to waste. The stairs before her reach down into the earth, their path concealed by low-hanging blooms from the north. A statue of the dream goddess Kaiduko stands by this hidden space, hands clasped and pointing down into the dark. Rahat gulps down her fear as she bows her head to the goddess' image.

Her heart comes to a still, calm rhythm. The darkness reaches up for her out of the earth. The dew in the air makes it hard to breathe as she takes those first few steps down into the unknown. The flowers grow up over her head, blocking out the stars, and the darkness feels like a weight on her shoulders as she descends.

Although not hidden, the den of the oracles is not a welcoming place. The magic surrounding its entry usually deters anyone wishing to enter—Rahat's skin is crawling, trying to force her away. She swallows the revulsion lapping through her in waves. This is something she must do. *For Iliyah.*

With each step, the light is strangled, swallowed whole by what's to come. As if they've spelled away the stars. A shiver races through her.

She says a prayer to the gods, a short one because she can't think of what to say. The main thought is please. *Please let me be right on this.*

Cheeks flushed, legs shaking, she reaches the hall at the bottom of the stairs. It's pitch-black down here. The faintest of shadows are cast from above, the light like a blessing from the gods. Looking back, she says goodbye to the last wedge of light weaving its way around the curve of the staircase.

She moves forward to find she's standing beneath a gargantuan arch. She's never set foot down here—the waves of revulsion still wash through her, setting her stomach upon the seas. Usually it keeps her from wandering too close to Kaiduko's statue.

It's so cold that her breath rises before her in a frosty mist. Tall carvings decorate the arch above her with tigers and bears in battle. Bears—the Lyra Lands. Something in the back of her mind goes blank. She feels like she should remember something, that she should know this story, but nothing comes through the fog of her mind.

Upon taking a step, she hears a solitary stone roll across the cobblestones. Old cobblestones—older than her kingdom—stretch out before her as her eyes adjust to the humming dark.

She hears the cat-like sounds of a shadow dancer as she reaches out, finding a wall a little to her right. Her knuckles sing out, stinging with split skin. The warmth pulses through her hand, for the wall has drawn blood; she's sure she's smeared it across the rough-hewn stone. As if in response, a croaking sound travels down the tunnel, the sound threatening to bowl her over. A sweet-smelling flower reaches her nostrils, tangling about her. Stories say the oracles dwell beneath every palace you've ever laid eyes on.

The sweat trickling down the back of her neck tells Rahat that there just might be something else down here, too.

Those tentative fingers dance upon the rough surface until she can't stand the apprehension any longer. *Grab the tiger by the tail*, she tells herself. *You can do this.* Taking small steps, she follows the wall with her hand still pulsing in pain. Up ahead, she can't yet see the shadow dancer she hears scurrying about the catacombs. A soft glow builds slowly, almost unnoticeable to the eyes. Her ears pick up every sound around her, alert without sight to rely upon. A light breeze whispers along the corridor, confirming the space she's in. In such darkness, she could find herself lost walking in a straight line.

Panic jolts through her as the wall drops out and she halts, unable to feel where it's disappeared—and remembering that even the goddess' chosen can play tricks. This part of the palace is so old, it might still be laden with traps. And Rahat doesn't particularly want to find herself tumbling off the edge of some cliff she has no help in the realms of seeing. Down here, the light is snuffed out; the cold is frigid, and her breath is festering hot against her cheeks.

A tiny spark jumps to life, making her squint through the black. The tears sticking to her face are sticky, making the cold worse to bear as they're heated by breath and frozen by the dank air.

A word she doesn't understand is muttered into the void. The word is sharp, clipped, as it echoes about her. *So there is a drop*, Rahat realises. *But where?*

The darkness hums. Rahat hears the gentle *tap-tap-tap* of a staff. The oracle Taeng stops down the long hall with a start, over the other side of the drop. Although the pit is only five-feet deep and once harboured venomous snakes, it has been empty for hundreds of years. Only those who have the Sight are able to navigate these halls; Rahat's done well to get this far by herself.

The oracle's shoes hiss like silk as they graze the stone floor. Her staff sounds hollow against the stone underfoot. Though Taeng is blind, she detects Rahat from her breathing. The gentle sound draws her close.

Blind in the dark, Rahat turns to the sound, and jumps at feeling the woman beside her so soon—for the pit is only three feet long, just long enough to fall down.

'Rahat, what are you—? Oh.' The oracle trails a hand down the girl's arm as she wipes the tears from her face. 'Come with me.'

Feeling invisible eyes upon them, Taeng leads Rahat around the pit and down what feel like long haunting halls, right into the heart of the catacombs. A faint glow continues to built somewhere; she isn't sure where. Eyes adjusting to the dark, she scans the room. Shelves, where bodies had once been, are laden with flowers, bottled potions, and beasts (some alive and some less so). In the corner of the room glows a shadow dancer, the cat-sized dragon of Antëasynë, the goddess of dancing lights. The creature's golden glow casts that soft shadow across the room, making Rahat able to see—to an extent.

Shadow dancers adopt gender at will; though most remain somewhere in between, switching between the days. Hen, she remembers, is the creature's name, and to her knowledge, they have never shown signs of choosing.

Taeng releases the *rajkumari's* hand only when she's sure Rahat can see.

The dome of the crypt is deathly silent. Over all the possible noises that could creep out of the dark, all she hears is the heart battling in her chest—it's the rapid heart of a shivering hare. Her bare feet feel frozen against the marble floor, laid here by her great-great-grandfather, Adhiraj the Grand, to replace the rotting cobblestones so worn by death.

In a waterfall, Taeng's black hair cascades in silken lengths over her shoulders. Small buns at the base of her crown keep the golden fans decorating her head in place. Her red and peach-coloured robes are traditional to her western homeland of Sylong; and while the fabric covers every inch of her, it clings to her powerful arms. The warm flesh of her face is pale in the flickering light, a shade lighter and rosier than Rahat's.

As the *rajkumari's* eyes roam over the oracle, she is careful to avoid her unseeing gaze. For to gaze into the eyes of an oracle brings more pain than you can imagine. Visions, nausea—there are even tales of some who have travelled time through these women's eyes. *All fairytales.* And then, of course, there are those stories of death, of men peering into the Sight of an oracle only for their hearts to stop.

Firelight licks at those high cheekbones, as if begging her to sneak a peek.

'You know of the soul?'

Rahat swallows, her throat suddenly tight. 'No,' she says, surprised by how her voice is consumed by the dark.

Darting between their feet is Hen. The shadow dancer purrs like the menagerie's serval cats, their light dancing about the decrepit crypt. Spiderwebs are aglow, and if she weren't shivering, Rahat would think this place part of a dream.

'Humans know little,' says the oracle, spooking Rahat from her thoughts.

She follows her to where she stands by the shelves, selecting vials and blooms with practised hands. 'But *you're* human,' she points out, and Taeng's laugh sends sparks up her arms.

'Oh,' the oracle chuckles. 'Am I?'

Light glints in the white of Taeng's blind eyes and Rahat has to tear her sight away. Had Taeng been angled a little more toward her, she would be writhing on the floor, clawing at her skull to rip it apart to stop the visions. The visions of oracles have driven even the sharpest of minds to destruction.

Rahat is careful not to be one of them.

The oracle waves a hand and Rahat obeys, dropping to the pillows piled about the floor near a small cauldron. Something bubbles in its depths, but upon peering inside, she finds only darkness there. Whatever it might be, she's not sure she wants to know. 'Hen,' the girl mutters, catching the creature beneath her feet. Hen miaows, tail curling as they approach Rahat on the floor. The creature's heat will be welcome—down here, the cold air presses right through them, freezing Rahat to the core. She knows that this air doesn't come from any outside tunnel. It's from something deep down.

Rahat asks a question in the gods' tongue then, making Taeng whorl on her. Arms full of concoctions and ingredients smelling of earth and bone, she grins. 'You enjoy language, then.'

She wraps her arms around herself against the cold. The light-weight silks of her *lehenga choli* aren't nearly thick enough to keep her warm.

Grinning, she recites, 'Language is the most valuable treasure we have,' quoting her father from a day where she and Iliyah had argued as children.

Taeng nods her agreement distractedly as she lays down her staff to sit across from her, and unstoppers a vial to pour the red liquid into her palm. Rahat hopes it's not blood, but in this poor light, it can't be anything else. 'The *shehzadi* Iliyah...' the oracle muses.

To fight the trembling, Rahat scoops Hen into her lap. 'They said she was—that she was—' She can't say it; it won't come out.

'Well, not quite,' Taeng decides at last. Rubbing the blood—it's that coppery tang that reveals it—over her hands, Taeng rests her fingers flat over her eyes before dragging down, streaking her face in blood. Dragon's blood, if the soaring heat along Hen's back is anything to go by. The red smears across the oracle's summer skin; she closes her eyes when they start to glow. 'The soul is complex,' she explains. 'Story goes, after it has been taken from the body, the victim has but one day to find where they wish to remain. Then—'

'How do they know where they want to die?'

Taeng strokes the air with her spider-thin hands. 'It will have meaning, usually tied to childhood, but not necessarily. Find the place that is most important to her, and you will find Iliyah Ameha there.'

'And if I can't find her,' asks Rahat, 'what will happen to her?'

A smirk plays upon the oracle's lips; her eyes are closed but gleam with light, open to the gods. 'Her soul was taken on a day of Ilori's Sunset,' she says. Her hands flutter, as if illustrating the setting of the third sun in the six-day cycle. 'She has hidden herself today, on the Fall of Teos.'

'So...?'

'You must find her before the Rise of Perrinopë ends in three days time. Otherwise, Iliyah Ameha will die. Permanently.'

Ice bites down on her heart, hard. 'What?'

Looking up, the oracle tilts her head, though her eyes remain downcast. Her hands fold in her lap, and Rahat notices that they're shaking. And even without stealing a glance, she knows that those eyes have become a brighter white against the dark blood marring her skin.

'I cannot detect Iliyah's certain touch of magic. It is as if she is lost in the fog... *waiting*.' Those hands coax the air, as if they might conjure the words. They do not come. Taeng's shoulders slump as her hands return to her lap. 'Three days, Rahat.'

Hen stretches in her lap, pushing hard against Rahat's legs and forcing her to move so the shadow dancer can rest their head on her thigh. But the creature's scales *burn*. Careful, she hooks her hands under Hen to throw them off her exposed skin, which stings as if sunburnt.

Landing on their feet, Hen flexes their wings and hisses, allowing the women to glimpse that glowing black tongue like cooling lava.

'Don't mind Hen,' says Taeng, flicking at the beast and sending them skittering from the crypt. Now that her closed eyes no longer glow and she's wiping the blood from her face, the oracle looks younger. As if the magic has passed through her and left her unscathed. 'They're so like cats, they're almost annoying,' she laughs.

The shadow dancer flees, taking every flicker of light with them and plunging the women into darkness. Rahat blinks once, twice. The darkness encroaches, the cold creeping in again. As if some foul beast were raking its hands down her back. A cold descends. An emerald flame flickers with a spark at the altar farther down the hall of domes, making Taeng pull the *rajkumari* to her feet.

'You have to leave,' gasps Taeng, the urgency in her voice a threat.

'What—'

The emerald dances, flashing darker, and Taeng gives her another shove.

A voice rumbles, the vibrations of it shaking the very air. Jars lining the shelves rattle; sleeping creatures wake with cries of protest; and the girls look to the destruction around them as debris scatters dust across the marble floor.

'An earthquake—?' Rahat begins, but she's cut short by that deep roar of a voice. It's a bark, a growl. The very rumble of the earth.

A goddess. The realisation's like a slap.

'You have to—'

'I need a light.' The girl steps just out of Taeng's staff's reach, and without question, the oracle snatches a sprig of thyme from a jar on the shelves. She breathes life into the sharp leaves with a quick puff, and the sprig sparks to life in flames. Taeng thrusts it into Rahat's outstretched hand—and to her shock, it doesn't burn her. The flames barely lick at her fingers.

'It'll burn steady till you're out,' she tells her. And with that, Taeng disappears farther into the crypt, her senses finding in the dark what Rahat's cannot.

The girl spares a glance in time to catch the explosion of jade and emerald flame that consumes everything while burning nothing. When that eerie voice fills the catacombs with that ancient language she'd spoken moments before, it steals the air from the room. Rahat's heart stops with a quiver. And, shaking to the bone, she flees.

The voice follows, breathing down her neck like some Lyran Mountain troll as she grasps through the darkness, almost plummeting into the pit. She stumbles over with a muffled yelp—

—and thanks the gods for the sprig. Although flaming, it does not burn to ash in her hands. Just like the room. A shiver rolls through her at the reminder of the All-Mother's voice she'd only just escaped. That voice has sent armies mad.

That green, she thinks. It will be burned into her mind till her last days.

Reaching the stairs and racing up into the light feels like all the air in the world is trying to dive down into her lungs. The revulsion swirls in her stomach. She splutters, choking and clawing at her throat to breathe in this clean air. She doesn't even realise that the sprig has sputtered out, having trampled it underfoot by Kaiduko's floor-length robes.

The moonlight is warm, welcoming: it banishes the sensation that thousands of hands are grappling at her, ripping at her. Rahat spies the covered bowl at the statue's feet, full to the brim with red ashes, and everything starts to fall into place.

She knows where to find Iliyah.

*

The Praitosí *shehzadas* refuse to believe a word she says.

'Iliyah wouldn't put herself out in the open like that,' protests Tahir once she's finished explaining. Weary, the Praitosí pinches the bridge of his nose between his fingers. He's never been able to resist pandering to Rahat when she looks at him like that.

Zehran shakes his head from where he stands by the floor-to-ceiling arched windows. Latticed walls cast moonlit shadows across the polished-granite floor. The bags under Zehran's eyes are haunting; by the looks of it, the journey had been a rough one. It's been a long day. And he could have done without Rahat storming into their guest chambers this late. Not that there will be much sleep tonight with what has happened.

Crossing his arms over his broad chest, Zehran draws Rahat's attention. In the privacy of their chambers, he's stripped down to something more comfortable. A sleeveless *qamis* reveals bulging biceps. Despite the strength in those arms, he squeezes himself like he'll never be warm again—like Iliyah's departure will always leave him cold to the bone.

Tahir rests his forehead in his hands with a heavy sigh. 'Iya's smarter than that,' he says. Elbows on the table, he can hardly stand to look at his bride. She'd stormed out when they heard the news; she'd practically pushed him aside—and had made more of a scene than anyone else had dared. Karnan had done his best to hide his sister's behaviour, but... Tahir sucks in a deep, shaking breath. 'She's gone, Rahat,' he whispers. 'She's gone.'

The stillness in the room makes Rahat uneasy. The resignation in his words is enough to tear at her heart—*Tahir knows*, she remembers. *He* knows.

But the rage in her is subtle, giving way to temperate calm. 'I know,' she says, her hands outstretched on the mahogany table and begging for understanding. The sweat trickling down the back of her neck makes her clothes stick to her skin. The slick silk scratches. 'Please just listen to me,' she pleas.

Tahir catches her gaze, the look in his charcoal eyes torn.

'Okay.' The word is sharp, critical, barked. Zehran turns from the windows with that calculating stare he's perfected over the years. He's the third son; he won't ever rule. A soldier in every way, his rigid stance demands attention. Their eyes never leave him as he crosses to the table and pulls out a chair to take a seat. All the while, Rahat doesn't leave his sight. 'Then tell us,' he says.

Tahir is about to object when Zehran makes a gesture for silence.

'Taeng's never been wrong,' she starts, and Tahir laughs—a cruel sound.

'We know nothing of this oracle.'

A frown creeps its way onto her brow. 'But I just told you.'

Leaning back in his seat, he sighs. Beside him, Zehran remains alert, annoyed with his brother's behaviour. If Saadi were here, he knows Tahir would be behaving differently. Gone would be the brute before him, brooding by the elbow of his bride. Another sigh rolls through him. 'It's been a long few days. We came here all the way from Rahala to find that our brother has done nothing, and our sister is *dead*.' He chokes on the word, forcing it out. He turns on her, and the look on his face is heartbreaking. A little peek into the man beneath the soldier. '*What* do you think you could possibly do, Rahat?'

Taken aback, all she can do is stare. At his grief-contorted face, his eyes brimming with tears. And the pure, searing-hot rage that lurks beneath. That intimidating man is all but gone; she never thought she'd see this.

She forces herself to look at him, to look at the pain she's sure is reflected in her own features. If she can only convince him she's right—that Iliyah *is* alive—then that's all she needs. Just one person to believe her.

'The clearing is the only place I can think of as being important to her. If she's like me—and Zehran, you see it, don't you? You see she's like me?' She pauses for his nod, only continuing after he deigns to bow his head.

Relief washes over her. 'I feel it in the very *pit* of my being, Tahir.' She doesn't realise she's speaking so desperately, so passionately, till Tahir cocks a brow. It makes him look more bird-like than his father. 'Iliyah's in the clearing by the fire god's temple,' she says again.

Tahir presses in on his eyes so hard with the balls of his palms that he blinks back black stars. 'And what makes this clearing so important, hm?' he asks, the tone of the question shooting down whatever hope she'd had that he might believe her.

Restlessness plays just beneath her skin. 'It's just important,' she says, willing him to look at her. 'You have to trust me on this.'

'And why should we?' he demands, standing so suddenly that his chair screams with protest against the granite floors. 'We know nothing of what you're speaking of. We do not know this oracle woman. How do you expect us to trust her?'

'I'm not asking you to trust her. I'm asking to you trust *me*.'

Zehran's shoulders slouch a little as he looks to his brother. But the look on Tahir's face makes Rahat's heart sink. It's almost as if—*but no*. There's no way in the realms that he would bring it up, not in this moment.

His sigh is pained.

Zehran's still staring up at Tahir when Rahat finally turns away. Something in her says that she just can't bear to look at them anymore. That their faces are too similar to Iliyah's. Zehran has her eyes; Tahir her smile. 'Just—' She stops herself before she can say anything stupid. It's one thing for them all to understand the truth of the situation; it's another to say those words.

Clearing his throat, Zehran makes her glance up through her lashes. Her cheeks are burning at feeling the words balancing at the tip of his tongue. Now if only he could just say them. Yet the glance Tahir flicks his way keeps any emerging thoughts at bay.

'What?'

The brothers exchange that look that's always set her on edge.

'What is it?'

Tahir paces as he speaks. 'Iya's smarter than that,' he says again, his voice dark and smooth as adamant. 'She won't be in some filthy field in the middle of a crowded jungle. She can hardly walk a pace if her slipper is the slightest bit tarnished—what makes you think she'll be out there in the wild?' His smile becomes vicious, a viper's like his brother Saadi's. 'Why would she choose a clearing by the temple of a god who hasn't shown his presence in *years*, when she's only been there once—if at all? And when was she there, Rahat? How can that lump of earth possibly be important to her?'

'Saadi would have stopped her,' Zehran chimes in, but no one's listening.

Rahat's blood is too busy being frozen in her veins. Steeling her features, she begs them not to betray her fear. They can't find out. 'You just have to trust me.'

He's still pacing; it's an intimidation technique. She's seen Saadi do it before, when they were children. Tahir knows Rahat's hiding something.

'*Fine.*' Rahat almost trips on her voluminous skirts as she gets to her feet, her chair clattering as it hits the polished floors. The sound reverberates through the drawing room, making the Praitosí men flinch. For a moment, she catches Tahir's mask slip into fear. It's the same fear coursing beneath her skin—the same fear she can spy in Zehran's rage. 'If you—'

Zehran raises a hand, stopping her from spewing whatever insult she might have hurled from her lips. Gods forbid she call off the wedding. 'I'll ride out at dawn with my most trusted,' he says slowly, his eyes trained on Rahat.

The blood seeps from her cheeks as she stares at him dumbfounded.

'Haroun, Malik, and Wahab will be up for the journey—Qadira will join us, of course,' he says, and his brother nods in that knowing way. Even as his training companions, Rahat had never had much to do with Zehran's fellow warriors. They were always too busy dismissing her to pay attention to her. 'Even if Malik decides to stay here with his wife, Qadira will more than make up for his loss.'

Tahir flicks a hand as if he were a Conqueror already. 'Fine, fine.'

'We'll find her along the Opaline River somewhere close to the palace where she hides after fights with *Baba*,' he says, and again, there's another nod from Tahir as he paces. Zehran's fist remains balled on the table. 'I doubt Saadi would have known where to look.'

'The *palace*,' Rahat repeats slowly, the idea reverberating. The palace of Rahala is nowhere near the fire god's temple.

Both brothers turn their eyes on her, and she feels herself quake beneath their heavy gaze. Still standing, she leans against the table, placing her hands on the smooth surface for support.

'Yes?' drawls Tahir.

'The palace is in the opposite direction of the fire temple,' she says blankly.

Tahir stops his pacing with a frown. 'And?'

That red hot anger boils up within her, so putrid she feels fit to vomit. 'You might as well slit her throat yourselves if you think you'll find h—'

Tahir moves so quickly that it's all she can do to suck in a breath. One moment he's across the room, and the next—in little more than two strides—he stands so perfectly still before her that she clamps her mouth shut. He's so much taller than her. So much more muscular. She feels like she's standing beneath him as she bows her head, already playing the role of a wife to the Empire.

No. She refuses.

Lifting her head, she stares him in the eye. 'She'll die.'

Those dark eyes flicker. 'She's already dead.'

A breath.

'Zehran.'

The youngest *shehzada* does his best as he stands to look like he hadn't been watching them intently. Shoulders pulled back, his stance rigid. But he can't tear his sight from the rebellion written across Rahat's face. She will certainly prove a handful.

'Get a full night's sleep; you'll need it when you leave. I'll send word to the others to be ready at your call.'

The warrior gives a single nod to his elder, and bows to his future sister-in-law as he makes his way from the drawing room to his private chambers. Rahat's hair sticks out in every possible direction, strands of beads from her performance tangled in those dark locks. Red powder still stains her face, her cheeks. Even chaotic, she has her own sort of wild beauty about her. The gentle hook of her nose, the slight downturn of her lips. Zehran looks her over one final time as he glances back from the door, all too aware of the tension hanging between them. Fear and pride rolls off of them like smoke. A small voice in the back of his head nags him not to leave as he pulls the door closed behind him, leaving Tahir alone with his bride.

As soon as the door closes, Tahir releases the breath he'd been holding. His sigh rolls off of him like he'd been carrying the world. And in a way, he has been. For he is as much of a sacrifice as Rahat—the second son thrown to a foreign country as a symbol of peace. A *symbol*, yes. Of course. But Rahat knows he will oversee her rule of Delorran and decide the country's future under the ideals of the Empire. Her brothers will give up their gods-given rights to rule as the eldest children. Her people will thrive, out from under direct control of the Empire, but they will still be kept in line. Her heart sinks. Her people will be freed, but... There are limits.

He trains those eyes on her, resting a hand at her tangled hair. A gentle kiss to her forehead makes her pause—and curse herself for her audible intake of breath. She can feel his smirk against her skin as his voice becomes a husky purr.

'Rahat, I know you're her dearest friend, but I think my brother and I know our sister better than even you.' He pulls her into an embrace she has no hope of escaping. Arms enclosing about her, she feels claustrophobic. She can't do this. Something about him feels wrong.

'You don't know her,' she challenges, scolding herself for letting those dread words escape.

The *shehzada* goes still, the *rajkumari* in his arms. Those muscled arms tense around her, and that's when she realises just how much of an idiot she's been. She knows better than to get ahead of herself, especially alone in a room with the enemy.

Enemy.

The word makes her pause. Her future husband, the enemy to her people.

What have I gotten myself into?

'All right.' Those arms relax. 'Tell me something of my sister I don't know.'

He might as well be squeezing her to death with how her heart's racing. The smell of him, like dew and hot sand and lilacs and sandalwood... it's heady. It clouds her senses, the scents locking in her nose. She looks up at him to find him looking down at her, a tiny woman in his arms. A tiny woman who knows how to wield a sword better than he. That is, when dancing.

For a second, for some stupid second, she almost considers telling him outright and confirming his fears. A calm smile passes over his face like he understands, relaxing his features until he almost becomes someone she could genuinely love. Until she realises just how wrong that is. She's felt this moment before, this want to turn her back on what is true and forget what she wants for the sake of her people. For Tahir already knows that she will never love him. You cannot talk yourself into loving someone—not that she hasn't been desperately trying. If only for her mother's sake.

'I can't say it,' she says at last.

And that's where the moment ends. The Praitosí drops his arms and backs away a step. Red is smeared over his face and stains his *qamis* where she'd rested against him. He takes in the sight of her, exhausted and dishevelled and covered in drying sweat. The shine in her eyes is crazed, breathless.

'Can't say it?' he echoes, his tone sharp as a viper's.

Gods. Think. 'No,' she says, her voice unshaken, 'I don't think there's anything you don't already know.'

It's a challenge. They both know it is.

Slowly, the *shehzada* nods. His brows jump a little in surprise as he considers it with a shrug. Rahat keeps waiting for that wall of his to slam right back up, but the jolt doesn't come. With no one's eyes upon them, the boy before her is relaxed. There's an easiness to his smile. But there's still that shine in his eyes that makes her uneasy. 'Well,' he says softly, brushing a hand over her hair, 'you had better get some sleep. It has been a long day for us all.'

It's better not to say a word, she decides as she turns, looking toward the servants at the door whom Tahir signals to with a flick of his hand. But she turns back before he can open his mouth. Her movements make the servants pause. She mashes her lips together, unsure.

'Yes?' he presses with a playful chuckle, but his features remain tight.

Opening her mouth to speak, she stops herself. Hands fluttering before her, she can hardly keep still. She's a mess, all nervous energy and regretted thoughts. As if reading her mind, Tahir takes her by the hand and pulls her close.

At feeling his breath caress her face, she gazes up at him. Charcoal eyes melt, warming at the sight of her. It takes all but a second for his lips to graze hers, ever so gently. And while she feels the pulse of lust racing through him, his heart quickening against her hand at his chest, she feels no warmth within herself. Just a wrongness that makes her stomach sink.

'Thank you,' he says upon pulling back.

She furrows her brow, pressed to his as he remains close. 'For what?'

'For sacrificing yourself for your people.'

'Well,' she laughs gently, 'it wouldn't have worked if you didn't agree.'

An exaltation like a chuckle sends warm breath into her face. He mumbles something she doesn't hear before pressing a slight kiss to the very tip of her nose. Again he mumbles the word, something she still doesn't catch.

He agreed to marry her after she proposed the idea. Even as a child he was ambitious. She can feel that now —that false affection placing a smile at his lips.

Feigning reluctance, she moves away, taking her hand from his grasp. They're both playing a part. Yet the way he looks at her makes her feel as if she's ripped her touch from him in revulsion. His eyes linger on her, but only for a moment before again flicking a hand to the servants by the door. 'Take the *rajkumari* safely to her rooms,' he orders.

Balling her fists and hiding them in the pleats of her skirts, she's about to lose her temper—ordering *her* servants in *her* city. In *her* home.

Then Tahir calls her back, barely breathing her name as if he can't quite bear letting her out of his sight. 'And Rahat?'

Her eyes find him over her shoulder, where he stands by the table. 'Yes?'

An odd smile flickers across his chiselled lips. 'Don't do anything stupid.'

4

The dancing lights above the mountaintops are hypnotising. Flashes of green, red, and dusky purple flit across the skies with pinks in their afterglow. She watches them each night from her window. Yet there's something about the lights tonight that screams danger. They twirl about the snow-capped mountains visible from the border of the Lyra Lands. Her mother once told her the lights were magic; that the Lyran people could not mourn their loss of the faeries, and so immortalised their bones in the sky, burning and projecting them across all the north of Abrecan.

But the lights have existed for longer than that; she remembers them from before the gods fell. Even the old folk cannot name when they began.

Exhausted, Rahat wipes the stray tears from her lashes. Her mind hasn't quietened since she left Tahir's chambers.

'Have we got everything?' she asks Hazel, keeping her strained focus out the window. The mountains feel a lifetime away. She doubts she will ever have the chance to see them up close and experience their wonder.

Yet under those reflecting lights, the city of Ajrapur has never been so beautiful. The green-topped roofs glimmer almost directly below her, the houses rising high up on Delorran's second-tallest mountain. It's so close, Rahat feels she could reach out and touch it, if she only just dared. Lights blur before she realises her eyes are brimming with tears again. Taeng's words have been playing on repeat in her mind, intermingling with Tahir's resigned disappointment.

'What else do we need?' she asks.

Hazel rummages through her knapsack, muttering to herself, 'Food, enough water to last till the first river, a change of clothes if we need it, salt, knives, and—' She points to Rahat's bag. '—fairly sure you've got the whetstone, ropes, map, and any bandages we may need, plus a few snacks.' A frown hovers at her brow before the redhead nods. 'Yes, that's everything.'

Rahat almost collapses back onto her lush bed with relief. A nervous laugh escapes her as she shoves the last few things—those that she'll need to keep quick at hand —into her saddlebag. Her arms are sore already. Her hands shake. 'What would I do without you?' she laughs.

Hazel gives her a once-over. 'I don't think you want me to answer that.'

Faint sunlight creeps over the horizon. The emerald-roofed houses in the city shine beside tin- and gold-roofs in the lazy light, their shine subdued till high-noon. A breath-taking sight. 'I sure will miss this place,' Rahat mumbles, making Hazel grimace from across the room.

'It's not like we're not coming back.' A beat. 'Right?'

Her words are met with a silence that makes her uneasy.

Outside, they can hear the horses being saddled in one of the courtyards. By the sounds the beasts make, Rahat recognises them as highly-trained desert horses—not the titanium creatures that she and Hazel will ride.

Titanium horses: the *lindélofs* of legend, created by gods to be the hooves of the wind. They can gallop through middle-mountains without harm, dance upon the midnight breezes, and most importantly: need no food or water. Which means less provisions that need packing. Only two of these mythical beasts remain in the royal stables, on the other side of the palace from the guest stables. One belongs to Rahat; the other is Karnan's pride and joy.

The horses whinny, making Hazel peek out the window beside her cousin. With the dancing lights streaking across the sky, morning is creeping ever-closer. The dozen or so men below mill about, preparing their leave, though it's difficult to say when that may be, with the sun being so stubborn this morning. As if he doesn't wish to rise and put Iliyah's soul at risk.

The best Rahat can do is make out the faces of riders she only vaguely recognises. But no one could forget Qadira. The disgust on the *kehrasa's* face at being on horseback is almost palpable. A desert-wanderer, the faerie's more used to travelling on camels than horses. With a glare at the men, she dismounts.

Rahat straps her vambraces tight. 'When do you think they'll leave?'

Hazel stands on her tiptoes to glimpse the horses below pawing at the stones about the gates. They're growing impatient, kicking up clouds of desert dust that's become trapped in the cobblestones. 'With the sun, I'd say, though who can say when that'll be.'

Rahat loops the leather of her breastplate through its buckles as she approaches the windows. The humidity is only getting worse as the day approaches. She knows she'll curse the soft leather later. But for the moment, it sits comfortably against the band of her *sirwal* pants that brush gently over her skin.

Green, purple, and a rusty orange dance across the starry sky. The twisting lights are fading, the sky lightening and casting the world in blue. The arms of Teos creep over the horizon, a reminder of what little time remains. It seems that not even the gods can prevent time from unravelling.

'Soon, then.'

*

Sneaking through a guarded palace before dawn breaks is trickier than Rahat had thought. Add open windows and breezy curtains of gossamer to the mix, and you're asking to be caught.

Knapsacks on their backs, boots lightly grazing the polished marble, they're careful with each corner they turn. Weaving through the corridors and down stairs and around spirals, Rahat almost feels dizzy. As if she had never realised how labyrinthine her home is. Bright walls of turquoise fade back through pinks and purples to bright oranges, mandalas mosaicing their way in intricate patterns from room to room. Moving so quickly through the half-darkness feels like moving through art —the paint mixing and mingling with each step.

They stick to the walls, watching for anyone who might prevent their escape—after all, someone is bound to question their attire. They're not exactly dressed for wedding preparations, which is what they *should* be doing. That little voice nags at the back of Rahat's mind. If today were normal, she would be confirming all last-minute decisions and overseeing the preparations.

Yet there's hardly a sign of life past the royal chambers. Despite almost wandering upon a meeting of servants in one of the back corridors, this is going surprisingly well. *And now that I've thought that, something's bound to go wrong.*

The slap of Hazel's hand on Rahat's catches her off-guard. The younger girl leans back, pulling Rahat against her to stop them rounding a corner. Hazel flattens her cousin into a doorway as an old aunty wanders by, rubbing at her eyes and clutching prayer beads in her gnarled-knuckled hands. The symbol of the sun goddesses twinkles at her forehead, painted in liquid gold and vermillion pigment. Garbed in white, she's a religious leader.

Warm breath caresses their faces. Hot, sticky breath.

When Hazel glances Rahat's way, she's shocked to find their noses nearly pressed together in the small space. 'Sorry,' she gasps out once the aunty has passed. Quick as a mouse, Hazel emerges from the sliver of the doorway and disappears around a corner. Rahat follows without a sound.

There isn't much time left. Her brothers will be awake soon, and they'll be the first to notice her absence. Especially when Ashrit won't be able to find her to share a breakfast of pomegranates fresh from the trees in the gardens. The thought that everyone will suspect she fled the wedding is what makes her pause. Her people will think her a coward. After years of being oppressed, they deserve better. *The* rajkumari *has turned her back on her people!* they will cry. They will fear she has abandoned them. The thought lingers in her heart, pulling at the cage of her chest.

Only her brothers will know otherwise; they will placate the masses. And in doing so, they'll buy her time to return—*if* she returns.

Taking those first steps outside feels like stepping into the firing line. Into the silence, they run, cursing as their bags *clatter* and *clunk*. Though the promenade is covered by shadow and lacing vines, the noises echo across several levels of the yards. Each step brings a new noise they fear will get them caught.

And if they get caught... what happens then? Depending on who catches them, it could mean condemnation, even calling off the wedding. It could mean a call to war. For is fleeing a wedding meant to free her people not an act of war? It could be the death of thousands in one simple burst of anger.

After all, the Praitosí have a *kehrasa* at their disposal.

Passing under the final aqueduct, Hazel glances back to her cousin to catch the pained look on her face. She nods, hoping Rahat understands what she means—that it'll be okay, in the end. And if it's not okay, it's not the end.

At last, they reach the doors to the stables, the handles hardly visible under this cloak of darkness. Hazel keeps watch as Rahat snaps open the lock on the doors, before slinking inside to safety.

They're greeted by Rahat's *lindélof* Prakaash and his affectionate soft whinnies. It sounds like the whirring of gears and the purrs of kittens. Handing her pack to Hazel, the *rajkumari* goes to the titanium beast's side to run a hand over his cool muzzle; he needs to keep quiet, and thankfully, he understands. 'You're all right, Prakaash. Everything will be all right,' she coos, making the horse tilt its head.

The air feels sucked out of the stables when they hear a whistle from without. And it's coming closer. Hazel drops the bags behind a wall, looking about in panic for somewhere to hide. Over the faint din of the city awakening outside the palace walls, that foreboding high-pitched whistling becomes all-consuming. It's one small reminder that they can be stopped even before leaving the palace walls. They haven't got a chance.

Hazel keeps her eyes on Rahat before throwing herself behind a stall wall when the door swings abruptly open. It creaks as it goes, to reveal Zehran standing there, apple in hand. Rahat's sight flits to where Hazel's hidden as the girl sweeps her feet out of sight. She moves her eyes back to the prince. Sleep-ringed eyes tell Rahat of the *shehzada*'s sleepless night, of the hours spent crying.

He grunts. 'You're up early.'

Thank the gods. 'Couldn't sleep,' she says, returning her eyes to Prakaash.

His sigh is heavy, burdened. He takes a bite of that crisp apple, its juices running over his lips and down his chin. 'I have to find Iliyah,' he says, his voice rising almost to hysterics. But he shuts down the panic before Rahat can see too much—and before the woman who's crept up behind them can witness much more.

'The horses are ready,' the woman purrs in her deep, rumbling tones. Those dark cheetah's eyes keep Rahat pinned over the *shehzada*'s shoulder. The black stripes beneath those eyes flash, catching the light. As the woman grins, she reveals pointed teeth like a big cat's. *Damned shape-shifters.*

Robed in black with her whip at her belt, Qadira stands with her arms over her chest, demanding all attention. The mere sight of her makes Rahat quake. Over the woman's shoulder, Rahat spots two men she vaguely remembers from years ago: Wahab and Haroun, men who had served the Empire during the first invasion. They'd burnt down the palace gates.

Rahat clears her throat.

'As your brother keeps telling me,' she responds at last, to Zehran, and only Zehran. Summoning indifference from the very pit of her being, she smothers all hatred and channels her mother as she glances at the woman in black. 'Qadira.'

The *kehrasa* flashes those sharp incisors. 'Rahat,' she says, with a shallow bow as she dabs her fingers to her forehead.

Turning back to Zehran, she tilts her head, forcing Qadira to understand that much longer of an interruption and she'll be in trouble. Although she's under the control of the Empire, Qadira is not immune to outside orders. As a faerie in their land, she must abide by mortal rules.

The *kehrasa* glances to Zehran who nods, and she withdraws from the stables, closing the doors as she takes her leave. The two men behind her stand oblivious.

'She's...' Rahat can't find the word.

'I know,' agrees Zehran, his brows knotted. 'She's been a little tense lately.'

Tense. That's one word for it.

He takes another bite of his apple, smiling openly as he watches Rahat with Prakaash. As children, she'd wanted nothing more than to ride—away from her captured kingdom, he assumes. Whatever the want was, he'd never asked.

A rustle comes from the stall over, making the prince look up. A light kick to the stall gates and Rahat tenses. If she's lucky, Zehran will dismiss it as one of the other horses. 'When will you leave?' she asks, before he can move to where Hazel is hiding. Most likely, Karnan's *lindélof* Bijalee has nuzzled her a little too playfully.

Zehran shakes away his curiosity like a hound does the rain. Shoulders sag. 'Soon, if Qadira's any more anxious than before. She says the air doesn't feel right... whatever that means,' he says, keeping his voice soft. All manner of things can be racing through his mind as he takes in the sight of Rahat dressed in riding leathers instead of a morning shawl. A frown etches at his features. 'You're dressed ready to ride.' He sounds shocked as the furrow of his brow deepens. 'So early?' he presses, approaching with that confident puffed-out chest. The half-eaten apple is discarded to the straw-coated stone underfoot.

Prakaash moves before her, barring the *shehzada's* way. An exhale of steam wavers before the beast's nose as it stands face-to-face before the soldier. A challenge hangs in the air, one Zehran pushes aside as he demands, 'Why are you wandering the palace before dawn?' His strides are smooth, controlled, as he moves about the creature to reach her side. Prakaash tosses his head, training his glowing blue eyes on the boy. All thoughts of Hazel in the next stall are forgotten—but if he were to glance over the wall now, she'd be discovered. All it would take is a glance.

That can't happen.

'If you couldn't sleep, as you say, you would be in the gardens, waiting for your brothers—where we always used to find you,' he says, his breath now hot against her exposed neck. She can feel the moisture of his mouth at her skin, can hear it sticking in the back of his throat as he wets his lips. Like some kind of predator.

She gives Prakaash's saddle ties a tug. Eyes don't dare meet. 'A lot can change over three years,' she dismisses.

As he places a possessive hand at the small of her back, he slides the other along her arm. She has to fight the urge to rip herself from him as that hand wanders across her stomach. 'How much, exactly?' he ponders, breath hitching as his fingers glide across the buckle of her leathers.

The air goes still. The heat spreading through her as she lifts his hands from her soars to excruciating heights. Sparks flood her cheeks till the rage becomes dizzying. It's only then that she catches his eyes lingering upon her chest. Hands become claws. 'I may be the bride of your brother,' she hisses, 'and I may be in love with your sister—'

His gaze snaps up to meet hers, eyes wide.

'—but that does *not* mean that I will *ever* be interested in having you.'

With that, she backs away, claws ready at her sides as she passes behind Prakaash, where the boy will not dare follow. Against the *lindélof's* cool hide, she feels her hands relaxing as the beast moves closer, guarding her.

That shock morphs as Zehran's face contorts. He clicks his tongue, and Prakaash whips the boy with his tail of spun titanium. A hiss from the creature sends the boy skittering from the stall like a cat. There's no way in all the All-Mother's realms he'll try that again.

'I don't think he likes me very much,' purrs the *shehzada*, biting back the insults written across his face. Rahat can almost see them, etched in black ink.

She lifts her chin. 'He doesn't take kindly to strangers.'

'Strangers?' he echoes.

Silence meets him.

But when he clicks his tongue once more, she can't help it. Fingers drum against Prakaash's hide with a rhythm. Despite it all—the rage, the harassment—she has to tell him. 'You're looking in the wrong places—'

He pulls away. 'I heard enough of this last night.'

Turning on his heel, with not a glance to Hazel's stall, he saunters off. Like the brooding child he is. His knock at the stable door sees it opened by Haroun and Wahab as he glances back with a sneer. 'Sorry I'll miss the wedding.'

The well-aimed dagger sinks deep. Icy claws dig into her stomach, making her feel fit to burst. When she refuses to speak, staring him down, he turns his back on her with a muffled yawn.

Haroun and Wahab examine her with wary eyes as they close the doors on her, locking her in with the metallic horses. Their eyes had been unforgiving as they took in sights of what they wanted to see—with thoughts of nothing near noble.

Rahat bites her tongue to stop the scream climbing up her throat. Fingernails dig into palms so hard she slices half-moons into life-lines.

Only once the steps of the Praitosí company have faded from the courtyard does Hazel rise from Bijalee's stall. Coated in straw and her hair sticking up each way, she looks like she's been rolled out of a cart. 'That,' she says with incredulity, pointing to the door in accusation, 'was *way* too close.'

Rahat keeps her eye on the doors; somehow, she doesn't trust that they're completely alone. Have they posted someone outside? The Zehran Rahat knew as a child never would have done so, but he's become more like Saadi over the years. And Saadi would never trust to leave Rahat alone. Not now.

'Zehran's not the boy I used to know,' she says in a half-whisper. 'And I don't know why—it's stupid—but it hurts. He never would have put me in that position in the past. *And to suggest that we—*' Sucking in a deep breath, she shakes her head. 'And if... *if* Iliyah's not there, where she *has* to be, then he'll be all I have left to remind me of her. He has her eyes...' Stubborn tears refuse to roll down her cheeks, instead blurring her vision. 'And I don't think I could do that to her, Hazel.'

The Asthori stands firm beside her Delorrene cousin. With a tentative hand, she pats her shoulder, making her smile before embracing her outright. This is a game to be tread lightly, and they are breaking through the game-board. So close to the wedding, it's deserving of war.

And if Zehran suspects her of fleeing... The game might already be over.

'If it's any consolation, he's not that attractive when he's such a jerk.'

Shocked, Rahat slinks out of the embrace.

'What?' The defensive shrug almost makes Rahat laugh. 'I mean, he's always going to be a *liiiittle* attractive and kind of, well, *gorgeous*, but give me some credit. He's a jerk. He shouldn't have put you in that position, and he damn well shouldn't have touched you. Quite frankly, he needs a punch in the—'

'Slow down, tiger,' chuckles Rahat. 'You're getting ahead of yourself.'

The girl blushes, those snowflake cheeks blooming with a wink.

In his open stall, Prakaash exhales imposingly, growing impatient. Rahat reaches back a hand for his muzzle, and the titanium creature bends into it, his metal smooth in her palm. 'I'm okay,' she says, though she isn't sure who she's speaking to—the horse, or to her cousin. Both come from foreign lands.

As the cogs inside Prakaash tick beneath his immortal hide, the slight vibrations ringing through Rahat's fingertips, she takes a deep breath of her own. 'We'll find her.'

The *lindélof* blows toasty-warm air in her face.

If her suspicions are correct, then the Praitosí company will depart from the eastern gate, leading them over the bridge and almost directly over the border. Which leaves the northern gate to the jungles as their best option.

Securing the saddle about Prakaash's middle, she watches as Hazel leads Bijalee from his stall. The black-adamant *lindélof* is smaller by a foot, rising still a head above Hazel. The creature whinnies as they mount, their robes gliding like silk over their metallic mounts. Their leathers are soundless as planned; even Hazel's leather riding pants are silent as she settles into the saddle.

They're really doing this. Steeling their nerves, they share a nod. If Zehran thought he could lock her away, he has another thing coming.

There's a path in the gardens she knows that'll lead them out of sight, leaving them invisible to anyone who might be searching. If even one pair of eyes spots them, Rahat's certain she'll be locked in her rooms till the wedding.

There's too much at stake here. She doesn't want to imagine the look of disappointment on her mother's face. It won't be long after they've escaped that the Maharanee will discover that her daughter is gone. And she'll think it was fear that drove her away. She'll think her daughter a coward.

But now is not the time. The sun is blooming across the sky, spreading its light over the canvas of the All Mother. Rahat mutters a prayer that they might remain safe. A glance back at Hazel; a nod. They can do this.

Behind the stalls, Rahat presses her hand to a stone in the corner. With a groan of old stone, it opens the secret passage behind the wall of saddles. While Hazel suppresses her gasp, Rahat nudges Prakaash onward. She can't remember the last time she'd used this entrance. The glimmering spiderwebs dangling from the ceiling confirm it: there hasn't been movement through here in years. 'Ew,' she hears Hazel mumble from behind her.

'We're headed into the jungle; might as well get used to it.'

With wide eyes, Hazel leads Bijalee through the thin corridor of stone, rotted wood, and thick spiderwebs. 'Nope, I'm good,' she squeaks, hands clutching the reins so tight her knuckles shine white. 'Fairly sure I won't get used to it.'

Rahat laughs through her nose as she tugs the reins, making Prakaash follow the narrow path to the left, which will land them near the menagerie. The small sounds of larks chirping and singing their morning songs wind their way down through the wind-tunnels. Soon, the other animals will start to wake.

The dank air breathes through Rahat's hair. She sighs into the breeze as, behind her, Hazel keeps a hand over her nose and mouth. 'I don't know how you can stand that smell,' she bleats through her fingers.

The *rajkumari* shrugs. 'Wait till you smell the old blood in the oracles' den.'

Hazel only shakes her head like a spooked toddler. 'No, thank you.'

Again she laughs, the sound echoing around them, bouncing off every wall.

'Somehow I feel like this is a bad idea,' demurs Hazel. The sunlight is blinding as they emerge from the spiders' den. Rahat didn't realise how quickly the sun would rise—but then anything seems bright compared to that pitch black. There's a small wave of revulsion that rolls through her; she's near the Kaiduko statue by the entrance to the catacombs. A shiver races up her arms. Shaking it off, she steers them onward, down promenades so slim their boots scrape the walls.

The serval cats within the menagerie's walls bleat over the sounds of snow-tigers roaring and zebras yipping. Far-away beasts, all of them. The snow cats hidden behind those walls are creatures big as bears—from the north of the Lyra Lands, they're beasts of nightmares compared to the Delorrene tigers only half their size. Beneath all those layers of sound, the *lindélofs'* cog-works and hooves are hidden. But there's something she can't quite understand.

The gates are open.

Who would be up this early?

The handlers do most of their work at night. And if they're about during the day, they go unseen. Morning brings many of the foreigners out to behold these exotic creatures, but this is early by anyone's standards. And the gates are open, lazily discarded.

Must be Karnan. He's sure to have visited Taeng before sunrise.

Taking the lead, Hazel disappears around a corner in the low-lying gardens. Her pale skin glimmers like ice in the dawn's blue light.

'What are you doing?'

It feels like someone's grabbed her about the throat. A squeak is all the noise she makes as her brother sprints to her side. His hands spread over Prakaash's flank and the *lindélof* leans his head toward the *rajkumar*. Yet Karnan only has eyes for his sister.

'*Bhai*,' she gasps out, the saliva sticking in the back of her throat.

'Need help getting out?' he asks, that wicked grin spreading over his face.

And what can she say to that? Clamping her lips shut tight, she nods. Karnan might be the only thing that will keep them from being discovered.

Without a word, the *rajkumar* pulls his scarf tighter about his shoulders as he bolts to where Hazel's wandered before them. Laying a hand at his *lindélof's* side, he makes her stop with a fright, before leaning close to explain the situation. After a moment, Hazel glances back at Rahat, who gives a gentle nod.

Turning back to Karnan, Hazel rolls her shoulders in a shrug.

Her brother beams at her, and seconds later he's scouting ahead in the gardens. Graceful, he hops between bushes and along the paths, stopping at moments in foliage so full of flowers every colour you've imagined that he disappears amongst them. The scarf about his neck flutters in the slight breeze.

Above them, the palace is beginning to wake. Shutters are thrown open with a sickening creaking of hinges. As each window opens, the girls on horseback slink into the dying shadows. All it takes is one look, one ray of sun to give away their position. *Lindélofs* aren't exactly inconspicuous creatures.

The closer they come to passing the eastern gate through the clusters of blooms, cloud-seeker trees, and fountains, the more Rahat's heart sinks. There's no way of avoiding this. The sounds of swords colliding scream from across the courtyard. The crack of a whip echoes off the stone walls.

Hazel mutters something unintelligible under her breath. Just beyond the wall lay the only people that will be able to stop them. Another crack of Qadira's whip makes her flinch. Bijalee tosses his head, just smothering a snort.

Karnan glances back at his horse with a frown. At the look, Bijalee calms under Hazel's hands. But the gleam in Karnan's eyes is one of foreboding.

Rahat pulls short on the reins, making Prakaash tug. His soft braids of spun titanium whisper as they fall against his neck. Rahat has no doubt that the *kehrasa* can hear them over the wall; soon enough their minds might give them away.

Through a small crack in the wall, Rahat can spy Qadira coiling her whip in her hands. The woven leather and silver-tin gleams in the growing sun. Threatening and deadly, the *kehrasa* narrows those animal eyes. Tall and lithe, she is on the alert, shoulders tensed and pointed ears straining for any sound of trouble. A head-scarf wrapped about her head conceals most of her hair from the sun. Her sharp eyes survey the yard as she stands back from Wahab and Haroun sparring, their swords clashing like bursts of lightning. As those eyes settle on the garden wall, a jolt runs through Rahat. Yet the *kehrasa* turns her sight away.

Zehran stands by the gate with his brother, all in black and speaking animatedly. Something's happened. Squinting, Rahat is only able to make out one word on his lips—*Saadi*. Their brother's done something.

With them so distracted, this might be a tad easier than thought. Overhanging trees bearing fruits and blossoms obscure their view past the garden walls. The courtyard just beyond is barren of all colour, all growth. Rough gravel lines the path; gravel which will *crunch* underfoot. Qadira turns her back on the open path leading through from the courtyard. As if she knows... *Impossible.*

Rahat kicks Prakaash into action, only for Karnan to hold out a silencing hand.

Prakaash halts. Rahat slouches back in the saddle.

Without a word, Karnan peeks around the corner. Wahab and Haroun still spar, their swords sparking as Qadira keeps watch over them. Meanwhile Zehran and Tahir continue to argue in the shade, throwing about their hands as they speak.

Again, Karnan holds up his hand, as if expecting them to shoot forward. Rahat wants to shake him when he turns back, winks, and straightens his robe. 'Watch this,' he mouths, oozing confidence.

Smooth, controlled motions lead him around the corner with his hands laced behind his back. That cocky grin plastered to his face doesn't falter as he takes in the sight of Qadira preparing herself for a fight. The whip makes a creaking sound as she bends it through her hands. 'Morning,' he grins, brushing his forehead with his fingers in welcome. 'Hope you all had a pleasant rest.'

It's apparent by the silence on the other side of the wall that they're staring. Rahat can only imagine the look on Zehran's usually-so-controlled face. The two have hated each other for years; that's apparent to anyone. Rahat has to stop herself from peeking over the wall —and the temptation is almost too strong.

Like the cogs clicking in the creature between her thighs, her brain ticks over the paths of the palace grounds. If Karnan can distract them for long enough, they just might have a chance. There are two paths from here. One straight ahead, if they can make it past the open promenade. Knuckles glowing white at the reins, she steers them back—for this path is too risky. There's a corridor through the hedges and labyrinthine stone corridors which should see them through to the northern gate safely. If no one catches them first.

A demand cuts through the air in Qadira's quick tongue.

For a second, Rahat's heart stops. As a child, she only heard that guttural language a handful of times: Qadira uses it only when she wants Zehran and Tahir's attention.

'I thought you were leaving by the southern gate?' asks Karnan, his words like a quiver in the silence after Qadira's harsh words. 'Or do you believe your sister may be elsewhere?'

Rahat can picture the upheld chin of her brother as he stands with feet firmly planted in the earth. It must be a staring match between he and Zehran by now.

Again, that ancient language rings out in the courtyard.

Sparks like spiders' legs race up Rahat's arms. Oh, Qadira *definitely* knows what they're trying to do. A glance back at Hazel—and it's clear she's keeping her mind off of the task at hand by the contorted concentration on her face. It's the only way to get around Qadira without the *kehrasa* knowing their exact plans.

When Rahat was younger, she used to continually sing the same song in her mind until the *kehrasa* finally gave up trying to delve through her thoughts.

'Why are you out here, Karnan?' Tahir's voice is deadly low.

Rahat can almost see her brother's purposeful strides as he joins them by the fighters which have stilled. He shrugs, silent for a time before turning his attention to the princes. 'Couldn't sleep,' he says, by way of explanation. 'I'm sure you all had the same trouble.'

A silence stretches out between them, making Rahat's nerves bubble.

Hazel shoots her a glance, a slight frown. Rahat dismisses it.

For if there's anyone who can get them out of this mess, it's her brother. Karnan, who strolls through the courtyard as he inspects the Praitosí desert horses with their packs loaded for the journey. 'Quite a way you'll be riding,' he says. 'A shame you only just arrived, really.'

Zehran's snort is his only response.

'You never wanted us here anyway.' The words are quiet, spoken by one of the other men—Wahab or Haroun, Rahat can't be sure.

From across the courtyard, Tahir has to yell to be heard. Standing by the crank of the gates, he rests back against the carvings of the outer-wall. Rahat gulps. If it weren't for the small gap in the wall's stonework, she might have been able to get through this without feeling guilty. There are so many things that can go wrong. For example, the path which lays ahead of them is exposed to the courtyard for nearly a metre. Yet they stand within a labyrinth of sandstone walls which tower over them.

The shadows feel like they're mocking them. Shadows tracing the sun's movements onto the walls.

Rahat tries hard not to think of how she's already sweating.

'My only problem with my brother leaving so soon is that he won't be here to take part in the wedding ceremonies.' Tahir's voice rings out like a knife to the chest. Rahat spreads her hand over her shoulder, her fingers digging into her tense muscles. If only *mehendi* didn't mark her skin so. The delicate red lines lace her hands like blood. 'Iliyah will be by the God Mountains, just north of the palace. It is Zehran's task to fetch her body.' The prince shakes his head, his brow pinched in pain. 'Respect that this is not a game.'

Karnan raises his hands in surrender, turning his back on the princes. Subtly, he glances at Rahat and Hazel, but his sight is drawn upward. His eyes widen just a little. Someone else might not notice it, but she knows what that means. *Trouble.*

Between her thighs, Prakaash stirs. A toss of the head, and his reins almost rip from Rahat's hands. 'Prakaash,' she shushes, quiet as a breath. Only it's too late.

Karnan folds down the two middle fingers of his right hand. *Look up.*

With a heart beating harder than thunder, Rahat looks up—

—to find Qadira standing atop of the wall above them.

Rahat gasps, 'Run!'

She spurs Prakaash into action, the *lindélof*'s whinny echoing off the labyrinth's walls. Hazel follows without protest, nudging Bijalee into a gallop. The hooves kick up dirt underfoot. The sandstone walls blur together.

Above, Qadira cracks her whip and raises a call to the skies—a *whoop*ing Rahat's never heard before. Her voice expands in the air like it might in the desert, filling up every space to echo in their ears. Her calls grow louder as she snaps the whip again and follows.

Her lithe limbs are strong and powerful as she sprints after them, her slippered feet silent against the ancient sandstone. Leaping to the next wall, she beats them to the next corner, making Rahat pull up hard on the reins. She doesn't know which path to take.

Desperate, Rahat steers Prakaash left. He careens, hooves sliding on the old stone.

Another cry from Qadira, this one more of a rhythm'd gasp. Rahat doesn't know the exact moment the whip catches her cheek—only that it explodes with pain.

As the blood dribbles down her face, she can only imagine the chaos Karnan's facing in the courtyard. The *kehrasa* follows without a fault, gliding easily from wall-top to wall-top. The black of her skin becomes mottled, ochre fur poking through as she bears her teeth to the winds. Power surges through her, thick as blood.

'STOP THEM!' she cries, her words heavy with that Rehmayan lilt.

On the other side of the garden wall, Karnan battles against Haroun and his weighed net. The warrior fights gladiator-style as he lurches forward with spear raised. The spear tip barely grazes Karnan's forearm as he blocks the blow, forcing Haroun back.

Only he isn't able to defend himself from a kick to the back of his knee from Wahab. Karnan hits the stone with a hollow *thud*, his kneecap feeling about to crack. A whimper, and the men turn from him.

'NOW!' Qadira screams, vanishing mid-air to reappear right as her feet hit the ground. The smattering of shadow and sand is hypnotic, almost distracting, as Rahat and Hazel burst out from the labyrinth and into the courtyard—the courtyard they were trying to avoid.

Chaos erupts.

A roar rips from Karnan's throat as he throws himself at Haroun and Wahab. His arms catch the men about the neck as he yanks them from the horses' path.

'NOW!'

The scream throws Bijalee off-kilter, the horse darting between the men and raising up on his hind legs. He strikes the air, eyes wide and full of fear as the courtyard crowds with bodies. There are so many of them.

'Hazel?' Rahat yells, throwing her sight back over her shoulder.

By the garden wall, Qadira roars, her magic quaking as she takes aim. The coiled tin whip catches Bijalee about the neck, pulling the beast back. Bijalee tosses his head, desperate to escape—and Hazel hits the old stones hard.

'*Hazel!*'

Prakaash rears, striking his hooves down upon shields carried by servants. The servants crumble to their knees as Rahat pulls him back.

Hazel rolls to her side, narrowly missing the beat of Bijalee's hoof.

Qadira catches the motion out the corner of her eye and tosses her whip, making Bijalee lurch to the side— away from Hazel's grounded body. Hazel scuttles back, desperate to rise to her feet. Following her movement, Qadira unsheathes the dagger at her side. The way the *kehrasa* brandishes the blade makes Hazel feel sick. It shines in the rising sun's light like the call of a god.

The faerie's face shifts, the dark strokes beneath her eyes flashing like the blade in her hand. They're meant to reflect the light like a cheetah's markings, but it seems they're swallowing it. Qadira's carnelian eyes glow.

Hazel fears it's the end.

Throwing Haroun and Wahab off, Karnan careens into the faerie's side, sending her staggering across the courtyard.

Tahir yells something Rahat doesn't catch as she takes Bijalee by the reins.

Before them, the gates still creep to a close. The creaking of the metal screams as the men work the crank. Rahat's torn between her brother by Qadira and her cousin on the ground. 'Quickly,' she gasps out, jerking Prakaash out of reach of Haroun's weighed nets.

Hazel throws herself atop Bijalee's back while Karnan keeps the faerie distracted. By the outer wall, Tahir no longer yells, but has gone quiet. Over the din of battle, Rahat cannot hear Zehran weaving his way through the chaos.

'Rahat!' he calls, barely heard over the whinnying of their horses. 'Rahat!'

Her heart gallops, and she's not sure if it's breaking or if it's guilt; it thuds as loud as Bijalee's hooves against the stone. Prakaash's flank grazes the closing gate as she makes it through into the outside world.

At last, Qadira pushes Karnan aside and raises her whip hand.

The gate is almost closed. The left door is forced into place as the right is slowly brought to meet it. Rahat's blood freezes in her veins as the door rattles and the men flee, scattering themselves about the courtyard as the *lindélof* with the glowing eyes barrels through.

And makes it.

Hazel makes it.

That cry of triumph screams from Rahat's throat as she punches the air, the both of them already soaked through with sweat. The tears at her cheeks coax a smile from Hazel as she gallops past at full speed.

'That was easy,' she gasps. 'Now *run!*'

It's Zehran's order that brings her back to the task at hand: 'OPEN THE GATES!'

Prakaash skitters as the gates are yanked open, as if by the force of demigods. Tugging on the reins, Rahat pulls him back as he rears—and is barely able to keep herself astraddle his back. A call cuts through the air, agitating the *lindélofs* more as it cries out, filling every inch of space.

Qadira.

Through the gates, they spy her sheathing her dagger. The faerie stretches her neck and shoulders, preparing herself. The whip, however, stays firmly in hand.

Behind her, Zehran mounts his desert horse in swift movements. It won't be long before they're atop them. Yet Rahat feels frozen to the spot. Petrified. What has she done?

Prakaash's hooves hit the ground and Rahat turns him about, but the damned creature is moving too slow.

'*Rahat!*' Hazel's cry is exasperated from metres ahead. The *lindélof* responds before his rider can, taking off with such a speed that he almost knocks Rahat from his back. She has to bite back a yelp when she spots a flash of red—Zehran's riding cloak. But nowhere does she see Tahir readying himself to ride. He won't be following them. Casting a glance over her shoulder, she spots him first: there, standing by the gates like a statue, eyes glued to his runaway bride. There will be no coming back from this.

The jungle swallows her whole. As if the goddess Ghera has opened her arms to conceal the *rajkumari* from danger. Amongst a lush smattering of greens and vibrant hues, it will be hard to find her. Trees, vines, flowers, creatures—life all blurs together as Prakaash carries her far into the jungle after Hazel and Bijalee.

'Rahat?' The girl's voice echoes from up ahead.

Haroun's hunting cry stills the jungle.

Prakaash gallops harder—though she didn't think such a thing possible. The wind is deafening in her ears. And above, she can hear the piercing cries of a falcon. They're hunting them.

At the call, Hazel doubles back, steering Bijalee with such speed that he raises dust clouds. The girls share a breathless smile, triumphant and nervous, before Hazel catches sight of their hunters over Rahat's shoulder. 'Keep riding,' orders the Asthori, taking off in the opposite direction to meet the Praitosí head-on.

'Haz—' Rahat catches herself at realising the girl's plan.

While Rahat remains out of sight around a fork in the path, she watches as Hazel storms straight into their hunters' party. Veering to the left, she spooks their horses into rearing—and spurs their riders into following. In all the confusion, they've thought Hazel to be trailing Rahat.

Qadira's quick words echo through the trees, growing quieter the further they're lead south. By how the trees quake, Rahat knows that the faerie is in the treetops, weaving through the vines as she dissolves into shadow and re-forms just in time to pounce. She's only seen it a handful of times, but it has always been terrifying. To watch someone disappear before your eyes to become smoke and sand, then reappear moments later—if Rahat's telling the truth, nothing has scared her more. What might Qadira uncover with a skill like that?

And what if Qadira had been there, during any private moment with Iliyah?

The thought stops her dead. Prakaash keeps his hooves planted firm as they listen to the sounds dying away. Every muscle in her body wants to turn back for Hazel, but the risk it could pose to Iliyah stops her.

'We've come this far,' she says to herself, steeling her nerves. 'Escaping is the hardest part.' *You are the earth, the gods-sent, the ruler of your future*, she tells herself with each deep breath, remembering the words from some tale her mother told her as a child. Her pack doesn't hold much food, she knows that—but a map is more valuable than food out here. The jungle is full of food. The knives strapped to her thighs will provide enough meat, if she can catch a hare or monkey in time. Not that the thought is appealing.

She sighs, 'We can't turn back.'

The dark glimmer of black through the trees is all she needs to run. The faint shine of silver sends a jolt up her spine. The Praitosí are still close. And like a true Praitosí hunting party, they make no effort to be quiet. That's as much a part of the hunt as the pursuit—to hear your pursuer creeping up on you, your breath quickening to vomit-inducing levels as each moment you feel they could leap from the trees.

Yet as their triumphant cries fill the air, they grow quieter, further away. The earth is swallowed by powerful hooves; the company will have Hazel soon. Rahat can't stomach to think what they'll put her through—what her own father might put Hazel through, to get her back.

He will do anything to avoid another war.

Bounty hunters are rife in the Summer Lands since the faerie Rapture, and it's only a matter of time before they're sent for her. *There's no use thinking of it*, she scolds, spurring Prakaash into the darkest parts of the jungle. It opens itself to her, the jungle a great cavernous mouth from which she might never emerge.

*

There goes the idea of *ever* being a knight. Sweat makes her shirt cling to her feverish skin; the sun glinting off Prakaash's face is blinding. How can people boast about quests when they're like this?

Yet it makes her wonder. Would Hazel have become a knight, if she'd stayed in the Asthore Isles? In both the Lyra Lands and the Asthore Isles, it's not uncommon to find a woman's face behind a jousting helmet. It's an honourable profession, if not a short one. For any woman who fights for their Queen strikes a fine match of her choosing—and then must hang up her sword. The Queen herself is whoever bests her adversaries; the ruling family changes generation to generation.

One day, Hazel hopes to return home one day and become queen. Start some changes. Though Rahat's not too sure how. Her father made it clear when she left that he never wanted her in the Isles again. That hasn't stopped her from dreaming, of course.

'She'll be okay,' Rahat assures herself, knowing that speaking aloud in the middle of the jungle with nothing but a metal horse for company is not exactly the most common sight. 'Hazel always pulls through.'

They ride on till sunset, her stomach grumbling all the long way, till Prakaash draws them away from the path, the smooth earth having been lost somewhere in the trees long ago without Rahat's realising. The vines become denser; the foliage underfoot more lively. Everything about this place is lush—except for the mosquitos. She could do without the mosquitos. And without the stinging ache where Qadira's whip had caught her cheek.

The *rajkumari* glances to where she might have thought the path would be, to find the jungle staring back at her. It all looks the same. This is unlike anything she's ever seen in the palace gardens. No wonder the architects had never planned for a jungle; there'd be no way of containing it. The scratching and scurrying of small animals leaping though the boughs above is comforting. The canopies almost look comfortable. If she can just climb up there, she might be able to...

'No.' She shakes herself awake, rocking a little in the saddle. 'Awake, stay awake. You don't have time for sleep.' An inhuman sound gurgles up from her stomach as if pleading for the dried goat meat in her pack. She grimaces, feeling the pain in every inch of her being. Even her eyes hurt. The handful of nuts in her pack won't be enough and she doesn't want to eat all the goat meat at once. Perhaps she hadn't thought this through.

A light whisper bubbles over the breeze. Rahat strains her ears as Prakaash guides them through the trees, leading over mounds and under low-hanging vines laced with likely-poisonous flowers of every shade. A rush of cool air kisses her cheeks, making them sing. Over the low *whooping* of langur monkeys, she hears water trickling over rocks.

Water?

They shouldn't be anywhere near a river. Ripping the map from beneath her leathers, she searches with dirty fingers. Having travelled a full day's ride north of the palace would place them *about...* Nowhere near any stream marked on the map. In fact, there shouldn't be water near for half a day more.

Emerging from the thick cluster of trees, Prakaash is careful with his footing in the freshly-tilled earth. Any wrong move, and they could sink through, devoured by mud and gods know what else. The image of just her hand sticking out of the undergrowth in a last failed attempt to breathe sticks in her mind like glue. Yet the trickling of the stream is so enticing, and the babbling water's so clear.

'You're sure this is safe?' she asks of the *lindélof*, who nods irritatedly, as if to ask who is the eldest between them. 'Okay, okay,' she holds up her hands in surrender with a laugh, barely keeping ahold of the reins, 'but if it's poisoned somehow, that's on you.'

He nips at her shoulder when she dismounts, almost collapsing at the strange heaviness of standing on legs which have somehow configured themselves of jello. *This isn't fair*, she scoffs, the tingling in her legs searing with pain. *No one tells you of this in the songs.* Glancing back at the map, she frowns, feeling the sweat drip into the furrow of her brow. 'Why isn't this stream marked?' she thinks aloud.

Prakaash ignores her as he sniffs at the riverbed. His muzzle gleams, bouncing light into Rahat's face and making her blink back stars. Truth be told, *lindélofs* have no need for water; this is what makes them such valuable mounts on long quests. But while there's no need for it, there are some like Prakaash who enjoy the fresh zing of freezing water against their metal tongues.

He splashes Rahat when she doesn't move from her spot, making her jump back. '*Prakaash*,' she whines, wiping the water from her lashes.

The coolness against her cheek is euphoric.

There's no reaction from the horse. The water runs over his mouth, and if it were any colder, it might freeze Prakaash's mouth wide open. Rahat can feel the temperature of the stream from several feet away, making her hesitate. To be so cold, this stream must come from the snow-capped mountains of the Lyra Lands..

Again she refers to the map, tracing her fingertips over where they roughly ought to be. A little above the palace, in a valley of nothing but green. *Great.*

'There.' Her fingers leave a smear of sweat upon the parchment. 'Maybe a day's ride out from the next village, if the map's right.'

A glance to Prakaash, but he still drinks greedily from the stream.

'And let's be honest,' she sighs, tucking the parchment back into her leathers, 'the map's probably wrong.'

5

She could not erase the wrongs of her father. She could not even fathom how to undo the monstrosities of his father before him. So much blood had been spilt. So many lives ruined. She should have taken Rahat to the sea, where the warm waters could wash over them. The sand would squelch between their toes. But instead there's only this murky golden-green of the jungle in the summer's sun.

'Rahat?' Iliyah couldn't count the times she'd called for her as she worked through the jungle's low-hanging vines. This far from the path, she wasn't sure they would be able to find their way back to the carriages by themselves.

Bhadraa would be sick with worry as the only servant set to watching them.

But of course Rahat had to race after a shadow dancer in the undergrowth. They're not usually creatures which come out in the sunlight: translucent skin leaves them burning hot, or perhaps that could be the lava that they're rumoured to live within.

'Rahat?'

Up ahead she could hear the langur monkeys leaping from tree bough to tree bough. Whooping, they called to each other, with only their tails visible from so far below. Iliyah discarded her slippers a while back, resigned to keeping them clean; Bhadraa would find them on the way. Yet with the way the earth wiggled between her toes, she could not say that she regretted it. She smiled as she pushed aside the vines to enter the clearing.

Though it was only a small space, it felt as if it could have been carved out of the earth. In all the crowded spaces of the jungle, this was the only grassy knoll. The only field which they had come across on the journey home from Rahala.

It had taken months for them to pester the Maharaja and Emperor into allowing them to journey together. Now they were putting all of that trust at risk.

Iliyah's eyes skimmed the clearing to at last land on Rahat, who stared up into the canopies. It must have been where the shadow dancer disappeared.

'You caught up,' Rahat said, without turning to look at her. There was a marking of red smeared across her forehead—a blessing. But in the middle of the jungle?

Curling smoke rose over the tops of the trees. Not far off lay the Temple of Estevao, the god of Flame and husband to the Oceans. He gave all life its sacred breath, all dreams their beginning. With that red across Rahat's brow, the god had placed his blessing upon her, that she may have a strong life. For strength is what she needed.

'And you ran off,' Iliyah countered, crossing her arms over her chest.

Even at fifteen, the look on Rahat's face could make Iliyah weak at the knees. Her mothers had dismissed it as a foolish crush, one that would fade. She'd felt this way about boys, too. Had even kissed some. But Rahat's kisses felt like home.

'Where did the little beast go, anyway?' Iliyah asked her.

Rahat's smile faded, though she turned her sight back up into the trees. 'Away,' she said, in a voice so small that Iliyah almost didn't catch it.

But she did notice the eyes staring at them from the trees beyond the clearing. A woman with night-dark skin and glowing green eyes. With a red hood pulled up over her head and a bird's skull hanging from a cord about her neck, there was no denying it: she was a red priestess.

A glance down at Iliyah's hands. She wore the same markings as many of the priestesses scattered across Abrecan, even at sixteen. Her gift for dream weaving had developed before she could even speak. As she grew, the gift had only gotten stronger. The palace oracles had never seen such a thing. But then, trapped down in the dark, she doubted they'd seen much.

'Who goes there?' Iliyah demanded of the scarlet-cloaked woman.

She emerged from the trees, her blood-red cloak heavy as she stretched her arms wide before them. Fresh blood freckled her face.

Iliyah took a step toward Rahat, who was closest to the priestess. The woman dipped her head, reaching a hand for Iliyah's touch, for like calls to like. The priestesses brushed hands, their marked hands singing along their lacework. Iliyah's dark mehendi—which one day would soon be tattooed by the gods—scorched at caressing the priestess' silvery markings.

Rahat took a step back, though this woman had clearly blessed her not moments ago. And the priestess dragged her back, the look in her eyes soft as she analysed them together. 'Together?' the woman drawled, with an accent thick and unfamiliar. Yet with her midnight skin, she could only have been from somewhere in the north.

The only indication Rahat gave that she'd heard her was to look at Iliyah with pleading eyes. This had all began with whispers between sheets. So many nights they had spent together, swapping stories of grand gestures and gods and monsters, and cuddled till dawn broke over the horizon. Now this was real.

Iliyah took a deep breath, entwining her hand with Rahat's. 'Together,' she said.

The Northerner's eyes rolled into the back of her skull as she raised her head to the skies. Her hands fumbled in the leather purse at the cinched waist of her robes to produce a swath of red cloth. As she tied the cloth about their entwined hands, she murmured blessings in a language Iliyah had never heard. With each brush of their skin, the priestess unwittingly brought memories to Iliyah's mind.

Memories of the future.

Quick flashes, of the dissolving of ink in water like Qadira's shadow-singing; the crinkle of Rahat's eyes when she smiles; the screeching of a newborn, pawing for the sky; the tossing of blessings from balconies as, below, Rahat and Iliyah walked side-by-side with their hands once again entwined—only years from now.

The priestess tied the knot about their hands as Iliyah was brought back to the present. She shook the images from her mind, but her brain mulled over one in particular. One which they would share forever: Of Rahat and herself, so recognisably themselves, being blessed for a life together.

As the priestess whispered in her lilting voice, she could not hide her radiant smile. She'd never seen Rahat grin like that— so at ease, as if she were free.

'In the sight of the gods who rule us, I swear you as one, ir-revocably Bound, never to leave each other's side on your jour-ney through this life. May the path treat you well.'

Reaching into her leather pouch, the dipped her fingers in blood and ash. One heavy-handed line down their foreheads, and it was done. With reddened hands, the woman gestured for them and the girls complied, pressing their foreheads to-gether as they had seen many others in Binding ceremonies do.

For no matter what would happen in the future, Iliyah al-ways wanted to be by Rahat's side. Even if that meant turning her back on the Empire.

The priestess had smiled as she unbound their hands. But they didn't let go.

'Your Highnesses!' The cry came through the trees.

In a second, the scarlet woman vanished, consumed by flames which had leapt out of the nothingness. That bursting light blinded them, the roar deafening their ears to the servants calling for them.

'Rajkumari! Shehzadi!'

'Your Highnesses?'

The cries continued, growing louder and louder with each step.

Iliyah's heart thudded in her throat. They both knew that there would be consequences to what they had done that day. And all because Rahat had hurried after a shadow dancer. The Empire might disown them for this disobedience.

But Iliyah could live with that—if it meant she wouldn't ever have to let Rahat go. That no matter what, because of what they had done, the gods would keep them together for eternity.

'Rajkumari!'

They exchanged a look. Rahat squeezed Iliyah's hand tight.

'Shehzadi!'

There was no time to think of an explanation. Licking her hand, Iliyah rubbed at the red marking her forehead; Rahat followed suit. The red was coming away, but the fluttering in their stomachs wouldn't fade.

Yet they knew: no matter what happened, no one could find out.

*

That icy tremble races down her arms, from her shoulder-blades to the tips of her tattooed fingers. She should have seen this coming. The field of her childhood dreams stretches out before her. So many times she has visited this place in her dream wanderings, but today she is finally here.

Iliyah should have expected this.

Her aunt Nisha had threatened action before Iliyah was even born. So many years had passed that they had thought her threats null. They never could have known this would happen, that Nisha would strike before Iliyah could tell anyone of what the Neverworlds showed her.

The ice in her chest clenches, sending her to her knees. Not but a day ago, she was meditating in the High Temple. Now the earth beneath her slippers is dry, the jungle stripped of its life under the glaring sun.

She's not sure how she came to find herself here. It should have been impossible, all the way from the palace of Rahala. Yet here she stands in Delorran, in a field which she's found difficult to forget. Not four years ago, she had been Bound to Rahat by a priestess in this exact spot.

Running her fingertips over an old arcing tree-trunk sends a shiver up her arm. If only Rahat were here now. If only Rahat were hers.

The black tattoos lacing her hands feel heavy against the bright light of dawn. From the tips of her fingers to her first knuckle, her fingers are stained black. She still remembers the day it happened. She and Rahat were swimming in the opalescent river below the Ajrapurian palace when the pain struck. The pain was so strong she was pulled under the water by it. Her sight left for a time, and when she returned to the surface, it was under Rahat's arm as the *rajkumari* pulled her to safety. And while the oracles questioned the black-out, not one spoke a word of the black markings now coursing over her hands.

Somehow, things were simpler then.

Dragging her hands over the earth, she pushes to her feet. What might her brothers do in this situation? *Well, she considers, they would not be here.*

In the trickle of a memory, Iliyah can feel the heavy-handed stroke of the red priestess as she marked she and Rahat in red. Bound them.

Somewhere through the trees, she can feel her—Rahat, her breath weaving through the jungles to reach her, as if *knowing.*

You'll find me, she thinks, hoping the words carry though knowing they will not. She isn't close enough within range. *Perhaps it is the weakness,* she tells herself. A stiffness in her bones is all she needs to understand that this will not be simple. Here, she is well and truly trapped. Just as she is by the bonds to her gods which keep her from Rahat. *It could have been me,* she thinks, with a shake of her head.

But now I am lost.

The earth rumbles. A gasp is ripped from her lips as she's forced again to her knees. The jungle spins, green and blooms blurring till she doesn't know which way is up or down. It broils, turning and churning. Her hands hit the dirt hard as she shakes sense into herself. This cannot be real.

Unable to move, her limbs locking as the earth rocks like the ocean's waves, she watches in unblinking horror as the sky rushes up at her. It fractures and molds itself about her like magic. The scream catches in her throat.

Icy winds whip at her face as she realises that no, it is not the sky which has moved, but the earth beneath her. Before she can come to her senses, a fortress rises about her. The ground rips apart, pressurising itself into stone and glass and crystal—as if it were something hidden beneath the field all along.

The memory of Rahat's smile flits through her mind. She might never see that smile again.

No.

Shoving her hands down into the earth, she fights against her binding. Yet the tattoos at her hands glimmer as if illuminated from beneath. She cannot stop the tremor in her hands.

The Tower swallows her whole. Crystal arches overhead, blocking out the sunlight as it frosts over, the *cracking* like ice as it forms rock-hard.

'No—'

The words are stolen from her as the Tower flashes cold. Before her, her breath becomes mist. Her hands tremble, her legs seize. This palace is not safe.

Fighting against the cold, the *shehzadi* stretches her limbs before her and lowers herself to the earth as it turns to stone beneath her touch. The stone is rough-hewn, scratching against her skin.

A moan, and she rolls onto her back, wrapping her arms over her chest to keep warm. She tries to speak, but finds she cannot. Black stars swim before her sight. The air is so thin up here, and she is so cold. Her breathing slows, the pattern of her chest rising and falling stretching longer and longer until she almost cannot feel it. The stone beneath her trembles.

There's a light touch to her hand, and her fingers curl, yearning to reach out and find Rahat's hand in hers.

And as Iliyah succumbs to the cold of her Tower, the ice forms a chrysalis about her form. It hardens, locking in all life which might be preserved.

6

'The girl won't talk.'

In fact, Hazel hasn't said a word since Rahat left her sight. Qadira knows this. The *rajkumari* had been so close. Right in her grasp.

And she let her go.

Why? She still can't believe it. Her orders had been to stop her; she's never disobeyed orders before. The hiss of her whip against Rahat's cheek was a mark of authority and almost satisfying. But when Hazel sat before her with her hands chained to the floor, for the first time in a long time, Qadira had felt sick.

'What do you mean, she won't talk?'

The *kehrasa* lifts her head to the Maharaja in time to catch the recoil from her gaze. It's the eyes. Always the eyes.

'Would you be so kind to—'

'A faerie without wings should make you comfortable enough,' she snaps. All this time, she has been waiting for that question. As if somehow it might be easy to hide the truth of her people stamped so clearly across her face. Thick black lines to reflect the sun; eyes the colour of carnelian, bright as sunlight.

Cursed humans.

The Maharaja shifts uncomfortably beside his wife. The blonde Maharanee rests a hand at her husband's arm. Her eyes haven't left Qadira from the moment she walked in. The *kehrasa* has to admit, to the humans she's an intimidating sight.

Awkward, the queen wets her lips. 'I'm sorry to say, but it's a little hard to believe my niece could ever keep quiet.' Despite the weight of her words, a smile plays at her lips. 'Talking is a specialty of hers.'

Yet everyone remains silent.

At his father's side, Ashrit looks to Karnan beside their mother. The *rajkumars* had been worrying about their sister's marriage—not her escape. They never thought it would be an escape that would bring them to this.

Not to mention that nothing has been said of Karnan's involvement. If his father knew, there would be blood. Qadira had even considered telling them, but in the end she had been the one to keep Zehran from throwing himself at the Delorrene. Since, the boy's been struggling to keep his eyes off of her. But it's not like the others. There's no fear—not even the kind that doesn't show. If she could decide what it is, she might call it suspicion.

'I have tried every one of my talents without causing harm, and I haven't discovered anything we don't already know,' says the *kehrasa*, when it becomes clear that some of them cannot bear to stand her presence. The few courtiers gathered about the throne room, even some of the Royal Guard, haven't lifted their eyes from the floor the moment she walked in.

It's not like she's an oracle; though she can feel Taeng pacing down in the catacombs, almost directly beneath their feet.

But both she and Qadira are creatures of the long-dead past. Why should these people have to look at her? She balls her fists, curling her fingers about the handle of her bullwhip. 'We all know Hazel is fiercely loyal to her cousin. I never expected her to betray their plans,' she says with exasperation. 'To think Hazel would give her up is like hoping my gods will return.'

To that, the silence grows painful, seething into every corner of the hall.

Zehran clasps his hands behind his back at Qadira's side. A hint to stop talking. Foul words stick to her tongue; they wish to emerge. She's over three hundred years old, older than anyone in this palace—in this gods forsaken realm. How can they expect to order her about like some little lap dog? Ignore her as if she's a kitten caught in a blanket.

Again, Zehran lifts a hand, grazing it over the small of her back.

'What *I* don't understand is why she would leave,' breathes Satiyavati from the corner, as if the cousin had had no doing in turning Rahat against Tahir.

Tahir, who hasn't said a word from his seat. The *shehzada* still can't believe this is happening. He had thought they were content—that they were going to be content together, despite Rahat's want for his sister. And the wedding is tomorrow.

Was tomorrow, he reminds himself.

Light plays off the mirrors scattered across the ceiling. Why they're in the larger audience chamber, similar to the Hall of Mirrors but with pools along the middle of the floor, Qadira isn't sure, but she has a feeling it has something to do with the humans. She can feel the fear radiating off of them like ripples. They can't keep still.

The open window tosses its curtains like a cat with a ball of yarn. Tangling, rubbing, the gossamer gives a soft hiss as it's tossed, twirling like palace dancers. It's almost distracting. But she could not be more thankful for the fresh air.

Of all those gathered, the northerner Satiyavati Naidu was the quickest to recover from the news of her cousin's escape. As if happy about it. Qadira keeps watch of the glances the girl sends Karnan's way, but as she'd noticed before: the *rajkumar* won't let her out of his sight. What had Qadira missed last night, when Satiyavati had come as they had left? She would give anything for that information.

The handle of her whip is cool in hand. Welcoming. A sigh rolls through her as she relaxes her shoulders. Holding this whip always reminds her of home. It had been given to her by her sister, the only one of her fourteen siblings to survive through the Rapture. To her knowledge, all their brothers had perished. But Adilah had always been the best at hiding, even in the dunes of Rehmayan. It's no surprise it was she who survived.

'Why would she leave?' asks Satiyavati again, forcing shock into her words.

It's too much. Qadira's grip on the whip could break it, if it weren't faerie-made. The fire roars in her chest, lengthening her teeth like the monster they fear she is.

Before she can speak her mind, Zehran claps a hand at her arm, but it's too late. Her eyes scan him before she looks to the smug smirking cousin seated behind her aunt and uncle on the dais. 'If you really couldn't see that Rahat has been in love with Iliyah all this time, then you're blind.'

Again, silence. In which all that can be heard is Qadira's heavy breathing. It had come out in a snarl with a gnashing of teeth. Like a monster. Which, by the look on the Maharanee's face, is all they suppose she is.

Those pale cheeks flood red before the colour stills, fading back to alabaster. As if even her face doesn't know how to show her mind. The Maharanee's thoughts are frantic and stilled all at once, blurring before moments of clarity. It will give Qadira a headache if she listens too long.

All eyes creep to Tahir—Tahir, who has known this whole time, and never said a word except to his brother.

That's it.

With those probing eyes off of her at last, Qadira can breathe. The heavy fall and shallow rise of her chest feels human to her. She can't stand it.

Turning on her heel, she takes her whip in hand. The *crack* as it snaps against the floor drowns out the thoughts of everyone gathered. She doesn't care. It sends a current of sound through them, distilling them as their eyes are again brought back to the woman who should have died long ago. The stems along her back ache as if fresh. They will always ache.

She would give anything to fly again.

Pushing the doors open, she slinks from the mirrored chamber, unable to bear it anymore. *Humans never learn.*

*

The gardens have never felt all that welcoming to Qadira. The very idea of a garden has always been one to escape her. How humans think they'll ever be able to tame nature, she doesn't know. The humans were never able to tame her people. She suspects it's always been something to frustrate them. Faeries are elusive, after all. *Were.* The word stops her.

Faeries *were* elusive.

'Dear Serpent of Ages,' she curses. How many years has it been now?

Enough to now remember there's almost no one left.

Resting back against the rocks, she's sure no one can spy her from up here. She's never seen any of the humans attempt a climb like this. Basking atop the waterfall in the main gardens, she leaves her whip within reach. The fresh air caresses her sanity; the spindrift from the slow-trickling waters as they crash over the falls are like hundreds of precious kisses. There's almost no water in Rehmayan. You'll be lucky if you find it after days and days of wandering. It had always been a game to them as children. Long, long ago now.

Shaded by the standing stone, she's concealed from sight even if there were to be a procession below. Good luck to anyone trying to find her. Not even the windows that open onto this side of the palace will be able to glimpse her. Content, her long spotted tail flicks, fur dancing in the fractured light. No human has seen her tail—not even Zehran.

She's kept so many secrets from the boy. But how can she begin to explain? After what happened in the Chamber of Mirrors, she doesn't exactly feel like taking orders. Especially those which may send her after Rahat.

Her cheeks are warm in the sunlight. Her hair in braids lays wet about her head. This is freedom. Well, as close to it as you can get these days.

*

The latticed windows feel like a prison, casting bars of shadow across the chamber floor. A four-poster bed stands proud centre, its pillows lush and oozing onto the floor in a cushiony mess. This is *much* too much.

Last night she had waited outside the door listening to Zehran with Tahir and Rahat. As soon as she spotted the distraught girl sprinting down the halls, she couldn't resist following. Not that the *rajkumari* knew she was there, of course. Shadow-singing is her specialty. A puff of smoke later, and she was trailing the dancer over-head. What she'd heard hadn't surprised her. She'd known Taeng long enough to understand the boys wouldn't listen; just like Qadira, Taeng is from a lesser land in their eyes. If it wasn't obvious by the shape of her eyes, it was her drawn-out vowels that gave her away. In all the time Qadira has known the Praitosí, she has never known them to trust a woman of the West.

The door creaks as it opens behind her. Careful steps, light on the balls of their feet. *Zehran.* The scent of him tangles in her nostrils to the point where it makes her feel sick.

'You put on too much musk,' she barks. 'It overpowers the amber.'

While she remains staring out the carved window, the *shehzada* takes a seat at the edge of the bed. The sheets whisper as they ruffle beneath him. Silk on silk. Of course, Zehran isn't dressed for a journey.

And the buzzing of his mind shows her he has no plans for one, either. Huh.

Oh. Oh, no.

'Qadira,' he sighs.

'No.'

'I couldn't find you.'

She turns to look at him—and instantly regrets it. The look on his face hits her in the gut, hard as a blow. 'I didn't want to be found,' she demurs.

He nods like that's obvious.

An exasperated breath deflates her chest. What can she say?

Zehran levels her with that look. 'You might have just started another war.'

She turns back to the window, hissing, 'Don't you think I know that?'

In Zehran's lap sits his blade, unsheathed and shining. Careful hands polish at the edge sharp enough to slice through adamant, given force. He'd almost taken the head off of a sphinx with it—*Gods, that was a bad day.*

Outside, the sun is almost set, like it's just hovering at the horizon with the taunt of returning again. The sky's dusky purple fades to ultramarine in the time of a breath. The colour makes her suck in a gasp and press her hands to the latticework over the window. If only her sight weren't hindered by the rosewood.

Though she knows Zehran is watching her, not once does Qadira glance back.

The sky is the colour of the Rehmayani dunes, seconds before sunrise. She has known that colour all her long life. Each sundown is just as stunning.

Slowly, the city below twinkles. Thousands and thousands of lanterns are brought to life with the flickering of flame that's strung between houses. Magic; that's what keeps this city alive. The musky caress of smoke and roasted spices reaches her through the latticed window at her side, making her mouth water. What she would give to be out there with the locals, tasting their food as they taste it: with warmth and life and *yearning*.

A distant memory plays in her mind, tugging her lips into a smile. Her father had been a smart man as he sold his wares—weapons and jewellery, all forged by his fourteen children. Yet the most talented of them all had been Adilah. The smile falters upon remembering that that had been the moment that Qadira had become the less-favoured daughter. *What good is it to only fight in this world?* her father had growled at her, from such a young age it almost hurts to think so far back. *I will not allow you to become like our people.* Each time she reminded him that the *kehrasa* were bred as assassins, he had ignored her, as if something like that could be ignored.

It's in her blood. She can feel it, coursing thick and strong.

Her long fingers unhook themselves from the latticework. 'I want to be alone.'

Zehran sheaths the blade at his belt. 'Too bad.'

'Fine.'

The *kehrasa* fades from sight. She becomes the desert, a mixture of sand and heat and shadow. The *shehzada* growls his frustration, scanning the room for where she might have disappeared to. The silver-leather whip rests peacefully in the centre of the mattress. Against the blue silk-woven sheets, it almost looks pretty. Till Zehran notices the dried blood marring its shine.

'Qadira, please,' he says, reaching out with his hands as if he can catch her.

The world swirls about her like ink as she weaves her way through it. She is the desert night; she is fear. Soundless, she appears behind Zehran on the bed with that grin she knows he hates, and takes the whip in hand.

'You wouldn't,' he challenges, but he already knows her response. He watches helplessly as the faerie again fades to smoke, and the tendrils curl their way out of the window, away from him. 'Qadira, I'm sorry.'

Ignore him. Determined, and knowing she can't go anywhere she'll be interrupted, she looks over the palace grounds. Dozens of courtyards spread out before her in an array of colours. Brilliant golds and vibrant flowers are all she can see from up here, the colours wedged between motifs of marble and stone. Just past the courtyards lays the cliff-face, and the smaller palace of the three inter-connected buildings that form the grounds. Stranded in the centre of the lake lays a courtyard impenetrable, except by the towering stairs of the cliff. It would take a team to find her there.

When her feet touch the ground, the air is sweet. Yet the scent does not work its way into her hair; it would of, had she been able to fly. There would be leaves and the open air trapped in her braids, making her smell of freedom. Alas.

Today the water's smooth as silk. Not a ripple marks its surface. The cool salty air brushes Qadira's cheeks like a lover's caress. Here, she can breathe. Her shoulders relax as she takes in her surroundings. Only once has she been here; a performance ground, this space is usually reserved for dancers. Faint memories of girls spinning in yards of damask and silk, their limbs painted red, flit to the front of her mind. This space has known happiness.

At the centre of each boundary stands a covered platform for small audiences. Within the largest stands the dais belonging to the royal family. The alabaster is smooth beneath her bare feet, stained red by hundreds of years of inking them. Her scarlet toes are stark against the gold-work beneath them, the patterns wrought long ago by hundreds of hands. The impression of sound makes her ears twitch. As if someone plays dhol drums in the distance, so that the beat may float down upon her. In all the palaces she's traversed, Delorran has been the most musical. A twinkle traces its way by her feet, the small ponds of water built as a part of the mandala-painted platform swarming with tiny fish.

Pink blooms roll at the corner of the clouds above. There may yet be rain.

Flicking her braids over her shoulder, Qadira twists them into a long coil that lines the whole of her back. The knot sits at her thighs, her hair swinging like a ceremonial flag with each step. She can feel the magic with every breath as it works its way into her senses. It has been a long time since she's felt a place so alive with the old folk, with her own people.

Like a vision, a dancer twirls its way into her mind. Hips twist as she dances, her soft voice rising with the slow and calculated beating of drums. Behind her, women move into formation, swaying along with her movements. Skirts splay around them as they spin, raising their hands into the air to trace intricate patterns.

'Stop it,' the *kehrasa* growls to the platforms, and the images fall away.

The lack of music is startling; it almost makes her wish she'd kept it, or at least the woman's sweet lyrics.

Now all she hears is the silence, the unending depths of the water and its blackness. The palaces on the cliff tower overhead, blocking her sight of the rising moon. As if sensing her agitation, the space begins to glow, scattering patterns of gold across her face as the magic swells about her.

The fountains remain still, however. The only times they have come to life is during performances. A sigh rolls through her, as heavy as the dawn.

Zehran wants her to seek Rahat and bring her back; he himself will give orders to Saadi to find Iliyah's body. Even Tahir thinks she's simply wandered to the healing pools of the God Mountains, a few hours from Rahala. Only, they're so old and crumbling that no one dares go there. No one, save Iliyah. Saadi's likely too terrified to risk his life in searching for a corpse.

But Iliyah cannot be dead.

Qadira finds her whip in hand, feels the way it uncoils as she lifts it from her side. Some of the twinkling subsides, as if falling back from any wound she might inflict. As if magic is something that can be harmed.

Out the corner of her eye she catches movement on the cliff's stairs. A gangly silhouette. *Tahir*. He has always known how to find her, even as a child. She re-members the way he'd looked at her on that cursed day.

The handle of her whip is heavy. Knuckles crunch as she grips it tight, curving her whip up in an arch. The followthrough takes her breath. It spins, the silver reflecting the light of the magic lingering at her feet. The warmth she feels down her back tells her that her tail's showing. In the dark she doubts Tahir will see it.

The added limb lends balance as she twirls, up on the tips of her toes as she cracks the whip, the sound echoing and reverberating off the cliff walls. The sound comes back at her from every direction, the harshness of the *crack* growing more threatening each time it sounds.

Her *sirwal* pants fan out above the knee as she twirls, quick on her toes as she dances back and forth—as if, were she human, she might dance the Khumaani alongside Rahat and her sisters.

But she is not mortal.

Water bubbles. The lake remains calm, though the ponds ripple with soft lapping waves. As the fountains spring to life in a flash of golden dust and magic, she has to bite back the yelp of joy. Every sound she makes can be heard throughout the valley; Tahir alone plays witness.

The *kehrasa* keeps the performance going, weaving in and out of the whip's fall as it lashes the night. The *shehzada*'s growing closer; she can hear his steps now.

Slowly, the moon is rising, dispelling the darkness. The flitting magic only grows brighter as it captures the moonlight. She feels it stick to her tail, the magic working its way into the thick fur. And it tickles. Against all thought or feeling, Qadira laughs. Truly *laughs*. The sound bubbles around her, reflecting back at her from the cliff-face in chords she has not heard in years.

Tahir's soft steps are at the bridge now. A small path of stone across the black water, the path shines like silver. 'And what are we laughing at?' calls the boy on his approach. She can hear his smile.

The magic strokes her skin, making her drop the whip as it works its way up her spine. Qadira cries out, stumbling to the ground with a heavy *thud*. Landing on her stems, she gasps. The magic quickly turns her numb.

Stained feet stretching out before her, she wraps her arms over her middle as the assault continues, the golden magic wrapping itself around her, recognising its kin.

Born of the old desert, Qadira is magic.

Rubbing her head against the ancient stone, she works the magic into her hair. The ebony braids bob about her face, wispy woollen locks free and golden at her hairline.

When Tahir reaches the platform, he pauses. Maybe he should leave Qadira to her happiness, however fleeting. There has never been the right time to ask of her something so dire. But this is war.

He clears his throat. It's been a long time since he's seen that smile on her face, making her eyes reflect the light of the magic attacking her. The *kehrasa* doesn't move, save to lift her legs to her stomach, as if that could protect her middle from the magic's tickling touch.

'Qadira...'

The hunter lifts her head, ever so slightly as the laughter bubbles in her throat.

'I need a word.'

A heaviness settles on the *kehrasa's* chest at hearing those words. Thank the gods Tahir has never been so like his brothers, who blurt their thoughts—or feel like they're screaming at her from their minds. In fact, Tahir remains silent, leaning against the platform's structure, his skin flushed in the heat of the night. Qadira knows he won't move from that spot until she allows him to.

With a nod, she waves her hand, sending the magic skittering back to wherever it came from. Suddenly the little platform out on the lake is so dark. The moon creeping across the sky provides little light, still trapped behind the spiralled plinths of the main palaces. They cast brilliant shadows across the black water.

'You found me,' she pants, with a voice thick with laughter as she lays back and laces her hands behind her head. There's a glimmer in her eyes Tahir cannot explain.

The *shehzada* shakes his head, as if that can shake off the wrong feeling in his stomach. It's been plaguing him since he last saw Rahat, racing away from the palace—away from *him*. 'You're never easy to find,' he sighs.

Qadira can feel the magic still lingering in the stones beneath her; the power pulses through the muscles of her shoulders, still pressed to the ground. She pats the smooth stone by her side, and Tahir joins her on his back. The sky above them is rich and thick like velvet, as fuzzy as the creatures of the dark. Slowly, the moon reaches across the stars, illuminating them in all their millions of stories.

The *kehrasa* sighs. She only speaks when Tahir turns to her, rolling onto his side to watch her face. She closes her eyes. 'I forgot how much I missed magic.'

'I've never really known what it feels like,' he says, making her smirk.

'Imagine every fibre of you is aflame. Each time you feel it near you grow warmer and warmer as if struck by lightning—before levelling out, and that heat disperses into the cool lapping waves of the world. It stays with you; you're never truly alone when there's magic around... You become more than yourself.'

Tahir keeps his eyes on her. An instinct deep down wants to reach out and hold her hand, hoping to bring her comfort. But he doesn't; there are laws when it comes to extending anything to faeries. As soon as humans were brought into the world, the faerie gods created laws to separate their races. The faint glimmer of tears shine at Qadira's closed eyes. He's never seen her cry before. He wasn't exactly sure faeries *could*, for that matter.

'I know what you're about to ask me, Tahir.'

Those words are so full of resignation that he sighs. The breath rolls through him as he turns back to stare up at the stars. They twinkle, sparking and bursting to life like millions of explosions. The skin of the All-Mother is a beautiful thing.

Tahir closes his eyes, unable to look at her. 'And yet I must ask it.'

'You know I can't say no,' says Qadira. Embers light the gold of her eyes, flashing like the stars overhead. The magic still swirls about her, unwilling to leave its kin in the dark. 'You found me when I was in need. By faerie *law*, I am your possession.'

But the *shehzada* shakes his head. 'The faeries are gone,' he tells her gently. 'You don't have to obey their rules anymore.'

For a moment, all is silent. Even the soft lapping of the waves against the stone structure. The air is warm in their lungs, curling up inside them like kittens. It's almost suffocating.

Qadira's hands are coarse against the smooth stone. In the darkness, they look stained with blood, although she knows it's blessing powder. The priestesses here are flamboyant with it at best; she's been covered with the damned stuff ever since she got here. Smearing some of it across her cheeks, she doesn't know how to proceed. To tell the boy, or to keep quiet? Well, it's not like they can kill her.

'I bribed the guards to get Hazel safely out of the city,' she says suddenly, making Tahir's eyes snap to her. The shock in his features is like a slap to the face.

'But she's—'

'A child. Exactly.' Pushing to her feet, Qadira looks down at the boy through her glowing eyes. She raised him, in her own way. That he's surprised she would let the girl go feels like his hand is elbow-deep in her chest. 'She should be safe in the jungles by now; she can go after Rahat and keep the girl safe. Gods know that one won't survive out there by herself.'

To stop her leaving his side, Tahir reaches out a hand. The shadows hovering before him swirl, half Qadira and half the stuff of space. Only her face remains by the time she turns, feeling his stirring the air. 'Then you understand why I must ask this of you,' he tells her. The desperation in his eyes is heartbreaking. She'd seen that look on his face earlier, when Rahat had left. 'Please.' Tahir's never begged for anything in his life.

Her form swirls, the smoky shadows like fog as her body forms out of the darkness. Slowly, her limbs appear from the shadows and sand. She shakes her head. 'Tahir, I—'

'You're a good person, Qadira. You're a good faerie.'

'If I were a good faerie you wouldn't have to ask this of me,' she growls back. Her features are contorted— teeth sharp, eyes wide like a hunted beast. The mottled markings of her skin push up from under the illusion she uses to conceal the truth of her face. 'If I were a good *kehrasa*, I would be dead.'

Taking a slow breath, Tahir shakes his head. 'No. You're exactly where you need to be,' he says, not really knowing what to say. Over the years there have been sentiments like this, but never before has he realised that maybe, just maybe, Qadira is struggling. 'But I need to ask you. And I'm sorry, but you have to—'

'Go after Rahat.'

'Yes.'

Those amber eyes catch his; her gaze is heavy, resentful.

'Only to make sure she's safe,' he says, climbing to his feet. Slipping his hands into his pockets, his subtle movements tell her he's not armed. Her own whip lays a little way away, its silver thread sparkling against the moonlit stone.

'You really care about this girl?'

He holds her stare. 'I cannot take Delorran without her.'

Resigned, she lowers her head. 'Then I will go after her.'

7

The unmarked town rises up from the riverbank in orbs of glowing light. Lanterns hang from cords woven between houses. Small paper globes, they gleam with vibrant colour to illuminate the tiny village. The colours only grow as Rahat approaches from along the stream. This village perched on the low-rising cliff over the river isn't marked on the map in her hand. There's only the river, forking off to the north and north-west.

From along the riverbank, she can see little more than the lanterns. And all she sees clearly is the hall reaching over the low cliff to meet the guard-tower standing directly in the centre of the forked waters. Were the trees closer to the guard-tower, she might think it were a bridge spanning into the larger expanse of a town. But it is only a tower, solitary in the stream.

The lights dance on the water, darkest under the hall where their reflections are moving paintings. In the blue dusk being swallowed by black night, it's something like magic. Red, purples, yellows, rich carnelian—it's like something off the palace walls.

Hooves gliding through the water, Prakaash's approach is near silent. If Rahat knows anything, it's that they should go around the tiny village rather than under it. After all, she has no idea of what lays in that elevated hall.

By calculation, this village shouldn't even be here. Yet with hardly more than two dozen homes clustered about the standing hall, it's not large enough to be acknowledged by royal map-makers.

When cries of praise lift into the air and the lilting music of a sitar travels downstream, Rahat realises with a jolt that it's the sixth day. The holiest of days, to those who worship Niabi most devoutly. She is the Life-Bringer; a daughter of the All-Mother and Sister to the Oceans.

If this is a village of Niabi, then she should not be contemplating stealing from them. Passing over the earthen skin of the goddess to reach Iliyah, surely it is she who must give thanks upon this day. She should pray that the earth be kind on her journey.

Her boots crunch in the gravel and sand, lukewarm water lapping at her toes. The water is gentle, like a wind-chime forever moving, calling out in sounds not unlike the faeries' forgotten music. It's dark in the night, glimmering under the smiling moon. *Oh gods*, Rahat curses. It's later than she thought, if dusk has given way so quickly to night.

A voice of the heavens fills the night, soft tones cascading upon its listeners and making tears prick at the back of Rahat's eyes. It's a voice that can only come from one descended from the faeries, generations ago. Or, if the purity of sound is true, this is a faerie woman singing. The voice rises and falls, over and over in a tale of lost loves regained. The tale of the Lady Vanja and Lord Maris of Belanós—a story from the Lyra Lands. Rahat remembers it well; it had always been a favourite as a child.

The song comes to an abrupt end, and the tears brimming her eyes spill over. She wipes them away with rough hands, not understanding why such a voice should affect her so. But she can hear the clang of swords, the rush of the ocean winds, and the crashing of waves in each fold of syllables. When she finds herself wishing to hear those words again, that voice of ice and wind and summer breezes, she can hear the voices of children echoing through the hall, calling for the woman to perform her serenade again.

Their silence rings out, blanketing the night. No doubt the performer projects the appearance of being humble and refuses to take pride at first; but if she is truly one of the old folk, then she will be a proud creature. Of course, with a talent such as hers, it's almost a sin not to oblige her listeners so enamoured.

This time, Rahat is close enough to hear the beginning of the fable. Of a man called upon by a king to rescue his intended from the Isle most dreaded.

From the fields of gold to the waves of night...

The words drift down upon Rahat as she forgets her way, following the stream to beneath the hall and pausing where the stream meets the widest part of the river. If she stays to listen, she may be caught. But she can't help it when that voice calls to her.

Seeking the dead became his plight.
Alas, alas, say now the king,
'I will offer no hand in this fight.'

The several lines which follow are in the tongue of the Lyrans. Rahat shouldn't be here; she should keep moving. Like Maris, she is taking a deadly risk.

Far from his land, a ship he would steer
Into beastly waters to isles of fear
To find the land of the dead—
A journey that cost them their years.

Prakaash moves to the riverbank, his hooves never once slipping though the water becomes deeper. It seems that even he is drawn toward the hypnotic lyricist. The voice calls to them, promising to whisk them away into a world where women's souls aren't stolen from their bodies. Perhaps this woman was once a Court performer, in the height of the faerie kingdoms. Perhaps she was celebrated.

Stopping directly beneath the singer in the hall, Prakaash lays down, his belly rubbing in the damp earth. Rahat hesitates before joining his side; she shouldn't have allowed them to come so close. Could this woman be a siren? There is no sense in stopping to listen. *But—*

No, there is no excuse. By now, not only are Zehran and his company likely to be hunting her, but she can't stomach to think what manner of bounty-hunters are on her tail.

Yet the night is settled. All life has stilled as the earth allows that voice to fill the void where the sounds of dark should be.

The fair Lady Vanja was who they sought,
The bride of the king for whom they fought,
And they found her there, without a care,
To find this journey for naught.

Brilliant images of towering black trees reaching for the skies with vibrant fuchsia leaves fill Rahat's mind. Although she's only seen one cloud-seeker in her life—the single one in the palace gardens—the Isle of the Dead is said to be full of those trees of eternal life. She sighs.

She could listen forever, if only she had the chance. But the night is growing darker, the river has stilled, and there is no sound but the singer's voice and the collective held breath of her audience.

Long nights were spent like this once, with Rahat and Iliyah and their brothers. All had gathered about the Maharanee as she told them tales from the Asthore Isles, which had felt so exotic to them as children. Life was different there: the people paler, more hardened to life and its cruel lessons on the seas. Never will Rahat forget those stories.

A part of her is tempted to sing as the woman comes to the close of her tale; she's failing to truly listen to the lyrics as that voice wraps around her mind in curling fog. Nothing she's heard before has been this beautiful, this tragically sombre.

Her grumbling stomach shatters the ideal. This is no sliver of perfection, but a chance to steal enough food to last her. There won't be another chance like this so readily handed to her.

Climbing upon Prakaash's back, she gives his belly a squeeze before he lurches to his feet. Unwrapping the strips of cotton from her hands, she balls them in her ears, blocking out the dangerously seductive song. Still, it does not block out all of the appeal. An apology falls from her lips to Prakaash, truly sorry to tear him away from such music, but they have to keep moving. With how her eyelids droop, there's too much danger in falling asleep beneath the hall and being found come morning. That would land her right back at the palace. Or right into Death's claws.

Silent, Prakaash leads them out from under the food hall and along the stream into the darkness of the jungle. Beneath the moon, they blend into their surroundings of dark greens and blues and purples. The river is lit differently on this side of the bridge: the colours of the globe lanterns illuminate the water, and the rocks glimmer in the dark. The orange candlelight is a fuzzy glow overhead that makes her blood run cold. Stealing a glance over her shoulder, she discovers that the hall is open to the river on this side.

No one can see Rahat—yet. But all it will take is a quick turn. She will be safe as long as the faerie woman sings. She daren't think of what the woman may be planning; the old folk have always been ones to fool humans into their demise.

The siren's voice carries into the distance upon the last lines of the song she's drawn out through rising notes:

> The green girl could not stomach the king,
> So she chose the dead lands that could sing,
> But with Maris' heart, the Isle she would part
> And the king remained a lost thing.

The careful feather-light voice deepens on the last word of each line, making the hair on the back of Rahat's neck stand on end. The silence after reverberates into the darkness, so quiet that the whispering of Prakaash's hooves pressing half-moons into the damp earth can be heard. Full of warmth and alert to the bone, they make their way to the fringes of the jungle, passing the village's mango grove on their path.

The fruit dangles low to the ground, boughs heavy with thick, juicy fruit. Rahat wonders how she hadn't smelt their sweetness before, downwind. Carefully, she removes the cotton from her ears to hear... nothing. Absolutely nothing. The hall remains silent, the people within settled as if frozen in the night.

While Prakaash steers them out of sight, Rahat keeps her eyes back on the hall above the stream. These people have no idea she's passed through, forgoing filling her knapsack with as many mangoes as she can before, leaving the village behind.

*

There's a flickering through the undergrowth. Dancing orange light looks captive within the bars of the trees. Whoever would be foolish enough to light a fire on a night black as this, she doesn't know.

Rahat keeps her eyes on the jungle moving about them as Prakaash weaves through the trees and their low-hanging vines, silent as a mouse. The flickering flames swallow the darkness, casting shadows through the trees which appear like nightmares. The twisting images dance about Rahat on her mount as they emerge from the ghost trees in silence, to find a man sleeping by the fire. Dark skin, raven-black hair. He's Delorrene.

From what she can spy, he's the only life nearby. That is, if you ignore the monkeys bristling in the canopies, and the lithe-limbed ebony martens leaping from bough to bough. Rahat takes a moment to still her heart as she dismounts to warm her hands by the fire. Never does she let her eyes leave the sleeping knight.

Her legs ache from a long day's ride; Prakaash by her side flicks his head, shifting from hoof to hoof as he keeps his glowing-blue sight out over the trees, where the firelight cannot reach.

The man sleeping by the campfire doesn't stir. His breath floats the hair draped over his face; it sways with each inhale, exhale. Arms tucked around his body tight, Rahat thinks he'd be ready to strike at any moment if awoken.

And while she can see no sign of a horse in the makeshift camp, she cannot rule out the possibility of a mount nearby. Over the crackling of the flames, she can't hear a thing. Keeping her hands by the fire's warmth, she hesitates as she looks the man over. He's handsome enough. The scars in his hard leathers are deep, as though many have tried to kill him in battle. Then there's the scars at his face.

By his head sits a leather satchel overflowing with...
nothing important. *Hm.* Scraps of food wrappers,
scrunched balls of parchment that've spilled out onto
the sparse grasses, and a thicker piece of parchment
that refuses to be held within the bag's confines. Rahat
dares a closer step as she leans over the man, to find it's
a map. A lord-commissioned map, by the looks of it.

A stone skitters into the flame, and she's careful with
her next step. Her boots hiss in the long grass about the
knight; if she's lucky, he's a deep sleeper.

She glances back to Prakaash—but he's nowhere to
be seen. Rahat pulls herself upright, stretching to see
around the weeping trees, to spot the faint glint of his
titanium hide not but a few feet away. A heavy feeling in
her gut makes her wish he were closer at hand.

The voices of her brothers echo in her mind as she
edges closer, hand outstretched for the map. She dares
circle the man, for fear his horse may be close enough to
spot her in the darkness. Her white shirt and trousers
aren't exactly inconspicuous. Foolishly, she approaches
him directly, hand hovering over his head as she totters
for the thick, new map. It has markings on it she'd kill to
see.

'And if you scare him enough, he'll kill *you*,' echoes
Ashrit's voice in the back of her mind.

Biting down on the fleshy inside of her cheek, her mouth fills with that metallic tang. *Damn it.* Sweat trickles at her brow, but she can't afford to wipe it away. Never had she considered what it would be like to run into others on the road; it'd never crossed her mind while she'd been packing bags with Hazel. Or rather, while Hazel had been packing the bags for her. A pang of guilt laces its way through her chest to her stomach, making her feel sick. *Hazel's out here somewhere,* she tells herself, before pushing the thought away.

She leans further over the sleeping knight.

'Watch his hands,' her mind's Ashrit snaps.

'Be quick as a mouse,' chimes in Karnan, the laughter missing from his voice.

Shutting out her brothers' voices, she focuses on the task at hand—the map only inches from her fingertips. The closer she comes, the more she's able to see of the man. She curses him sleeping in a nook of thick tree roots; this would be easier if there was more space.

There's the dull shine of a bone-hilted knife in one of the satchel's side pockets. Not many blades are crafted with bones anymore; it's a weapon of the old folk. Which means Rahat needs to grab the map and get away before anything can happen. The knight's hair keeps his ears covered—there's no way of knowing if he's part faerie or just a risk.

The *rajkumari* senses Prakaash lingering behind her, waiting and watching the trees for signs of life. He knows there's someone nearby. But where? A stilled breath, and she makes the final reach over the comatose man. As soon as the parchment brushes against her fingertips, she feels that rush of triumph.

A second later, and she's across the campfire from him and deep in the trees with map in hand.

Swiping her own haphazard map from her pocket, she flips it over to reveal the differences: the knight's map marks the small village she had passed through, and the stream which cuts through it. Hers hadn't even marked the smaller forks of the river. Where had Hazel even picked it up? And why hadn't Rahat thought to steal one from her father's offices? Surely a vizier would have had a better reference. Even her uncle Badal.

Surveying the map, she returns to Prakaash's side to utilise the light provided by his glowing eyes. Soft lines reach through the map's linen fibres. With a frown she turns it over, to find a sketch of a castle forged of stone and glass and what looks like it could be glimmering crystal, if the depiction can be trusted. *An artist, then,* she thinks with a glance back around the tree into camp.

Somehow, the tower feels familiar. At the bottom of the page beneath the sketch is a smaller map, handdrawn with cross-marked squiggles. Several areas are crossed off—like he's looking for something. Looking for what? *Iliyah*? Another look to the knight, and she shakes her head.

'Who are you?'

She whorls on the voice. The boy—the *squire*—stands perfectly still, taller than Rahat and larger built, though he can't be any older than eighteen. If it comes to a fight, she doesn't want to think who'd win. He carries a horse's rein in his hand by his side. The brown beast a little ways behind him stares openly at the *lindélof* glinting with the firelight.

'I—uh—'

That's when he notices the map in her hand. A step back, and he screams.

His master by the fire jolts, and after stumbling to his feet, comes running.

Gods.

Rahat staggers back, desperately reaching for Prakaash, but the steed is spooked out of reach.

Sword drawn, the knight is a threatening sight, no longer the peaceful creature sleeping by the flames. A deep scar runs down the cheek which had been hidden. With a glance to his broadsword, she feels fear. The odds are against her with a broadsword.

'And what do you think you're doing with that?' demands the knight.

If she had more space to move, she would have swung up onto Prakaash's back and fled, but their proximity doesn't allow for such an easy escape. A flick of her hand beckons the *lindélof* return to her. He obliges, though reluctant.

Hand tightening about the parchment, Rahat forces herself to look the man in the eye. He hasn't made a move against her yet. She could just... give it back?

'I was curious.' She shrugs. 'My map wasn't matching up so I thought I'd—'

'Steal it?' suggests the squire, making her grit her teeth.

'*Borrow* it,' she corrects with a tight grin, hoping her voice is steadier than her hammering heart. 'But what I'm most curious about is this drawing,' she says, pointing to the knight, 'did you draw this? And where is it? I've never seen anything like it.'

To his credit, the knight doesn't say a word. He simply keeps his sword raised. His hand adjusts about the hilt as he looks over the girl before him. Rahat's stature —her posture alone—marks her as a woman of noble birth. And that's forgetting the embroidery of her garments, the smooth and shining leather of her armour. A *very* high born lady.

Not that that should bother a knight. By code, he should protect her.

But this is the jungle.

'The Praitosí *shehzadi* is in danger of dying and the Emperor's listed a reward for anyone who finds her,' he says by way of explanation, clipping his words. He doesn't make any move to lower his weapon, though Rahat's arms would be shaking by this point. Her fingers itch to draw her sabre, but she knows that the second she does, she'll be dead.

'There's a price to be won upon her return to her brother Saadi.'

Gods. Obviously, these two won't be the only ones out hunting for a sign of the *shehzadi* when there's a bounty. Saadi has always been efficient. His birds are some of the best trained in all the realms. It's no surprise word has spread so quickly. But if she has to battle her way through swarms of knights and ruffians to reach Iliyah, she might not find her in time. None of them must know this quest is so time-poor.

'So these locations you've crossed off—?' she presses.

The knight surveys her with a flick of his tongue. 'Where I've looked, yes.'

'And no sign?'

A furrow of his brow, and his grip adjusts on the hilt. Her illusion of the clueless girl is well and truly dead. Bounty hunters can be anyone, after all, and the best assassins are those you don't expect. 'Hand it over,' he orders, jerking his head to the squire who reaches a hand for the map.

Still, she grasps it tight. 'No.'

The squire unhooks a dagger from his belt, brandishing its sharp point. The men stand still as statues with their weapons when Rahat reaches a hand for her belt. There's not a sliver of fear in her stance; inside, she quakes. *Think of the stories*, she tells herself, taking her sabre in hand. A light, swift weapon. Perfect for confined spaces like this. *This can't be too hard.*

But two-to-one for her first real fight hardly seems fair. Sizing up the broadsword in the knight's hand, she takes a deep breath, steeling her nerve. 'Gentlemen,' she begins, making them hesitate. The squire narrows his eyes. 'If we are to fight, I'd like to know the names of those I defeat.' *A show, Rahat, give them a show.*

The squire spits at her feet. 'You wish.'

'All right, You Wish,' she grins, knowing well that she's set the boy's cheeks ablaze, 'have at it.'

The boy's mettle falters as his gaze shifts to his knight master. Firelight casts a shadow across his face.

Only a breath's warning, and she leaps to block the knight's blow with her sabre.

The force reverberates up her arm, and she realises that the ceremonial sabre won't last long against such a heavy piece of metal. 'Why—' she gasps, panting, realising with a flush that the stories are lies: Talking while sword fighting can cost you your life. Fighting against screaming, she forces him back with an off-balanced lunge. '—fight?'

The knight doesn't offer an explanation. He's as laboured for breath as she.

The squire moves around them as Rahat fights off the knight. Struggling to keep her eyes on them both as the squire approaches Prakaash who rears, she screams and leaps off a tall-standing tree root. Her kick collides with the squire's thigh, making him stagger back. Prakaash rears again, his hooves drumming the earth to scare the boy away. He dashes to the other side of the flames, so bright in this darkness that they're blinding.

The darkness is a friend, she reminds herself, thinking of Taeng. The oracles have remained safe for thousands of years in the thrumming dark. *Confuse them.*

Her sudden scream catches them off guard, making the knight stumble back as he clammers to cover his ears. Sabre coming down on his broadsword, she is a flurry of quick lightning strikes.

The squire bows out, knowing a strike of his own may result in the injury of his master. The firelight dances across them, casting shadows that confuse the flustered knight. To Rahat, the man is a silhouette against the bright flame.

'Ansh, *no!*' cries the knight, making Rahat whorl around.

She ducks the blade which narrowly misses her head. The squire—Ansh—had been about to decapitate her. *Holy Hells.* A flash flows through her—shock, she knows it's shock as her fingers start to shake—as her hold upon the sabre becomes precarious. With a pulse of adrenalin, she stamps on his foot and slams the hilt of the sabre up into the side of his head.

Ansh goes down like a sack of rocks.

The horse somewhere nearby whinnies, and Prakaash sounds his own metallic whine in return—drawing the attention of the knight.

Rahat attacks, swinging her blade down upon his, halting with a panic when she feels a *crack* that races up her arm. The sabre won't last much longer against his heavy blade. Maybe one last strike, if she's lucky. She catches the look in the knight's eyes as she makes her way over the tree roots, bringing them back to the full firelight. Toward the satchel. She'd noted the dagger inside earlier—a strong one, with a bone hilt. A faerie knife.

The knight leaps over the roots, his boots hitting the ground with a cloud of dust. 'And where do you think you're going?' he pants after her. His eyes flicker to the satchel and he springs to life, dashing after her with a stagger.

She has enough time to dive for the bone knife, praying it isn't cursed, before he's over her. But from this angle she doesn't have to do much to knock the sword from his grasp. A well-aimed kick upward catches his arm and he drops the weapon with a stifled cry. The sword's sent scattering into the campfire, the flames curling about the biting blade. She scrambles to her feet, heavy blade in hand. This isn't going well. The shocked look on his face is enough to give her pause, before remembering that the knight had no qualms with the prospect of killing her. *So why should I?* She raises the blade.

'All I want is the map back,' he pleads with an outstretched hand.

Rahat glances over her shoulder to where she last saw the squire, but he's nowhere to be seen. The tree roots distort her sight; he might be hiding.

Sweat stings at her prickling skin. The hairs at the back of her neck stand on end, covered in the blanket that is her thick hair. The heat rolls off her in waves, battling against the flames too close for comfort. If the boy's wandering, closing in on her, she won't have enough time to make it back to Prakaash. Even close, he's too far away. Rahat's breath hitches in her throat at the heaviness in her hand. The flame throws shadows so dark across the knight's face that she can't make out his expression, but there's a glimmer in his eyes. Still, his offered handshakes as he waits for her to return the map, and the sketch upon it.

'Why do you need it so badly?' she asks quietly, all too aware that the boy could be anywhere. This could end all so terribly.

His voice is like a whisper, he's so laboured for breath. His armour must be searing hot. It's the fire, sucking all the oxygen from the air, pushing its warmth into their noses, their mouths. The leather gleams with moisture—its insides must be blistering. 'There was a vision,' he pants. 'Like it was magic. The most beautiful woman I've ever seen, trapped in a tower—I had to draw it. It had to have been magic.'

'The magic left with the old folk,' spits Rahat, levelling the sword to his throat.

The knight rests back, hands tangled in the grasses. 'There are—others,' he says instead, blinking the sweat from his eyes. 'Many seek the glory of rescuing the *shehzadi.*'

She casts another look for the boy. *Nowhere.* She's playing a dangerous game. 'How many?' she demands. Gods dammit, if only Hazel were here.

'I'm not sure.'

'*How many?*' she demands again, holding the blade so tight it draws blood.

'I don't know! *I don't know!*' he screams, raising his hands over his face, almost uncaring for the blade so close to his jugular. He has a handsome face, Rahat assumes, by the little she can make out of him from the dancing light.

He drops his hands to his sides in the grass. 'Maybe...' The knight's voice wanders as he watches something far in the trees to the west. The howl of a wolf climbs the skies. Rahat daren't turn; much longer in this place, and she might draw the creature near. 'Twenty,' he tells her.

'*Twenty?*' This may be harder than she thought. *If I have to fight them all—* She stops herself before she can calculate the probability of Iliyah's death. It feels too real right now. Because Iliyah could die—

—if she's not dead already.

She interrupts his babbling, and he pauses. 'Where are you next headed?' When he refuses to speak, that glimmer of defiance in his eyes becomes hateful. She touches the tip of the jagged knife to his throat. 'Need I remind you, one quick strike and it's all over?'

He glares up at her, spitting out, 'Estevao's Temple.'

Her blood runs cold despite the sweat drenching her leather gear. If he'd considered searching the temple or the jungle nearby, he couldn't be the only one with the idea. It's not exactly like the temple's a secret. 'Why there?' she asks, failing at keeping composure.

In answer, his brows jump. 'In the vision, there was the smoke from a temple... Wait, the vision was true?' His sudden burst of laughter is maniacal. 'You've spoken to the gods and they've told you too?'

The gods... The only source of magic left to mortals.

Of course.

Though Iliyah refuses to call her gift magic, there's no denying its source. And a gift like hers works on proximity. Rahat allows her sight to drift to the skies— she must be close. But the blade in her hand is still of the old folk. And if any of the knight's behaviour is to be judged, then it was stolen. From where?

The old folk cursed their knives with madness if stolen. And if used, it needn't matter who was the thief. But bearing the dagger also attracts the gifts of dream weavers. The knight never would have known it was drawing him to Iliyah.

Slipping the blade into her back pocket, she draws forth her sabre from where she'd discarded it. The tip grazes the knight's throat, and he goes still. Despite himself, he gulps, forcing the skin against the sword's edge and drawing a trickle of blood. 'What do you know of the Temple?' she asks, with a voice heavy as stone.

Eyes lingering at the blade, he looks up into her face. Obliging, Rahat lowers the tip from his throat by an inch, allowing him space to breathe. The air about them is still, save for the crackling fire behind them. Although unwise, she daren't spare a glance at their surroundings. Not now that she knows of the faerie weapon he may have had for gods know how long. And not when he could so easily reach for the blade and turn it against her if he tried.

'She knew a girl there, once,' he explains. 'Something happened.'

Had Iliyah told him this in his dream?

Unsure, she bites the inside of her cheek. 'And that's all you know? That something happened?'

A laboured shrug. 'That's all I remember.'

The silence stretches out between them, and in that silence, Rahat can hear that the squire will not be found. The sounds of night cannot even be heard over the fire devouring the knight's sword. Sparking *pops* send Rahat's heart skittering. Prakaash remains still by the trees, surveying the multitude of colour flashing in the warm light. Not a breath can be heard save her own and the knight's beneath her. Rahat's shoulders slouch a little—with relief or defeat, she's not sure. All she feels is fear, thick as it swills in her ribcage.

'No one should care what happened in that place,' she says at last, 'what will happen there, what might be—'

The knight's nodding stops. 'While I must agree with you, I must ask.'

She frowns. 'Yes?'

'Would you care to lower your sword?'

'Sabre,' she corrects.

Though he must feel terrible, he chuckles. The dark rings under his eyes look like they've been pressed in with hooves, these half-moons lining his face and making him look years older. His lips are cracked. His eyes water. 'Yes, I know,' he says, aiming for dismissive but sounding strained. 'You're a Delorrene Lady,' he says, digging his hands into the ground to stand. When he makes a move, Rahat flourishes her sabre, the blade too near his nose for him to consider standing just yet. Raising his hands in surrenderer, he sits once more. 'It's anyone's guess who you are though, with that attitude.'

'And what is *that* supposed to mean?'

'Well,' he says, eyeing her up, 'how many high-born ladies would have a sabre ready to pierce my throat?'

Squaring her shoulders, she sneers. 'You mustn't know many high-born ladies.'

Considering his bulk, she takes a step back from him, allowing enough space to shimmy back in the grass from the fire's deadly heat. The blade of his sword is still pinging away, the sound an assault to the senses. The man sighs with relief as he crawls away from the fire-pit, paying no attention to his flaming weapon.

'Now I've a question for you,' she says softly, once he's regained his breath and wiped the sweat from his eyes. The world about them is too quiet, even for the night, and it's only when he looks up at her, exhausted, that she speaks again. Some small part of her feels that sharp panic. '*Where* is your squire?'

Sharp pain explodes in the back of her skull in answer. The fire seems to attack, rising up and coming at her as she collapses to the earth beside it, the darkness swallowing her whole.

8

With a head screaming, she wakes to the bright dawn.
It's well after first-light. Larks flitter overhead, monkeys
howl from yards off in the canopies above. As her eyes
adjust, the sun becomes blinding, forcing her to blink
back tears. Slowly, the night comes back to her. Only,
she has no idea why she's standing; her feet tingle,
heavy against the hard earth. She moves to wipe her
eyes, but finds her arms bound. They spark painfully,
twisted at an awkward angle to reach around the tree at
her back. She tugs, panicking as the bark rubs against
her hands, drawing blood from her freshly-healed palm.
Her wrists pull against the restrains as she balls her
fists, careful not to cause a strain. The hot trickle of
blood on red raw skin itches. Her skin feels tight, pulled.

Turning her attention to her surroundings, she takes in what is perhaps the lushest, greenest sliver of the jungle. Something here might be able to help her. If she can find a sharp stone and—and what exactly can you manoeuvre without your hands? *Holy Hells*, she curses, taking in the jungle. Thick moss the colour of emeralds glimmers with morning dew upon tree boughs. The vibrant red-and-orange wings of paradise birds can be spotted through the high canopies which block out the sun. Her eyes pulse with pain when she moves her head; it feels like her brain's being squeezed in a child's impatient hands. The strange sensation she doesn't recognise is the crust of dried blood matted in her hair. *How hard did he hit me?* The flash of memory comes with a jolt of panic that almost makes her cry out.

Another tug at the restraints.

Not four feet away is the campfire, smothered by wet leaves. And where the kindling had burnt rests the knight's ruined broadsword, melted to ore in the black dirt.

The men sleep without disturbance. Sweet sleeping faces hide the aggressive nature beneath. Her bonds are tight. Rahat can practically feel her fingers turning blue. The humming cold shoots pain through her hands.

'Prakaash?' she calls softly, resisting the urge to whistle for him. From across the makeshift camp, she spots movement through the trees. Or rather, the flash of stark light as Prakaash shifts from hoof to hoof, artfully making the sunlight glint off his titanium hide. There's the temptation to call to her mount again—but he won't approach. Can't, in fact. A chain tethers Prakaash to a thick-trunked tree beside her adversaries' horses. Rahat bites back the string of curses at the tip of her tongue. It's a faerie chain, forged from the bones of immortal creatures. *Bloody faeries*. Even dead, there's no escaping them. The knight must have ransacked one of their dead villages.

The sun glints, heat raining down on her through the bent trees where the shadows cannot protect her. It's the middle of the year of high summer—something left over from when the old folk ruled all the realms of Abre-can. For thousands of years, it has been the same. The faeries pulled together their strength long ago to create what are now the seasons: a year of each, providing time for each of their cultures to thrive. And ultimately, sur-vive. An incredible feat, Rahat has to admit, if it weren't for the fact that this is the worst time of the season to be anywhere remotely within the suns' reach. It's already unbearable just after first light. She doesn't even want to think about what the temperature will be like by mid-day, especially under all this leather. But surely there has to be a river on the way... *If I can get out of this mess.*

Which doesn't seem very likely.

The jungle surrenders nothing of where they are. Sunlight filters down through the canopies, and the breeze is all but silent. By the shadows, she hazards a guess she's to the north. Not that that realisation's very helpful. *There has to be a way out,* she thinks, if only to keep herself sane. Two more days... That's all she has to save Iliyah, and already too much time has been wasted. She should've been half-way to the field by now, if she'd continued through the night.

Gods know where she is now.

Another glance at Prakaash, and she knows there's no way she'll be able to reach him—even if she does somehow manage to free herself—without waking the knight and his squire.

A rustling in the undergrowth draws her attention to her feet. Her boots glisten with the dew of morning. And to her surprise, it's evaporating, steaming.

What—?

A shadow dancer curls about the tree trunk to emerge between her feet. Shadow dancers don't usually venture out into the sunlight. The gods themselves have ordained it. Forged of light and stone, the small crea-tures are only found in the dead of night where they race through the treetops like fireworks, lighting up the dark. Although Rahat's never seen this display herself, it's said that those who have the honour will again relive it in the moment of their last breath. She doesn't doubt it. They're truly magical creatures. As the tales are told, those who die of natural causes have their souls carried upon the shadow dancer's wings. But what could one be doing *here*, and out in the sunlight? Taeng's creature Hen has glowing skin in the darkness of the catacombs. Yet the beast before her—its skin is like translucent stone, if there were such a thing.

Rahat shifts her feet, making the creature pause. Their ears twitch. They're blind in high sun, she remembers, as she prays to the gods that this one can see. And feels utterly helpless when she realises they cannot.

Raising their nose to her strange scent, they stare up at her with glowing slitted eyes. The creature's mouth hinges open, revealing the tongue that glows like molten lava in their mouth. It's a wonder their paws haven't burnt prints into the earth—which is even more magnificent when you consider that they've never set these jungles aflame. The animal—she decides on the name Neeru, the name of her first pet caracal—tilts their head when Rahat clicks her tongue. The sleek-backed dragon purrs, the whirring sounds making her think of waterfalls, as they arch their spiny-scaled back. She's never seen one without wings before. Two deep scars run down the beast's back, making Rahat pause.

The spiked scales are bunched, dug into the silken smooth skin. Someone tore off the little creature's wings.

She clicks her fingers gently, and Neeru's ears twitch twice. A quick glance up assures her that the two men still slumber. Curled in on themselves, heads pressed together; she hopes it will take them hours to wake, after the exertions of last night. For she'll be long gone by then.

'Neeru,' whispers Rahat, her voice barely more than a breath. The creature tilts their head again. 'Neeru,' she coos. The animal at her feet comes closer, tentative with each step, as if walking over unsteady ground. In a glimmer of sparks that could blind, Neeru darts back around the tree, taking all of Rahat's hope with them.

Resting back against the tree, she beseeches the sky. The bark at her head aches, sending splintering pain through her brain. The one thing that could have helped her... and she scared them off.

The sun becomes blinding overhead, shining so stark a white that her eyes water. Not for the first time, she wishes Hazel were here; she always knows what to do. Even now, surely she would have *some* idea how to get out of this mess.

'Neeru,' she hisses again, her voice whipped away by the sudden wind. 'Neeru?'

There is no sound from the little beast, not even the light hiss of scales as they move against the tree bark. The grass underfoot crunches beneath her boots, and she halts, listening close. A whisper of grass as the creature brushes against it with scorching skin makes her grin. *But where is the little beastie going?*

'Neeru?'

The gangly squire rolls onto his side, groaning at the hard-packed earth beneath him as he rouses from his slumber. It had not been a comfortable night, and needless to say, they'd both fallen asleep during their watch of the girl.

'Neeru,' Rahat whispers, failing to quell her building panic.

Ansh the squire frowns, the name echoing through him as he realises the prisoner is awake. A quick hand at his master's shoulder rouses the knight. At first, the knight protests, swatting at his squire's hand like a pesky insect.

'*Devak,*' growls Ansh, shoving at the knight's back until he rolls over.

'*What?*' he complains, pushing up onto his arms. Hair falling in his face, Devak is not a graceful man, and by no means a morning person. Lip curled in a sneer, he turns on his squire. That rage fades when he catches sight of Rahat over the boy's shoulder. 'She's awake,' he mutters, making Ansh nod.

'What do we do?' asks the boy, and Rahat realises that even though his baby-face makes him look young, he's probably older than her. A gentle hand at Ansh's shoulder makes her eyes widen a little, making her wonder. Is Ansh simply a squire, or something more?

That they have no idea what now to do with her soon becomes unbearably clear. Obviously they hadn't thought this through. And why not simply kill her, if they hadn't thought ahead to this very moment?

The light sound of scratching in the tree bark draws her attention back to the shadow dancer. She can feel the heat through the dark bark. Neeru skitters about, soundless as a cat as they reach Rahat's bonds. A shock runs up her arm when she feels the full heat of the wingless dragon's mouth. Their teeth are needle-like, piercing. She winces, trying her best not to let on to her captors the truth.

The knight rolls to his feet, making a grab for the knife sheathed at his thigh. Beside him, Ansh turns over the parchment map crinkling with the morning damp as he rolls it back into the satchel.

Devak approaches with knuckles shining bright on his blade. In his other hand he holds her sabre, the tip having been snapped off in last night's battle. Rahat would bet anything it's deadlier now than in one piece; the broken metal gleams with malicious intent. Tearing her eyes from her blade, she catches the scorn on the knight's face. As if he was hoping she wouldn't be here to deal with come morning.

The suspicion in his eyes dances; as soon as she'd mentioned the temple, to him she became a prize. For one does not simply stumble onto magic. Or at least, that's what those unfamiliar with it believe.

Rahat presses her back harder into the tree, as if this will somehow keep her from meeting the bite of his sword. Why would they keep her alive through the night if they planned to slay her under the morning sun?

Arms stretched further back, she gives Neeru has more space to nibble away at the thick rope keeping her bound. The light touch of one of their paws on her forearm makes her tense. Eyes go glassy and wide. She would give anything to scream—but to scream would end her. There will be a blistering burn later; the colour might even match the puffy purple of her cheek.

The creature balancing at her hands jumps about, tearing at the ropes. Neeru will be quick, but perhaps her death by the knight's hand will not be.

She wriggles, outraged as he grows closer. The blunt tip of a dagger's sheath butts her in the ribs as she twists, and she could almost laugh for relief. Her sabre is ruined—but the armour-piercing dagger strapped beneath her tunic may just get her out of this. The men had been foolish enough not to search her. Gods willing, she'll live.

The single sun glints through the trees at an angle that hits Rahat square in the face. The first sun is the largest, the brightest. The most deadly. Soon the second sun will rise. She can almost taste its warmth; the hell of the heat alone is making her stomach feel tight. Only in the summer do the days taste this way.

'Care to offer up who you are?' says Devak.

She holds his stare but remains silent.

'You're a noble lady,' he says, his grip on his blade lightening ever so. It's clear he has no true intention of harming her as he shrugs, but she doubts the same could be said of the squire at his shoulder. 'That much can be guessed from the gold in your purse.' So they *had* dug through her pockets. 'And the sabre you carry—' He brandishes the broken thing, demonstrating just how ruined it is. '—is unlike any I've seen, and I've met many fencers like you. It's a Zaborian sport, is it not?' A light toss, and the sword lands almost perfectly in his hand. 'Sport isn't the same as fighting, so it's useless, but admirable in a way, I suppose.' Another toss of the broken thing. 'Light, too, even *with* its tip. It would've been perfectly balanced.'

'And how do you know I didn't steal it?'

The look he gives her would send a shiver down any girl's spine. 'You don't look to me like the pilfering kind.'

'How can you be so sure?' she counters.

Dropping the sabre to his side, he moves closer. The smirk that plays along his lips is deadly, cocky beyond belief. Yet his sour breath makes her flesh crawl. 'Wedding *mehendi*,' he purrs in her ear, and she goes rigid. 'The *Rajkumari* Rahat Brijesh is said to have fled, and so close to her wedding...' Leaning back to watch her face, he grins, flashing those sharp teeth. 'By the look on your face, I must be right.'

Not even for a second is she foolish enough to think he'd release her on that merit alone. Being a princess means nothing. Not out here. His grip on the sabre lessens till it's balanced precariously between his fingers. He's captured the third in line to the throne; one day he may have to bow to this woman. That smirk twitches at his lips as she glares. Rahat's ransom could change their lives.

'The *lindélof* you ride—' He throws back an arm, dismissively waving to Prakaash across camp, '—is old. So I'd say he's your grandfather Adhiraj's.'

The heat engulfing her hands becomes unbearable, as if the molten lava of Neeru's tongue is flaying the skin from her arms. Sweat pools between her shoulder-blades as it becomes harder to breathe.

'So why are you alone?' asks the knight after a pause.

Her dark eyes narrow. Devak reminds her of Zehran so much he almost makes her skin crawl. 'Care to tell me where you're from?' she demands. 'If you're going to kill me, I'd at least like to know where I can send the restless Retrievers.'

A chill rolls down his spine. The Retrievers—a tale told at night to children, or truth? Women with skinless backs who haunt their world, to destroy the lives of evil men and claim their souls. Devak clears his throat, forcing a chuckle. 'I believe you said something of the sentiment last night... Although I'm sure you thought it was *we* who would fall by your hand.' His brows jump, mocking. 'No? Well, I remember it went that way.'

Behind him, Ansh remains silent, his mind still lingering upon the Retrievers. To him, such creatures are irrefutable fact.

Sweat trickles at Rahat's brow; it rolls down her cheeks like tears. The salt licks at her wounds, making her hiss. Chewing her lip, she wills Neeru to hurry. *Surely the heat's burnt through the fern rope.* If not at least eaten through the bark. The smell of burning reaches her nose and she freezes, muscles tensed as she realises that Devak and Ansh can smell it too.

'What's that smell?' Ansh mutters. 'What is that?' He speaks more to himself than to Devak as he crosses the camp, stamping the cold fire-pit underfoot. Making a wide circle around Prakaash, the boy disappears into the trees in search of the smell. Fire means trouble, but Rahat thanks the gods he's upwind of her.

A sharp pain ricochets through her arms as the weight of the rope loosens. Neeru's got their paws on her wrists again. The sizzle of her skin makes her stomach churn. Then the pain eases, before hissing as oxygen rushes to the wounds already cauterised. A soft pitter-patter, and Rahat knows the shadow dancer has fled up the tree.

Before the rope can hit the ground, Rahat whips her arms around, producing the small dagger from beneath her tunic as she punches Devak square in the jaw. The *thwack* of her knuckles against his face makes her wince.

Thank you, Neeru. From above, she hears their small tittering.

Devak had been about to speak when she struck him. The knight flexes his jaw, groaning as he grips his knife tight—and notices the blade which Rahat now holds to his throat.

'Remember this?' she grins.

A sick laugh builds, bubbling up and through him. It makes her hesitate.

Hearing the laughter, Ansh returns through the trees at a sprint. Staggering, he almost collapses when he sees Rahat holding the blade to his master's jugular. One foul swipe, and it's all over. This could end terribly.

Sweat makes it hard for Ansh to keep ahold of his small knife, the blade barely longer than his hand. It shakes in his grasp; he's never done anything like this before. And the Retrievers—they're stuck in his head, hounding him. The only thing that stops him completely is spotting the red marking the woman's skin, reminding him of who she is. They'd known she was the *rajkumari* as soon as they'd bound her to that tree. To kill her would be a death sentence.

'One move and your master is dead,' hisses Rahat. She denies the tremble in her hand, but Devak's eyes never leave her face. He's too busy trying to turn himself to stone.

The squire takes a hasty step, and Rahat's arm goes taut.

'*One* move.' Even she doesn't believe the desperate tone in her voice. It's erratic, foolish. But it's enough that Ansh doesn't attempt another step.

'You're no ruler,' Devak spits out, throat scraping against the knife with each word. Hatred distorts his features. 'You're nothing but a—'

Yanking his hair back, she pushes his throat tighter against the knife. He halts, statuesque beneath her hands. 'You're practically begging for this knife in your throat,' she spits back at him.

Ansh opens his mouth to speak; the sound of him sucking in air makes Rahat glance up—before the boy stops himself. If he says what he wishes, he knows Rahat will be sure to slaughter Devak where he stands.

Then Ansh would be next.

He isn't foolish enough to press the matter further. The royal families of the Summer Lands have never felt trouble at having blood on their hands. What makes this woman before him any different? Ansh drops the knife. The shining dagger bounces, so sharp and unnatural against the lush green.

The camp around them is still sticky and burnt with the heat of the extinguished campfire. The black earth seems to swirl up at her, like a great gaping mouth. Eyes roving over camp, Rahat notices her belongings scattered amongst her captors'. Getting away may be harder than first thought.

'You.' She flicks her head at the squire, who goes rigid under her molten gaze. 'Return my belongings to my saddle. And free my horse while you're at it.'

He follows her order, almost tripping over his feet in his haste. Thankfully, her things haven't been removed from their bags; the boy sighs his relief—until he reaches for the *lindélof* who watches him with glowing eyes.

Rahat turns her sight back on the knight, his hair sweaty in her grasp. All she's done is aimed a weapon and gritted out orders at what have now become her captives until the knight flashes that smirk. It's sickening, much too overtly sweet and knowing to bring any comfort. It's only then that she realises she has no idea in Hadria's Halls how to get out of here. *But at least they've no weapons*, she reminds herself hastily.

The man before her, dressed head-to-toe in thick armour, is still smirking. He's unable to make too sudden a movement without struggle, even if desperate. To her relief, he carries no other weapons—otherwise he'd likely have spilt her belly upon the earth by now. But even if he has weapons at his disposal, she doubts he'll do something so mindless as to move with a knife at his throat.

'What do you want?' asks Devak, when it becomes clear that she's unsure what to say. She's locked herself into this. Though they all know that one minuscule move—anything that may become a threat—and she will slash his throat. And she thinks she just might be able to do it.

'I will give you anything if you drop that knife.'

She looks between them, the knight and the squire now spreading placating hands. Ansh is perfectly still, standing by the edge of the trees and evaluating her every move. There's nothing he can do but watch. She considers the pair, how Ansh's panicked eyes stay on Devak and never on the blade.

'Don't follow me,' she says softly, and the knight nods his head as best he can with death at his throat and her hand in his hair. 'Don't come looking for me,' she continues with a shaky breath, 'and give up your search for the *shehzadi*. Or I will hunt you down when this is all over.'

Again, Devak gives a small nod.

'But finding the *shehzadi* means—'

'Means *what*?' snaps Rahat at the squire, but her voice has lost its bite.

Holding her gaze, he daren't stare her down. There's too much pain in his eyes to do so convincingly, and she looks crazed, this runaway bride. A deep breath as he looks to Devak. So much pain in his eyes. 'You wouldn't understand,' he says quietly. The knight edges back from the blade at his throat, the back of his skull pushing harder into her hand. He's trying to look over his shoulder at Ansh. If Rahat were in the same situation and Ansh were Hazel, she'd do the same. Yet there's something different about Devak's eyes—as they dart back to the woman threatening him, she feels that glimmer of confirmation. It takes all the time of a single heartbeat for Rahat to relax her arm and drop the blade to her side.

'I do,' she says softly, taking a step back from where Devak might reach for her. 'Understand, I mean.'

Ansh fights every instinct not to run to Devak. They're both still wary of the blade in the *rajkumari*'s hand.

'We won't follow you,' says Ansh in the silence, making Devak lift a brow. Yet a moment later he nods. A hand at his neck searches for any serious damage. His fingers come away bloody, but there will be little scarring.

Across the burnt earth, Ansh retrieves his knife from the grass to return it to the sheath at his belt. Not once do his eyes leave Devak.

In the sunlight cascading through the canopies, the knight's hair is a deep chocolate brown. He would be dreamy, Rahat supposes, if he weren't so grubby with the jungle. His lilting accent leaves it obvious to assume that he's from the north of Delorran. From the cusp of the Zabor Mountains, perhaps, where they built the wall to block out the creatures that didn't die with the faeries during the Rapture. Horrible beasts with manes of fire and teeth the size of hounds. How the faeries had lived amongst them will always remain a mystery.

Slow as a glacier, Rahat crosses camp—with Ansh like a mirror to her movements as he reaches Devak's side. A step away, and the knight envelops the squire in his arms, breathing in the scent of his dark wavy hair. The younger man grasps at the knight's back, holding him close, and Rahat hides her smile when she reaches for Prakaash, now untethered. Prakaash whinnies, a sound of shared relief, when she pulls herself up into the saddle. The jangle of a saddle pocket gives her pause.

Leaning back, she takes the purse in hand. These two would've kept her captive for as long as they had to to gain a little coin. Without it, they may continue their search for Iliyah, no matter their promise. And confined within Rahat's purse is enough to purchase safe passage to the Southern Lands, to the East, or even the far-off Kirramaloo. There, they might find solace together, away from whatever they're running from.

Before she can change her mind, she tosses the small bag of gold. It *clinks*, coins singing together, when it lands within reach of the embracing couple. They jump at the sound, eyes wide as they stare up at the princess on horseback. 'I cannot say that I agree with your methods—' She waves a hand to stop them both interrupting, no doubt about to point out that she'd been as bad as they. 'Nevertheless,' she continues, 'that should be enough to grant you safe passage across the southern seas.'

Surprised, Devak bows his head. 'Your Highness...'

'Look at me,' she orders, and slowly, the man raises his head. His dark eyes dance—with suspicion, gratitude, Rahat isn't sure. 'I am giving this to you in faith,' she says, straight-faced. 'You will not follow me, you will not pursue the search for Iliyah Tyrikaara, and you will not speak of who gave you this gold. Understood?'

Again, they nod. 'Thank you,' says Devak, with a voice that quivers. Beside him, Ansh gives a small smile. He still doesn't trust her, or what lays in the purse at their feet.

Rahat gives a sharp tug on the reins, making Prakaash flick his head. The *rajkumari* shakes, jittery as she loosens her hold on him. 'Good luck,' she tells the men at last. She's got to get out of here.

Squeezing Prakaash's belly, she takes off, the twigs of the undergrowth snapping underfoot. The trees and vines rush by in a whorl of green, and she prays to every god she can name that they stay true to their word. *Because if not...*

Colour speeds by. Rahat yells as she cracks the reins, leaning her weight forward as Prakaash bolts through the jungle.

9

The jungle looks no different from above than it does
from the ground. Wind whispers through the treetops,
delivering news of things to come. The far-off cries of a
macaque give Qadira pause as she shifts her weight in
the tree boughs. Small monkeys and martens skitter
about overhead, leaping through the very tops where
they can become one, disguising themselves with the
wind-spirited leaves. A sweltering wind blows back the
kehrasa's hood, tossing fly-away strands out of her face.
The ebony tresses whisper, brushing at the faerie's
cheeks as she listens close to the winds. They're warm,
coming from the south where they breathe off the Shallow Sea.

Paradise birds flutter their wings above. They call out, throwing their voices far as they search for others. Bright feathers, a plethora of colour. It's almost like home.

Never before has Qadira been through the jungles of Delorran alone. Alone, she can almost mistake these jungles for being peaceful and not full of nightmarish creatures like the rest of Abrecan. They prowl the night, roaring their paths. She doubts any of the creatures below know that *she* is the reason they're so on edge. The magic that flows from Qadira's skin alone is enough to make the tigers scream into the night. Her magic feels like the void—at least, that's how she's heard Tahir describe it, in secret audiences with his brothers when they thought she wasn't lurking. Their own fault for keeping a faerie as a pet.

A scent tangles in her nostrils, though it's not the scent she's expecting. For hours now, she's kept on Hazel's heels as the girl pursues the *rajkumari*. That it's taken Hazel this long to find her way has honestly been a little surprising. Qadira sniffs again, taking in the scents that tangle amongst the trees. Dank earth, smoke, burnt wood, myrrh, and... the faint tang of death. It makes her recoil. The *kehrasa* bares her teeth, sharp as a big cat's, as she approaches the smell. It only grows stronger with each step, though the scent is an old one. A lingering one. In the back of her nose, she catches the jasmine in Hazel's hair and the sour sting of sweat as the Asthori steers her *lindélof* through the trees, away from the scent her human nose cannot detect.

Something must be protecting this place.

But to follow the girl or to follow death? Hazel will not fare far—all it takes is a breath for Qadira to regain her position. The girl doesn't even know she's being followed.

Again, the death calls to Qadira. Wrapping itself around her nostrils, it yearns for her. *Come to me*, it purrs, with a deep rumble of the earth that rattles her bones. *Come to your people. Come to your home.*

The call wins. Turning her back on the redheaded Asthori, Qadira rests a hand at her whip as she follows, the scent near visible in the air. A fine mist, it tangles in the trees. *Qadira...*

Great Serpent of Ages. The jungle is all but silent. Birds ahead still, their feathers ruffling as they take their perch at the tops of the trees. The wind whistles, brushing against Qadira's face as if she were a lost friend. The blessings scrawled across her forehead burn; she knows their scars burns bright, ink carved deep into her skin. It has been a very long time since she's felt magic like this. It echoes through her veins, making her buzz with each step closer. It's ecstasy, a dream, madness, and a cry for contact that all roll into one. Running her hands through her hair, she feels each touch a thousandfold, making her sigh. This is what it is to be faerie.

Come home.

This voice is different, shifting. The approach of the phrase, somehow feminine. A voice cast on the wind from the far north-east. It pricks her ears. *Could it be?* Qadira shakes the thought, though her mind's zeroed in to that voice. It's the voice she's needed to hear.

Qadira, lost sister... Come to me...

Again, the rumbling. Her knees wobble, unsteady as she leans into a thin bough. It takes her weight with a careful step as she springs into the next tree. This—this is what they used to call dancing amongst her people. Where there were no trees, but desert, and those who were family about you. A faint song comes to mind, the singing growing closer as her heart pulls her through the jungle.

Below, she feels the presence of greater animals. Large things covered in stripes and spots and silky fur. Nearby sleeps a jaguar, its coat so shiny a black it's painted by midnight.

My lost one... Qadira...

Louder, more laboured, the voice reaches out for her, grasping her about the throat as it pulls her closer. *Come to me.*

And through the trees she sees it. It freezes her to the bone. The voice loses its hold, the call dies away, and her heart stills. Tree roots snake their way across the earth like veins, weaving their way down the side of a short mountain and through the spaces between where homes once stood. Several huts stand in a circle formation, gathered about a village square which was once asunder. Qadira can see it all. The scents tangle in her nose as she stands staring down at the lost faerie village.

Flames lick their way to life, lighting the village in the night that it was destroyed. The images fill her mind before she can stop them. They force their way in. The men—men wearing the uniforms of the Praitosí Empire. Their uniforms, once white, are stained with blood. *So much blood.*

The villagers are unsuspecting, though the elders are full of apprehension. Gnarled-knuckled hands turn a-flutter as they speak, words swift as the winds and full as the river's current.

Brows furrow as the jungle before her empties.

Birds flee from their perches overlooking their huts. Hundreds of creatures hide, burrowing down into the earth or disguising themselves with magic as tree roots. These are all the signs. The elders exchange a look, and the eldest snatches a seashell from her belt. Blows.

The horn sends the villagers into slow-motion. Faeries scatter, looping their children up under the arms to pull them in close. Those with wings ready themselves, about to shoot into the skies, when the first arrow strikes.

Arrows—more than can be counted—rain down on them.

Qadira cries out, but this is a dream and she is helpless. Her grip fails on the tree trunk and she slips before quickly regaining her footing, not daring to enter this place of death.

The arrows keep coming. Wings are shredded. Children are skewered. And the elders disappear in a puff of darkness, dragging whoever is close to safety with them. Those unlucky enough to be out of reach stay, and are frozen with fear as the first Praitosí soldier cuts his way through the jungle. The machete in his hand drips with blood and the sap of fertile trees, cut to the core. Behind him an archer approaches, arrow posed to fly. These are men with harsh faces, frozen features. They do not like their orders but must obey. But as they filter through the trees, surrounding the helpless village and those trapped and bleeding, there are some amongst them who curse the faeries still living.

A wave rocks through the *kehrasa* as she stares into the past. The sights, sounds, feelings—she feels it all. And all of this is after the Rapture. Faerie families who survived the death of their cultures and managed to band together... and here they are, being torn apart by man.

A haughty general struts into the madness as faeries un-
leash themselves. The confidence on his face is despicable.
Blood fills the air, its tang more than metallic, making the men
splutter. Black and blue and red and golden faerie blood. It
slicks over the earth, the trees, the men. It shrivels, the men
screaming in agony as the blood burns through their skin.

Warriors with shredded wings keep fighting, keeping their
broken wings tight against their backs. The talons of each fold
shine, their silvers and golds glimmering as they move about
the arrows trapped in the membrane.

It's an agony Qadira remembers. The stumps down
her spine scream out, stealing her breath as she remembers what it was like. Blinding pain and a breathless
scream stolen from her lips as the air was knocked from
her lungs. There hadn't been enough time to scream.

The people keep fighting before her, even as it becomes clear
they will fail. But they keep fighting, until the last of them is
standing, panting and wielding mirrored moon-blades. Slicing
and dancing about the bloodshed as if this were a performance
and not a massacre. Tears stream down their face of mottled
fur. If this is the end, they will make it one to remember.

On the other side of the fire pit, Praitosí men start piling the
bodies of the dead. Wings, talons, horns, claws, tails, they all
become one. A mass of faerie blood and life, snatched away
without cause. And after all they've been through.

She can't breathe. If Qadira had known...

But she never could have. No one would've dared tell her, not when she's the deadliest creature they've ever known. The *shehzadas* would have denied it— Tahir would have— *No.* They were trying to protect her.

It doesn't stop the revulsion rocking through her.

The faerie keeps fighting, fighting to his last breath as he turns on them, throwing out his armoured tail to strike. From above on the side of the mountain, a soldier takes aim and lets his arrow fly. Bull's eye. The faerie screams his wrath, his tail puncturing a shield as he rails. Darkness floods out of him, humming like an aura as he tugs, finding his best weapon caught. This is it.

With one last effort, he strikes out, taking two soldiers with him as he roars, his lion's lungs filling the jungle with fear.

The soldiers smart enough start back, retreating from the faerie as his fur bristles. He's coated in blood, the fur of his arms slick with it. A worthy soldier, against a cowardly enemy.

Qadira feels a rush of pride, of sorrow, of loss. She may have been able to prevent this, had she known.

But that's his last blow. The blood of his enemies rains down on him as, faster than he can detect, a soldier grabs him by the scruff of the neck.

And forces him into the fire.

Qadira recoils, clawing at her ears to keep the screams out. She can feel his pain, his loss, his defiance as it feels that he's staring at her—staring *right at her.*

The *kehrasa* clamps her eyes shut, as if that can shut out the images in her mind. As if trying to hide will help at all. She feels like she's being torn apart.

When the faerie at last falls silent, the soldier drops him to his knees. The armour clanks as it glows red-hot in the growing flames. The soldiers spread the fire to the pile of bodies, ridding this place of all evidence of their massacre.

But you cannot rid that kind of blood from the earth.

Qadira wipes the tears from her cheeks as her vision clears, till all she can see is the village, ashen-coloured and forgotten. A whispering on the wind makes her pause before she steps off the tree-branch, expecting her wings to whisk her into the air—before the darkness embraces her, and she reappears with her feet on the ground. She rolls her shoulders, trying to forget what it felt like to have such a weight at her back. Her wings once were beautiful.

The earth feels uneven beneath her feet as she enters the sight of the massacre. The stench of death is so strong it makes her stomach churn. What happened here should never have been. Her people should still be thriving. After surviving the hells of the Rapture, they deserved it. But living in peace would never be possible, when humans think themselves fit to rule the realms.

Standing in this place, Qadira's very bones hum. The magic flows through her, still rich and full of life even though its people are long dead.

Magic will always live on, if only you know where to find it.

A darkness like shadow dances in the ashes of the fire-pit. It's only the wind, she dismisses, though the buzzing tells her it might be something more. It moves like ink in water—like the shadow-singing of the *kehrasa* people. It's the same darkness that roils off the bodies of Eeries in the daylight.

A shiver claws down her back, raising goosebumps even in this humidity. The touch of frost passes over her heart, the ice seeming to spread through her as she takes in her surroundings. A dozen huts, standing in a perfect circle about the fire-pit by her feet. The pit itself is a concave, a foot down into the earth. She can almost make out the stench of singed hair on the air. The ash sticks to her boots as she turns. They're huts forged of pine; some are of turf. The faeries who once lived here were species scattered from across the Northern Continent. The turf wall-houses of the northern Lyra Lands, the pine of the Summer Lands, and the canvas tents of the Rehmayan deserts. There were no *kehrasa* in the vision, but it doesn't stop her from wandering. There aren't too many old folk with wings. And despite their different cultures, their different species, here they all were.

Linking the huts are tiny lanterns strung up on twine that's held strong. The lanterns are leafy globes full of faerie light—the spirits of lesser faeries, the small ones you may find in gardens, once they've passed on to the Neverworlds. After all this time, they still shine bright as the moon on a cloudless night. A soft green glow, their warmth caresses Qadira's cheeks lovingly.

She runs a hand down the canvas and leather of the Rehmayani-built tent. So like the one she and her sister had constructed when they'd tried to run away. My, that was long ago. Adilah had had so many ideas of where they might go.

The *kehrasa* stops the smile before it can distract her.

In lands touched by death, you must remain vigilant.

The shredded remains of her wings itch at her back. They've always itched, aching to be free of her clothing though she refuses to show them.

Not that there's anyone wandering about. She casts her eyes about before catching sight of a pink-faced macaque, sitting at the mountainside as it cleans its fur. The monkey watches the *kehrasa* as closely as she watches *it*. Wiping the tears from her face, she furrows her brow. How long has it been watching her?

The juvenile macaque whoops, its soft sounds like a child's laughter. Slowly, it tilts its head, copying Qadira. The *kehrasa* grins, the glint in her eyes making the creature bare its teeth in a way similar to a smile. She places her hands gently over her pointed ears. The monkey follows.

'Monkey see, monkey do, huh,' she says with a chuckle, shaking her head.

Adamantly, the macaque shakes its head like *it* is leader.

Qadira trills, the sounds rising and falling over the creature as it raises its head—as if watching the sound cascading over itself. As before, it follows suit, keeping a close watch of the faerie.

'You're kind of cute,' she says, daring to step closer, 'aren't you?'

But the monkey shakes its head, making her frown.

'But I—?'

It waves a hand, beckoning her close. Something tightens in her chest as again, it beckons, waving fingers too long to be any normal macaque's. Its eyes glimmer, dark as the glittering pools of death.

Too late, Qadira takes a step back, only to find such an action impossible. The monkey twists its hand, flicking at invisible bonds which force her closer. It bares its teeth, sharper and darker than before. Black teeth.

Dear Serpent.

The monkey climbs up onto its paws, resting back as it reaches a hand for her. Its facial features ripple, and the realisation hits her.

Devourer.

The Devourers should all be dead. And yet here one sits, its foul teeth baring up at her. Alive. *Dear Serpent of Ages, no.*

'I know who you are,' it breathes, the voice of death wrapping around her like fine silk. It holds her tight, binding her in place as the creature analyses her face. Those tiny furred hands reach up to grasp her cheeks. Its breath curdles, making her every instinct scream to run. A grin plays at its lips. 'Qadira of the stolen wings,' it purrs, with that disembodied voice.

Only once before has she run into a Devourer.

It didn't end well.

Carefully, Qadira levels her breath, even as the Devourer leans closer, the little hairs of its nose bristling against her chin. The creature rises up on its hind paws, using its whip-like tail for balance as it brings its eyes to hers. The glittering darkness of the void meets Qadira's feline gaze with a start.

'I have never beheld a *kehrasa* so far from the molten sands.'

'And it's not likely you will again,' she pants, feeling the creature sucking the air from her lungs. That silken hold tightens; she shouldn't have done that.

Those monkey's eyes never blink. They keep her pinned, but slowly, very slowly, she feels its hold lessen. Its tail flicks again, held high above its head as it slaps her cheek once, twice with those clawed hands.

She daren't drop her eyes as she edges her fingers to her side. To the whip where it hangs at her belt. If she can just...

Those furred hands turn her head, forcing her to bare her neck, looped with scarves. 'Your fear is delicious,' it purrs against her cheek, its hot breath caressing the tender path beneath her ear. She shivers. 'And your blood is singing. It is the song most heavenly in these humbled worlds now toppling.'

The sweat slicks down her neck, glistening before the Devourer's wide eyes. Just one bite, and it's all over. Through its teeth, it will devour her soul before tearing her open and swallowing her heart in one mouthful. She has seen the bodies destroyed and discarded by the Devourers along the border of the Rehmayan deserts. The first time was as a child; it was the first body she'd ever seen.

'I can see your dreams, Qadira. Your past, your future, your very *heart*.'

Now—she needs to get that damned whip now.

A burning tooth brushes against her neck and she bites back a scream. The creature grips her face in one hand, squeezing so hard she fears it will crack bone. Talons form, making her cries louder. And like a cobra, she strikes. The whip is in her hand in a moment and she cracks its length.

The macaque dances back, baring those unbearable teeth. Their black's so dark and brittle they're molten rock. The Devourer screeches an unworldly sound as it throws itself at her from the rocks. She flinches back, throwing an arm out. The whip uncoils before her, quicker than the nightmare.

Those teeth are a breath from her face. The hot wetness coats her face as she yelps—

—and the heat retreats, pulled back by her weapon.

The Devourer screams his defiance as it struggles with its feet bound by her silver-threaded whip. Those teeth. Those *teeth*. There isn't time for her to think as she unfurls the whip, casting it across the village. It drags the Devourer off the rocks, scraping its fur against the age-old sharp stone. Its cries of murder grow louder, and as it makes a grab for her, she vanishes into smoke and ash and darkness.

The creature cannot follow as she tosses herself far from the forgotten village, far from the stench of faerie blood which coats the earth, and far from all that can harm her as she lands in a stream, the cool water lapping at her skin.

One breath. Another.

About her the world is silent, save the running water. Clear, opalescent, it runs free with fish that speed by, their scales glittering like thousands of royal jewels. *Serpent of Ages*, she sighs. The Devourer had ripped through the sleeves of her tunic, exposing night-dark skin. There's no use.

Tearing the cotton, she rips away the sleeves, leaving her shoulders and arms to gleam with sweat in the light of the dual suns. Two suns. There isn't much time left. She hisses as she tries to move, to scrape its scent from her. That rotten-flesh still clings to her scarves. But washing the marks of fear away will take longer than a quick bath in the stream. The water is cool, but her chest feels heavy with cold. Death had come so close she had stared it in the face. Only once before has she come so close.

Ten years ago, that man tore her wings from her back in broad daylight. Just outside Rahala's gates; she had been lucky to be so close to a city, even a mortal one. But she did not expect the cries of the people who first saw her. They're the screams she's unable to forget. Screams that will always haunt her. For after the Rapture, humanity had let itself believe the old folk dead. Their bodies became commodities; their ashen blood a delicacy. If you were to get your hands on the wings from a corpse, you would be a rich man. But the fresh wings of a living faerie? Well, apparently that had been too good to resist, for one such man. A greedy smile, a false kindness, and he had attacked as soon as she turned her back. Greedy, *foolish* humans. He had fled before she awoke, finding her way back to life through the throbbing mist of agony. She had made him pay for it, later. But the wings were never found. Wings of glittering ebony. They had been the envy of all who saw them.

But amongst the humans, it had only been a matter of time.

Qadira had stumbled, near-blind and dying through the palace gates. How she passed the guards, she can only assume she flitted with darkness, alerting the city-dwellers. The screams still ring in her ears, but she doesn't remember much past the moment where the *shehzadas* were called to dispose of her. Like the children they were, they had pleaded with their parents to help her.

And so she became their pet, owing them a life-debt as they nursed her to health. As they sharpened her into their deadliest, flightless blade.

Qadira scrubs at her arms until they grow sore. As if she might be able to scrub away the pain, the betrayal. The boys who had once saved her had sent a raid on her people, condemning them to the deaths they had escaped. What if she had been one of them?

10

Around her, slowly, there's a scene forming into focus. The stark white fades, embracing colour like blood seeping through water. Even before that light sensation of being drunk weaves through her, Rahat knows this is a dream. The smoky scents of saffron and tamarind and perfume linger in the air, growing stronger as her eyes adjust to the light, to the fuzzy feeling spreading from her toes to her fingertips.

This can't be real, she thinks, wiping her face with the back of her hand—a hand free of wedding tattoos. *Oh.* The sea-green of her *salwar kameez* glitters under the candlelight, the warmth replacing that artificial white glow. A room forms about her, fading into being and solidifying until she's standing in the Hall of Mirrors.

The gasp is on her lips before anyone can speak—she's surrounded by hundreds of people, though no sound can be heard. Dozens of conversations and dances are being had, and all in silence. Confused, she reaches out a hand jangling with golden bangles to touch the nearest man's shoulder. He's dressed all in white; a holy man. But as her hand sinks through him she flinches back, moving through the bodies of dozens of lords and ladies. The ground underfoot is polished marble, soundless under so many feet.

Desperate, she searches for her brothers, but there's no sign of them. Her *salwar* tells her this is the memory of her nineteenth birthday, not four months ago. It was the last time she saw Iliyah alive.

A phantom wind weaves through the open room, forcing open doors to lower balconies. Now this is something she doesn't remember. Casting a glance across the room for Hazel or a familiar face to confide in, to try understand what's happening, makes her realise that all these faces are strangers. From other Courts, other countries, all shades of skin and styles of dress.

Women in brightly-coloured *sarees* twirl like flowers in the breeze as Rahat ducks in and out of their way to reach the doors. The midnight sky beyond beckons, the warm air a promise of some kind.

The fuzzy feeling isn't fading. There's a warmth building in her chest as she approaches the open doors which no one has yet seemed to notice. The heat of summer embraces her as if she's stepped from the snow of the Northern Lyran mountains into the tepid, lapping waters of the Shallow Sea. The open air is inviting as she steps onto the balcony, out under the fuzzy blanket that is the night sky. Out here, the perfumes are diluted, hidden beneath the scent of lilacs and orange-blossoms.

The heat in her hands grows, stinging like the blistering skin which, here, does not exist. 'Neeru?' she calls in a whisper, though she knows the little creature hasn't followed her to this place.

'Who's Neeru?'

Rahat whorls on the voice she's played over and over in her mind, to find her standing there. *Her*, with her hands clasped behind her back as she grins, that mischievous glint in her eyes as if she's just done something the guards won't be pleased with finding later. 'Iliyah.' The name rolls off her tongue with such adoration that the Praitosí bows her head before Rahat can notice her blush. Her very skin glitters with silken black tattoos as she tucks loose strands of night-dark hair behind her ears. Those captivating eyes glimmer like a cobra's; Rahat can't keep herself from staring. 'You're alive,' she gasps.

Iliyah looks down at herself, at the *choli* swathing her in brilliant colour. It's what she wore the last time Rahat held her in her arms, the last time she'd whispered of the universe. The bright watermelon-coloured skirt trimmed with golden embroidery and fading to the deepest of blues is subdued in the lantern-light. She wraps her shawl about her slender shoulders, the royal blue is a translucent gossamer that shimmers with its golden stars, offsetting the jewels about her neck.

'You know,' she says after a long moment, her eyes moving over Rahat as her voice shakes, 'I'm not too sure about that.'

Reaching out a tentative hand, Rahat attempts to close the distance between them, but the air is thick and creamy. Like wading through clouds.

'Oh,' breathes Iliyah, the sound haunting over the silent party just beyond the doors. The tone catches Rahat off-guard—was it surprise, or something closer to dismay? 'This is only one of my dreams,' she says, those bright eyes flashing. 'I was hoping...' A glance about their surroundings, to the party behind them in the crowded Hall of Mirrors. 'But then,' she says, 'this is only magic.'

In that moment, Rahat wishes more than anything to feel the soft, supple skin of her cheek beneath her fingertips. 'But you're real,' she says.

Iliyah lifts her head with a sad smile. 'Yes,' she agrees, at seeing the hurt in the other's eyes. There's a pull deep inside her, an ache to be close to her, just to hold her hand and feel the warmth that's always been there for her. She hadn't realised how much she'd yearned to see her Rahat. 'I may be real, but this place is not. Simply a memory my mind has locked on to. And you're here.' Her hands drop to her sides to prevent her from ripping at her nails. Priestess tattoos encircle her wrists like a prisoner's bonds. 'You must be close, then.' A nod.

'The knight and squire didn't follow you, by the way,' says Iliyah suddenly, keeping her face void of emotion. 'They were true to their word. So you're not dead like me... You'll wake up.'

Rahat gives her a sidelong look as she drops her hands, accepting that she won't have the embrace she's been craving. An embrace from Iliyah would wash away all the fear that's been jumbling around in her chest since she first stood before that mirror in her wedding dress. 'I thought magic only works when you're alive,' she says.

Iliyah simply shakes her head. 'No,' she says, her voice soft. 'It lasts much longer than that.'

Out of the silence, music swells like a tidal wave. The girls turn, hair whipping into their faces, to see the commotion inside. Never had they thought the music of festivals this loud, until it leapt from the silence. People inside gather, taking dance partners. And through the mass of dancers, they spot themselves: Rahat and Iliyah, a true part of the memory taking form as the dance begins. They twirl in time with the music, hands reaching for the sky as they tap at the ground with their painted feet, keeping light on their toes.

Iliyah—the real Iliyah—places a hand over her mouth to conceal her gasp. 'So that's what we looked like.'

Their smiles are brilliant, their dancing breathtaking.

They can't pull their eyes away. If she thinks hard enough, Rahat swears she can still feel the lingering touch of Iliyah's hands at her sides.

'You must be alive,' says Rahat, searching for the words that battle on her tongue to escape. How much can she say without revealing what she's always wanted to say? Watching them dance together, their hands twitching with nervous energy to *touch*, she almost has a feeling that Iliyah knows. That what happened when they were younger wasn't a flighting fancy. 'Iya,' she sighs, unable to look at her, 'you have to be alive.'

The Praitosí sighs. 'I don't have to *be* anything, Rahat.'

Abruptly, she tears her eyes from the visual memory, and the way she looks at her—Rahat can feel it in her bones. There's that warmth again, spreading through her like ink in water, and she realises that perhaps it isn't Neeru in the physical world, snuggling up to her. Maybe it's Iliyah, here. 'What are you doing?' she asks softly, before realising that this is in no way a rational question. Her eyes remain on their dancing, joyous and leaping—everything Rahat thought they might have, might be able to have. If only Iliyah weren't a priestess.

Frowning, Iliyah pulls an odd face out the corner of Rahat's eyes. 'I'm not doing anything.' Her eyes linger on Rahat's hands by her sides; her knuckles have gone white with how tightly she's fisted them. Sweat gleams at her brow. 'Though I would get out of the suns, if I were you,' she says.

The moon shines brightly above them. 'Suns?' she echoes.

A pause, and Iliyah closes her eyes, taking deep breaths. 'There's someone with you, right now, in the physical world.' A hand goes to her temple, fingers pressing hard against the bone as she massages out the twinge of a headache. 'You need to wake up,' she says, opening those brilliant eyes. They say more than she could ever voice, more than she'd dare. 'Only a day and a half to find me,' she says without a hint of emotion. 'And you will, Rahat.'

'How can you be so sure? Things keep happening and I'm scared you'll—'

Iliyah takes a step forward, making Rahat cut herself off. When the girl stands before her, Rahat has to look away from how they dance in the memory over her shoulder. Slowly, the space between them closes, until Iliyah stands so close that Rahat could reach out and touch her.

But Rahat's hand passes right through Iliyah's when she reaches to hold it. The pain in Iliyah's face is a mirror of her own as they hold their gaze.

'Iya,' she begs, 'what if I can't find you?'

Iliyah's eyes remain steady as she reaches to place her hands, suddenly solid, at Rahat's shoulders. And though the Praitosí's hands are stone-still, she feels the sensation of being rocked awake. Her heart hitches in her chest, making her gasp. And, almost aggressively, Rahat pulls the girl into her arms, the warmth of their bodies spreading through them. They are magnets, pulled together and unwilling to part. At her ear, Iliyah mews like a scared animal. She can feel the moisture of her mouth against her ear as Iliyah sucks in a breath.

'I'm not ready to die.'

Rahat fights against the invisible hands at her shoulders shaking her so violently. The dark swoops in, locking her out of the memory, away from Iliyah, and keeping her from consciousness. A dark and slippery feeling crawls around in her chest, making it hard to breathe.

The suns are too bright.

The hands at her shoulders are too tight in their grip. Pain shoots through her side and she yelps, protesting as her watering eyes creak open to the sky. The tears trail down her cheeks to her mouth, where they taste oddly sweet. Her hands shoot up, brushing away the grip at her shoulders as she stares Hazel in the face. 'Hazel, what in Hadria's Halls are you—'

Then it hits her.

'*Hazel?*' Rahat scrambles up onto her elbows, ignoring the hot tears at her cheeks. 'But how are you here? How'd you find me? What happened?' A shake of her head, clearing the fog from her thoughts. 'This is impossible, you were taken back to the palace; I saw you— Qadira *had* you.'

Biting her lip, Hazel ignores the bombard of questions. 'You're behind on schedule,' she says, as if that is obvious enough to explain her story. There's an odd look in her eyes, old and haunting, that Rahat has never seen. Hazel wipes the dirt from her face and kneels beside the *rajkumari*. The Asthori rubs her sweating palms against her leather pants, but it's no use. She only smears the wetness across her thighs. 'I was hoping you'd've found Iliyah by now, but here I find you in the middle of the jungle, *grossly* closer to Ajrapur than the fields, looking like you've had a bout with the gods.' She cocks a brow. 'And why are you sleeping in the middle of the day?' A hand goes to her cousin's forehead without second thought. Small grazes and cuts cover Rahat's face and neck; not taking into consideration the bruised welt where Qadira's whip had caught her.

Hazel recoils when she finds the burnt and blistered skin of her wrists. She doesn't want to imagine what other kinds of injuries might lay beneath her clothes. 'Did something happen?' she demands. 'Did you run into hunters?' The sounds of the jungle become so loud that they scramble her thoughts as she tries to understand, but comes up with nothing. 'Rahat, none of this should have happened,' she says.

But Rahat's too stuck on that word. 'Hunters?' she echoes, still fighting to wake even as the sun forces her eyes closed. 'What hunters?'

The girl hesitates, sitting back on her knees. 'More knights than I can count are searching for Iliyah—and Zehran's sent orders for Saadi to search around the God Mountains near Rahala. He...' Hazel sucks in a deep breath, unsure of whether to tell Rahat this bit. It's the look on her face that makes her say it. 'He sent Qadira after you. When they caught me, I wasn't sure they'd let me go.'

'Why did they?' The question's out of her mouth before she can stop it.

A small quirk of her lips. 'There's a bounty of a thousand línare on your head. So Qadira let me go.'

'She—what?'

Hazel's lithe hands go to Rahat's hair, matted with blood, smoke, and gods know what else. Without a word, she begins unravelling the *rajkumari*'s hair and rebraiding it. 'Did you split your skull or something?' she asks, fingers grazing the tender bump at the back of Rahat's head.

She flinches at the touch. 'Something like that.'

Those hands pause in her hair, tugging on loose strands. And before the Asthori can ask, Rahat tells her everything that's happened since they were separated. The tiny village with it's age-old weaver of words, a siren singing the Lyran song of Vanja and Maris; how she hadn't heard that story since she was a child; how it had made her start to hope again that she might find Iliyah. How she had almost given up, when she found herself tied to the tree in the high morning, cowering from an arrogant knight and his frightened partner. And finally, her dream of Iliyah—of seeing them dance the way they had when they were happy. Of holding Iliyah in her arms one last time, as Iliyah's gift reached out for her across the jungle.

'It was so real it almost hurts,' she explains slowly. 'I always knew Iliyah could do that—that as a dream weaver, that gift is why she's a priestess. Why she can't...' Tearing her sight away, she clears her throat. 'Why she can't marry and hold station like a normal princess. I *knew* she could do that, but I've never been a part of it.'

All the while, Hazel is silent. Now-bloody hands tying the ends of her braid, she sits back on her legs and considers her cousin. There's a new light in her eyes, a certain degree of wonder, that makes her believe the stories. Or makes her *want* to. 'Well,' she says at last, 'you haven't had the best run of luck.'

'And neither have you,' says Rahat, finally noticing the bruising at Hazel's collarbone. It's obvious that the greenish-yellow of her skin has only just stopped swelling. 'What did that?' she asks.

Hazel's hand instantly jumps to the bruising. 'Oh,' she half-laughs, fingertips light against the split, swollen skin. 'Zehran got me with the butt of his sword.'

Horror makes her heart stop. Blood runs cold. 'He *did that* to you?'

'It was my fault,' the girl says. 'I was trying to pull him off his horse at the time.' That mischievous glint flashes in her eyes and Rahat has to bite down on her lip to stop herself from laughing. 'They took me back to

Ajrapur and demanded to know why you *fled*, as they put it. They thought you were running from the wedding—your father was *furious*. But not as mad as the Emperor. You should have seen it.' She rips at her nails as she tilts her head, remembering these last few days. A laugh makes her nostrils flare, in turn making her grimace as she stretches, feeling the pain pulse at her collar. 'Uncle Ram didn't want to let me go; he wanted to keep me because he thought you'd come back for me. In the end, I think it was Karnan who must've convinced Qadira to let me go—because there is *no way* that I can believe she didn't know there were guards smuggling me out through the tunnels.'

'How is he?' she interrupts, biting her lip. 'Karnan, I mean.'

Hazel shrugs. 'He's Karnan,' she says with a gentle laugh. 'He's a little worried. And with good reason,' she adds with a pointed look at her cousin's hands. 'I can't believe you were so foolish. Damn the map, you *should* have kept going.'

'Yeah, yeah.' She brushes off, climbing slowly to her feet with a groan. Her limbs are stiffer than she'd thought, sleeping on the hard-packed earth. 'Nothing we can do about it now. I don't think they're following me, at any rate.'

The Asthori sighs once up on her feet. She's a good head taller than Rahat, though she's never felt it until now. She casts a shadow over Rahat's face. 'We should get going.'

11

A blush lingers at her cheeks as the air floods back into her lungs. She hates saying goodbye. But the suns' light is glaring, illuminating the world enough for her to make out its jumbled silhouettes. Up here, out of the tunnels, the world is overwhelming. The shadows blend together.

Karnan lingers behind, his hand suspended in a wave, not yet wanting to say goodbye. It's so sparingly that they see each other now. Her blush deepens when she thinks of Rahat's birthday, of how the prince had snuck away to dance with her in the gardens under the full moon. He had forsaken the parties and all the well-born ladies throwing themselves at him... for her. She still can't wrap her mind around that—that she can make the prince blush as much as he can steal her heart.

A sigh rolls through her as she is soon swallowed by the familiar darkness. The disorientating shadows no longer dance across her mind. Over her shoulder, she feels Karnan still standing there, his hands by his side but hyperactive, wanting to pull her back to him. He waves again, unsure, before she turns her back on him. This isn't right; they both know that. The Maharaja and Maharanee will never allow it. What kind of prince marries a woman who can hardly look someone in the eye without killing them?

But Karnan has done that, every now and then—opened his mind to her, just to get a look at her eyes without pupils, and how they swallow the light in their blinding white nothingness. 'They make your skin glow,' he'd once told her, on a midnight stolen. 'They being what?' she had asked, for him to reply: 'Your visions. You think no one can tell, but... they make your skin glow.'

It had taken months to rid the memory of the feel of his smile that day from her mind. She was so hypnotised by how that slow smile morphed his face into something godly that she knew it was wrong. Every time she sees him, that feeling grows. And there's nothing to stop it.

The descent of stairs is almost maddening. Deeper and deeper into the dark. So many stairs, all trampled underfoot for centuries, all worn slippery under her silken shoes. Her sigh echoes off the tunnels that break off in every direction.

Reaching the bottom of the stairs, she pauses, feeling something unfamiliar creep over her. As if she can almost hear the soft breath of Karnan atop the stairs, where he always stops to hear her footsteps growing quieter and whisper an 'I miss you.'

The words weave their way down to her, making her bite her lip to keep in whatever humiliating squeal wishes to escape. Standing in the darkness, alone and missing the warmth of him, she listens to that heavy breathing.

It takes less than a second for her to realise it's not Karnan. The shallow sound is close. Too close. Snatching her robe's dagged sleeves to her sides, she becomes a statue, holding her breath as her ears struggle to listen. Beside the Sisters of the Order, there should be no one down here.

Unless some creature is foolish enough to waltz down here, she thinks, not daring to move a muscle. Before her, the catacombs are as they always are: halls and overhanging arches and towering marble altars and shelves of creatures and potions. What lays before her is empty. She is alone.

And yet...

Steeling her nerve, she releases her breath. Even if something is standing before her, she fears she will not know it.

But down here, each stone feels like an extension of her. When she was a child and first arrived, the dark had seemed to move, as if wishing to trick her into losing her way into the mouth of some fearsome beast. Now, she can feel the vibrations down every hall like they're her veins.

A shadow dances across her vision. Whipping her hands to her eyes, she rubs at them in vain, hoping to produce some semblance of shadowed sight. *This helplessness is what humans feel*, she thinks. She blinks once, twice. The pitch blackness moves like the ocean at night as her eyes adjust again, small fragments of light meeting her until she foolishly takes a deep breath.

And allows the creature in. Claws itch her skin—but this is not a creature of the ground. She is alone, and she is not alone. Slowly, she recovers her breathing, matching it to the taloned beast's which remains steady, controlled. The wetness of its mouth whispers at the exposed flesh of her neck; the sharp nip of a tooth at her lobe makes her go still. Fighting all instinct to flinch, she stills her heart. *Breathe*, she tells herself. This has never happened in the halls beneath the palace, though she knows this creature.

This beast has held her before.

Somewhere down the hall, a strange light flickers. Violently bright and forged of colour she can barely make out. Jade, emerald, moss, turquoise, and deep sea green. Taeng knows who it is. All colours dance against the walls, reflecting like the moon on a still ocean. They are devastating. Beautiful. She knows the image projected into her mind.

Those claws sink into her skin, drawing blood and making her cry out. The mouth laps at her neck. This just might be it. Taeng tries in vain to squirm from its grasp, but those claws dig deeper. She feels the scrape of her bones. Blood pools about those sharp talons. They feel like ice shards against her muscles. The arctic courses through her till she stills herself.

Slow, achingly slow, her blood heats about the creature's claws as they retract, taking with them slivers of skin. A shiver rocks her and her heart falters, skipping before painstakingly returning to natural rhythm. Though now working much harder. The air stings against her skin, raw and exposed. *Don't cry out.*

The moist breath at her neck retreats the moment she feels its teeth pressing against her jugular. *Stay still.* And just when she fears it may bite, it leaves, disappearing into the nothingness.

In the silence all she hears is her panting. Her stomach roils at hearing the creature—whatever it is—licking the blood from its talons. It disappears down one of the corridors.

If that monster is in the most sacred of places, then Taeng doesn't want to think of what her Sisters may be doing. That *thing* should be dead. Along with its god.

Palpitations make it hard to breathe. Tears roll fresh down her cheeks as she sucks in deep breaths, fighting against sobbing. She doesn't want to take another step further. Karnan is just up those steps—but she refuses to drag that creature up with her. From the path up the stairs, she hears not a sound. He will have heard nothing. She says a silent prayer to the gods for that.

And while the blood courses down her arm freely, giving no sign of the wound clotting, she remains where she stands, listening with bated breath. No use panicking if there's another one down here that'll come along and end it all. But it wasn't a Devourer—she knows that. This creature had membranous wings like those of a dragon; sharp teeth like deep-sea fish; it smelt like death. Anxiety makes her mind whir. The corridor swirls before her, flashing lights nearly knocking her off her feet. Yet she knows that the moment she gives in, she'll die. Balling her hands into fists, she does her best to clot the wound. Her robe is marred by blood, the folds slick with it. The scent alone makes her feel sick—that coppery *wrongness* of her life leaving her.

Down the halls, that light continues to pulsate across her sight. Taeng sucks back her tears and forces herself to watch. The blankness is being transformed around those vibrant colours. As if it sizzles. *Which means the god is near.*

She'll only have one shot.

The light splatters itself across these old walls, almost throwing itself. Where Hadria the All-Mother cultivates emerald light, this is the green of rotted flesh. The All-Mother has visited this labyrinthine temple for as long as Taeng has been here; always she has appeared as a body of light so she could see her. But if Taeng is right, there will be no body of light. There will be flame and smoke. There will be rancid ash.

Tentatively, Taeng takes a step into the first room, passing under the etched carving of bears and tigers in battle. There's no hint of the bright, flickering ashen light here. The world is too dark. All altars are aflame upon an audience with the mother goddess. Yet now they remain dead. Her vision is unclouded; the dark welcome. This is not her. The realisation sinks deeper and deeper. She's not sure she will be able to face him. Not again.

Praise be Ohren that Karnan will not worry; she casts her prayer to the god of luck. Her mind dances about the name of who she will face, refusing to conjure such a cursed title. Conjuring it only makes it real.

'Hen?' she whispers, calling for her shadow dancer. Each time Taeng leaves to see Karnan, Hen has waited at the bottom of the stairs for her return. But not today. 'Hen?' When not a sound answers her call, her heart thuds.

Almost instantly, she recognises the light pitter-patter of the shadow dancer's prancing gait. They sound close. She starts when Hen emerges as if from thin air, having dulled their glow to nothingness while the taloned-beast was near. Light bounces off the walls, disorientating her as Hen approaches.

'Hen,' the girl sighs, almost dropping to her knees with relief. The blood is hot and sticky down her arms, dripping from the tips of her fingers. Hen mews, nudging her legs to move her on to the heart of the catacombs. The blood drips with the light sighs of rain, leaving a red trail behind.

The air feels thick. It swirls about her like the ocean's floor, kicked up with every step. Keeping her fists balled tight, she sucks in one last breath—tasting of dust and decay—to hold. For as long as she can remember, this has been a skill of hers. Her mother had taught her from

when she was a toddler; she remembers it being important. That voice, nearly lost to memory now, chimes in
with those words in a language she hasn't heard since:
'Hold your breath near god-flame. Breathe in the flame,
and you breathe in the darkness.' As a child, it had always felt a foolish reminder. The hot lick of fire in her
nostrils when she got too close was always enough of a
warning. She'd just never understood why it was so important until the day it happened.

Taeng follows Hen as the creature bounds ahead, toward the flickering flames so like the sky's dancing
lights. A disconcerted chord rings out of the silence, a
chord played on repeat by a musician's practiced hand.
A lyre, closely followed by what she can only assume is a
crudely-fashioned flute. An ancient sound, like something that crawls up out of the ground in nightmares. It
makes her blood run cold. And, as a voice joins the instruments, she halts mid-step. Though she knows not
the song, she knows that the language is not one of mortals.

They are conjuring Destruction.

Again, that name floats to the surface in the scramble
that is her thoughts, but she sinks it. Never—she told
herself she'd never think of that foul beast again.

At her feet, Hen curls around her as if begging to follow. The animal stares up at her with wide eyes until she

has to loose her breath. It feels like all the air in all the world is trying to force itself into her lungs. The music continues, that voice haunting as it caresses and soothes the darkness, forging from it a lover, a dark deceiver. Every urge in Taeng tells her to flee. The scars across her body scream. The nightmare that had attacked her at the bottom of the stairs was no coincidence. Whatever is happening, in the heart of the catacombs where the cremated bodies of oracles are kept, they wanted to keep Taeng away.

Further down the hall she travels, growing weaker by the second. Pain throbs at her shoulder, stinging like a thousand deaths, but she pushes it away as best she can. There is no time to collapse to injury. Not if they're about to unleash what she fears they are. And if she's right about which god this may be, then there's no time at all. The roar of fire plays in her memory, joined by the screams of her villagers as they cried for the gods that they are dying.

Around the bend, she follows the light, Hen staying close. The light becomes blinding as she walks toward the closed door at the end of the hall, the door like a beacon shining with those colours of the rotted earth. There's a silver glimmer to it, sizzling at its edges. That can't be good.

Each step down the hall feels like she's walking on nails. Pins and needles run down her legs as she forces herself to keep moving, Hen mewing at her to turn back. The winged beast nuzzles against the door upon reaching the end of the hall lined with dozens of crypts. Dead kings and queens, and those gifted oracles of old. Yet behind the door lay the most powerful of all.

The singing comes to its end, and Taeng hears a glass smash. A scream cuts the air before all goes silent. So silent. As if the air has been snatched from the world.

Flashes of fire play across Taeng's sight as she rests a hand at the door. Beneath her touch, it opens without force, and Taeng is left standing in the open corridor. Before her, her Sisters surround the high-built altar in the centre of the room. Jaya, Deepti, Kumuda, Amritha, led by the elder Aiah, a Tehrarsi by birth. The second-eldest, Ewah, turns her burning eyes on Taeng. At spotting her, she sneers, her wrinkles etched deep into her face.

In the corner, the youngest girls play their instruments and raise their voices again to the skies. At their feet lays the broken glass which clinks as they tap their feet. One of them had dropped an offering to the god they so desperately call to.

The heat in the room makes it hard to breathe; it forces Taeng to relive dark memories. Flames swarm—

and Taeng hurdles into the room as if fleeing the memory to barricade the door. Hen hangs at the foot of her robes as she stands between the women seated about the altar. The altar—smeared in metallic blood.

The altar—aflame in green. Emerald and jade and moss dance like the flash of dragon scales as they meld together, forming the face of an evil master.

It's too late.

She's too late.

From the flame, smoke plumes like the tallest cloud-seeker trees. Pumping the room full of smoke, it steals all oxygen. And slowly, the elderly women lean back in their seats, breathing in the smoke and feeling the effect of the thinning air. Aiah turns her sight on Taeng, old eyes lined with kohl and deep wrinkles.

They know not what they have done.

'Why?' screams Taeng, feeling a hand at her bloodied wrist.

'Because war is coming,' croaks Aiah, 'and we must be ready.'

Taeng wrenches her hand back despite the pain. 'You fool.'

The smoke grows darker, thicker as it continues to rise, the roaring sound of it overwhelming the bird-wing soft falsetto of the singing. The hymns are choked off into absolute, humming quiet as the nightmare forms before their eyes. As Ewah tenses in her seat, eyes wide as she realises the truth of her actions, Taeng trembles. Smoke clings to the blood at her arms, fresh and sticky and hot.

Soon, the room is too small to contain them all. The smoke stops growing.

The green light shines through the ashen cloud, illuminating the twisting form as it comes into shape. A man, if it were, coming out from the cloud of ash and ember. She feels him forming about her. Taeng could not have stopped this.

The flutist watches on in horror as her mouth runs dry; the lyre-girl pauses, hands trembling as the instrument clatters to her feet.

A mouth forms in the moving dark. Then a pair of eyes glowing like embers. The apparition stretches, arms moving through the high archways and through the bodies of the oracles, who have fallen asleep at the ancient god's smoking feet. An explosion of pain at Taeng's left arm makes her scream. The god turns its eyes on her with intent, the embers narrowing as it swarms, the air thick as it swirls about the room and over the heads of those who now dream.

They have conjured him to save them.

And he will destroy them.

The handprint of a scar at Taeng's arm glows red, red as blood, as the god approaches. A gruesome grin stretches over its face.

'Soooooo.' That sound, she has only heard once before. It is the roar of flame and the crashing of an earthquake, the tumbling of mountains and the screams of the dying. It is destruction and terror. The deep voice of doom. 'You held true to your promise,' the god hisses, conjuring the memory of the day her life was stolen away.

She was only a child. While her father and mother lay burning in the confines of their hut, the god had cornered her by the well. It had stared into her blinded eyes as it does now, detecting the difference in her with a sour breath. Taeng never forgot the way the god reached to caress her chin, where there remains a scar from his scorching touch. The god had stared into her soul that day—and she had refused to beg. She would not lay down her life. So the god laughed and told her: 'Summon me when you feel it is time to die.'

That was before the faeries had fallen. When they fell, she believed the ancients gods dead too. And they had been... Until this one was awoken. Not for one moment would she stoop to summoning him and returning him to the realm of the living.

Today, her Sisters have sealed their fate.

Reaching out with a still-forming hand, the god makes for her chin to repeat that scarred mark. As he grows closer, she winces. For while the rest of her body has become near-numb with the loss of blood, the pain at her wrist is all-consuming. Like fire. Like scorching kisses laced into her skin. She screams, but it doesn't help. Screaming never helps.

'God of Bones,' she gasps at him, before the nightmare can lay a hand on her. It hesitates at her word, and she takes a stifled breath. 'I am sorry your people are gone and we cannot bring them back—' It comes out in a tsunami, the words tripping over themselves as the god listens in patient quiet. 'There is no way to bring them back or atone for what humanity has done, but I beg of you, be lenient. I did not summon you today, but my Sisters have committed themselves to the task. I cannot think what they wished—what made them *so determined* that they would conjure Death to banish the Empire—but I have questions before I die.'

To this, the god tilts his head. The figure of his form becomes smaller, less imposing, as he surveys the oracle. Bleeding before him, she is like the sacrifices of old, willingly given. It appears his creatures have had their fun with her. 'Go on,' he purrs, in a voice sweet in the way that lava is sweet and heady.

'Tell me,' she gasps, 'tell me my world will get better. Tell me Rahat changes the Empire's future—changes everyone's future. Please. *She has to.*'

'You speak as if I have control of such matters,' the god croaks, his smoke swirling about Taeng. It forms a cocoon about her, threatening to swallow her whole. 'My children were kinder on this matter,' he purrs by her ear, making her jump. 'No wars over power, no... *empires.*' A seductive laugh surrounds her and she holds her breath as her mother taught her. *Breathe in the flame, and you breathe in the darkness.*

'Why do you seek my aid for such a thing?' the god asks at last. His embers caress her exposed skin. As her eyes follow his movements, Taeng realises that the blood has stopped freely flowing down her arms. The wound is clotting. 'You being an oracle, I would assume you *know*. But then...' The god takes a good look at her face. 'No, you wouldn't, would you?'

She makes the mistake of breathing deep, the god's face inches from her own. He chuckles as he comes closer—close enough to kiss her. 'A curious thing, a girl,' purrs the God of Ash and Bone. The Faceless God. The Stranger's Son. Father of the All-Mother. There are too many names rattling about her skull. 'Curiosity, you know,' he goes on, keeping those embers pinned on Taeng's white eyes.

A curt nod. 'I know.'

'And what does the little one seek of me *really*?'

Another stolen breath. 'Tell me where to find them.'

The Ashen God retreats, his form filling the crowded room until he is once again the only thing around her. The heat grows unbearable. The smell of him is still tangled in her nose, bitter and sweetly sour like sulphur.

'Tell me where to find my family on the Isle,' she says again, and it's only a moment before the Ashen God charges. In the space of a blink, that searing cold becomes a scorching flash as he dives at her. Jaw opening, prying back like a cobra devouring its prey—

—Taeng spies the lost galaxies upon his tongue of embers.

Bones are caught between his teeth like insignificant meals. Like sacrifices. Taeng screams, the sound engulfed by the god's wide mouth.

Skittering up the door and onto Taeng's shoulder, Hen rears with a screech and dives at the incoming attack. The shadow dancer disappears right through the god's mouth as its jaws wrench back even further, revealing the contents of his stomach. Lost worlds, the skeletons of faerie creatures, and beasts screaming to be released from their prison. Those teeth come at her, stealing away her screams. Hands raised above her head and tracking blood, she knows this is it.

It's intimidating, to say the least. Taeng can't remember the last time she stood in the audience chamber—or before so many people. The Maharaja and Maharanee stare through her like she's a projection upon the sunlight streaming in through the wide-arched windows.

The views out of those windows are breathtaking but lost to her: the jungles and the Opaline River; the spiralled towers reaching into the sky from the city of Ajrapur, a splatter of the rainbow with its many districts. The audience hall is long, and her footfalls echo unbearably as she makes her way, flanked by guards, to the dais. A dozen or so steps keep the royal family above her at all times; narrow pools of water lining the path keep her from the courtiers' reach. As Taeng keeps her eyes on the floor, she ignores theirs, which roam over her as if she were entertainment. And, in a way, she supposes she is. Oracles have not been seen by many since the final fall of the old folk. Once, Taeng and her kind may have conversed with those ancient people. Now, they're no more than a dream to her, as accessible now as the Isle of the Dead is to one living and without a ship and a weathered crew.

A deep bow of the head upon reaching the bottom of the stairs, and Taeng hopes she's keeping her sight on the feet of the Maharaja and not on his sons. Though she supposes their screams would alert her if so.

Ashrit sits beside his father, resting on plush cushions with a plate of dates and almonds and mangoes within arm's reach. The Maharanee nibbles at a date, its scent crisp and sweet. Pale as the day, she is a wonder in a room of dark skin. As much as Taeng is, with the peach-tinge of her skin marking her as different, as an enemy of the Praitosí people. Taeng doesn't let her mind linger long on the troubles her people have faced in Sylong and Hrathī as the Praitosí Empire stripped her homeland of its culture and forced them into servitude.

She can feel their eyes on her. The Tyrikaara-al-Hiraj family have spread themselves over the sides of the pools, hands folded in laps as they sit watching the audiences. Taeng knows she is one which no one expected. The rigidity in Karnan as he sits bolt-upright is one indication. A turn to the *shehzada* Tahir, and she knows that no matter what she says—even about his sister—he will never believe her word. Not only is she the woman who drove his bride away from him, but she is of a servant people. She almost fears to open her mouth, for fear that her lilting, jolted accent will betray her as Other.

'Taeng,' greets the Maharaja when she raises her head, returning her eyes to the food at his plate. His voice is gruffer than she remembered; a tingling in her fingertips tells her he's been crying. 'What news have you brought?' he asks, leaning forward.

The oracles never bring good news.

Keeping her hands hidden within the folds of her robe, she remains controlled. Being in such close proximity to Karnan without touching him is torture. Seated beside his mother, he remains silent, barely acknowledging her save for his alertness. While no one has said a word of her injuries, his eyes scan over her, cataloguing the damage. Again, Taeng dips into a short bow. 'Your Majesties,' she starts, not knowing exactly how to begin. When she'd awoken in the abandoned crypt, surprised to be alive, there hadn't really been a plan in mind. Only a need, a screaming in the back of her head, to *Go*.

The Maharanee raises a hand, beckoning for her. Taeng's lip is split; blood splatters her face in a swathe of cuts, grazes, and bruises. She isn't sure how long she had laid there in the cold, unconscious and close to death. Even with Hen now clinging to her shoulders, she cannot feel the creature's warmth. The blood at her exposed shoulder has dried, the wounds clotted. Yet even dry, they are ghastly.

'Would you care for some food?' asks the Maharanee. As if knowing that the girl cannot glimpse her face, the woman throws all concern into her voice. 'Perhaps a drink may refresh you.'

Taeng knows, without a doubt, that after this audience the Maharanee will order for Taeng's care and her wounds will be pieced together by someone gifted with healing magic.

Once, Taeng had had nothing. Now the Maharanee is the closest thing she has to a mother. And it's an easy fit; Odelia's face feels like her mother's had, with long hair that cascades in waves, both women preferring to keep it braided over a shoulder. Both women have almond-shaped eyes, cunning as a feline's. Though she supposes their colourings must be different.

The oracle grins, slowly using her staff to make her way up those steps until seating herself a few levels from the top. From here, the Maharanee hands her a date, pouring with her own hand a glass for the young oracle.

Here, Taeng can almost feel Karnan's breath on her face as his mother hands her the glass. Greedily, she gulps it down, not having realised how thirsty she was. 'Excuse me,' she whispers, wiping the water from her lips as she casts her sight away. 'Thank you, Your Majesty.'

'Taeng,' says the woman again, wanting to reach for the oracle's hand but knowing the better of it. 'You do not often come with news.'

Still, Karnan remains silent. In her peripheral, Taeng notices Ashrit glancing at his younger brother. Karnan's affection for the girl is no secret to him. Nevertheless, it would not be something noticed by the courtiers spread throughout the room, watching the interactions greedily.

It is more silent than the catacombs. There are no whispers from them. Their eyes all stay upon the foreign woman in her foreign robes with her inhuman eyes and accented words. *Entertainment*, indeed. Some small part of her hopes they'll realise just how wrong they are.

Carefully, she raises her sight to rest at the Maharanee's chin—it is as close to her face as she will allow her eyes to roam. 'Auntie Odie,' she breathes, the familiar name too low for anyone but the woman in question to hear, 'you have always believed in me.'

The Maharanee nods, laying a hand at her husband's knee. As if answering, he leans forward to hear the oracle's whispered words.

'These are not matters that you would wish to have subject to the ears of Court.' She can't help reaching out then—Karnan shifts, uncomfortable in his seat, and leans in so he might catch her words. It's mere hours since he'd last seen her, unscathed and smiling. And now...

Each breath in the room is suspended for one hair-raising moment as Taeng moves closer. Too many people in this room wish to hear; the shift in the air tells her of the Tyrikaara family moving closer to the shallow pools, the Emperor knocking his goblet into the water. The splash echoes back at him from every curve of the hall's domed ceiling.

'Perhaps this is a matter to be discussed in personal quarters,' suggests Ashrit slowly, keeping his voice steady so as just to be heard.

The courtiers' collective breath is released.

After a pause, the Maharaja nods. With a sweep of his hands, he and his family and Taeng are on their feet, leaving up the steps and through a narrow hall for a more secluded audience. Taeng trails behind, and the guards trail her. Their footsteps are swallowed by the whispers that fill the vast cavern of the audience chamber, speculating over what the matter could be. An oracle with a shadow dancer does not appear in the middle of the morning carrying news. It is no secret that many believe her kind false. Taeng can almost feel the frustration of the Praitosí gathered.

Keeping a step behind his brother, Karnan reaches back with a subtle hand, which Taeng envelops in her own. He gives it a squeeze, which she returns, hidden within the falls of her sleeve. A familiar warmth, a tingling, spreads up her arm with the feeling of home. She wishes it would never end. Karnan runs his thumb over the back of her hand, ever so gentle. *You're alive*, that touch seems to say, *And I'm never letting you go.*

Every sound echoes in the small corridor. Before them the royal family brushes by the chiselled walls that explore the tales of lands once ruled over by the old folk. Each painting is more painful than the last, their stories of love soon turning to those of darkness. Yet none display the Rapture. At the end of the hall stands a towering door of thick dark wood, smelling gently of sandalwood and roses. It must be the scents lingering in the room beyond. At reaching the open door Karnan hesitates before releasing her hand, wishing to keep that *rightness*. At last, he lets go, filtering into the room behind his family.

Hen hisses at her shoulder as Taeng passes through the door. Claws digging into her muscles, the oracle yelps, hands instantly reaching to grab ahold of the creature's body, but Karnan is by her side before she can ask for help. Deftly, he scoops the boiling beast into his hands before passing Hen to the floor. Their paws pad lightly against the freshly-polished marble. Mewing, they explore their new surroundings, so bright and open to the catacombs.

The guards on their heels stop at the door, turning to remain outside when Ashrit gives them a nod. 'Fetch Doctor Chaudhary,' he orders, and one of the guards leaves at a run. Those remaining right themselves, sword and shield poised outside the door. No one will make it past them.

With a cursory glance, Ashrit closes the heavy wooden doors, closing the latch from inside. They are alone, no one wanting to move in this pregnant silence.

At last, Ashrit touches a hand to Taeng's shoulder, careful of the blood and gauged skin. The look on his face is one of pain. 'May I ask what happened?'

The deep gauges of where the nightmare's claws had been pulse with unbearable heat. The urge to scratch until she's bloody is overwhelming. Her nails bite crescents into her palms as she balls them tight, hidden in the folds of her robes. 'The Ashen God has returned,' is her only response.

And it is as if all life has died.

A chill descends, making Karnan wrap his arms around himself. But Taeng is immune to the cold. Since the moment the god swallowed her in that cavernous mouth, every movement of her body has felt wrong. As if the Nameless God has violated her skin and turned it into something that is *his*. Wrong and shapeless and evil. The more her nails bite into her palms, the urge to scratch her skin to ribbons becomes stronger. She grips herself tighter.

'The Son of the Stranger,' Taeng starts again, pausing on hard breath.

As if understanding why, Ashrit crosses to the windows, where he throws one open. Instantly, the summer air whooshes into the room, warming them through their cores. A glance about the shutters tells Ashrit they're alone. If arguments become tense, none of the neighbouring balconies are within earshot.

The Maharaja slumps into a carved wooden chair, resting his head in his hands. The gods of the faeries had once been a worry to all the realms of Abrecan where humans dwelled. Some have been optimistic enough to believe many of them dead; the Maharaja, it appears, is not one of these men.

'Why did he come?' he asks, in a voice hardly louder than a whisper.

In response, Taeng rolls up the sleeve of her left arm. Blood flows freely from where her skin has broken, but she ignores the glistening red that smears her red-and-pink robes. It's hardly noticeable—as long as they don't look too closely. There on her exposed skin, that red scar of a handprint stares back at them, explanation enough.

'I am one of the Marked, left living when he destroyed my village as a child. Everyone was burned, and I was left standing in the fires of destruction. The god came to me, told me to summon him when I wish to die—' Not being able to see Karnan is the only thing that keeps her voice from shaking. Even from across the room, she can sense his want to sweep her into his arms. '—before he branded me.'

The slight breeze flowing through the window tosses the loose hairs of the Maharanee's blonde braid. The tresses spark around her crown like a halo. Her brow remains furrowed as she looks to the girl's marked arm. 'I've seen scars like these before,' she admits lowly. 'Those who have them don't survive long when the god is living... *How* did the god come within the palace walls?'

Confused, Taeng shakes her head, before Ashrit explains in a dead voice:

'The walls are warded against the old gods. He shouldn't have been able to breach those spells unless someone powerful enough summoned him.'

They know that Taeng alone cannot wield that kind of power.

The Maharaja sighs when they fall silent. 'Did someone summon him, Taeng?'

She won't raise her head.

He brings his hand down with a massive *thwap* like thunder on his leg, and she flinches, lifting her gaze. '*Taeng!*' he roars.

'Yes,' she gasps out. Her hands thread over her mouth as if she has sinned; the words claw their way up her throat, burning with intensity. Allowing her unseeing eyes to roam the room is the only thing that keeps her from shaking. 'The Sisters were gathered in the Inner Crypt, singing the songs of the old folk when they—' Her sight alights on a tapestry lining the far wall. It's the one Karnan described to her once. Though she sees nothing more than the light streaming through the windows, she feels something deep down rebelling at what surrounds her.

Spanning at least four metres, the tapestry on the wall depicts a battle between humanity and the faerie people. Blood and gore and shining metal and beastly steeds. Taeng can almost hear the clash of swords and the cries of ravens, as if she were standing in the very thick of it. A chill rolls down her spine. Her skin feels feverish, the temperature only growing. '—when they were summoning him. They thought he could save them —that he could destroy the Praitosí, and...'

Revulsion rolls through her the longer she stares at the jumble of the tapestry. But she can't look away. The colours bond together, reds and browns and blacks blending into the truth of that unbridled violence. The hand at her mouth is the only thing that keeps her from vomiting, though her stomach is determined.

All she feels is the god's anger, fierce as a storm.

'Taeng?' It's Karnan. Without her having noticed, he's crossed the room, closing the distance between them. His parents remain silent when they notice the way he looks at her now, brow knotted and lips parted. A hand at Taeng's waist makes the oracle jump, before she leans into that touch. 'What's wrong?' The *rajkumar* looks to his mother, but she only shakes her head.

'I was drinking from that glass moments before her,' she says.

Desperate, he looks to his father, now on his feet. He removes his turban.

Taeng's hands claw at her neck. Her staff clatters to the floor. Mewing in alarm, Hen darts about their feet, almost tripping Karnan up as he attempts to calm her, to figure out what's happening to have halted her tongue. A darkness comes over Taeng's face, bubbling beneath the skin and infecting her eyes. Clouding them black.

'Karnan,' she gasps out, a hand gripping him by the collar as she holds on to him for fear of falling. 'Cover the tapestry—'

Without question, Ashrit dashes to the far wall. He gives a tug, but the tapestry doesn't budge. The woven fabric protests against his hold, and his sword is in hand before he can think better of it. This is a tapestry older than the Brijesh family reign.

'NO!' The Maharanee leaps up the stairs to the far wall after her son. Before Ashrit can bring the blade down upon the fabric, she shoves him in the chest, knocking him back a step. Thinking fast, she throws a blanket up over the corner nearest her, beckoning for her son to do the same as he recovers his footing. His sword *clangs* to the marbled floor when he reaches for it.

As soon as the tapestry is hidden from sight, the darkness fades from Taeng's features, curling off of her face like mist. Karnan watches wide-eyed as wisps of smoke curl from her eyes, returning them to their pure white.

'What was that?' he asks her.

The Maharanee stands in the corner of the room, panting from the steps she had to climb to reach the tapestry's corner. She readjusts the fall of her *saree*, draping it back over her exposed shoulder. 'That looked like smoke to me.' Brushing her hair back from her face, she looks between her sons. 'How close did you say you came to this god?' she asks.

Then all the questions come at once.

'Can you see now?'

Ashrit. 'Was he forged of smoke?'

'Is he gone now? Where did he go?' The Maharanee.

'Who summoned him?'

'Are you hurt?' Karnan's hands are light at her sides as he looks her over. The dried blood is dirty at her shoulders; it coats her arms, her hands, her face. She is a walking battlefield after the battle has been lost. 'What did it feel like?' he finally asks.

She feels the way his eyes bear into her—it feels like sunlight against her skin, like the caress of the breeze on a starless night. Shaking away the feeling, she releases Karnan's collar, suddenly feeling embarrassed. Through the episode, she hadn't realised she'd kept ahold of him so tightly. She collects herself, smoothing down her robes. 'It was... like death.'

Ashrit sheaths his sword as he approaches. Something about his step is heavy, as he keeps his eyes trained on the oracle standing, still, by the door. 'What was it that brought you here, Taeng? It can't only be the god's presence, though I'd assume he's gone, by all that blood.' He jerks his chin at her shoulders, as if it weren't obvious. And some deep part of her wishes she could look him in the eye, to see that veiled strength she can feel in his voice.

'I have had... fleeting visions of Rahat.'

Everyone in the room goes still. Before they can interrupt, she continues:

'She has been injured and will face more than you can imagine. Now that the god has been summoned again—' She stops herself, finally understanding the familiar feeling in the back of her mind. It makes her words feel like sludge as they leave her tongue. Her heartbeat quickens, and she speaks faster. There isn't much time. The god will consume her soon.

'When I spoke with Ewah after we woke, she told me of how she has seen glimmers of darkness around the Lady Nisha. I thought this was because of her rotted soul, warped by jealousy, but perhaps it is not so.'

The blanket shifts, gravity tugging at its tasselled ends.

'Perhaps... maybe...'

With the delicate whisper of fabric, the blanket crumples to the floor.

In an instant, Taeng is gripped by that exploding pain of rage. A scream rips through her, so loud it could split every atom of her being. Her skin feels like it's boiling as she feels the wrongness trying to push itself out through every pore. Through her open mouth, the smoke and embers escape their host. Taeng groans in pain, eyes flooding with tears as she doubles over, her very bones protesting. Karnan reaches for her but is pushed away. She screams. The tears are violent. The darkness leeches from her skin, turning her black and red all over before it seeps out in tendrils of smoke. Embers burn through her skin like blisters as the god is forced out in anger.

All they can do is watch in terror. A second more passes of her screaming, before the Maharaja leaps from his seat. He's by the oracle's side quicker than Karnan can push him away. Ram shrugs off his son and grabs Taeng by the shoulders, forcing her to look at the tapestry.

'*Ram!*' scolds Odelia, pulling at his arms. But he holds strong.

'It's the god,' he explains, panting as he struggles to keep Taeng on her feet when she bucks. 'Ashrit, Karnan—help me hold her.' He grits his teeth, almost roaring to fight against the god inside the oracle, as his sons come to his aid. 'To save her life we have to evict the god.' His words come out in gasps at best.

'*Odelia,*' he calls, and she appears by his side, water goblet in hand. Where she'd gotten it from, he doesn't know, doesn't care—only that it's here. 'Make her drink,' he orders.

Not without questions, the Maharanee does as she is bid. It's a fight to raise the goblet to the girl's mouth without it chipping her teeth as she thrashes. As if the god can already feel the water in its host. An inhuman roar shakes the room where they stand as Taeng gulps the water greedily.

And collapses.

Falling into the men's arms, she is kept on her feet, but only barely. The Maharaja hands her over to his sons as he wipes the sweat from his brow, hardly believing what has just passed in this small room. He dares a look at the tapestry, something he had once viewed as harmless, and finds himself grinning—perhaps inappropriately. His wife scowls at him, shooting a look to the girl unconscious in their son's arms. 'The poor girl,' he murmurs.

The Maharanee's shoulders sag with relief as the last tendrils of darkness rise from Taeng's body like the smoke of a candle snuffed out. 'I hardly know what to say,' she whispers, more to herself than anyone else. 'Ram,' she says, with a hand perched at his arm, 'how did you know to do that?'

Out the corner of his eye, he spies a tendril of darkness escaping the window.

'When I was younger, an oracle told me that I would face a dead god.'

The Maharanee's eyebrows shoot up, taken aback.

Meanwhile Karnan leans over his love, an ear pressed to her chest.

The Maharaja flashes that grin at his queen. 'I was confused too. So I studied everything there is about the gods. There's not much written on it, unless you go to the Obsidian City of Sarrin.'

Taeng's hand rests at Karnan's cheek, making him look up. Her eyes glimmer, their all-white forming a deep chestnut. She blinks back the smoke with a fighting grin. 'You're... beautiful.' Her thumb falls across his jaw as she rests back in his arms.

Easing the girl to the floor with his brother's help, Ashrit's head snaps up to look at their father. 'Sarrin?' he echoes, incredulous.

Beside him his brother is still.

'But their people have been cut off from the continents since their empire was overthrown,' continues Ashrit. '*How* did you get there?'

The Maharaja narrows his eyes, ordering his son quiet. 'Very carefully,' he drawls, never able to forget the horrors he had witnessed during his travels to the forgotten land. 'The seas are littered with monsters for a good reason, my son.'

'So what does it mean?' asks Ashrit. Leaving the oracle in Karnan's care, he stands, ready to approach his father. 'What was she trying to tell us before she passed out?' He can't help his pointing, all thinly-veiled fear gone now that the oracle's inhuman eyes are not turned on him.

And that's when they notice it. Notice the tears streaking down Karnan's blood-smeared cheeks. In, out. In, out. Or—that's how Taeng should be breathing. Charred in places, her feverishly hot skin is slowly losing its lustre.

But Taeng always survives. Karnan's light touch trails over the scar at her left arm, the wine-dark red raised under his fingertips. It was a mark she'd shown him only once before, when they'd had a whole night to themselves thanks to a religious festival he'd taken no part in. There are other scars—some he knew he would not see for a long while. Taeng has seen so many places... and Karnan hardly any. He may have sailed a ship about the great island of Ellasí; he might have even saved Hazel from her fate. But he has never had to run from a god. Karnan had always known. Taeng had never tried to make a secret of it from him. And she had seen him. In that last moment—she said he was beautiful.

The slight part of her lips falls. Her bottom lip, once luxurious, is losing its colour. Hair sweaty and gritty and burnt by embers, she is his Taeng.

And she is dead.

The sob rips from his throat before he can stop it.

'So he can be defeated,' whispers the Maharaja. At his side, his wife slaps his shoulder to go to her son. He doesn't lift his head when she reaches the oracle's side. The burning of flesh lingers in her nose.

'My child,' she breathes, placing a hand at her son's arm.

Karnan rests his forehead against Taeng's cold shoulder. Cold, so soon. The life in her eyes is glassy, gone. Dead. Only hours ago they had shared kisses, shared whispers of their future. Ideas of running away and finding their own place in this world.

No more.

Across the room, Ashrit wipes the tears from his eyes as their father paces.

'To keep from the confines of death the god *must* bind himself to his host to truly claw back to life. Otherwise they'd be fighting the—'

'*Ram!*' roars the Maharanee, tears lining her face. 'Have you not seen that a girl has just *died?*' Her eyes implore him for compassion.

But the Maharaja continues to pace, his son statuesque beside him. Ashrit cannot tear his eyes from the girl mangled on the floor in his brother's arms. Her Sylongí skin ripped open, burnt, destroyed. Her now-brown eyes rolled back to the ceiling. Her body already showing the signs of death.

'If the host is destroyed, the god is destroyed,' continues his father's mutterings. 'If Nisha is working with this god to destroy the Empire and at last take it for herself, then she must be stopped. Stop her and stop the god.' His eyes alight on his sons, before the realisation truly sinks in.

Karnan's face is hidden in the shoulder of the girl he loved; his howls of agony cleave them in two.

At the door, there is a knock.

'Doctor Chaudhary, Your Majesties,' comes the guard's call.

With everyone so frozen, Ashrit forces his feet toward the door. With shaking hands he unlocks it, pokes his head outside. The pinched, worried face of the doctor searches the prince's for confirmation.

'How?' is the only word the doctor speaks.

12

The air is so hot she can taste it. It roves over her skin like unwanted hands down her back, her thighs. Now that Rahat and Hazel are travelling together, they move faster, putting their minds to work as they steer themselves in the right direction. Or at least, what they hope is the right direction. Qadira's been following them for so long she feels they just might have hope.

Considering there is but one day left.

Hazel rides a little way ahead of Rahat, head down with her hands at the reins. For a while now, Rahat's been thinking of how ill-prepared she has been for this quest. With all the faerie people gone, she hadn't thought it would affect the amount of creatures roaming the jungle.

Typical, thinks Qadira. Her people were once the finest hunters in the world—no human could best them. Before they turned their bows and knives upon them all.

The creatures slinking through the trees at Qadira's side were once sport and hunted accordingly. Mortals have no idea of how population culling works; that is, how to do it properly without making the creature extinct.

Flicking her braids over her shoulder, Qadira narrows her eyes in on Rahat travelling slowly behind. The girl's tired. Her slumped shoulders might even lead to a fall, if she allows herself too much slack. Qadira's almost tempted to yell to see what the girl might do. But no.

It won't be easy to take them captive. Or rather, it could be, if she doesn't let herself think about it too much. But up here in the trees, all there is to do is think. Think of why Rahat went on this quest in the first place. She easily could have demanded Qadira go in her stead; Zehran would have allowed her this. Especially when pressured by Tahir.

Tahir, who only wants to keep Rahat happy. For what reason she isn't sure—but she knows it isn't love. Even so, the *rajkumari*'s life could have been simple. But she left with no aid, had told no one, didn't pack enough food, didn't account for being separated, and had never even considered that one of them might be captured by others in the jungle. Luckily enough the *kehrasa* is following, her scent in the wind warding off any creature that might dare attack them. Pity all their food's gone.

'I'm thirsty,' whines Rahat down below.

No answer from ahead, though Hazel's shoulders pull rigid.

They ran out of water a while back. Qadira's lucky enough to have her own water reserves, as all faeries do. It's something they've hidden from humanity for millennia. For if mortals knew the old folk can survive weeks without water, she might be in trouble. Saadi has never been kind with her in the past. Suggestions of execution, torture, depravity... She knows never to doubt his contempt. Who knows what he might do with that information?

Shaking the thought away, she forces the image of bound wrists from her mind. She'd almost lost a finger the last time he'd scolded her for simply existing. That high-strung *faerie-killer*.

'Sorry,' gasps out Rahat, making Qadira's ears twitch. 'I know you're thirsty too.'

Hazel remains silent as she leads them through the thickest parts of the jungle.

Flexing her fingers, Qadira leans against the tree-trunk. The dark bark is nearly the same black of her skin; it makes the threads of magic in her hair spark.

Spark, like blue flames so hot humans cannot even glimpse them.

The chirping of birds flurries about them. Yet the closer Qadira comes, the more the birds move ahead—sensing her near and fearing her presence. The flapping of wings whoosh through the trees which shake as they take flight. Hundreds of birds in all colours take to the skies and soar, fleeing the jungles. Up ahead, Rahat and Hazel don't take notice. They haven't recognised the warning signs.

Overhead, the clouds cluster. Wind whorls through the trees, forcing Qadira to steady herself against the tree's thick trunk. The highest branches of the canopy whisper, bending to bring themselves together as if that might help them survive. Below, Qadira catches the moment Rahat glances skyward. The *rajkumari*'s eyes remain unfocussed as she swivels back to the Asthori.

'Hazel?' she calls quietly, making the girl pull her *lindélof* about.

'Come on,' whines the girl, her sunburn smarting, 'it's just a little storm.'

But Rahat isn't convinced. She kicks Prakaash into action, bringing him up beside the Asthori who continues upon Bijalee's back. *There isn't time to be spooked,* Hazel's look seems to say. This far out of range, Qadira can hardly hear the zapping of their thoughts. The jumble of their minds. Out of doors, her brain has always had difficulty picking up on certain targets. The swirling clouds overhead only make the world more of a jumble.

Her sight clouds, but with a curse she shakes it off. If she allows herself to be fooled like the mortals on horseback, then this is the end. In a place like this you have to move forward no matter what you must do.

As the tree boughs creep together, blocking out the sky, Qadira follows on. Prakaash and Bijalee have picked up speed, though their riders are unsure, knowing the creatures detect something they cannot. A certain darkness rolls through the trees, a ghostly fog creeping along the jungle floor.

Frost meets Qadira's fingertips high up in the trees and she yelps, only just able to bite back the sound. How she plays this could be the difference between life and death. And like all the creatures before this, these ones should be dead. They should all be.

But her people have not been hunters for years now.

The frost slithers up her fingers with a painful sting. There's only one thing to do. Throwing herself through the trees, she stays on path. From branch to branch, her feet are nimble. The smoothness of her run, the grace of her turns—she hadn't realised her tail had appeared, steering her with certainty. The tail balances each movement, keeping her on her feet. A twitch of the ears and she hears each protest of the trees. She can feel the creatures disappearing and hiding themselves, burying deep into the earth in an attempt to escape.

They all know what is coming.

The *lindélofs* just might keep them safe.

Below, the fog thickens. The trees strangle the light. It won't be long before they cannot see what lays before them. She'll have to be quick.

Like sand kicked up in the waves, the fog becomes a tangible thing. The trees become further apart as they approach a field. Most are thinner than the others; a patch of cloud-seeker trees. They won't take her weight. Qadira leans back as she trails down the branches, analysing her movements. The next tree that might carry her is but eight metres away. She'll have to jump.

Instincts force their way through her chest. She can feel the cheetah's nerves racing through her; the power of each muscle, the coil of each intention. She can't remember the last time she felt so alive.

The *kehrasa* leaps. Reaching out with calculated hands, she prays to her lost gods that she might make it. There's no telling what that fog will do against faerie skin, though the mortals racing before her seem unaffected. The horses, on the other hand—their movements are erratic, their glowing eyes wide in terror.

Desperate fingertips grapple for the branches coming closer as she falls through the air. *Come on.* Qadira's hands graze the nearest branch. Her heart leaps into her throat as her hand catches the next bough. The bark firm in her hand, she grits her teeth against the jolt of pain in her arm, the pull in her tendons as the momentum shakes her.

Behind her, she can feel the darkness growing colder. There's no time to waste.

If she were younger, she might have dared to challenge them. If Adilah were by her side, she wouldn't hesitate. This would've been a game. But without her wings and without her whip, she cannot fight against such beasts. At least, not for long.

Qadira steadies her balance once she pulls herself up onto the tree-bough. She can just make out Rahat and Hazel in the distance. But it won't be enough. Racing on, she's all too aware of the growing darkness and the way it devours all in its path. But it isn't the darkness she fears. It's what lays within.

The bough shakes as she pulls herself to her feet and throws her weight across to the other side of the tree. The cold ricochets through her with each breath. Ahead, they still race.

'What *is* that?' comes Rahat's startled gasp.

Hazel chokes back a scream as Bijalee clears a fallen tree. 'I don't think we want to know!' she cries. Her lips already gleam with purple frost.

Along her limbs, Qadira feels the ice quaking. It's been years since she's faced this creature. Her chest hums with fear. Her mind muddles, but she sucks down the scream that crawls up her throat. No matter what happens, she has to protect Rahat. Rahat has to live. Tahir had asked her to protect the girl.

Choking on the arctic air, Qadira forces herself to keep going. Frantic eyes search the jungle for what she can feel lurking below.

Out of the undergrowth and the fog, they emerge. Not one, but three of them, their ivory horns glimmering with liquid gold like blood and their feature-less faces staring forward. Hunched shoulders beneath their robes end in spikes, the creatures slinking along the jungle floor as if they were crawling over it with hundreds of little legs—though Qadira knows, from when she first saw them, that they've only six. When they stand on their hind legs to their full height, Qadira hurls herself into the next tree. They sniff at the air and bare their teeth, dripping with ichor.

They know a *kehrasa* is near.

Racing through the strangled light, the faerie girl would give anything for her wings. With them, she would soar into the canopies and fight her way out of their hold. She would flee into the sky and return home, never to see these beasts again.

If only things were so simple.

Creeping through the jungle, the creatures reach out with their middle arms, carving their claws into ancient bark. Eeries. That's what these creatures are.

All three follow their scent upward—and lock eyes with Qadira the exact moment that Rahat screams a bone-rattling scream that sparks down their spines. The creatures tear their eyes away—toward the mortals up ahead.

There's no time to think. Qadira dissolves into smoke and sand, hurtling herself through the darkened canopies. The trees spin about her, so hazy in this light. They're close. Rahat screams again and Hazel cries out, spurring them on faster. The *lindélofs* are quick, but the Eeries are quicker.

Throwing herself back together, Qadira appears from the smoke and sand before Rahat and Hazel. They have enough time to yank the reins, urging their mounts to a halt before they can collide with the faerie. But Qadira raises her hands, pointing them away from the creatures trailing them. '*What are you doing?* RUN!'

Rahat glances to Hazel. The Asthori furrows her brow as she cracks the reins, spurring Bijalee into a gallop. Still, Rahat hesitates.

'*Run!*' demands Qadira, her sunstone eyes wild.

When the *rajkumari* doesn't move, the *kehrasa* charges at the *lindélof*. Neither of them move. Rahat's chest rises and falls like a hare's. Eyes wide, she can't move. She's in shock. *Gods be damned.* Qadira *thwaps* Prakaash's flank, sending the creature skittering through the trees after Hazel and Bijalee.

'Seek out water!' Qadira yells after her. 'It will keep them away!'

Rahat has enough sense in her to grip the reins and lean into Prakaash's neck as they disappear into the trees.

The Eeries slither closer. Once again, she is their focus. With each of their breaths, she can feel the cold air of the Lyran Mountains. Their black robes ripple around them like shadowed flame. Her legs tremble. They've no idea whether to crouch into a fighting position or flee. The Eeries are within metres of her; it's already too late. Dissolving again would only turn their attention back to the mortals fleeing.

Qadira searches the nearby trees for anything that can be used as a weapon. Her whip belongs to the Devourer now. The titanium blades crossed over her back will only last her so long against the Eeries. She knew she should have brought obsidian with her—fire glass is the only way to slay these things. Obsidian, and adamant.

Adamant! Fumbling in the belt of her tunic, Qadira's fingers shake as she reaches for the throwing blades she'd stored away. It had been a stretch to pack them. But you never know what you will face in the jungle.

Four throwing blades tumble into her hand. Four. If her aim stays true, then gods be praised. If not...

Focus, you fool.

Keeping the blades in her right hand, she takes one in her left. The smooth adamant glitters against her skin. Shining, calling for death. She's not sure what she might have done without them. Yet her legs still quake.

Two of the Eeries drop to their paws, their six legs working like an insect's. It makes her skin crawl. So unnatural, these things before her. How the gods had ever thought to create such things, the world will never know. The darkness curling off of them like smoke makes her stomach roil. Her fingers shake, making her grip on the throwing blade precarious.

FOCUS.

They're close enough now that she may have a clear shot. Close enough now that if she lets a blade fly, she knows the others will be on her in a flash.

That's a risk she'll have to take.

Raising the blade level with her ear, she takes aim and lets it fly. All in the space of a breath. Her hand shakes with the lack of weight in her hand as she reaches for another adamant blade. And watches the Eerie easily step out of the weapon's path. They move no faster, even with Qadira aiming at them.

Like they know she'll miss.

Taking another piece of adamant in hand, she doesn't hesitate before letting it fly. This one sinks into the tree over the middle Eerie's shoulder. *Gods. Oh gods.* Taking fevered steps back, she offers herself time. It won't be long now. *Oh gods. Oh gods.* Shaking fingers make it almost impossible to take the next knife in hand. Its sharp blade slices her fingers, making her hiss.

The scent of blood makes the dark monsters lift their heads. Her blood draws them closer. The middle Eerie drops to its paws—

—and all the sounds of the jungle die away.

They are suspended in the silence. Qadira with her desperate aim, and the Eeries with their featureless-faces trained on her. Even as her muscles grate, throwing off the freezing cold, the *kehrasa* struggles to focus. They're too close now. *Too close—If I can just…*

The third blade leaves her hand, this one sinking into a horn of the middle Eerie. It screeches, rearing on its hind legs and opening itself as a larger target. In a single arc, Qadira throws all her hope into the final dagger and watches with baited breath as it sinks through the Eerie's chest cavity, ripping the creature open and banishing it to dust.

Either side of it, the two remaining Eeries shriek. And Qadira's no weapons left.

Oh gods oh god oh gods

They launch themselves at her, wrenching their jaws back like cobras. The scream is stolen from Qadira's lips as they tackle her to the jungle floor. Knocking the wind out of her.

And clouding her vision red.

*

'Do you think it's still close?' whispers Hazel, glancing back over her shoulder from where she stands in the little stream.

Rahat shakes her head, shock glazing her eyes. 'Qadira sacrificed herself.'

Hazel scoffs, an undignified sound that makes her cousin frown. 'Who says she's dead? She's survived this long, she'll outlive us all.' Yet beneath that smile, she has a darker feeling about it. Stories—fantasies alone—tell of people surviving against the Eeries and their monstrous talons of night.

'Yeah.' Rahat bobs her head, keeping her eyes on her hands at the reins. 'Yeah, you're probably right.' But the words feel wrong on her tongue. She should have stood up for the *kehrasa*; she should have done *something*.

Those were Eeries. Eeries, the dark messengers of the Ashen God. The god who is meant to be dead. Rahat glances Hazel's way before she shakes off the feeling. There are a lot of things in this world but the Nameless is no longer one of them.

'The Temple is close,' breathes Hazel, keeping her eyes firmly planted on the jungle path before them. The ice-laced stream before them quivers. Its surface ripples over soft stones made smooth by years of erosion. The soft trickle *ping*ing against the hooves of their *lindélofs* is the only sound they can hear from the jungle. Everything else is silent. Waiting. Dreading.

A deep, dark, and terrible sound makes her heart skip a beat. It's a growl, a strangled scream, and the roar of flame. Searching the trees in the path they'd come, neither Hazel nor Rahat can find the source of the noise. The scent of melted wax tangles in their nostrils.

'Do you smell that?' comes Hazel's gasped whisper. Her eyes are wide, so wide Rahat can see their startled whites. 'Do you think it—' Her voice strangles itself off as she falls silent, her sight rooted to where they'd emerged from the trees.

A darkness falls through the jungle, the fog creeping toward them but stopping at the lake. As if there were some invisible wall dividing them, protecting them. They watch in wonder as the darkness hurls itself against that wall of air, its tendrils like tentacles as it prods and recoils. And it happens so slowly that they almost don't realise it, but the fog begins to fade.

Before they can see the clear air spilling through the trees, they look to the sky. To the trees bowing back to their true forms and allowing the suns to glare down on them. Instantly they feel the heat from the suns' rays which were suppressed by the Eeries' presence. Rahat and Hazel watch in amazement as the pitch black of the jungle becomes a vibrant painting of greens, oranges, purples, pinks, and yellows. There is so much life surrounding them as the sound returns. The worried calls of a monkey fill the air above them; a babe calling for its mother, who leaps between the trees, using her tail for balance.

Hazel releases the breath she was holding. 'Do you think... do you think they're gone?'

Rahat looks to Hazel, unsure. Her brow furrows. 'I suppose so.' A glance back over her shoulder to where the fog had been moments ago. It's all gone.

'I've never seen an Eerie in person.'

Running a hand over Prakaash's neck, Rahat dismounts on shaky legs. She's just about to stumble into the shallow waters of the stream before she relinquishes all care to sit on the tallest of the scattered rocks. The sparkling clean water seeps into her pants, soaking her through, but the warm ripples are welcome. Like a caress. Again, the warmth returns to her skin, albeit painfully slow. A moment later Hazel joins her in the water, discovering that her own legs don't want to work as she tumbles from Bijalee's back.

'If Qadira hadn't've saved us,' sighs Rahat, 'Iliyah would be better off dead.'

Hazel's eyes go wide. 'You can't mean that.'

They share a look before Rahat has to look away. 'I do,' she sighs, the air leaving her in a laboured *whoosh*. She splashes water over her face, cleaning off the sweat, dirt, and blood. She hadn't even noticed how dirty she'd become. Sliding a tentative finger over her forehead, she decides a shallow cut along her brow isn't anything to worry about. 'Think it will come back?' She casts a look at the jungle but cannot spy anything even remotely dead.

The Asthori shakes her head. 'I don't think so,' she says, 'but it might be best if we stay the night by the water—no matter how close to the Temple we might be.'

To spend the night here means another day gone. It means another day leaving Iliyah out in the wild. But it also gives them time to rest. And Rahat feels like she could collapse at any moment. Hesitating, she agrees.

A silence spreads out between them. The sounds of their surroundings fill the quiet. It is only now that they realise how much life they have been engulfed in during this journey—in the palace there is only tamed wilderness. Through the trees, pygmy deer yip and graze. The langur monkeys above them flit from tree to tree, speaking in soft sounds, while nearby yellow birds chirp to one another, singing a song over the stream that they could easily fall asleep to.

'My mother said I would never see life like this,' says Hazel, shocking Rahat back into reality.

Shoving away her thoughts, the *rajkumari* drops her eyes from the trees. 'No?'

'There isn't much life like this in the Asthore Isles. There are wild horses and bears and squirrels...'

'What are *squirrels*?' asks Rahat with a look, making Hazel laugh.

'Exactly.'

'There are monkeys that sing here. The macaque and langur—they're everywhere. But on the Isles... you're more likely to find deer or foxes. My mother never could have dreamt of this place, where trees have wet bark and there is such warmth. She never even saw it when her sister became the Maharanee. Home is... *her home* was... it was birch and snow. It's so different, it's worlds away.' The way she regards Rahat makes her think. 'And if she hadn't've died, I never would have found a place like this.'

'If your father had responded to *any* of Ma's letters, then Karnan never would have landed in the Isles to see if you were still alive. We were worried; Ma was a wreck.' A sigh makes her chest fall. 'Your sisters were married off; they were safe, but... Karnan wouldn't have brought you back with him if he thought you were better off there.'

'And for that, I'm grateful.'

Rahat is quiet a while. It's only a matter of time before night will fall—and so quickly as it does in the summer, the world pitched into darkness as the All Mother wills. The fluffy langur monkeys in the canopies pick at each other's fur; as they watch Rahat can't help but smile. Who would have thought that a girl from oceans away could have found her way here, to become the only pale face is a sea of brown skin. 'The Summer Lands are life itself.'

'Father said that to be before I left... He was happy to see me go.'

Rahat splashes her gently, only a handful of water splashing down Hazel's stomach. 'I know. Karnan told me.'

Resting her hands against the rocks, Hazel can feel the stiff cold seeping from her skin. Her fingers stretch out, curling around small pebbles by where she sits. Her knuckles ache. Skin tingles. 'This water is so clean,' she thinks aloud, scooping it up in her hands. The warmth splashes over her face and she rubs it into her pores, finally starting to feel clean again. The dirt and sweat washes away, leaving her face fresh. 'We should fill the canisters while we're here.'

'Prakaash,' beckons Rahat, and the *lindélof* leans forward just enough for her to snatch the empty canister from his saddle. The lid protests as she twists it off, but the canister fills quickly. Taking a swig, the *rajkumari* sighs. 'Didn't realise how thirsty I was,' she says, wiping her mouth with the back of her hand. Downing the contents of the canister twice, she fills it one last time before resting it in her lap. Rahat curls her legs to her chest, hugging them tight.

'I didn't think things like this could happen,' she says, her voice barely more than a whisper. When Hazel looks confused, she explains: 'Eeries. I didn't think they were even real, if I'm honest. They're just a bedtime story so you won't wander off, right?' When she glances up to

Hazel, she sighs and shakes her head. 'Guess that was naïve of me.'

'I don't think so,' Hazel tells her. Brushing the water through her hair, she takes a deep breath. 'When I saw them, I didn't know what to do. If Qadira hadn't've been there...' She's silent for a long moment, breathing in like she's about to speak. But the words don't come. A sigh, and then: 'I used to think it was bad to be scared of something.'

'Yeah?'

'... yeah. I thought it was cowardly and terrible, and now I think... I have never been so scared in my life. Not when my mother died, not when I first came here and didn't know a word of Delorrene. But seeing that—that *thing*?' She swallows hard like she's about to vomit. 'It's hard to explain, but it makes sense now, when they say that fear is good for you. Fear keeps you alive—we would have died if we didn't run.'

Rahat cradles her head in her hands. 'Thank the gods we did.'

Hazel laughs; she can't help herself. 'Thank the gods.'

The breath in Rahat's chest struggles. The air about her feels dense, too thick to push through her lungs. Yet the birds fluttering overhead keep soaring in the trees. 'Part of me fears what Ma will think,' she says at last.

'Hey.' When Rahat doesn't lift her head, Hazel grabs her chin, forcing her to look her in the eye. 'Aunty doesn't care that Ashrit likes men. Why would she care that you happen to like women too?'

A nod, before Rahat shrugs her off. Hazel's hold of her face leaves red marks along her jaw. 'It's just—What will she say when I tell her I can't marry Tahir? I *chose* to marry him. *I proposed!*' Her thick hair matts between her fingers as she runs them through. The crusted blood at the back of her skull flakes off, sending a spark of pain down her neck. '*To save Delorran.* This was my idea. And I thought it would be okay—I thought I could grow to love Tahir too, because I think he loves me and he's conventionally good-looking but...'

'But?' presses Hazel, concern wrinkling her brow.

Resignation hangs her head. 'I can't do it.'

'You mean—'

'I *mean*,' Rahat interrupts, with more force than intended, 'that I can't marry him. I can't love him.'

'Cousin...'

Rahat wipes the growing tears from her lashes. 'I thought I could love him, if I just convinced myself that I like men too, but I... He's a friend. Tahir will never be more than a man who I grew up with, who I feel safe with.'

Hazel reaches for her hand, holding it tight.

'I love Iliyah. I love women.' She pauses on a hard breath. '*Only* women, I think.' Hiding her eyes behind her hands, she shakes her head adamantly. 'I don't know; this is all too confusing. How did Ashrit ever figure it all out? How can you rule out an option when you've been told your whole life that *that* is what you have to want?'

'Rahat—'

'And then, what if your whole country is relying on you to marry a man, when you can't even stomach the thought? A light kiss, fine. Whatever. Anyone can do that. But *more*?' Rahat gulps. 'I don't think I'll ever feel that way for a man.'

Hazel waits for the *rajkumari* to fall quiet. Rahat wipes at her face, slapping away the traitorous tears. She gives another squeeze of her hand. 'How long have you felt this way?'

A scoff is all the answer she needs.

'Okay.' Hazel nods her head, focussing on what might be some kind of option. Nothing comes to her mind. 'Just think,' she says, wetting her lips as she sits up on her knees, 'they might write a song about you.'

Rahat's laugh is strangled, but it's a start.

'Wouldn't that be incredible?' Hazel muses. Her light giggle is the plucking of a sitar's chords, brilliant in song. '*The quest of the Delorrene Rahat, so fearsome, none would dare!*'

'Jovial,' Rahat comments with a wet chuckle. 'But I don't think it would be any song like that.'

'No?' There's an odd glint in her eyes, a question there that begs an answer. 'No,' says the Asthori, 'I suppose it would be something grander—like the song you heard in that village, maybe.'

'Maybe,' she muses, sniffing back tears.

*

Through the night, they feel a light tickling sensation as they sleep curled into the sides of their steeds. The starry night above is dark enough to leave them in the shadows, but the shadow dancers that skitter over them light up the stream like a thousand suns. Their glowing scales shimmer in the reflection of the waters. The creatures guard them in the darkness, from the cold that still lingers upon their breath from the attack that almost was. Deep in their molten veins, the cat-like reptiles can sense how close these girls had come to death.

Opening her eyes before the dawn, Hazel is amazed to find so many shadow dancers climbing over them. At least twenty, all keeping their glow dark so as not to burn them. Bound together through the centuries, these little beasts curl up, sleeping side by side or keeping on the prowl about the stream. The largest one sniffs at Hazel's shirt, at the sweat that's soaked it through.

'You're right,' she whispers to the little dragon, who appears to wrinkle its nose. Hazel slides her shirt from her torso, relieved to be in the cover of darkness without the eyes of Eeries upon them. At the thought she goes rigid; she can't see anything beyond the tree-line. The shadow dancers will keep them safe, their glowing scales letting her see where they wander in the branches above like the langur monkeys that sleep there now, their fluffy tails hanging from the canopy.

Without disturbing her cousin, Hazel kneels with her legs in the stream's waters as she scrubs her shirt along the stones. She's relieved for the quiet, for the peace that surrounds them like these living night-lights. If only they could cure the shame in Rahat's heart. 'Thank you,' she breathes to the creatures, who dip their heads as if they understand. 'By all the gods, thank you.'

*

When Qadira wakes, she's alone. Left in a tent, to be precise. Ochre-coloured canvas draped haphazardly over a low-hanging branch and wrapped about the trunk protects the camper from anything that may dwell outdoors. She gropes about on the mattress—hard and thin, worn right through. Wherever she is, it's been the home of someone for longer than she cares to think. The dirt in the mattress comes off gritty on her fingers. Against her midnight skin, it's a faint blush. Odd.

Pulling herself up onto her elbows, she suppresses the grunt that rises up with the spinning of the tent roof. *That's not good.* Squeezing her eyes shut doesn't much help, either. This may be a trickier escape than she'd imagined.

The spinning of the tent only stops when she notices the sheen of ice against the canvas walls. Shivers arc up her arms. Her breath turns to mist before her very eyes. The Eeries are still near.

Great Serpent, she curses, lolling back onto the mattress. Without a pillow the back of her head *cracks* against the worn-through down. The Eeries may not have knocked her unconscious, but whatever they did to her likely won't wear off for a while.

Gods be willing, she won't be killed. Though she's not too sure she wants to go outside with those creatures so close. *Oh—* With fumbling hands she searches her tunic, fingers flitting over her weapons belt for anything she might be able to use to protect herself. *Well, the whip's gone.* A grimace makes its way onto her face as she realises the rest of her weapons have been stripped, too.

Tingles run along her arms as her body fights off the cold. In the back of her mind she can feel her brain reaching for any skill that might get her out of this. So many skills she has accumulated over the years, and she can only think of one that may help her: shadow-singing. Fleeing. *No.* If this is something that can affect the rest of Abrecan, then she has to fight.

The sparking at her fingertips shoots pain through her elbows in this cold. Looks like she won't be able to use that particular skill. The powers of darkness won't work against creatures made of the black of nightmares. And she hasn't had the chance to murder anyone with the gifts of flame to steal it for herself. Sand-whispering, shapeshifting, shadow-singing—the most common talents of Rehmayan. Some gifts are born; others stolen. Qadira's lucky enough to possess both kinds. Even embering—but such a skill cannot be used on something immortal.

A wolf's howl cuts off all thought. The sound ricochets through her, chilling her to the very bone. It's a sound more deadly than anything the Eeries could ever inflict. Her toes feel frozen in her boots, ready to snap right off.

Because a wolf means only one thing: dead magic.

Forcing herself to sit up, Qadira swallows down the bile that threatens to escape. Her stomach roils. *What did they do to me?*

A growl rumbles through the air. It's close, much too close for comfort.

Swinging her legs over the mattress, Qadira feels her bones creaking. It feels like she's been aged a few years. She's only 347; for a faerie, she's still a child. Right now, though, she feels almost human.

The tent canvas whispers. A wet face presses against the wall as another sound reaches the *kehrasa*'s ears: a slithering and a deep snarl. The Naj. *Gods let me be wrong.* All her life, the Naj have been hunted by her people—but no longer. The faeries have gone, and the Najir have thrived.

The jungle may be vastly different from the deserts of her homeland, but in the end, they have all become infested by these monsters.

The sniffing at the tent stops and Qadira feels her heart stuttering back to life. To have come so close... She feels the back of her head, relieved when her hand comes away clean of blood. If she had been bleeding, this may be a different story. As the growls outside the tent grow louder, she knows she can't put this off any longer. Climbing to her feet makes the tent spin once more. Her mind grows fuzzy and she reaches out a steadying hand which catches on nothing.

The tent flap opens before the *kehrasa* can touch it. Her eyebrows shoot up as she peeks outside to find the tent surrounded by Najir. Heart launching into her throat, she sucks down a gasp. Fingers shaking, legs quaking.

A growl has the Najir backing away submissively with their heads bowed. Their slimy scales glimmer in the light cast from a single lantern hanging in the tree above the tent. They almost look wet—it's the venom they secrete.

But Qadira's attention is drawn to the wolf that had made the creatures back down. It is a creature unlike any other. A grey-dappled wolf with a brown-furred spine, upturned ears, and an evil glint in its eyes. *No normal wolf;* she reminds herself to keep on guard. By the look of the Najir, the wolf is the true threat.

Daring to lift her eyes from its dappled coat, Qadira finds the Eeries lingering at the edge of the makeshift camp. Their darkness rolls over the trees, obscuring any way which the *kehrasa* may make an escape.

Ducking to exit the tent, Qadira's fear only grows when the Najir do not move further away. Only a few steps before her, if one decided to strike she would be dead. For the venom of the Naj is the most potent in the world—it can kill a grown human in less than twenty minutes. Slow-acting, in truth, if you forget the agonising pain that comes with its bite.

The Eeries' fog creeps into the camp, scattering with each footstep. About the wolf the darkness hums. Instinctively, Qadira reaches for the whip at her side before her hands freeze. The Najir closest rile, their scales raising like the hackles of the wolf they obey. Another growl from the creature sends the Najir scattering into the spreading darkness, leaving the *kehrasa* and the beast alone with only the Eeries for company.

'Hello?' she dares to venture, holding her hands out by her sides, clear in view.

The wolf sniffs the air before shaking its head and scratching at its own face with its paws. There's blood on its muzzle, Qadira realises, when it again looks her dead in the eye. It takes a step closer.

Great Serpent, please...

With each step, the creature transforms. Grey-dappled fur becomes deep Praitosí skin as the creature stands on its hind legs. Each step brings some ghastly moment stuck in the throws of transformation. The *kehrasa* takes a hesitant step back; whoever this is, they were not born a shapeshifter. Their movements are clumsy as the body configures itself into something new —something Qadira might have been able to recognise, had this woman's face not sparked with eyes of coals. She smells of ashen faerie blood.

'Hello,' purrs the shapeshifter, her voice deeper than her growl. Brushing her fingertips over her forehead, the woman makes Qadira's eyes go wide.

'Nisha,' she gasps out, knowing it's already too late.

With a dip of her head, the sorceress Nisha grins. The tinge of bruises play at her cheekbones, so sharp they could cleave the mountains in two. Her short hair curls about her pointed ears—and Qadira sees with horror the scars that coat them. Nisha broke open her own ears to give the illusion of being faerie. She did this to herself. The *kehrasa* takes a cautionary step back. Her heels skim the canvas of the tent, which whispers against her legs.

'It's been years,' says Nisha, looking over the faerie before her with hungry eyes. Those eyes freeze her in place. They were more at home in the face of the wolf than in the face of this woman. Most disturbing of all is that this woman's features might have once been sweet. It is no exaggeration to claim that her niece Iliyah was always going to grow up to look like her aunt. Qadira can almost see it; but it's the eyes where that illusion falters.

The *kehrasa* holds her ground. 'Years,' she echoes in quiet agreement. Sending out sensors, she analyses the shape shifter's every move. Standing so close, any fight will be over in seconds. But as Nisha said: it's been years. The sorceress was not always a shapeshifter; who knows what other skills she may have acquired?

The woman takes a step closer, her hand reaching for the *kehrasa*. The gleam of sweat at her brow makes her skin feverish. Her fingers shake as she reaches out. Qadira doesn't need to breathe deep to smell the madness on her. Something happened when she was banished from Praitos. Hells, Nisha should not even be able to step foot inside the Summer Lands. Its borders were spelled against her presence years ago. The sour tang of desperation curls in Qadira's nostrils, so strong it makes her feel sick.

Over her shoulder, Qadira notes the Eeries still lingering by the outskirts of the camp, hiding in the midst of the trees. The clearing where Nisha has placed her camp is small—small enough that it might not be noticed. Even the canvas of the tent has been dyed a darker colour to blend in with their surroundings. And despite the self-mutilation and the madness gleaming in her eyes, it's clear the woman has thought this through.

'Nisha?'

Qadira's attention snaps to the unfamiliar voice a few steps to her right. With all the distractions, she hadn't picked up on the heat signature of another woman. This one, dressed head-to-toe in red. A small bird's skull sways on the cord about her neck; the bone beats against the woman's sternum, strapped in red cloth. A priestess of Estevao. Qadira's brow furrows. After all that has been, she didn't realise humanity still worshipped the fire god of the old folk.

The priestess wipes the back of her hand across her mouth, smearing red powder with it. *Ah yes.* The sharp smokey flavour of the red dust is enough to give it away. *Of course they devour the blood of faerie corpses.*

Nisha slips Qadira a glance before waltzing over to the woman in red. The woman—younger than Nisha, the *kehrasa* sees, as they approach—lifts her hands to her head, draping her hood over her matted hair. Dirt rubbed into her cheeks, she looks like she's been living in the wild. There is more than one way to become one with nature, after all.

Overhead the stars glimmer, their glow dim as if wishing to keep unnoticed. The trees bend, their boughs stretching out to entwine themselves like woven blankets to become the clouds of the night. Yet their arms are not strong enough, and the trees remain with their limbs out searching, unable to find each other.

The weapons are all gone. Sliding her eyes over camp, she knows there's no place Nisha could have hidden them without her knowing about it. Though the woman's insane, she knows better than to try fool a *kehrasa*.

Qadira starts at the fur she feels speckling through her skin. The soft downy fur bristles in the night air—but this is not the time to show her true self. Taking a deep breath, she suppresses her instincts and curls her tail into the back of her tunic.

But Nisha already knows of the *kehrasa's* peculiarities.

The woman in red whispers something quick in the sorceress' ear. Qadira hopes they may forget about her long enough to escape. Alas. They both turn their sights on her—Nisha's burning black eyes, and the red woman's vibrant green. Such a contrast, in the subdued lantern-light.

'Dispose of them. No witnesses—and I want that sacred child alive.' Nisha nods, her mannerisms alarmingly more animal than human, as she dismisses the woman in red. Hesitant, the priestess gestures to Qadira, only for Nisha to scoff.

Qadira arches a brow.

Yet before she can think of a retort, the woman vanishes into the darkness.

'Travel well, dear Kiden,' purrs Nisha after the woman.

And whether she conjures the dark of her own abilities or slinks away into the Eeries' fog, Qadira might never know. But not being able to detect the woman's essence sends a chill down her spine.

Alone once more, Nisha tilts her head. Her calculating gaze soon grows cold as she watches Qadira's hands instinctively reaching for where her weapons should be. It feels like being raked over hot coals, to have Nisha staring so long.

Not an ounce of magic can be felt humming in the air. That is what most unnerves the faerie standing before the imposter. As Nisha slowly makes her way back to Qadira's side, the *kehrasa* searches for any inkling that this woman might possess magic. The tendrils of her gifts hit flat walls of force each time. Again Qadira reaches, only to hit that wall of nothingness. *Nothing.* So how?

The tip of her tail flicks against her shoulder-blades with curiosity. *How how how?* Nose twitching, she pulls her shoulders back to look Nisha in the eye. Again, her attempts at seeking out the banished woman's magic fall short. *HOW?* Qadira feels her incisors lengthening against the inside of her lips. *Great Serpent...*

'Fight for me.'

She balks. '*What?*'

Nisha's eyes narrow. 'You heard me.'

In the full light of the lantern, her dark face is drained, painted feverish. Qadira can't help but recoil for the feeling of *wrongness* about this woman.

'Fight for me,' she demands again.

'And why on the Serpent's Wings should I?'

'Because,' purrs Nisha, growing too close for comfort. Her breath caresses the *kehrasa*'s face, making Qadira want to claw at her skin. 'I can give you your wings.'

The world feels like it's cracked in two, opened up the earth and swallowed her whole. Her heartbeat jolts to a stop. As if knowing. As if knowing that this is the only thing in the world she has ever wanted.

She pushes the feeling down. 'My—what?' A shake of the head. 'No,' she laughs, her voice hitching in disbelief and—*want*. 'You can't.'

A sickening smile spreads over her face as she nods once, twice. A muscle twitches in her cheek as that smile grows just a little too wide, revealing scars along her jaw. Scars, whether inflicted or fought for, stretch white against her dark skin. 'Oh,' she whispers, much too close, 'but I can. All it takes is your fealty.' Those eyes gleam, going dreamy as her mind wanders, but the blackness keeps Qadira pinned to the spot. 'Swear your fealty to me and stop my niece from being awoken, and I will give you your wings.'

A tremor in her hands forces her to ball her fists. 'My wings are gone.' The words grate up her throat, each one as painful as the last. 'They were taken.'

Nisha's hands work their way around Qadira's throat, massaging her shoulders and neck as she takes that step closer. *Madwoman*, her mind screams, urging her to back away. But beneath that scolding gaze she is powerless. 'I will give you new wings, to whatever design your heart desires...'

The temptation to say yes presses firmly against her gut. 'No.'

Inches from Qadira's face, Nisha growls deep in her throat, making Qadira go rigid as the Eeries disappear past the tree line. They leave only their mist behind as the glowing of their ivory horns disappear into the nothingness of the night. Nisha's hold tightens ever so slightly at Qadira's throat.

'No,' she says again, at feeling Nisha's claws through her tunic.

Nisha wets her lips. 'What if I told you you could see your sister again?'

She halts, muscles going taut. Dumbstruck. 'My sister?'

So terribly close, and Nisha only nods.

Qadira swallows, cursing her dried throat. It has been too many years since she last saw Adilah, and she has always known it would be many more. What is but a few more years to wait when immortal? But...

This may be my only chance.

The deserts of Rehmayan are impossible to traverse without the aid of wings. With only your feet in the dunes, it will take years—maybe even a lifetime—to reach your destination. But with wings? Maybe only days.

The shapeshifter lifts a brow. That silent question hangs between them.

Those eyes are molten, so deep a black they could only belong to the abyss. They're the eyes of a god; Qadira can't explain how she knows it. That unnerving feeling creeping over her, pushing down on her shoulders, makes her tail flick with nervous energy. Deep down, she knows she is dealing with the whims of a god. And who is she to deny a god?

13

It is a truth universally known that the sphinx guards the temples of Estevao. As the red god's sacred creature, it is also against all laws of Abrecan to take the life of such an anomaly. With nothing to do to defend yourself against the sphinx, you must pray it doesn't devour you. Because like all things in the jungle, it will. Standing as guardian to the flame god has been an honour passed down through eternity from the moment the creature was welded by the god's own hand.

Yet all it takes is a riddle to survive. Protector though the sphinx may be, they are the guardian of the gates invisible to the human eye which keep Estevao's temples safe from harm in the Neverworlds. Each temple straddles the cracks in the skin of the All Mother, opening up Abrecan to the worlds that lay beyond.

The sphinx is the last defence in line, both against humanity and the monsters of the deep. Only those who prove themselves worthy are able to enter this realm between the nothing and the everything. Three riddles must be given to those seeking the temple, and only three. If the traveller speaks but one wrong, their flesh then belongs to the beast. If answered correctly, they are free to pass.

*

Rahat runs over the ancient rules in her head, dredging up memories from her childhood and hoping that there may be something there to protect her against the hideous nightmare she knows she will face. As a child it had never occurred to her that there may be a guardian —but then, the sphinx love children. In fact, were Rahat now a child, she would be able to pass freely, if she only promised to leave the boundless realm as it was when she came. Yet her memory is hazy; not even the blurriest memory relinquishes any reminder of a sphinx when she and Iliyah were younger. But perhaps the gaps between Abrecan and the Neverworlds were smaller then.

The *crack* of twigs in the undergrowth steals their attention. Rahat lifts her head, following the sound. Something's nearby. At the ready, she swipes the dagger from her boot—too many times have they been attacked to not be prepared. By her side, Hazel unsheathes the sword strapped to her back.

Still, nothing emerges from the trees. Rahat brings them to a stop, holding up a hand as they listen for whatever it was. They don't have to wait long. The sphinx slinks from the shadows of the trees, as she knew it would.

At laying eyes on the creature, Rahat wonders how they hadn't heard it sooner. She exchanges a look with Hazel, whose eyes have gone wide as they take in the creature before them.

At the sphinx's brow rests a headpiece of ancient coins of gold, all tinkling lightly with each step. The sound's so soft it's a lullaby. Striking features portray a woman of Sā-Mares, her large mouth sensuous even with the fangs that hang over her lower lip. High cheekbones direct all attention toward those teeth. But it is the sphinx's eyes that Rahat cannot tear her sight from. They glimmer like the golden coins woven over her forehead—only they spark like hundreds of tiny fires. Two sets of eyes stare the humans down as the creature pads closer. Her giant paws are a tan brown, soft as they move in the undergrowth.

The sphinx stretches her wings, lifting her head and almost rising onto her hind legs, only she pauses. For the beast carries a sleeping child upon its back. The child—a boy with a mop of dark hair—has his hands clasped about the sphinx's neck, securing his place in slumber.

Hazel's eyes twitch as she manages to drag her sight from the sphinx to Rahat. In the Asthore Isles, there are no stories of this creature; the god Estevao is not widely worshipped in such a land. 'I *really* hope you know some riddles,' Hazel gasps out, not daring to move even with her sword in hand, 'because I am bloody useless at them.'

Considering them, the sphinx tilts her head. Luscious locks of raven hair cascade over her shoulders, the shine so silky that there is no denying this creature comes from a land of water. A land of water, to protect a god of flame. But let us not forget that the flame god is married to the Oceans.

'We have been waiting for you, Rahat of the Delor-rene,' purrs the sphinx, in a voice so seductive that it sends thrills through her. Each word is so smooth it's like falling into a vat of honey: heady, sleek, and suffo-cating.

Rahat levels her eyes with the creature's. All four of them.

Beneath her, Prakaash shifts from hoof to hoof, uneasy so close to this monster of legend. As the sphinx prowls closer, Rahat's eyes rove over her. To the chest— so human at first glance, until you notice the fur that grows over nearly-human clavicles in beautifully orchestrated patterns. The meeting of flesh and fur is mesmerising.

Frozen to the bone, Hazel remains on Bijalee's back when Rahat dismounts. Her shaking legs stay true as she takes those first few steps to stand directly before the sphinx that so bats her eyes at the *rajkumari*.

'What is your name?'

Again, the creature tilts her head. 'Marama,' she purrs. A name which means *light of the world* in the Sā-Marish tongue. So explains her features. Sharing a smile, the sphinx bows her head, not daring to dip lower because of the child at her back. 'Any requests before I begin?'

'Don't eat us,' blurts Hazel from over Rahat's shoulder, drawing Marama's attention. Those feline eyes draw narrow, angered.

'Answer my riddles three and then we shall count our survivors.'

Behind her, Rahat can feel Hazel's revulsion rolling off of her in waves.

As if uninterrupted, Marama turns her eyes on Rahat once more. 'Ready?'

A slight nod, as she sheaths her blade back in her boot. 'Ready.'

Marama rolls her shoulders. The jungle seems to spread out about her, growing still as if relying upon her very breath. Those eyes which are at once electric and soothing halt, like her mind has landed upon the perfect question. A sickeningly hungry grin claws its way across her features, stretching the looping tattoos marking her face. She recites: '*If you have me, you wish to share me. If you share me, you no longer have me. What am I?*' There's a clever gleam in her eye as Rahat's heart sinks.

Behind her, she hears Hazel's gasp of total shock. 'A secret,' she answers, almost throwing herself from Bijalee's back. At Rahat's side, she spreads her hands wide, having dropped her sword to her feet. 'You're a secret,' she says again.

The haughty look on Marama's face remains even as her smile drops, turning her features feral. Rahat can't help but note the bone-shade of those sharp fangs, like they were only recently coated in blood. She dips her head. 'I am,' she affirms.

Forgetting the horses behind them, Hazel can't stop herself from jumping in excitement. Though it's only one jump, it's enough to wipe all charity from the sphinx's face. Were it not for the child a-slumber at its back, Rahat fears they may already be dead.

Before they can ready themselves for the next riddle, Marama tosses her head. Her wings flutter, feathers of speckled grey and tan spreading wide, revealing the pattern of eyes painted across her wings. '*I am everything to someone, yet nothing to everyone.*' Once again, that sick smile returns, as Hazel notices the elongation of Marama's claws. '*What am I?*' she riddles.

Oh gods. The girls exchange a look. As subtly as possible, Hazel shrugs a shoulder, completely failing at keeping the action hidden from the sphinx.

'Do you...?' mouths Hazel, to which Rahat shakes her head.

'Everything to someone,' muses Rahat, thinking aloud.

'*Yes?*' presses Marama, hunger wetting her mouth.

Hazel frowns at the sphinx before them as one might a child complaining. The *rajkumari* resists the urge to elbow her in the gut.

'*Everything to someone,*' she repeats, rolling the phrase in her mouth. '*Nothing to everyone.*' The tension pressing on her brow stings, making her eyes blur with black stars. The suns overhead are blinding, making the pain worse. Running a hand through her hair, Rahat sighs, resisting the urge to *rip*. '*Everything to someone,*' she whispers again to herself. 'Heart? Love?'

The sphinx takes a step closer.

'Hey!' barks Hazel, snatching everyone's attention. Marama pauses, taking a step back from them—those eyes calculating, always measuring. The Asthori's cheeks puff red, full of rage as she stares the monstrous creature down. 'She wasn't giving you an answer. You only said she had to answer correctly—not that she could speak *only* her answer.'

Marama levels the Asthori with that gleaming gaze. Four beady eyes blink up at the redheaded girl with her peeling skin. The sphinx is superior in every way, and yet... Marama bows her head, returning her attention to Rahat.

Rahat, who feels like she's going out of her mind. There are so many factors here. The sphinx who wets her lips in anticipation, who hasn't truly lifted her sight from the *rajkumari* from the moment she wandered across their path. Her riding leathers are slick with sweat; beads of it roll down her brow, her cheeks. This entire quest was a mad idea. To think that she might be able to save Iliyah from a fate worse than death, from a fate not heard of since the faeries died... *I must be out of my mind.*

—That's it!

The *rajkumari* turns, hair whipping in her face, as she strides before the Sā-Marish guardian. 'The mind,' she says, quietly at first before repeating herself: 'You are the mind.'

By her side, Hazel laughs. 'I never would have thought it,' she grins.

But Rahat's still focussed on the sphinx. 'Am I right? My mind is my everything, but my mind matters not to anyone else—it has to be right.'

Slowly, the sphinx dips her head. 'Yes. Well done, *rajkumari.*' Marama rolls her tongue, the purr of a laugh rumbling through her chest as she tilts her head. 'Perhaps I need to make this more of a challenge for you.'

Rahat stops Hazel from raising her hands in protest. She shoots her a grating look which soon has Hazel withering back to stillness. 'Sorry,' she mouths, fully aware of how closely the hungry sphinx watches them.

The child sleeping at Marama's back murmurs in his dreams. His words are a mumble against the thick fur of Marama's neck; they make her grin, almost pleasantly. It might have allowed them to forget that this creature wishes to devour them, had the sphinx not kept a watch of them out the corner of her eyes.

Hazel might never understand why anyone would entrust such a monster with their child. Or how a child might even step foot near one of these beasts.

Yet the smile at Marama's lips is soft, her facial tattoos stretched into looping patterns to reveal her fanged teeth. She oozes danger, and yet beneath it all, there is a mothering nature that Hazel cannot even begin to comprehend.

But it is not long before the boy at her back is once again forgotten, and Marama turns on Rahat. Without ceremony, she begins, sitting back on her haunches. *'I speak without a tongue and hear without ears. I have no body but live with wind.'*

When Rahat can feel the blood freezing in her veins, she knows the sphinx has won. All the threat of those teeth sinking into her flesh, and the creature has won. The trees about them still. The breeze dies. All sound is ripped from the jungle as the world quietens, waiting for bloodshed.

The *rajkumari* spares a look to her best friend, but Hazel's staring at the sphinx. Fists balled by her sides, cheeks shining red with pure *outrage*. After *all* they have been through, this is how it ends? *No.* Hazel opens her mouth to speak, but is silenced by a disembodied voice.

'You are an echo.'

The voice emerges from the nothingness of the jungle. Around it, sound returns—the bleating of monkeys, the chirps of birds, wings a-flutter. The breeze wanders through the treetops, making the canopies whisper.

'Marama, you really should not play with guests.'

The sphinx grits her teeth as she lays down, spreading her paws forward as she rests her face in the long grass of the undergrowth. Her frown is ancient, as if etched in stone it sits so deep upon her brow. She has been robbed of a meal. And yet her thorny tail remains aloft, flicking like a feline's as she closes her many eyes. 'The Lord of Flame never spoke to me of a coming guest,' she sighs.

'You lie, and you know it,' comes the voice.

Marama's only response is to blow a soft laugh through her nose.

Slowly, Hazel unfurls her balled fists. Her cheeks pale, though the sunburn keeps ahold of that rich red. Freckles blaze against the burnt skin. Her flame red hair shines like embers in the night.

A tentative hand has her backing down, but only after Rahat has shaken her head with a soft whisper of 'Please.'

The *rajkumari* searches the trees, from their trunks to their tops. 'Who's there?'

There's a rustle in the canopies, followed shortly by a grunt. And a woman in red drops from the trees. She lands like a cat, balled in on herself with an arm outstretched for balance. 'You may call me Kiden,' says the woman as she rises to her feet. Her flat facial features glimmer in the light, her skin so irresistibly smooth it is as if her skin were wrought from scales. Her face is painted in blood and white tattoos; Hazel fights the urge to drop to her knees in worship. Night-dark skin, her face freckled with blood, and her hood pulled up over her hair like an Eerie. Her eyes glow a pulsing green, hypnotising against her dark skin. Pointed teeth glisten from between her lush parted lips, as from behind her, a younger priestess approaches. Hungry for blood.

At spotting the smaller girl behind Kiden, Marama spreads her wings and takes to the skies, leaving a scatter of feathers behind. The shuddering of her feathers as she soars overhead makes Rahat gasp as they watch the sphinx in flight. The child at Marama's back simply keeps their tight grip through slumber, never once slipping as the sphinx dips through the skies, disappearing to somewhere that they might only ever imagine. For the sphinx live between worlds.

'Now,' says Kiden, her eyes scanning the skies though her head remains still. Once she is sure the sphinx is gone, she gestures for the humans to follow. 'Come with me.'

Before they can respond, Hazel drops to her feet. The younger priestess grins a ferocious grin—and Rahat sees then the markings across the young girl's face. Though her skin is as dark as Kiden's, it glows with the golden markings etched into her features. *A sacred child...* It steals the breath from Rahat as she drops to her knees before such a thing.

The sacred children seldom live to eighteen. To witness one in person... Rahat cannot wrap her mind around how great an honour this is.

While Kiden *tsk*s, the sacred child bows her head to the kneeling women. Lips painted bright red, she is free of the freckled blood, though she holds so much more danger in the flashing of her eyes. 'You may rise,' she says, with a slight giggle that tells them she hasn't been a sacred creature for long. Or, she may not have come to know humans in her brief life.

Again the child bows her head, beckoning for them to rise. She keeps her eyes on Kiden all the while.

But Hazel is shaking so much she fears the rest of her may go out. Out, pitch black like a candle, as waves of dizziness swell. It's the heat, she realises as she sways, a shoulder brushing against Rahat's. 'Come on,' whispers Rahat, aiding her cousin to her feet. Hazel has strength barely enough to swipe a sphinx feather from standing upright in Rahat's hair.

'Careful with that,' Hazel gasps out, dropping the sharp thing to their feet.

Rahat nods once, twice. Considers her, then the women beckoning them to follow to the Fire Temple. 'Okay,' she tells Hazel, helping her limp forward.

In all of this, the *lindélofs* have remained silent, like their magic has been stripped from them. But when the younger priestess turns back to ensure they're following, Prakaash whinnies and exhales steaming air.

The child ignores the temperamental steed.

On their feet, Rahat and Hazel stumble after the priestesses, the horses trailing them through the trees. It's only once the sacred child turns that they see the quiver hanging at her belt, and the bow strung over her shoulder. The graceful loops of her long braided hair are bejewelled by gold. Even the anklets at her feet tinkle like the singing of water wraiths.

There's an odd feeling that follows them as they navigate their way through the jungle. As the sphinx had stood her ground, they weren't far—but even a short distance is a struggle for Hazel. Pale as a ghost, her drained lips tremble. Throat dry, she's grateful for the water they now carry in their canisters. But whether it will last them through the last leg of the quest is another question.

The trees become further spaced, the distance growing as they come closer to the temple Rahat only remembers in her dreams. She had been to the temple once, a long, long time ago. So long ago now that it feels like another lifetime. And perhaps in some ways it was. Rahat had thought herself a completely different person, a girl who would become a woman with the love of her country and—well, she supposes now that it was clear all along whom she truly loved.

Loves.

Wetting her lips, Hazel frowns as she looks her friend over. 'Rahat?'

'Mm?'

That scowl deepens. 'Why do your eyes look different?'

Instinct throws Rahat's hands to her eyes. Before she can name it, her knees go weak. Ahead, the priestesses hardly notice as they continue their march. Hazel reaches out as Rahat's shoulders droop, her hand dropping to her side as the *rajkumari* falls forward. 'Rahat!'

The priestesses turn back just in time to see Rahat reach up for her cousin as she collapses to the grass. Rahat can feel someone shaking her, can see the faint outline of Hazel's red hair before her eyes cloud over. When her head hits the soft earth, everything goes white—ripping a scream for help from Hazel's lips.

The aching in the back of Rahat's head is skull-shattering. This shouldn't be happening. The earth beneath her seems to move, the sky flipping over and under beneath her and making her stomach roil. She's upside down, floating. Only—not. Trapped in her mind, she realises that this is not the real world. In the real world, Hazel is shaking her shoulders and screaming for consciousness.

Here, Rahat is alone. *All Mother, please,* she prays, knowing this is no normal dream vision from Iliyah. Something must be wrong.

What was it that Iliyah last told her about dreams?

FOCUS.

Reaching out with frantic hands, she again hits the earth, hard. Yet when she looks up, the sky is foggy. The suns are hidden away, though she can make out the distinctive rings of golden-white through the cloud. Confusion rolls through her when she looks down at her hands, only to find that they are not her own. A dusky shade of skin free of red, though tattoos lace up her wrists. A birthmark at her palm brings the truth home. *This isn't my body.*

This is Iliyah's.

The truth hits her as hard as the ground. Is this what having your soul ripped from your body feels like? A sharp blow to the stomach forces Rahat to convulse with a groan. Tattooed hands—Iliyah's—cover her face as she waits for the next blow from some invisible force. She's not sure what it is. She's not quite sure she wants to know. But as she slowly pulls herself to sit up, she can feel the strain in her muscles. As if she hasn't moved for days.

Oh gods. This can't be real.

'Rahat?' says Iliyah, with a quiver in her voice. 'Is that you?'

A feverishness pricks at her lips—Iliyah's lips. *Gods.* Yet no matter how she tries, Rahat cannot get a grasp on movement. It's all Iliyah; Rahat is merely a spectator here. Neither can she push through her thoughts.

'It... it *feels* like you. I don't know if this is real.'

All Rahat can feel is the rush of warmth in Iliyah's middle. Butterflies. She could cry.

'It just—it feels like you're here.' Flexing her hand, Iliyah smiles through the stiffness in her fingers. 'Like you're holding my hand.'

As Iliyah shifts her sight to their surroundings, Rahat's attention zeroes in on the billowing smoke rising from what can only be the temple. It's not far from here. Terrifyingly close, from this high up. Woven crystal keeps Iliyah protected from the suns above; it's a thick layer that might not be recognised from the ground. What in the gods' names did Nisha do all this for?

'Rahat, if you're here, I need to tell you—' The *shehzadi* cuts herself off with a gulped laugh, as if unsure how to say it. How to confess it. She collapses back on the mattress, the only thing in this room of crystal, taking away Rahat's sight of the outside. Taking a shaky breath, she clears her throat. Even forcing her body to stay awake without a soul for so long is taking its toll. Her stomach churns. 'Don't be too late.'

In an instant, Rahat feels herself ripped from Iliyah so violently that she screams. The bed beneath her evaporates into thin air, and the air swallows the Praitosí, her glass prison disappearing around her. Magic. Cruel magic. Screams are stolen by the wind as she falls. Hair whipping about her, Iliyah cannot see anything but her own black hair against the foggy sky. It's cold against her skin, like a frost giant's breath. This—this is where she dies. Heart racing, arms waving. Twisting, she watches as the ground comes up at her. Screaming so hard, her voice goes hoarse. Gravity and magic force her back, hiding the ground from her. Even beseeching the gods won't prevent this fate.

'RAHAT!'

Seconds before Iliyah hits the ground, Rahat bolts upright with a scream. Her heart races. She feels sick. 'Iliyah—' she gasps out, catching Hazel off-guard as she lunges forward. The priestesses remain a little way off over Hazel's shoulder. 'She was— I was—' Gulping down air, she fights to keep calm, to make her heart stop racing. Her eyes search the Asthori's face, full of concern. Rahat hadn't realised she'd grabbed the girl's jerkin to pull herself upright. 'I think she's... no.'

'Breathe,' Hazel tells her, keeping her voice soothing. 'Breathe.'

The priestesses keep moving. 'Powerful, your dream weaver,' muses Kiden with a curl of her lip over her shoulder, 'to bring you down while walking.'

While Hazel stares after them, eyes tracking the sacred child as she fiddles with her bow, Rahat shakes her head. Tears stream down her cheeks in soft rivers. 'She's dead,' she whispers, wanting to bite back the words as if that could destroy the truth. 'I saw it. She's dead, Hazel.' When Hazel shakes her head, the claims only become more fevered. 'Dead, she's dead, oh gods, she's dead.'

Hazel smoothes a hand over Rahat's hair when she ducks her head into the crook of Hazel's neck. 'It was just magic,' she tries to explain, keeping a watch of the women leading the way before them. Still visible between the clear path of the trees, there will be no risk of losing them. 'A bad hallucination,' she tells her, her words muffled in her cousin's dark hair, though she doesn't quite believe it herself.

The wetness against her neck makes Hazel want to bury them in the shadows. While the shadows may not be safe, they might lull the distressed *rajkumari* to sleep. If only they had the time.

'Come on,' she says gently, hauling them both to their feet as Rahat had done only minutes before, 'we have a quest to finish.'

14

The Temple of Estevao towers above the jungle. Rising above the canopies in great columns of black-veined marble, its arches are specked with drying blood. Or paint—Hazel hopes it's paint. Pikes stained with dark blood line one side of the temple, where decapitated heads or sacrifices might have once been. Hazel's stomach prays it was only something small. Bunnies—no, not bunnies.

As it is, the smell of burning hair wafting between the temple's columns makes her throat ache. *Perhaps I'll vomit*, she thinks, catching the grave look on Rahat's face.

The temple is just as Rahat remembers. White marble with veins which ripple as if moving. Smoke billows out of the spiral staircase that leads down into the earth; the black rises to the roof before clouding, being carried away by the breeze in black waves. And like the waves that lap the shore, the black smoke curls, crashing against the columns as it climbs its way out and into the sky's freedom. A distant humming creeps up their spines with each step closer.

There are no doors; there never have been to a temple like this. Simply the columns that hold up that imposing roof, carved of stone and with illustrations of history. Where other temples have tapestries and paintings telling of their past, the Temple of Estevao has etchings. Of battles, of sacrifices. Estevao is a vengeful god.

Approaching the steps of the platform, Rahat holds her breath through the waves of smoke. Behind her remains Hazel, though they're both unsteady on their feet. An odd sheen of green works its way through Hazel's features; she cannot follow, and the horses need watching.

'Remember,' says Rahat over her shoulder, her voice a rasp. 'If there's any trouble, call for me or one of the priestesses. There shouldn't be anyone nearby because of the sphinx, but you never know.' Rahat waits for her cousin's nod before stepping beneath the temple's heavy roof.

From a distance, this place would look like a porch of some kind, broken off from an archaic ruin. The instinct to flee works its way up Rahat's spine. Just like the catacombs beneath the royal palace. And judging by how no animals have been spotted since they encountered Marama, the wafting fear must spread into the jungle too. Rahat shrugs off the feeling, letting it slide as she stares down into the staircase that leads deep into the earth. It leads so far down that she can no longer see Kiden or the sacred child with her shining golden-laced hair. Like the rest of the outer temple, the staircase is marble, though the steps are worn the further they go down. Most surprising is that the black smoke does not rise up the spiral, but rather the ventilation shafts at the other end of the temple floor. Even so, she can hardly see a thing other than the faint shine of the marble in the sun's light. Entering the temple will be a blind mission. *As all things are, when it comes to oracles.*

'Wish me luck,' she mutters, swallowing hard before taking those first steps. If there is one thing to be learned here, it's that you should never navigate in the dark. Especially if you're choking on smoke. Her heart slams in her chest as she struggles to breathe; before she can catch herself, she whispers a prayer that the Nameless God is not hidden within the smoke's folds. After the Eeries, she can hardly trust the jungle before her.

A step down. Then another. And in the dark, she is blind.

Upon reaching the bottom of the steps, she's shocked to find herself alone—even as she stretches out her hands for a wall. Taeng would know her way down here. Another lunge for a wall, only to find there's nothing there. She's alone. Completely alone. This probably isn't a good time to tell you that Rahat Brijesh is afraid of the dark.

Taking a step back, her heart jumps into her throat when she feels that the stairs are gone. Disappeared. Evaporated, like her hope.

This vast cavern hums with energy. What kind of energy, she isn't too sure, but as it snakes up her spine with a scaled slither, she isn't sure she wants to know. Each step echoes, on and on until she's afraid that she's lost in the cracks between worlds. Raising her hands to cup them about her mouth, she's about to call for Kiden when she feels a hand at her wrist. A soft touch. Soft skin. A silken hood whispers as they take a step closer. *A priestess*; Rahat relaxes into the woman's hold. Only after a moment does the priestess retract her hand.

'I wouldn't call out, here,' whispers the woman—the *girl*, by the sound of her voice. The sacred child, with her golden-scarred flesh. Her voice is deep, older than one would expect for a child of twelve, but she is not destined for this world. 'Who knows what could be festering in the dark?' There's a sort of amusement in her words, however dark they be. This is a girl who has lived here her whole life, plucked from the cradle by the gods to serve and later give her life to keep their people safe.

'And Kiden?' whispers Rahat, unnerved by how her voice echoes.

She can feel the shake of the girl's head. 'She was sent to harm you, and now is unconscious,' she says, as she takes Rahat's hand and leads the *rajkumari* through the darkness. This is the kind of darkness that moves, the type of stillness that unnerves. It takes a moment to realise that only Rahat's footfalls are heard in this cobbled hall. *Perhaps the child wears soft slippers*, she tells herself, though she knows better.

Rahat feels nothing but the cobblestones underfoot, though she worries she may trip over Kiden's body. There are cracks so deep that she fears losing footing and falling into the Neverworlds. Or that there might be some archaic creature below, ready to snap her feet clean off. *Could Kiden be one of these monsters?* Shaking the thought from her mind, she can't help the fear burrowing in her chest. The child pulls her along without a word, without even a name; her grip tight around the wrist, she cuts off all circulation. Rahat's hand pulses; she can feel her fingers turning purple as they tingle.

Rahat opens her mouth to speak but is stopped when they emerge from the dark into a room that blazes with light. A scream leaps from her lips and the priestess turns, backing her guest against the wall. The forearm against Rahat's throat keeps her silent, pressed to the ancient stone that seeps blood. The flames of the brazier lighting the room feel like they're licking at her skin. *This is where the smoke is coming from*, she realises, keeping her eyes locked with the child's—who she's frustrated to see is taller than her.

So young, and there isn't a single emotion upon her face, only determination to keep the *rajkumari* quiet. As if their lives depend on it.

But the flames have swallowed them into its light so suddenly that Rahat's still blinded—more so than by the black expanse that was her welcome. Orange light flickers, and red is all she can see through her shuttered eyes. Her eyelashes feel like they've been scorched clean off by the simple heat of this broom closet.

'Move fast! I don't know how many more here wish you harm.'

Once again, the child releases her as quickly as she'd grabbed her to pull her around the corners of the room and through another invisible door. Into complete darkness. Again.

It's like being knocked off your feet. Before she can find her bearings, the girl tugs her along, her tight grasp moving to the upper arm. Stumbling along behind the girl isn't too dignified, but Rahat bets that grasping about blindly would be worse. Much worse, when you consider that the priestesses may be all around her.

A grunt from the child—a warning?—and Rahat almost topples over her feet as she's yanked up what feels like a towering staircase. Going up... *Thank the gods.* Boots knocking each step on the climb, Rahat feels sick to the stomach, ready to overflow. Not only is the smoke all throughout the temple sticking in her nostrils, but with each jolt of her boots, searing pain explodes at the base of her spine. From the fall, the journey, she's not sure. Whatever it is, she prays the stairs come to an end.

When they finally do, she's breathless. Expecting one last step, she climbs up, only to find that there isn't another, and almost collapses to the stone floor in relief. It smells different up here. They've climbed upward so fast that now she wanders if they could be above ground... but there had been no structures about the temple. *Are we... in the Neverworlds?* It's warmer than she'd thought it'd be.

'Where are we?' she demands, but is shushed by the girl leading her. 'Can we—'

Though she cannot see, she *feels* the girl's stare. 'No,' is her only reply.

She breaks into a run, her hold slipping from Rahat's upper-arm and back to her sweaty hand. Squeezing the fingers unbearably tight. The dark moves about them like a living creature, slithering by like the Great Serpent of Ages. As if this temple somehow encapsulates the world.

Just as Rahat adjusts to their pace, she's brought to a sudden stop. She's being pulled around like a rag-doll. A knock sounds at a wooden door, and Rahat prays—*Surely!*—they've reached their destination. Wherever that be. Rahat blinks hard, eyelids heavy, at seeing the outline of a door. There's a flame on the other side. Gods help her, it won't be like that other room.

Even without sight, she can feel the many other bodies around them. Women in red, as if the colour is tactile. The buzzing in her fingertips when the girl releases her hand makes her think—not for the first time—that maybe this is a bad idea. But you can never refuse those who serve the gods. You might as well be spitting in the god's face. And you know what that gets you.

With a haunting creak, the door swings open. The orange light escapes into the black space they'd been travelling through, for Rahat to see that it isn't so open at all—in fact, they'd travelled down a slim corridor for most of the way, only to emerge into this circular hall. Dozens of priestesses stand lining the walls, their eyes upon the *rajkumari* who has come to ask after her lover. Many of the red women lift a finger to their lips, dragging the fingertip down to reveal the inside of their bottom lip. Anywhere else, this is a cursed sign; but here, a blessing of luck. As if they know she'll be needing it.

Only a few hours left, she reminds herself, feeling the sweat that trickles down the back of her neck. When she is propelled into the lit room, she can't help her gasp. The force of the throw is in her lower back, which explodes with pain, making her collapse to the polished floor. The door closes behind her, once again casting the priestesses behind her into the dark. Rahat dares look up.

The brazier before her is much smaller than the last; and this room much larger. A cathedral in itself. Beyond the falling of light, she knows there is much more space to this room, though how much, she'll never be able to guess. Stained glass windows above stare out into the nothingness. If this were a cathedral of Abrecan, it would shine in the suns, a beautiful thing. But here, the glass remains black. Blinking as her eyes adjust to the dim light, she sucks in shallow breaths, trying to calm herself. The pain in her back is excruciating. Like the touch of a shadow dancer's tongue.

'Hello?' she ventures.

'Rahat Brijesh,' is the answering call, from the other side of the room. Or rather, from the other side of the brazier. A woman sits beside the flame, her face half-hidden beneath her silken hood. White hair cascades in waves from the hood and over her shoulders, making Rahat suck in a gasp. A Lyran, from the north. She's almost afraid to lay eyes upon the porcelain skin beneath that hood, and what is likely a pair of translucent white eyes. 'I have been expecting you,' purrs the woman, with an accent she's never dreamt of hearing fully. It's lilting, like a song is captured upon her tongue. Although it's only superstition, Rahat now believes the stories that say the Lyran people can sing the future and the fate of men.

Tradition dictates she stand, but Rahat finds she cannot. Without a word, the High Priestess seems to understand why. As she makes her way around the brazier, Rahat measures up the lithe woman who never pulls back her hood.

Rahat's eyes don't leave the woman as she grows closer. Her heart hammers in her chest, making the Lyran chuckle.

'There is nothing to fear, little one,' says the woman of ghost white. With fluid movements, she drops to her knees behind Rahat to place a hand at the *rajkumari's* back. 'You are injured from your fall, and Mahesa dragging you through the temple would've furthered damage.' The woman lifts Rahat's shirt with frozen-tipped hands to press a hand flat to her back. Rahat gasps; the oracle's hands are like an Eerie's. Then slowly, that deep-freeze sinks into her muscles and spreads with growing warmth. The muscles tense before they relax, nearly giving Rahat a headache. But when the woman retracts her hand and pulls the shirt and armour back down to cover her, she can't believe how the pain has disappeared. Carefully, the woman pulls Rahat to her feet.

'There are only two hours left,' she tells her, turning Rahat's blood cold.

'T-two hours?' she stammers. 'I was sure I had four— at *least*.'

The Lyran nods in understanding. 'Time passes differently between realms.'

Rahat holds up her hands, preventing the woman from even beginning to explain. There isn't time to understand how oracles live beneath both the mortal and immortal planes.

'Tell me your name,' orders Rahat, shocking even herself at the boldness of the request.

The woman dips her head, hiding her smile. 'It is unwise to ask a Lyran Eye for her name,' says she, with such promise of mystery that Rahat almost tears at her skin with curiosity. All the secrets of the world—*all* of them—are locked away within this woman's mind.

When not a word is uttered, the Lyran fingers the seam of her silken hood and uncovers her hair. Revealing her scarred face. 'I am Aegileif Golden-Born of the Skylla Tribe of Lyra,' the woman says, her voice echoing like a thunder's boom. Her name, pronounced *EYE-geh-leaf*, sends a spark up Rahat's arms. She has a feeling she's heard that name before. 'Golden-Born,' continues the oracle, 'and once Silver-Sighted.'

Rahat can't look away from Aegileif's lack of eyes. Where those glowing orbs should be, remains only scarred tissue—as if her sight had been burnt away. Before Rahat can ask, the woman waves a hand.

'Cursed to be an Oracle, I sacrificed my eyes to stay with my husband.' Her hands linger upon her cheeks, rosy and high-boned. 'Only he cared not for a blind wife, no matter her famed name.' Dropping those hands to Rahat's chest, the oracle's fingers wheedle under the shirt until her fingertips graze Rahat's heart. The icy touch makes her hold her breath. 'You will face much, as I did. You will endure hardship and betrayal, but you shall be triumphant. I cannot see when, but you wear the marks of motherhood.'

Before Rahat can pull away, Aegileif presses her hand flat against her heart. 'There is a dark force—a beast of flesh and blood and flame. There is blood, so much blood.' The voice grows quicker, and what she speaks is no longer Delorrene, but the words of the Lyra Lands. It doesn't take a genius to know this is bad. Very bad. For when Lyrans speak, many of their words become truth.

Or so goes the legend.

'—until the world is Ashen,' gasps Aegileif, and Rahat yanks herself back. The oracle's touch leaves her skin, though not without leaving behind a looping brand of silken white above her breast.

Running a trembling hand through her own hair, Aegileif lifts her hood over her features, again hiding her missing eyes. 'Give me a lock of your hair,' she says quickly, beckoning with one hand for Rahat to come closer. She doesn't move a step. The oracle grits her teeth in frustration as a pair of scissors appears in her hand with a plume of smoke. She gestures Rahat to come closer. But who trusts a blind woman with scissors? 'A simple lock is all I need,' presses the Lyran.

The air about Aegileif shifts. Wisps of her hair are caught up in the waves of life pushed off of the flame; a sign that perhaps they are not alone but in the presence of a god. Without second thought, Rahat takes a blade from her belt and cringes as she cuts free a lock of hair the length of her hand. It curls in her palm. And wetting her lips, Aegileif takes the hair carefully, sure not to drop a single strand. Rahat doesn't even want to consider how it is that a woman without eyes is fully aware of her surroundings.

'Ask the gods,' says she, as if reading her mind.

'Uh, what?'

'Pray to them that you shall emerge mighty, and defeat the Nameless.'

Swallowing hard, Rahat can only stare. 'The Nameless?'

The Lyran's voice is dire as she nods, only once. 'Yes.'

Dagger trembling in her hand, Rahat lifts her other arm. There is only one way to ask a blessing of a god. And only one way to pay an oracle for her services. Slowly, she glides the blade's tip over the outside of her forearm, where the wound won't affect her need to fight. Because, after all the obstacles, there is no way this will not end without a fight. Even as she holds her arm over the brazier, allowing the flame to swallow a taste of her blood, she cannot think of a single prayer. Knowing this will be the Ashen God makes the task harder. *Keep us safe*, is all she can think to ask of the gods. *I trust in you.*

At last finished, she nods to the oracle. Aegileif, on cue, whispers curses or spells—Rahat has no idea which, in that language—into the lock of raven hair curled in her ghostly palm.

It's sudden. The oracle blows upon the locks and they are drawn into the flame, igniting upon contact. Having sheathed her dagger, Rahat watches, cradling her arm and keeping pressure on the wound. Her only hope is that this will help.

Once her hair has been devoured, the room grows brighter. Bright enough for Rahat to snatch sight of a bone, just beyond where the light had first touched. A bone, and a piece of membrane. *Wings.*

A faerie.

The flames leap higher, forcing Rahat to take a step back—both from the fire and the pale woman. There is much left to say, but she settles on: 'Thank you.'

Aegileif bows her head.

'But I do not have time for this.'

Rahat turns on her heel, only to be jerked back as the oracle takes the *rajkumari*'s wounded arm in hand. She hisses in pain as ice spreads from Aegileif's hand, leeching up her arm and gathering about the wound. Blinding cold as if burning. Healed.

Aegileif retracts her hand without a word, turning her back on Rahat to level her eyeless sight on the flame.

'Thank you,' she whispers, but the woman doesn't respond. 'How do I find my way out?' she asks, shifting her stance. 'It took me hours to get here.'

She hears, rather than sees, the woman smile. 'To find the way out, one must only turn around.'

Exasperated, the *rajkumari* turns. She's about to ask the oracle what she means when she realises with a sudden shock that once again, she's plunged into darkness. A glance over her shoulder reveals nothing's behind her, but she is certainly not in the cathedral anymore. *By the gods...* Running a hand over her hair, she prays this is it. Smoke tangles itself in her clothes, in her nostrils, as she leads her way forward. Sliding her feet across the cobbled ground, she avoids the cracks between worlds as she comes to the bottom of a staircase. A staircase leading upward. Holding her breath, she reaches out—and her hand finds the handrail she'd followed down.

Thank the gods. Rahat leaps up the stairs. With each step, the world becomes lighter. She's almost out.

'Rahat?'

The worried call from Hazel almost makes her trip in her efforts to bound up the last few steps. 'Hazel?' she yells, to be immediately greeted with the girl's relieved sigh. As she comes into the light, an ache grows behind her eyes. She has been in the dark for so long now.

The last step. Walking across the clean marble between the towering columns of the temple, Rahat feels like this is a dream. It *has* to be a dream. Nothing like that could ever truly be reality.

'I was worried,' grumbles Hazel, who won't take a further step toward the temple. The Asthori cannot even bear to touch the marble. 'Two hours—and you're covered in soot. What happened?' The look of concern on her make makes Rahat whisk her into her arms. 'I thought something might have gone wrong,' Hazel says, her face smushed into the side of Rahat's cheek before she puts her down. Back on solid ground, she makes a point of straightening her clothes and taking several steps back from the temple.

Rahat keeps in step with her, watching the sky is change. It looks like two hours may be a stretch. Prakaash tosses his head as his master approaches, reaching for the saddle. 'Did anyone come along?'

The girl shakes her head. 'Not a soul.'

Silence fills the space between them as she mounts her steed. Up again on Prakaash's back, Rahat leads them west.

'Rahat... what happened?' Hazel's voice is small from her side. 'I was scared.'

'So was I,' says Rahat. Keeping her eyes on the jungle before them, she considers their way. If they continue on this path, the spires of the crystal fortress should emerge from the top of the trees. 'But now I know who we will face,' she says.

'And that is...?'

It pains her to say. 'The Nameless God.'

The colour drains from Hazel cheeks. 'The— Are you serious?'

'Deadly so.'

As they travel on, there is no life about them. No singing of birds, no crying of monkeys. The trees dare not even whisper in the breeze. Dead air. Still air. The silence hums, drowning out any other sound that wishes to emerge.

Breathing is all Hazel hears, but Rahat keeps on the alert. Aegileif had warned her that they will face a beast, but never named it. Which leaves *beast* very open to interpretation. Beasts of the air, land, trees, or the Other... In this silence which only grows, she daren't attempt to name such a thing.

Navigating on memory alone—for it is not a straight path—Rahat has to pinch herself when she realises Hazel's asked her a question.

'How much further?' the girl asks again, not wanting to embarrass her friend. 'The suns look... *precarious*, if anything.'

Rahat ignores this. Partially. Keeping her eyes on the trees, on anything that moves (that is to say, on nothing, but it could be anything), she's unsure. An indescribable scent hangs in the air like a dulled memory. She knows this way.

Yet doubt still holds her tight. Is this the way from a memory, or a dream?

Iliyah would know.

'Not far now,' she says at last, kicking Prakaash into a canter.

As the jungle grows sparse, Hazel follows. Only at spying the low-hanging fog ahead does she pull up hard on the reins. The more they ride, the denser the fog becomes. 'Rahat?' The call is strangled.

'I see it too,' she calls back, waiting for Hazel to reach her side.

When she breaks through the trees and through the fog into the clearing, she sucks in a deep breath. As if this were her last. The glimmering crystal fortress towers over everything, though its gleam is threatening. Cold. But it's the fog that unnerves Rahat most, even as she shakes off the remnants of the projected nightmare. Iliyah's alive. The fortress is *here*.

About their feet, the black smoke curls, as if from thousands of candles snuffed out at once. There is life within this smoke without flame. It sets Hazel's teeth a-chatter as Rahat pushes Prakaash to take another step.

'By the gods,' she mutters, at last understanding the truth of this quest. 'Taeng knew all along.'

15

Ashen, curling smoke. Embers glimmer like stars in the swirling dark, pulsing like death.

The *lindélofs* won't go any further. Each tug of the reins is met by iron-clad hooves pressed firmly into the earth. But even the girls can feel it; the revulsion races through them as it had at the temple, at every temple and holy place. Like a wave of sunlight, it cuts through them to the bone, the heat pulsing, burning.

Prakaash tosses his head, tearing the reins from Rahat's white-knuckled hands. The *snap* makes her hiss as she dismounts, knowing her beast will go no further. Upon Bijalee's back, Hazel takes a shaky drink before following suit. She shakes so, Rahat can see the tremors in even her hair. Wind-swept, with instincts forcing her backward, Hazel steadies herself with a hand at a thick tree-trunk.

'I don't feel so good,' she whispers, frightened of spooking whatever they may face. 'What is that?'

Rahat shakes her head, forcing her feet to carry her forward. 'I don't know,' she says, but Aegileif's warning rings clear in her mind.

The ashen fog sticks to her legs, gluing her feet to the earth. As if she might be dragging her feet through a riverbed thick with sludge. Her stomach roils. The *rajkumari* holds a hand back for Hazel, who takes it after slight hesitation. For the structure standing before them hardly looks like truth. A cloud-seeking tower, it stands solitary in the middle of the field—just as Rahat had hallucinated. Just as the knight's sketch had depicted.

Each crystal wall is translucent, catching the heat of the blaring sun. It's as if the castle isn't truly here; that it might be a trick of the light.

Rahat's heart aches.

Unsheathing her dagger, she wishes she were braver. That she might deserve to be a hero. That, at any moment, she might be able to do what must be done. Yet that feeling in the back of her throat closes over. Will she be able to do it?

Further into the fog, they feel it hit. The wave of exhaustion—as if they've been travelling weeks on end.

Hazel's hand goes slack in Rahat's, but the *rajkumari* tugs, pulling her to attention. 'Stay with me, Hazel,' she gasps out, though she feels dead on her feet herself. The smoke clings to their legs like mud, dragging them back. Each step makes it harder to move as they go deeper. 'We've come this far,' Rahat says, 'we'll make it.'

She's not too sure she believes it, though.

Dark hands move through the smoke, fully formed and reaching with gnarl-knuckled hands. It tries to pull them down, taking ahold of their clothes like tendons, pulling and forceful. Rahat swings her long dagger, slashing through whatever hold it takes on them. But the embers merely swirl above their feet.

'Iliyah will survive this day,' Rahat grits out, hardening her voice if only to convince herself. 'We haven't come this far only to fail.'

A strangled yelp from behind makes her turn. The fear written across Hazel's face makes her pause. *Hazel's only fifteen*, she reminds herself. 'Are you all right?' she asks, but the girl only nods, shaking off any further questions. Each second still brings more weight about them. Too soon, and they might find themselves frozen to the earth... or whatever it is beneath their feet. Rahat fears they might be in one of the cracks between worlds; as a child it had never been a problem. The creatures that walk between worlds never claim children—only those fully-grown. 'Are you sure?' she asks again, only to receive a dead-pan look from her cousin. 'Okay, okay.'

They forge ahead. If Hazel dies, Rahat is responsible. She's the one who dragged her into this mess. That heaviness settles in her chest, tearing her apart. The sickness settles in her stomach. She can't do this—not to Hazel.

'Turn back,' she whispers, having to grit the words out.

The girl pauses, faltering for a mere second. 'What?'

'You need to turn back.'

The air about them stills as Hazel yanks Rahat's arm, pulling her around to face her. 'Are you crazy? We've gotten this far—there is *no way* I am turning back now.'

Rahat shakes her head, unable to think of what to say, when Hazel rests a hand at her cousin's shoulder.

'Look, this is my choice. If I didn't want to do this with you then I wouldn't have snuck out of the palace when Qadira dragged me back, okay?'

Rahat shrugs, but Hazel squeezes her shoulder, forcing her to look up at her.

'If we die, then we die.' The words don't even falter. Her stare stills Rahat's nerves, forcing them into submission. 'But I would rather die fighting for something I believe in than running.'

'But—'

'No. I said I would fight,' she drops her hand, leading them toward the tower, 'so that's what I will do. For you, and for Iliyah.'

The sky is already streaking orange. There's isn't time to waste. Rahat nods.

'Scout the area,' she orders.

The girl breaks free without further order.

Staring up at the tower, Rahat grips her blade tight. 'I'll find Iliyah.'

Because Taeng was right. Because *Rahat* was right. And if she was right about where Iliyah might be, about where her soul would seek solace, does that mean—?

A scream interrupts the thought.

A jolt runs through her. '*Hazel?*' cries Rahat, the name ripped from her throat. Out the corner of her eye she spots the smoke swirling, forming the shape of a woman who stands over Hazel—the girl swallowed under by the embers and ashes. '*HAZEL!*' she screams. She cannot even see her red hair above the smoke. Desperate, she wades her way through the fumes that curl about them. It creeps up her armour and clings to her nostrils, making her feel faint. Feverish. This isn't just smoke. Embers burn at her skin, scratching her cheeks and searing her flesh. As she races through the darkness, her eyes search for Hazel.

Yet that creature is still forming. The smoke breathes, caressing whatever lays beneath as it comes to its full height. Dark, glowing eyes take shape.

'Hazel?' Rahat panics. There's no sign of her.

The sky fades, inciting a blind flash. Panic makes her eyes jitter as she searches, cursing as she fails to find her friend. She thought she'd had more time.

Another scream—this one a higher pitch.

'HAZEL!'

The solidifying smoke wavers. A travelling cloak billows out, the wind stripping the smoke away to reveal dark linen. The eyes burn dark, swallowed beneath a heavy brow. Rahat's heart leaps into her throat. The woman clad in black is part-wolf. That lupine grin pins her where she stands, shooting fear through her chest. The woman's skin is lighter than most Praitosí—but it's the eyes that give her away. That dark charcoal. It shocks Rahat to her core. 'Nisha?'

The woman laughs, a sickening sound as it reverberates through the smog. All along, Rahat knew that this would come. That Nisha would be standing before her at the end of the journey.

To know is one thing. To see, another.

It's an entirely different feeling; for no longer is it hurt, but betrayal that she feels. It's like embers peeling the skin from her cheeks.

Tears spill over, coursing rivers down her bloody face. Rahat can hardly breathe as she pushes further into the smoke curling about her legs. Praying to every god she knows, she cannot find what to ask of them. That she may live; that Hazel will escape this; that Iliyah will be saved...

'Get away from her!' orders Rahat, with a voice powerful and booming. The woman standing before her demands a fight by her deep aura. A darkness ripples off her skin as her wolfish features dissolve into that of a woman's. Even as Rahat levels her blade at her throat, Nisha flashes that predatory grin, ready to devour them both.

'Oh dear,' snarls the woman with mock shock, 'but you didn't think I'd be fighting alone, did you?'

The blade lowers ever-so-slightly as Rahat tears her sight to the shadows flitting along the side of the tower's outer-wall. The shadows, they dance. Rahat feels the realisation settle in before the *kehrasa* forms before her, leaping out of the shadows in the sky as if she's been dropped from the heavens.

'Qadira,' grits out the *rajkumari*, tilting toward the traitorous creature.

Qadira's sight doesn't waver as she stares Rahat in the eye. That bright carnelian flashes, the slit pupils more feline than she's ever seen them as they crinkle—in what? *Hunger?* No. *Kindness?* Definitely not.

'So this is what it's come to,' says Rahat, not for one second forgetting the sorceress at the end of her dagger's point. To her credit, Nisha hasn't flexed a single muscle.

A flicker pulls Rahat's attention away from the disgraced sorceress. *Was that... a tail?* A glance to Qadira, to spy the spotted cheetah's tail peeking out from her loose, billowing trousers. The *kehrasa* shrugs a shoulder, as if daring her to question it.

She remains silent.

But the *kehrasa's* eyes search the fog, combing it through as if it might reveal something. *Hazel*—the jolt strikes her hard. Rahat's hand tightens at her hilt; if the faerie finds Hazel, there's nothing she can do to save her.

Without magic, without help, Rahat will not be able to keep a banished sorceress and a three-hundred-year-old faerie preoccupied. In fact, she knows exactly how the fight will go. And it won't last long, either.

Yet there's a quiver in Nisha's cheek, a twitch at her eye. Does Nisha possess all of her power? There isn't time to find out. Qadira still searches the embers, the smoke that climbs up the side of the tower, and Nisha's eyes haven't left Rahat's face since Hazel disappeared into the darkness below.

'Where is the other one?' Qadira asks at last, her voice a purr, heavy and seductive the way it always is. 'The redhead,' she reiterates, when her master piques a brow in question.

Nisha gives an imperceptible shake of her head. A soft growl rumbles in the back of the sorceress' throat. Even under the smoke and burning embers, Hazel can be smelt—but where? Behind her, the *kehrasa*'s eyes narrow in on an area of the whirling darkness. Has she found her?

'Nisha,' barks Rahat, putting all her force behind the name in an attempt to distract them. Meeting those eyes, she's almost swallowed by the warm silver. They're sickening, smooth like velvet and gruesome like melted flesh.

The darkness moves at the wrong moment. As Hazel hurls herself up through the smoke, lunging at Nisha, the sorceress wrenches back her arm in a movement too quick for Rahat to stop. Nisha's fingers curl, going rigid as she contorts her hand back—

—wrenching Hazel back under the burning smoke.

Gods.

'What was that?' laughs the sorceress. 'You thought you stood a chance?' The laughter rumbles, grizzly like gravel. 'I'm afraid not.'

Tendrils of the ashen fog crawl up her armour. Rahat holds back her yelp even as she feels the darkness pulling her under; this is futile. 'Let her go!' she yells, fighting to keep her voice as the tentacles threaten to climb down her throat. The cries escaping her make her want to weep.

And Qadira merely stands there, eyes pinned to where Hazel had been wrenched down into the unknown.   The *kehrasa*'s tail flicks, violent like her whip, which Rahat notes is not by her side. The faerie without her whip...

Rahat struggles to keep her blade aloft as the ash envelops her. With each flick of her wrist, Nisha takes a step closer to tower over her like some malevolent god. And Rahat can do nothing against it. She is like the Ashen God, the Nameless One, the Stranger's Son.

Holy hells. Rahat inhales too much of the smoke at once, sending her a-splutter. Giving the sorceress enough time to grab her by the neck to raise her into the air. Her boots graze the earth, struggling to find their footing.

'You thought you could save her?' Nisha demands, her silver eyes crawling with something darker. As if they were a part of the smoke, too. 'You truly thought that you could *survive* this?' That laugh is so evil that Rahat fears it may rob her of her soul. Without any help from the dead thing inside of her. 'I hate to tell you, Rahat, but the villains are smarter than that. This isn't some bedtime story.'

The sabre drops into the waist-deep smoke as Rahat's hands go to her throat, grappling at Nisha's tight grasp. She pulls at her fingers, to no avail. Each breath is rasped, strangled. Dying. 'Haz—eh—' Her throat cries out in protest, red raw and aching.

Flexing her fingers, Nisha squeezes, making Rahat whimper. The blood is rushing to her head, making her temples pulse with pain. Her eyelids flutter; she won't last much longer. If only she could just...

Desperate, shaking hands fumble for the knife at her belt.

Qadira melds into the smoke, transforming herself to shadow as she flits to where Hazel remains hidden, pinned to the earth.

Watching Rahat's face, Nisha grits her wolfish teeth.

The world is spinning. And the world is balanced at the tip of Rahat's knife. With one last hope, the *rajkumari* brings her shaking arm up, breaking the bonds that kept her pinned as Nisha watches her with hunger.

Those clawed hands tighten about her throat, making the world fade red.

With her dying effort, Rahat swings up the blade, slashing. It happens so quickly that she doesn't realise she's caught Nisha's face till Rahat hits the earth with a heavy *thud*.

Pain screams through her arms as she lifts her head, squeezing her eyes shut against the embers. Coughing murders her throat as she tries to push up, only to feel a clawed hand snatching at the back of her tunic.

'HEY, WOLF-BREATH!' Hazel cries.

It's just enough of a distraction. Rahat feels the hand slip from her back and she scampers out of reach, daring to open her eyes against the ash. She can feel the blood on her hands, sticky and hot. The knife in her balled fist gleams with it. Yet she's no idea how much damage she's done.

Seconds later, she hears the *thud* of Nisha hitting the ground. Two deep gashes line her cheeks, tearing her face half-open from where Rahat had desperately slashed. A grunt from above forces Rahat onto her feet.

To find Hazel staring Qadira down, the *kehrasa* palming her mirrored blades. Hazel, *oh gods Hazel*. Wiping the blood from her face, Rahat hurdles for her, screaming her battle cry. But Qadira vanishes a moment before

Rahat can plunge a blade into her neck. She staggers forward, eyes meeting Hazel's, wide with horror.

'Where—?'

Tendrils emerge from the smoke, forcing Hazel onto her back. She gasps, dry-wrenching and sucking in embers which burn her throat. Her eyes water. Air tries to force itself down her throat but she splutters, winded.

A quick death—that's what she wants.

Because there is no way out of this.

Several metres away, Nisha hauls herself out of the darkness. The smile plastered on her face is animal. Her eyes flash murder. 'Think you can fool me?' she snarls. The wounds at her cheek gleam red, the gash glowing a strange colour that ends in gold around its edges. As if glowing with heat. The woman stops, hands smacking her face as she scratches at the wounds, desperate against the searing heat. It festers under her skin, making her flesh bubble. Her scream is inhuman, demonic, and the smell makes Hazel vomit in the dark.

Rahat re-adjusts her grip on her knife. She is the only one left standing.

But a sharp intake of breath has her turning to find Qadira at her back, blades in her fists. 'You tried to kill me,' she growls.

'Yeah, well,' Rahat begins, feigning a grin and lifting her weapon gleaming with blood. Black blood, she realises with revulsion.

The *kehrasa* leaps at her, arms raised to bring the knives down into Rahat's chest, but the *rajkumari* dances out of the way, twirling to bring herself up at Qadira's side. The faerie grits her teeth, bending to swing her blades, hoping to catch Rahat by the rib, but missing each time.

The air in Rahat's lungs feels stolen. Dodging blows, she searches for Hazel, nowhere to be seen. And Nisha... she must have dropped to her knees.

A blade almost catches Rahat in the neck and she leaps back, staggering through the thick darkness. It clings to her legs, keeping her pinned as the faerie launches herself at the mortal. Their blades sing out when they meet, making Rahat cringe.

'Why?' she spits at her, and the *kehrasa* pauses. 'Why are you fighting for *her*?'

Something shifts in Qadira's eyes. Shock, dancing in that sunstone brightness. Her slit pupils search Rahat's face, but the force of her blow does not lessen.

'Why?' she demands again.

The faerie opens her mouth to speak, but not a sound emerges. Her brows furrow, and she pushes herself into the knives, forcing Rahat to stagger back.

'Rahat!'

Hazel leans herself into her blows, forcing Nisha to deflect each with flashes of pure darkness. The sorceress struggles against Hazel's quick attacks, sweat dripping at her brow. Cropped hair, slick with sweat, sticks to her face. Hazel screams, combatting a low-blow that slices through the heavy-plated armour at her breast. She lunges forward, catching the sorceress off-guard.

Rahat whips around, fleeing from Qadira's double blades to bring her dagger down—only for it to be caught against those curved knives.

'Rahat!' Hazel grits out, as her head collides with the tower base. Nisha has her backed against the stone, smearing blood with each movement. But whose blood? Nisha's face is covered. 'Rahat!' she cries again, the name strangled.

Rahat catches a blow from Qadira, missing the second blow as she tosses her blade, forcing her back. 'Please,' she gasps. The sky is the deep orange of the faerie's eyes. There isn't time. 'Qadira,' she cries, voice thick with desperation.

Out the corner of her eye, Rahat watches as Hazel is forced under the smoke as Nisha grabs her by the hair. A sharpened dagger in hand, she angles it right.

'Please,' Rahat spits out, 'she'll die.'

Qadira levels her eyes on her. On the two battling at the tower's doors. As she drops her weapons, she dares steal a glance into the sky to the room where Iliyah resides. The glimmering orange sky peeks through the crystal stone.

Rahat chokes back her sobs. 'Please.'

Without another word, the *kehrasa* charges at the tower with her blades raised.

'Hazel!' Rahat cries, as the girl is wrenched up and pushed into the stone. Her head lolls, her eyes bleary from the force. But she looks up, her eyes catching on the blades sparking with sunlight in Nisha's hands.

Hazel doesn't look away. Staring death in the face, she remains calm, even as she feels the breeze of Nisha's movements raising the knife.

Qadira appears at the sorceress' back, daggers raised. And as she brings them down, Hazel screams at the sound the two blades make as they rip through Nisha's spine.

The hand balled in Hazel's hair goes slack as Nisha collapses against the stone base of the tower. The world about them spins.

Hazel can feel the blood at the back of her head, hot and wet and making her dizzy. The fog crawls over her, but she pushes herself back up to stand.

Nisha's face ripples, her features a-morph between wolf and human. Her sharp teeth gleam red in the arcing sunlight as she wrenches back her jaw to scream. Qadira stands panting behind her, staring at the damage she has inflicted. Blood coats her face in splattered freckles. On her dark skin, it looks like paint, but in her ebony hair, it matts. The *kehrasa*'s tail flicks with agitation as she takes a step backward, only for the witch to lash out, knocking the faerie into the darkness.

But before she can be swallowed, she vanishes, becoming shadow and sand.

With a sickening *squelch*, Nisha reaches back to pull the knives from either side of her spine. Blood bubbles up her throat, overflowing and coating her face in a fresh layer of it. Those silver eyes turn glassy.

Watching Hazel edge around the circular base of the tower, Rahat stands breathless. The darkness swirls about her feet, but it no longer feels like it's dragging her down. The weight is gone, stolen away by Qadira's mirrored blades.

'H-hazel?' she stammers.

The Asthori looks up, her face coated in the sorceress' blood. Eyes wide, Hazel can't tear her eyes from the carnage that stands before her. And she can't move away quickly enough.

Nisha takes the blades into her hands and lashes out, digging them into the stone by Hazel's head. 'Who said this was over?' she gasps out, blood dribbling with each word.

Whimpering, Hazel cannot look away. Her limbs refuse to move, and she is weaponless. Bloodied handprints about her neck make her look mortally wounded as Rahat approaches, having to drag her dead limbs through the dark. Shock, that's what it is. That's what she knows it is.

She's never seen a body so broken.

'Hazel?'

The Asthori grips along the walls by her sides, hands frantically searching for the handle to the armour-piercing dagger at her belt. It's a thin blade like a needle. With shaking hands, she palms it and shoves upward into Nisha's gut. She whimpers again as Nisha starts to fall toward her, almost pinning her to the cracked stone.

At the sound, Qadira reappears, perched high up in a tree by the horses. The *lindélofs* whinny, alarmed, as the *kehrasa* grips the branches tight to get a closer look.

Rahat crosses the darkness which parts for her like the seas. Relief floods through her as she reaches Hazel's side, only now seeing the true damage inflicted upon the sorceress. Yet she keeps fighting.

Reaching a hand for Hazel, Rahat takes a wide step, but it's too late.

'MOVE!' screams Qadira, but not before the blade slices through Rahat's armour.

Hot blood pools at the wound in her side. Rahat staggers back a step, staring down at the blood oozing from the slash. If it weren't for her armour, she would be bleeding out. But already she can feel the aura of death.

Her skin sizzles, discoloured and blood-slick. Her hands are shaking. She can't stop herself from shaking. The skin has peeled back, revealing the muscle beneath, and blood—too much blood. Fresh air stings the exposed meat as she sucks in a hissing breath.

Qadira evaporates, again appearing by Hazel's side in a moment.

'Hazel,' Rahat whispers, her dry throat crying out. 'Hazel.' Bloodstained hands reach out for the Asthori, but the girl swings her into the doors leading up into the tower.

'Run,' orders Hazel, pushing the doors open to shove her up the spiral stairs.

The *rajkumari* swallows, staring hard at her cousin and her company: the torn-apart madwoman still fighting, and the faerie who has betrayed them before.

'GO!'

'But—'

Qadira steps between Nisha gasping for breath and Hazel to place a hand at Rahat's shoulder. 'Go. While there is time.'

'But—'

'We will deal with the witch,' says the *kehrasa*, as they share a look.

Rahat mashes her lips together, unsure, but—there isn't time for this. She's right. As Nisha again raises her last weapon to attack, Rahat turns and sprints up the stairs.

The doors slam closed behind her. She hears the screaming of swords meeting as she ascends.

Through the crystal walls, she can see the suns and their light cast across the sky. A dusky orange, soon to be pink, then purple. Then gone. She has but minutes. The pain in her side screams, bringing her to a gasping halt. Minutes, if she's lucky.

Ripping back her split armour, Rahat reveals the blood and sweat about her wound. The skin is turning green, burning away with some kind of poison.

'Najir,' she gasps out, and it's almost enough that she gives up. If she's right and this is Naj poison, then there's no point. She won't even make it to the top of the stairs.

But she has to try.

Though her strangled cries echo within the spiral staircase, she pushes herself on. Each stair becomes harder. Feverish, she rips away her outer-armour, leaving her tunic in place. The air is so hot, it's sweltering. She keeps a hand at her side as she runs, putting pressure on the wound even as she feels herself approaching death.

The castle, once crystal, is becoming hard stone around her. The walls shift, the dark grey wicking up the glass like blood on a tapestry. The glass clouds over, blocking out the light until she's running in near-darkness. *Come ON.* Not much further. Iliyah is mere *seconds* away.

Yet her heart is overworked. She can feel the effects of the poison coursing through her blood. A pain at her neck makes her curse; she can feel the bruising already, colouring her a dark purple and green. Black blood seeps from her side.

She daren't stop. She isn't sure how much time has passed but it feels like longer with her heart beating so. Small windows the size of her palm start to appear in the now-stone walls, allowing her to glimpse the sky upon its descent. A dusky pink streaked with orange. A sob escapes her throat before she lets it.

'Iliyah!' she cries.

'Rahat?' comes Iliyah's voice, ringing down the staircase.

The *rajkumari* lifts her head. 'Iya?'

'Rahat? Rahat!' comes the call again, echoing all around her.

Hazel.

A glance over her shoulder, but she can no longer see or hear whatever is happening outside now that the crystal is stone.

'Rahat!'

Never pausing, Rahat runs with those two voices enveloping her. She's not sure if the venom is making her hallucinate—has she even come close to the top of the tower? Below, she can hear someone's boots on the steps. Hazel calls for Rahat again, but this time she's unsure. Witches play tricks like this all the time in tales.

She nearly collapses when she reaches the top of the stairs. She lurches forward, expecting more as she stumbles into the rosewood door. The beating of her heart is wild. She may be just in time.

'Rahat, we're okay!' Hazel's cry weaves up the stairs. 'She's dead, I think!'

Gritting her teeth at her limbs protesting, Rahat places her hand at the door. It swings open as soon as her fingers slide around the brass door-handle, to reveal the room from her projected nightmare.

The room is empty, save for a bed and a large window overlooking the smoke which billows from the Red Temple. The deepening sky peeks through, flooding purple and casting them in blue light. *No no no.* Wind brushes the hair from Rahat's face as she enters, holding her wound tight and staggering. Her feet don't want to move. Pain shoots through her with each step.

The bruises at her neck, at her back, at her sides... they pulse. But Iliyah is all she can see.

The door swings to a light close, silently clicking behind her as she enters the room. Laying there upon the bed, Iliyah's clean face is a shining beacon. Her ebony hair cascades over the sides of the mattress like a water nymph's. The lashes that brush her cheeks are long and precious. Long lithe limbs. Skin dark and creamy as night. In a *salwar* of turquoise, gold, and violet, she is a vision beneath the indigo light. Rahat's never seen her like this before.

Encased in a thin layer of crystal, she looks like she's sleeping. In the fading light, the glass gleams a faint blue like water. It's slippery under Rahat's bloodied fingers. A tug at the bottom of the crystal case, but it cannot be moved. Her muscles scream out in protest; even her blood feels like it's become heavier. Her eyes fade in and out of focus as fear grips her about the throat. There are only moments left. Mere *seconds* on a clock.

'Come on,' she whispers. Her escaped sobs ricochet through the tower, and on the other side of the door she hears two sets of feet which grow more frantic. 'Please,' she whimpers, leaning against the heavy glass. '*Hazel!*'

When the door flies open, Rahat nearly collapses at the sight of them coated in blood. Qadira's eyes rake over the scene; she's by Rahat's side in a moment, lifting the case from the *shehzadi*'s body. As Hazel helps guide the crystal over the side of the mattress, it thrums, shattering into hundreds of tiny pieces before hitting the ground.

'My gods,' breathes Hazel, as she stares at the glass strewn across the ground.

But the sky around them is almost night. Seconds remain.

And Rahat has no idea what to do.

Pulling herself around the bed to reach her, she hisses at the pain. She leans against the mattress, her blood soaking it through. Beside Iliyah's clean hand, the blood is wrong, dirty. Their hands feel like magnets, their touch thrumming through Rahat's fingertips. 'Please,' Rahat says, like it were some kind of spell. 'Please live.' Glancing up to Qadira, her eyes are pleading. 'I don't know what to do,' she admits. Tears streak channels down her sticky cheeks, her desperation turning to ice-cold fear. 'Please.'

Hazel's soft hand at her back only makes her flinch. 'Kiss her,' she says. Rahat looks at her with wide eyes before Hazel waves her hands, dismissing her fears. 'You're Bound! *Now*,' she orders. 'Kiss her now, you idiot!' Her eyes remain plastered on the sky as it fades to well past sunset. This might not work. Crossing her fingers, she prays to every god she knows.

Gazing down at Iliyah, Rahat gulps, before leaning over her and pressing her lips gently to the *shehzadi's*. The pain at her side makes her whimper, but Hazel's hand at her back keeps her in place. She feels electric— but that could be the hallucinogens in the venom, or the pain, or even death encroaching. Whatever it is, it makes it hard to breathe. She pulls back a moment later. Iliyah's lips are so soft that she's close to forgetting about everything else. Tears stream down her face onto Iliyah's, dirtying her fresh cheeks with soot and blood.

At Hazel's gasp, Rahat opens her eyes—

—To find Iliyah staring back at her. Those deep brown eyes glow with warmth, a thick gooey chocolate. Rahat's so shocked that she pulls back. 'Iliyah—' she gasps, before Iliyah silences her with another kiss. The second their lips meet is frantic, as if all these years have been building up to this. *This.* They lose themselves in each other before Qadira clears her throat, tapping a hand against the bed's wooden frame.

'You're—'

Rahat's legs give out and she hits the floor hard.

Without a second thought, Iliyah throws herself off the bed to perch by Rahat's side. Her head spins but she ignores it, her eyes zeroing in on the blood marring the *rajkumari*'s side. She looks up at Qadira. 'What happened? You're both covered in blood.' Realisation flashes in her dark eyes as she looks them over. 'My aunt. My aunt did this, didn't she?'

As if working on instinct, Iliyah plucks free the dagger from Hazel's belt to cut free the hem of her *salwar*. The golden fabric is so beautiful that Hazel can't help but wince at seeing it cut away.

The knife clatters beside her on the stones when Iliyah raises the length of material to Rahat's side. 'Qadira, if you would,' she says, without so much as a glance her way. The *kehrasa* obeys without question, shadow-singing to crouch by Rahat. When Qadira plunges a hand into Rahat's side to rid the poison from her system, Iliyah looks to Hazel—Hazel, who feels sick at watching Qadira's healing talent.

'Now, tell me what happened,' orders Iliyah.

Hazel swallows hard. 'I killed your aunt.'

The *shehzadi*'s sigh is heavy. 'Thank the gods.'

Hazel doesn't even know whether to be shocked, when she's watching a faerie with her hand inside the side of her cousin. The *kehrasa* pulls her hand out, gleaming with blood in the light of dusk, before producing a green powder from the pouch at her belt. Without a sound, she smears the powder over Rahat's off-coloured skin before pinching the wound together.

How that will help, Hazel hasn't the faintest idea.

'And?' prods the dark-skinned Praitosí, as she ties the fabric in her hand about Rahat's middle to keep her wound clean.

'And it looks like she poisoned Rahat,' Hazel says, with an obvious look to her cousin's wounds.

'Ah.' Iliyah watches with narrow eyes as Qadira wipes the sweat from Rahat's face, searching for any other wounds which may need healing. The faerie pauses at feeling the crusted blood at Rahat's crown, before moving on to press the bruising at her neck.

'The swelling will go down, with time,' she says quietly, resting her ear at Rahat's chest to listen. 'And her heart will be regular as soon as the salve starts taking effect.' Looking between Hazel and Iliyah, Qadira remembers her tail and whips it back into the folds of her trousers, as if it had never existed. 'Water?' she asks, to which Hazel shakes her head.

'My canteen's at Bijalee's saddle.' Only she is keeping a watch of the *kehrasa*.

'Please, sit,' says the faerie, and Hazel obliges with a hollow sigh. It's been a long few days.

Running a hand over Rahat's fevered forehead, Iliyah can't fight the small smile that works its way onto her lips. 'I don't know what I'd do if you'd died,' she whispers by Rahat's ear. 'Here, help me,' she says, gesturing to Hazel.

A moment later, Rahat is sprawled across the floor with her head resting in Iliyah's lap. 'Thank the gods there was enough time,' she says, not lifting her eyes from Rahat's face.

Qadira nods, crossing her arms over her folded legs. Anything to distract herself from what's happening. The tension between them feels like it's strangling her. She can only imagine how Hazel feels.

But Iliyah doesn't care. Placing a gentle kiss to Rahat's forehead, she breathes in the scent of her. It's a scent she hadn't realised she missed.

And finally, Hazel understands all those weeks of torment, of having to make excuses for them when she should have been with them. 'You love her too,' she says, and it isn't a question.

Iliyah doesn't look up as she caresses Rahat's cheek. 'Of course I do.'

Hazel drops her eyes to her cousin's restful features. 'I didn't realise...'

'I know,' she says with that sad smile, 'neither did she. Not really.'

Head in her lap, Rahat's eyelids flutter, her lashes like butterflies' wings. It takes a moment for her sight to focus on the face staring down at her. 'You... kissed me.'

The foolish grin on her face makes Iliyah laugh, though the tears make her choke. 'And you saved me,' she says. 'But don't you *dare* sacrifice yourself for me again. *Okay?*'

'Is that... not allowed?' Rahat asks with a cheeky grin.

Iliyah taps her cheek in a mocking slap. 'Of course that's not allowed. Dying is never allowed. You idiot—and you almost did die. *Gods.*'

The giggle rumbles up Rahat's throat before turning into a groan of pain.

Sniffing back her tears, Iliyah glances up to Qadira, who stares at the ceiling, willing darkness to engulf them. 'You should rest now,' the faerie tells her. She nods at Hazel, who offers a grin. 'There's a long journey come morning.'

16

The rosy-fingered dawn stretches across the sky. A triple sun peeks over the horizon, lighting the sky's canvas with golden paint. The world glows with blue as the darkness before the dawn fades, banished for another day.

Qadira's limbs tingle with weight, having slept at an awkward angle. Her nerves sing as she rests her head back against the base of the mattress to stare out the window over the bed. *So, this all really happened.* She lost the one chance she had left to save her sister.

What now? The Praitosí Empire will refuse to marry Tahir to Rahat, and no doubt there may be some protests against Iliyah and Rahat being together.

Rahat and Iliyah... The princess and the priestess.

The girls are spread out, Rahat resting with her head at Iliyah's stomach—and Iliyah, sprawled with her limbs about, one leg folded and the other about Rahat's side. How they can sleep like this, she isn't sure. Yet Hazel, at some point in the night, had climbed up onto the bed. *Smart girl.*

Tingling limbs give way to nothingness as she rolls her wrists. The others won't wake for a while. Of that, she is sure. But she doesn't doubt that they've worried over what will happen once they return. Their worlds will change. They will no longer simply be the princesses of an Empire, but different. Iliyah's own mother is married to both a woman and a man. She will not care that her daughter is bisexual, but to want to marry her brother's bride? And Rahat's mother is from the Asthore Isles; Qadira can count on one hand the queer marriages she's heard of from the Isles. What will *she* have to say?

The stiffness in her neck makes her groan. You'd think she hasn't sleep in weeks with the discolouration of her skin, faded and greying with exhaustion. *Speaking of.* The *kehrasa* peeks over at Rahat, at the wound which had been festering at her side. The *rajkumari*'s blood still coats her hands. She doesn't care; it's only blood.

The *rajkumari* shifts, wincing as her side stretches. Though it's fully-healed with hardly more than a scar,

Qadira knows Rahat will still be feeling the affects of the Naj venom for at least a week more.

Out the window, the dawn aligns. Three suns rise, dancing into the sky. Today will be a good day. She's sure of it.

Yet as Hazel shifts onto her side on the bed, the air begins to change. Something is wrong. 'Wake up,' she says quickly, jostling the princesses awake. By her head, Hazel swats a hand near the faerie's face, but Qadira catches it. '*Get up.*'

Her tone has them sitting upright, all save Rahat who groans as Iliyah moves beneath her. The *shehzadi*'s hands plunge into Rahat's hair, calming her as they raise her to sitting. The shadows under her eyes look bruised.

'How are you feeling?' asks Hazel, making the faerie scoff. The Asthori shoots Qadira a look. 'I meant Rahat.'

As Iliyah rubs a hand over Rahat's back, she groans, half-asleep. 'I feel better... if you can call this better.'

'You're at least not half-dead,' whispers Iliyah at her ear.

Rahat shakes her head. 'I feel it, though.'

The *shehzadi* laughs into Rahat's shoulder, making the *rajkumari* giggle. Tangling her fingers in her hair, Iliyah reveals Rahat's face in full. Covered in cuts and graces and slight burns. They all look much the same.

But only one of them is being showered in soft kisses.

It's only when Qadira clears her throat to stand that Iliyah stops herself. 'While I'm happy for you two,' she says, so heavy that she makes their bones shake, 'I can't help but notice that there will be more than a few problems when we return you two to Ajrapur.'

A strangled sound leaps from Rahat's mouth; she swallows it down before it becomes full panic as she entwines her fingers with Iliyah's.

The *shehzadi* only smiles. 'I'll take care of it,' she tells her.

'Right.' Hazel claps her hands and points to the sky out the window. 'Now that's sorted, I have a feeling we should start on home.'

At Qadira's stillness, they can't help but fall silent. The *kehrasa* listens, her ears straining and her face void as she picks up the sounds from below the tower. A strange, rumbling sound like ice cracking in the heat. A frown works its way onto her brow as she notices the girls watching her. 'Something doesn't feel right,' she explains, turning her attention back to the outside world. 'I can feel it...' she says, resting a hand over her heart. 'It's... a wrongness. Like the world is suddenly heavy.'

'What do you mean?'

She turns her eyes on Hazel, the colour of them unnerving her. 'I don't think getting home will be quite so easy as we thought,' she says. A peek out the window, the *kehrasa*'s feline portals flashing. 'I don't think it was only Nisha whom we were fighting.'

'Right, well.' Hazel puffs out her chest, stuffing down the fear that climbs its way up her spine. 'Guess there's no time like the present.'

The faerie scoffs. 'You're eager.'

'If I am going to die, it's going to be with my head held high.'

'Hey, hey,' Iliyah holds out a peacekeeping hand as she helps Rahat to her feet. 'Please, no one is going to die today.'

'Except maybe the evil guy.'

Rahat winces against the pain. 'Yes, Hazel, though I think that bit's implied.'

When Qadira gestures to the door, they all follow— but Iliyah tugs Rahat back by the hand. 'When we get back, everything will change.'

The *rajkumari* shrugs. 'Sometimes, change can be good.'

'I know.' She ducks her head. 'But I'm still scared.'

'If we could wrap this up,' drawls the impatient Qadira with a sardonic grin, 'I would greatly appreciate it. And before you give me that look, Rahat, I would advise you to remember who just saved your life.' As if the *ra-jkumari* might not believe it, she flashes her bloodied hands. Rahat has to look away, making the faerie smirk. 'That's what I thought.'

Ignoring them, Hazel approaches the door bathed in morning's light. The heavy door swings open without a touch, making her take a hesitant step back. 'I'm going to ignore that that just happened,' she says, giving Qadira a sidelong look. But the faerie nods, so she follows after as she leads down the stairs.

Silence follows them down from the room as their footsteps are soaked up by the weathered stone. Darkness swallows them, the only light peeking through the palm-sized alcoves in the walls. How this stone had come of glass remains a mystery. But as they come closer to the earth, even the mortals can feel that something's not right. The air hums, penetrating the castle's walls. The stones shake. The earth quakes. Qadira only grows more agitated.

Underfoot, the weathered stone slips, crumbling against their soles. Iliyah stumbles, gripping onto Rahat as she navigates her way in palace slippers meant for polished floors.

Qadira flickers, her form fading into the darkness before reappearing merely seconds later. Shame forgotten, the *kehrasa*'s tail curls, fading in and out of sight.

Even in this dim light, Rahat can spy the fur peeking out from under Qadira's skin.

'Qadira,' dares Hazel, her small voice echoing, 'are you okay?'

The *kehrasa* is silent for a time before she flicks her ears and peers back at them, the three mortal women following. They've survived so much... *Will they survive this?* 'I'm not sure,' she says, 'I haven't felt this in a long time... It should be impossible.'

Hazel asks, 'What's impossible?'

The faerie's attention is torn toward a sound the humans cannot hear and she freezes. All they hear is silence as the *kehrasa* dissolves into the dark.

Rahat clears her throat. 'Glad she got that off her chest.'

A breath later, the faerie reappears, her hands scraping against the castle wall. The creature's breathing is heavy, her movements jolted—again she becomes darkness, flitting about their heads before hurdling down the stairs.

Iliyah looks to Rahat, who shrugs. 'She raised you,' she tells Iliyah as she looks away. 'If anyone knows what that means, it's you.'

Yet Hazel's feet are stilled, as if imbedded in the stone.

Iliyah doesn't miss the girl's stillness. 'Hazel?'

Then the castle moves. The stones about them slide, jolting forward as if one side of the tower might sink into the earth, into the Neverworlds held at bay below. A scream is torn from Iliyah's lips as they're shot forward. Limbs graze against walls; skin splits open.

Light peeks through the windows which grow larger—and larger still.

The stones are collapsing. Crumbling.

Darkness glimmers above their heads, carrying a voice speaking only: 'Run.'

They follow the black mist at a sprint. They've come this far. If they can survive that, they'll survive this too. The stones crumble underfoot, and Rahat yelps as her foot shoots clean through a step. The rock rips through her boot to tear at her skin, the *rajkumari* stuck until Iliyah pulls her free.

'Come *on*.'

There isn't much time.

Ahead, Hazel is unseen, racing around the spiral faster than they can see. Her ragged breath bounces off the walls, but it's her scream that makes them pause. A scream, followed by a breathless laugh. It's only when Rahat sees it for herself that her blood runs cold. A crack between the stairs—there's six missing.

'We have to jump,' comes Iliyah's gasp, moments before she leaps.

Mid-air, she prays to the goddesses that keep them safe. Her slippers skid when she lands, the step beneath her feet tearing away so quickly she barely has time to regather her footing. She cries over her shoulder, 'Rahat!'

The pain in her side shoots up through her brain. But this isn't the time. Before she can talk herself out of it, she jumps, hoping it will be enough.

The landing is hard, punishing on her knees. A groan is ripped from her—but there again is Iliyah's hand, reaching out for hers. A questioning look is shared, but the *shehzadi* forces Rahat to keep moving. 'I'm not leaving you,' Iliyah grits out, as much to Rahat as to herself.

Behind them, Qadira appears out of the darkness. Light peeks through her visage, breaking her form apart as she shoves at Rahat's back, pushing them faster. 'You need to be quicker,' she yells at them over the roaring of splitting stone. 'There's a break up ahead. You need to move *faster.*'

The *kehrasa* disappears, spurred on by whatever sense her faerie-nerves are picking up.

A deafening *crack* makes Rahat's heart tighten. *No no no no no no no*

Iliyah squeezes her hand tighter. 'Please,' she gasps, her words too quiet to hear over the destruction. This is it. *'Please.'*

The side of the tower splits open, the rocks crumbling to the earth. Iliyah reaches out a hand for the nearest wall—only to find her support snatched away as it falls. Rahat yanks her back, keeping the *shehzadi* on her feet.

Tears glisten at Iliyah's cheeks. Gods only know where Hazel might be.

'Holy hells.'

Rahat keeps a steadying arm out to keep Iliyah from falling. 'What?' she demands.

Iliyah only shakes her head. 'Hazel's made it,' she tells her, not turning back.

Good. Because if Hazel's made it, then at least one of them will live.

A harder tug of her hand, and Rahat is pulled stumbling forward. Her unsteady legs betray her as the centre of the tower breaks away. It leans, the stone screeching as it falls impossibly before them. Iliyah yelps, leaning back on her heels in a failed attempt to slow. Behind her, Rahat does the same.

The tower sways, its mass falling to the earth. To the black, swirling earth.

The embers. They still burn.

But Rahat doubts she will see them.

Iliyah yanks Rahat to her side. 'Do you trust me?'

This is hardly the time. Yet one look has her thoughts scrambled. The word leaves her lips before she can comprehend it. 'Yes.'

Stones falls from overhead, barely missing them. The bricks fall apart, breaking away on their descent. They have never seen something like this.

'JUMP!'

Rahat obeys, betraying every instinct that yells for her to retreat. But there is no retreat from this. As soon as her feet are in the air, her heart is in her mouth. At the other end of her hand, Iliyah soars. The wind sweeps her hair into her face but the shehzadi holds tight. *Hold tight*, her features read, as she pulls Rahat toward the collapsing stone.

Falling. Flailing.

Calm. Rahat's shredded boots graze the stone of the tower's centre. Beneath her feet she can feel it falling apart. They've reached safety.

But below, Hazel is screaming. 'What are you doing?' she cries, hysterics flushing her face red. 'Jump! Jump! WHAT ARE YOU DOING!'

One sharp intake of breath. The ground is rushing up at them, green and black and deadly. The embers glimmer, sparking to life as they come closer. And closer. Another breath, and Iliyah gives a squeeze. It's time.

They barely muster the strength against gravity to leap from the destroyed falling stones. The *boom* rings through their ears as it hits the ground and an ash cloud envelops them. Too quick for them to spot the ground.

'Ugh!' Rahat's legs scream out upon hitting the hard earth and rolling. A tear in her side, and she's scared she's ripped herself open again. 'Iya!'

She hits the ground a second later, slurring curses through sharp breaths.

Rahat's ears ring, but she hears Hazel calling for them through the smog. The ash obscures all in a cloud of dust and stone and embers. *Impossible.* The *rajkumari* reaches out with desperate fingers, to find Iliyah shaking in the dirt.

'Iliyah,' she gasps, dragging herself across the dead earth to the *shehzadi*'s side.

The Praitosí lifts her head, seeing nothing through the darkness.

The ash cloud shifts about Hazel as she runs, feeling Qadira in her shadow-form by her side. 'I can't believe you just did that,' gasps Hazel. Reaching down into the swirling darkness, she pulls Rahat up by the arm. 'I can't believe you're alive after that stunt,' she says, bending to grab Iliyah.

The *kehrasa* gathers herself out of the dark, pulling her features together as the faerie usually portrays herself: smooth-skinned and without a tail. 'Never do that again,' the desert-woman growls, steadying them on their feet.

'Oh, believe me,' Rahat laughs, holding out her hands in surrender, 'I never want to come that close to death again.'

At her side, Iliyah nods with wide eyes. 'I second that.'

'Uh, guys?'

Hazel's staring off into the distance, watching the smoke forming, cocooning itself around something. A body. The black deepens as it wraps its tendrils about Nisha's body, pulling it up from the flat earth. Dried, crusty blood and puffy green skin stare back at them when Nisha rears her head. Only, Nisha isn't here at all. The ashen cloud dives in through her parted lips, pouring itself into her corporeal form.

Qadira goes still as Hazel digs her nails into the faerie's arm.

'Who did you say we'd be fighting again?' the Asthori whispers.

The *kehrasa* cannot tear her eyes away. 'The Ashen God.'

Hazel's nails bite into her palm the instant Qadira dissolves into shadow.

Iliyah's eyes linger on the space Qadira had occupied. She's known the faerie over half her life; she never thought she'd be abandoned. But they're alone now. The look in Rahat's eyes says enough.

'Whatever is to come,' says Iliyah slowly, 'it is an honour fighting with you.'

Rahat gives her hand a squeeze, relishing in its warmth.

'If I die,' she continues, after a sharp breath, 'then at least I got to see you, one last time.'

'You speak like we're already dead,' Hazel snaps. 'Stop it.'

Iliyah can't help her tearful chuckle, even as Rahat casts her eyes down to the mist. 'You're right,' she says, as her aunt forms before them in the smoke. The woman of walking destruction holds out her arms, summoning dual swords of night as she takes her first steps toward them with a demon's face. 'When this is done, Nisha will be the one conquered in Death's Isle.'

Yet the responding laugh of the sorceress sends a spark up the back of her neck. Through her monster's muzzle of lupine features, her words are slurred, growled, snarled. The sounds of thunder and beasts lurking in the dark. 'I might say that of you,' says Nisha, though it is not her voice. The shapeshifter twists the hilts of her blades with such skill that there is no doubt that this is not the woman they defeated. The Ashen God's voice of gravelled velvet purrs through the dead woman's mouth. 'All that work to bring down an Empire,' it says, its movements undeniably feline, 'and my servant is bested by *children*.'

Ignoring the pain in her side, Rahat reaches for her dagger.

When the god turns its eyes on her, her arm stills, useless.

At her side, Iliyah pulls back her shoulders and stares the god down. With the twisted face of Nisha's wolf form, this is no more a god than it is a dream. What was it that her mother always used to say? *There is always at least one way to win an impossible battle.* Digging a dagger out of the sheath at her thigh, she brandishes the blade. A blade cured with dragon's blood to protect against all things faerie. 'I suggest you stand down,' she says, with a voice so strong that it refuses to betray how she shakes.

The wounds to Nisha's face morph as the god reverts that wolf-face to human. The crusted red blood flakes as its mouth twists into a grotesque smile. The blood which had dribbled down the sorceress in her last fight has dried. The dark colours her, the sun reflecting each colour with each movement. Dark skin, dark blood. The smoke curls in the woman's eyes, now a glassy grey. Dead.

As the woman creeps closer, Hazel snakes a hand over her nose and mouth. There are many things she's smelt in her short life, but nothing matches this. The dead reanimated... Her eyes are erratic, psychotic. Glowing.

Lips the colour of muddy water split open with the god's smile. Blood cakes her face. Smoke oozes from her nose, her mouth, her eyes. The closer she comes, the grislier the sight. Rahat gulps down hard, fighting to keep her eyes on the monster before them as she looks to Hazel, white as a sheet.

'You don't have to fight,' she tells her. 'Find the horses. We'll catch up.'

Iliyah watches them out the corner of her eye. When Hazel's glance meets her eye, she turns her attention back to the possessed body of her aunt. 'It's up to you,' she tells Hazel, as she tightens her grip at her blade.

Slowly, the Asthori takes a step back, her eyes glued to the god not but a few yards away. Nisha raises a sword in her direction with the tilt of her head, brandishing the smoke which forces Hazel back. A scream is ripped from the girl as she's forced to the ground just past the trees, and the darkness forms a wall before her.

Iliyah raises her blade to attack but Rahat tugs her back, unsure.

The reanimated corpse flashes that grin, blood smearing its face as it turns on them. And sees how the wall of night curls in the wind behind them.

'There.' The god sweeps a hand back, reeling in the darkness about their feet. 'The girl is gone.' Then with the flick of a finger, the ashen cloud explodes. Darkness fills their sight, blocking out the light. The god's laughter fills the dark, enveloping them. Hair raises at the back of their necks. The smoke is steaming, *burning*. Embers stick in their hair, threatening to alight. Smoke plumes before their eyes. It sticks in their nostrils, strangles the air from their lungs. They cannot hear Hazel's screams.

And then it is gone. The cloud is wiped away as if time is in rewind. Air rushes into their lungs all in one gulp, forcing itself into their bodies as if they were drowning. Yet Iliyah stands firm, that cured dagger in hand.

All around them, the smoke stands in a ring, blocking out sight of the trees and leaving the ground uncovered. A precaution to keep them from being interrupted. Or perhaps to ensure that Hazel will not interfere.

The fallen castle lays strewn across the dead earth, stones scattered over blackened grass and stripped dirt. That cloud was living death.

No life could have survived it. Rahat's finding it harder to stand by the second. Buckling knees threaten to collapse beneath her. Her calves ache, her bones scream. Her side feels split anew. As the pain arcs, her blade drops from her shaking hand. She drops to her knees, unable to open her eyes against the pain that consumes her.

The Ashen God grins, flashing those sharpened teeth as it takes in the scene. Two are not here to battle. One is too injured to fight. And the last is nothing more than a dream weaver.

'Relinquish the body of my aunt,' orders the *shehzadi*.

The god tilts its head. 'I was under the opinion you had no care for her.'

'I don't,' she says, biting back insults, 'but she deserves a proper burial.'

As if considering this, the god drops its dual swords to Nisha's sides. Thinking it over, the god goes still, though the smoke roils from Nisha's nostrils like a freshly snuffed fire. Iliyah almost expects her aunt's eyes to open.

They do not.

Sparing a glance to her right, she finds Rahat grasping at her side. The Delorrene's broken out in a sweat. It smears the dried blood from the battle across her face.

The dead grass crunches under Nisha's feet. Iliyah dares glance up, to find the god still in place several feet away.

She turns back but nearly a second to Rahat, and the *rajkumari* screams.

'IL—'

Iliyah raises her dagger as she spins back, just in time to catch Nisha's silent double blades. The impact rocks through her as she takes a calculated step for balance. If it hadn't have been for Rahat, she would have been sliced in two. Or three. The double blades grit against her dagger, the *screech* making her cringe.

Slippers grinding into the earth, Iliyah slides backward with the force of the god's swords. She will need to hold out.

By their feet Rahat cowers, covering her wounds and gasping for breath. One wrong move, and it's all over. Not only for herself, but for Rahat. She won't let that happen.

Gritting her teeth, she pushes back into the twin blades. A grunt rips its way up her throat as she forces Nisha back; their weapons swing back down to their sides. Desperate to keep the god away from Rahat, she dances to the left. And maybe her prayers are answered when the god follows the feign.

Rahat groans, drawing the attention of the god back —

—and Iliyah brings down her dagger, only to be narrowly stopped before the tip of the blade can slice through Nisha's skin. Already covered in blood—and blood that doesn't flow—she cannot see whatever damage she may cause. But that doesn't matter. The gods eyes are glowing. She has but seconds left to prove herself before the god decides this little game is over.

Dancing back, she takes another swing, only to be forced backward by a swell of the darkness guarding them. Her scream rings out across the clearing as she's propelled into the ruins of the fallen tower. Against her exposed skin, the stone is gritty, smooth with blood. Her blood. Iliyah looks down at herself; her hands are split open, her forearms covered in cuts.

'What a weak thing you are,' the god purrs, taking lazy strides. 'I knew a creature like you once. A Sylongí girl.' When the god wets Nisha's lips in anticipation, Iliyah feels ready to be sick. 'She fought back, too. A little thing like that, I couldn't resist.' Reaching out a hand for Iliyah's face, the god smiles a feline grin. It's only when Iliyah bolts out of reach that the god growls. 'I ate what parts of her soul I could then threw her to the beasts.'

A jolt races through Iliyah as she stares up at her dead aunt's face. '—Taeng?'

The god simply laughs, that chuckle growing more ominous as it raises those twin swords. Iliyah brings her blade up to meet her metal. Keeping her eyes upon the face of the creature, she ignores the rotting features she once knew. Because this is not her aunt anymore. This is something worse.

Rahat watches, helpless on the ground as Iliyah faces the Stranger. The rotting sorceress seems taller, even as her reanimated form stumbles in its approach. Those unseeing eyes stare right through her.

Iliyah's blade catches Nisha's arm, but the god bats her away as easily as an insect. The *shehzadi* grunts, knocked back into the towering stones.

'*Now*,' purrs the god, turning its eyes to rest upon Rahat.

On her knees, Rahat scrambles away. The *rajkumari* tries to push to her feet but her side cries out. Her skin rips apart, forcing screams from her lips. Only a few strides, and the god is standing over the cowering woman. Sword raised.

'NO!' Iliyah roars.

The sword in Nisha's hand gleams. The sunlight bounces back at Iliyah, and it's the last thing the god sees. For as Nisha swings the sword, Iliyah plunges her hand through Nisha's sternum.

The bones slice through Iliyah's skin. She whimpers, but the look on Nisha's face is worse. The creature's face morphs. Ashen smoke spills from her eyes, coating Rahat in black blood at their feet. Iliyah daren't move closer to Rahat as the god looks down at the wrist protruding from their chest. Blood oozes afresh from the corners of her mouth. 'You—you are too weak,' the god whispers with a breathless chuckle. 'You wouldn't.'

But Iliyah doesn't care what it has to say. 'You knew how this would end.'

Iliyah gives a squeeze, making Nisha's features convulse. Those eyes slam open, bright silver and searching her niece's face. Alive. Part of Nisha may actually be alive in there.

'S-stop!'

It makes her pause, to see Rahat trying and failing to hoist herself up.

'She tried to kill you,' Iliyah reminds her. 'She tried to take you away from me.'

Nisha's sharp nails dig into Iliyah's skin, slicing it open with each desperate attempt to get her to release the heart. Though the possessed woman makes no sound, the expressions sparking across her face make them feel sick.

Iliyah swallows back the tears that threaten to topple. 'She,' she says again, choking back the emotion as she crushes the heart in her hand, 'she tried to take you from me.'

One last, final blow. Nisha's claws slice down Iliyah's arm as the *shehzadi* destroys the sorceress' heart. The darkness fades from her eyes, turning them glassy. And the heart in her hand becomes no more than dust as she wrenches her hand free from the chest cavity.

It's a sickening sight. Crashing to her knees, Nisha falls face-first as the ashen cloud dissipates. The wavering smoke looks like it's taken legs to creep into the jungle, fleeing the scene. But the sorceress is still, her life-force destroyed.

With disgust, Iliyah drops the dusty remains of the heart. The cuts covering her arm—from bones, from fingernails—sting beyond belief. Casting her eyes over the dead field, she at last takes a breath. Pain ricochets through her chest as the sob she'd held in bubbles over. Battling her aunt had been more a matter of the mental than physical, but the strength it takes to puncture someone's sternum with your fist is mind-boggling. The impact should have shattered her hand. Taking another deep breath, she fights against letting the pain overwhelm her.

'I-Iliyah,' Rahat gasps out from the ground where she's huddled.

Her eyes slam open. *Rahat.* Ignoring the tears at her cheeks, she refuses to cry for the aunt she just murdered. *Murdered.*

She refuses.

And yet, when she stumbles toward Rahat, she can't stop herself from giving in. On her knees she pulls Rahat into her arms and lets the sorrow engulf her. And Rahat is transfixed. She knows she should look away; she should give Iliyah privacy in grief. But she can't tear her eyes away, even in her pain. Iliyah's never cried like this before.

Bone-breaking sobs rock through her, forcing her back as she stares up into the sky. The *shehzadi* fights to keep her face hidden from her lover; hands running through her hair, she cannot even face the sunlight. The light feels too pure for someone like her now.

Through blurry eyes, Rahat watches. Over her shoulder she spies Hazel, the *lindélofs'* reins clutched in her hand. Metres away, half-hidden in the trees, and the Asthori cannot bear to take another step toward them, their faces hidden in each other as they grieve what they might have lost. But they're alive.

'It's all over now,' whispers Rahat to herself, her breath hitching at the spark in her ribs. Just in her sight, she spots a slithering of shadows. Qadira, reappearing in the trees now that her sacred god is defeated. The *kehrasa* watches them carefully, her features impartial as she surveys the grounds.

'There are no more demons to fight,' Rahat says, though she can't be so sure. There will be demons waiting for them upon their return. That they have kept their hearts a secret for so long has ensured that there will be blood.

Slowly, the pain in Rahat's side is subsiding. A glance to Qadira, and she can see the *kehrasa* muttering spells under her breath. If it weren't for Iliyah, she knows the faerie would heal them skin-to-skin. But for now, this will have to do. That tingling spreads through her, warming her to the core once more.

A light wind whistles through the trees. In the distance, martens call to each other. The silence of the field cocoons them, and Iliyah soon stills in Rahat's arms. The *shehzadi* only raises her head at the soft sounds of the *lindélofs* a little way off. Confusion spreads as she looks to Rahat, then to Qadira above them in the trees. The faerie ducks her head in a low bow before brushing her brow with her fingers.

Iliyah's eyes keep the faerie pinned as her face goes taut.

Without a word, the *kehrasa* disappears from the trees to appear by the body's side. A soft snarl, and Qadira embers the body. Without flame, the body bursts into a fit of heat, before drifting away on the wind as nothing but sparks.

'Come on,' says the faerie, her deep voice sympathetic as she looks the exhausted, bloodied girls over. 'We've a long ride ahead of us.'

17

Two whole days, and no one has said a word. The days are long beneath the scorching suns. The trees whisper as they pass, speaking of safe passage. And with Qadira leading them, not a creature has reared their ugly head. The darkness of the quest has lifted, the whole jungle rejoicing its freedom. For there is no more to fear, now that the Ashen God has lost its willing host and been banished back to the Neverworlds.

Upon Prakaash's back, Iliyah wraps her arms tight around Rahat. The wounds ripped open in the final battle were stitched back together by Qadira, though Iliyah's wounded forearms remain scratched but not bloody. Her *salwar*, on the other hand, is torn, the shoulders ripped open to reveal the creamy skin beneath.

Tight, her arms hold Rahat; tight, Rahat holds Prakaash's reins.

They've travelled like this for days, each one wishing to speak but unsure of what to say. Travelling by their side, Hazel keeps her head down.

The jungle looks different this way. The colours are more vibrant, the air is sweeter; there is no underlying dread lacing its way through the canopies.

So had the creatures only roamed the jungles because their master was alive? Iliyah rests her head at Rahat's shoulder. She keeps expecting something to go wrong.

'Rahat,' she whispers at the rider's ear.

'Mm?'

'Relax,' she says, running a hand over her arm, 'please. You've been tense since we started moving.'

Ahead, Qadira throws back a glance with a small smirk. 'One more day, Your Highnesses, I promise,' she tells them, wrapping herself in darkness before splitting into shadows and sand. Seconds later, she reappears a few steps ahead. The *kehrasa*'s image shifts, her tail flicking like a satisfied feline's.

Iliyah's warm hands at Rahat's arms make her take a deep breath. That touch... She has been longing for it to be hers for years. Now, it finally is. Tears prick at the back of her eyes as she rests a hand over Iliyah's. Their fingers entwine.

'Is everything okay?' whispers Iliyah at her ear, too low for the others to hear.

Rahat nods, allowing herself to rest back into her lover just a little. 'It's just,' she says, wetting her lips to smother the grin that threatens to make her cry, 'I almost died... We almost lost... And I've never been so happy.'

'Mm.' Iliyah presses her forehead into the crook of Rahat's shoulder. 'Me neither.'

Beside them, Hazel clears her throat and shifts in her saddle. A light kick at Bijalee's side has the *lindélof* traipsing to join Qadira up ahead. 'Should we think of settling in for the night?' she asks, her voice gruff with not speaking for days. 'Soon the light will be gone.'

In answer, the *kehrasa* lifts her head to the skies peeking through the canopies. The green reflected is such a deep shade it's like emeralds. 'We've an hour,' she says, eyes pinned on the sky, 'maybe more. We'll stop shortly.'

The *lindélofs* whinny, their tails tossing like Qadira's as they follow. Hazel shifts in her saddle, undeniably feeling the pain as she twists back to look at them. 'Why did Nisha attack you anyway?' she asks.

It's the question no one's dared to mention these past two days. Even Rahat has considered the reasons why and never imagined to ask. For at the mention of her aunt's name, Iliyah's arms loosen about Rahat's middle.

She had stolen the life of her aunt. Iliyah had murdered someone to save the girl in her arms. Gulping, the *shehzadi* shifts slightly at her back.

Only once does Qadira give Hazel a look. 'You should not have asked,' she purrs, in that deep and brooding voice. 'It is rude to speak of the dead so soon.'

But Hazel ignores her. 'I still don't understand. Iliyah, you're not the heir to the Empire. It doesn't make sense why she'd go after you and—'

Iliyah opens her mouth to speak, only nothing comes out. Still, Hazel hangs on her word. 'I,' the word sticks in the back of her throat. Her hands tense beneath Rahat's at the reins. The *rajkumari* can feel her body shaking. Another long exhale, another deep breath. 'Nisha, she, uh...'

'You don't have to.' Rahat gives her hands a squeeze.

'No.' With a shake of her head, Iliyah looks up to the canopies overhead to spy the langur monkeys with their tails swishing. So like the satisfied flow of Qadira's tail —she's never seen it so. Her sight is drawn back to Hazel as she brings herself to a slow. 'Nisha believed only the most gifted should rule.'

'Well that's silly,' Hazel says with a scoff. 'The eldest rules.'

Rahat fixes her cousin with a look. Qadira clicks her tongue.

'Careful, little one, if you keep on interrupting you may never get your story.'

Hazel pokes her tongue at Qadira's back, making the faerie chuckle as she continues to lead them over the short bridge of a stream. The cool waters bubble over the rocks, the sound so heavenly that Iliyah wants nothing more than to curl up beside its banks and sleep. As if she can hear the water wraiths singing.

'Nisha,' says Iliyah, her tongue stilling at the name. 'My father says she always thought she might be chosen by the gods as an oracle. And the gods *did* smile on her, when she was younger. She was good, and kind. A fine heir. But that all meant too much to her. Ma says it was obvious when she was my age—that there was something so different about her that it was impossible to miss.

'The gods' favour became everything to her. And as she gave more of herself to the gods, the more of herself she lost. The power went to her head. She became almost indestructible, and still, she wasn't an oracle like she wanted. My grandfather began to fear what she might do. So she was passed over as heir. And she killed him in an explosion that destroyed nearly half the palace.

'She was thrown into the dungeons and was there over a year. My father took the throne, he married my mother, and Ma was about to marry Safia but... She broke out. Melted the dungeon bars where they stood. The explosion drained so much out of her that she had to wait and build back those reserves—in the way that only evil magic works. Pure magic cannot extend itself. There are limits that stop that from happening. But, I think... maybe that was the moment she totally lost my father's trust. Before that, I think he thought she could still be saved.

'When she came back, she promised to take the throne for herself. She knew the palace corridors better than even those who had forged them. So she left. And my father lost himself for a while... They say it was only when Saadi was born that he became himself again. Nisha meant as much to him as his own soul.'

Iliyah drops her head against Rahat's neck, her brow pressed against her nape.

Ahead, Qadira's tail flicks with agitation.

'Wow,' Hazel breathes, unable to believe it—that Nisha had been good.

'And now you have your story, little one,' says Qadira, her form flickering in and out of sight.

Rahat watches the *kehrasa* and her cousin closely. The expression plastered across Hazel's face is one of shame. She should never have asked. But now the story is out.

She swallows hard, drawing their attention. 'Maybe we should stop for the night,' she suggests.

Before them, Qadira forms into sight. Her carnelian eyes focus on the *rajkumari* before she carefully bows her head. The *shehzadi* presses a gentle kiss to Rahat's shoulder, a silent thank-you. Qadira again lifts her gaze.

'I'll scout the area,' she says, and disappears in a plume of darkness.

Awkward, Hazel dismounts to lead Bijalee back to the trickling stream. 'I, uh,' she says, unable to settle her sight on Iliyah, 'I'll be right back.' She doesn't wait for their nods to leave them in the gentle quiet of the jungle.

*

In the winking firelight, Rahat watches the flames dancing in Iliyah's eyes. There was once a time where she thought none of this possible.

'I'm marrying your brother,' she says softly, watching as the realisation flickers across Iliyah's face. The *shehzadi* brings her palm up to cup Rahat's cheek.

'I know,' she whispers.

At their backs, Hazel is long asleep. Her quiet snores are enough to make Qadira nudge the girl onto her side. She's doing her best to ignore the princesses whispering between themselves. So many years, they have whispered in their beds, and all those years, they have denied what it truly meant for them.

'I'll call it off,' says Rahat, tracing a soft kiss over Iliyah's jaw.

'I'm sorry,' she says, making Rahat's brow furrow. 'For making you this way,' she reiterates, but Rahat only shakes her head. 'If it weren't for me, we wouldn't be in this mess.'

'If it weren't for you,' Rahat counters, 'I wouldn't know love.'

'But you'd be the Queen of Delorran,' Iliyah shoots back.

Rahat runs a hand over her hair. 'Only because Saadi forced my brothers to agree to abdicate if I married Tahir, Iya. It's just another form of control. I wouldn't *actually* be Maharanee. I'd simply be a servant, all in the name of peace. And Delorran would be lost.'

Iliyah shakes her head, but Rahat grabs her chin.

'No. Look at me.'

The *shehzadi* lifts her eyes to Rahat's.

'I love you, Iliyah.'

The *shehzadi*'s bottom lip quivers as she fights against tears.

Rahat says it again, putting more into her words. 'I *love* you. And I refuse to marry Tahir when I can have the future I want with you.' Her look has Iliyah captured. 'Okay?'

The *shehzadi* nods, wetting her trembling lips as she sucks in a sharp breath. 'I love you, too,' she admits. It's the first time she's said it.

A smile spreads over Rahat's face. 'Okay,' she says, unable to banish that smile as Iliyah rests a hand along her throat and kisses her. Kisses her like it's all that could ever matter.

When she pulls back, Iliyah closes her eyes, resting her forehead against her lover's. 'And,' her sharp breath fighting against sobs catches in the back of her throat, 'I want a future with you. I want to be happy.'

But as they drift to sleep, peace making the descent easy in each other's arms, Qadira lays awake, staring into the night. She doesn't believe it will be so easy for the princesses to simply take their happiness. The Empire does not forgive so easily.

*

The city of Ajrapur stretches out before them with the morning sun. Glimmering and sparking with golden-domed roofs and delicate turrets reaching into the sky. Seated at the top of a hill, the city is wondrous; it commands attention as it stares out over the jungles. Ajra-pur, the city of colour.

The gates stand open, allowing merchants and travellers passage. People of all lands enter the cit to find a world exploding with magic. Lining the city walls are mosaics of myths, legends, and heroes. Ancient ocean swells mark the left gate; the jungles and deserts of the north, the right. Music drifts down from balconies and platforms, the city scattered upon dozens of levels as it climbs the ambitious hill it stands upon. The people dance and sing, raising their voices as they rejoice this morning, a day of feasting. The people celebrate, but does the palace beyond the city gates?

Led by Qadira, they filter in through the crowd. Many pay them little mind, but the gleaming morning sun glints off the *lindélofs'* backs in a way that the crowds cannot ignore. Passing through the gates, they become one with the masses, filtering through the city's open streets. Women sit at balconies and weave on their looms. Children bolt through the side-streets, stopping to catch their breath when they reach the foot of the promenade so as not to be trampled. So many people. So much life.

Rahat had forgotten this feeling. Ajrapur, a city fit to burst at the seams. Magic, wonderment, the people, the music, the food, and the *smells*. Rich tamarind and garam masala floats through the air, the scents so strong they're divine. The sweat of the people, the warmth of the sun, the crisp taste of magic upon the tongue!

This is home.

It's so early the sun only just peeks over the surrounding hills. A soft pink, a dusty orange lingers in the sky's canvas, soon fading to that rich blue. It shines through the spiral turrets of the grand houses.

From so low in the city, they can hardly see over the walls to the palace that stands at its opposing side. There is only one way to approach the Royal Palace from the city: and that is through it. There are other ways, of course, if one wishes to avoid the fuss of such a place, but Rahat cannot not resist. It has been so long since she has seen her own city.

At her back, Iliyah beams as she takes it all in, this place of wonder. As the people begin to notice their *rajkumari*, life goes on. It is only once the children take in their gasps of wonderment that time appears to stop.

'RAJKUMARI! RAJKUMARI!' they cry over the sounds of the city.

While Qadira pauses, her shoulders going tense, Rahat smiles at the young boys who called out. Their faces are broad with grins, revealing lost teeth or bright blue tongues from sweets. Tiny children, all lined up along the walls of buildings to avoid the crowds.

'*RAJKUMARI! RAJKUMARI!*'

A deeper voice booms, 'THE *RAJKUMARI* HAS RE-TURNED!'

And the city-goers part like waves. Cramming themselves together, the people stop to turn and take in the sight of their returning princess. By their side, Hazel goes still, plastering that smile on her face. There are the cries of happiness; Iliyah spies a woman crying at her balcony, reaching out her hands as if she might be able to touch them. These are the people trapped beneath the Empire.

Of course they love Rahat so, she tells herself, bowing her head and smiling. For her own people have never loved her with such ferocity. *She brings them hope.*

And their hope has returned.

'A BLESSING UPON THE *RAJKUMARI*!'

A plume of coloured powder litters the air, raining down on them. Bright purples and yellows and reds. Rahat laughs, but doesn't shake the powder from her hair as Hazel does. Iliyah runs her hands over the pigments on her skin, amazed as the colour fades into her flesh, colouring it red. In Rahat's hair, it looks like magic. And perhaps it is.

Another cloud of bright red is thrown into the air, sprinkling them in bright blessings. Rahat raises a hand for her people, keeping the other at Prakaash's reins.

With Qadira at their head, the people are careful to mind her. They give her a wide berth before squeezing together to brush the sides of the *lindélof* they ride upon. Iliyah squishes in tight behind Rahat, flattening her body to hers in fear.

Archways overhead are decorated with dozens of people screaming their praises. When the *rajkumari* left, deserting them mere days before the wedding, their hope was stripped from them. But now with her return they may find peace again. They may find their lives no longer under the rule of the Empire.

Climbing the few steps up into the next district with thinner streets, the horses keep their heads down on the weathered ground. Little girls toss about rose petals, and a child upon her father's shoulders presents Rahat with a wreath of blooms. Without missing a beat, the *rajkumari* bends in the saddle. And to Iliyah's amazement, the child whispers a prayer for her *rajkumari* as she places the wreath about Rahat's neck. In return, Rahat kisses the child's cheek and traces a thumb over the father's forehead with a whispered 'Thank you.'

Back in the saddle, she sits upright—for once, not leaning back against Iliyah, though Iliyah wishes she might. Even as the daughter of an Emperor, she has not been in crowds so large with so little a guard.

As if sensing her trepidation, the *kehrasa* looks back to catch her gaze. Those feline eyes glint with the morning sun.

More clouds of purple rain down on them from some indeterminable balcony. Flowers lay strewn across the city steps. Even the air tastes warm, crisp on the tongue as spices waft from stalls stationed along the streets. Merchants call out, selling their wares and holding them high as the *rajkumari* passes on her shining steed. The sun in her hair is a welcome touch as she offers them smiles, smiles which send them into a frenzy.

Songs emerge from the masses, a soft tune carried by young women which is soon taken up by all. It's a song of home, a song of love returned. A song of triumph. And triumph Rahat did.

'Breathe,' whispers Hazel out the corner of her mouth.

The order almost makes Iliyah laugh; though she's glad to see someone has noticed how the people have almost entirely ignored her. Only a handful have reached out to touch her trousers as she passes, muttering their blessings for the revived *shehzadi*. She wonders, *Do they know what happened to her?*

Without warning, Rahat takes Iliyah's hand in hers and raises it into the sky. A triumph, she supposes. No, a *declaration*. The crowds do not waver; their cries and their songs grow louder, as if to say: *We stand with you.*

Out the corner of her eye, Iliyah spots two men leaning into each other, their arms entwined as they watch the impromptu procession. The smiles on their faces can mean only one thing: that they too are like them. Iliyah waves in their direction, and is relieved when they wave back. Though how anyone can see in this festival of colour is a mystery. Blues, greens, purples, reds, yellows—they all explode across the laneways, the arches, the paths, the turrets. Houses are painted thick with the powders thrown. Flowers lazily decorate the streets where they were tossed.

As they climb higher into the city, the silhouette of the royal palace grows. Beyond the city walls, it stands at the very head of the tallest neighbouring hill. From where they stand in the centre of Ajrapur, it lays before them, its towering gates imposing in how they are closed. And still, the people move with them. The towers of the palace reach for the skies, casting their shadows over the hill and against the city's outer walls. Imposing, intimidating, and unutterably beautiful. There is nothing else like it in the world.

The more districts they pass, the more colour there is to find amongst the people. These people are brown and black of skin, with few lacking any colour at all—Lyrans or Belanósí who crossed the borders for the Lands of Summer. The few pale faces in the crowd are flushed with heat, sweat beading at their brows, yet still they call out for the returned *rajkumari*.

Except, Rahat's eyes are set forward, and only forward. The palace before them grows closer, closer, and she cannot deny the excitement and trepidation. This place is her home, this grand palace of white, golden marble, and stone.

Iliyah still squeezes Rahat's middle. 'Breathe,' she whispers back, and feels responding Iliyah's smile as the girl leans into her neck.

'I'm fine,' she promises, though they both know it's a lie.

Rahat grips her hand tighter.

Deeper into the city they traverse, following the direct path through the towering buildings. The city gates grow before them, threatening to block out the light. Upon them are the myths of the Summer Lands: of the people all at once emerging from the sea's crashing waves, their skin as blue as the waters from whence they came. Long flowing hair moves in circular wave-motions across the wall, almost thirty feet high. They are beautiful, the mosaics crafted of thousands of glittering stones and precious gems. Before them the gates lay open, though few leave the city in pursuit of the palace.

As the arch welcomes them, a piece of Rahat wishes they might stay. That she might flourish amongst the love of her people, that they might teach her to survive out here, out from under the watch of those in the palace walls.

Perhaps I was never made for palace life, she thinks, with one last look back at the people rejoicing her return.

Uphill they trek with the palace shining before them. It grows before them in size, the imposing mansion of marble becoming almost impossible as they take in its pure majesty. Towers and turrets of white stone, multiple structures make up the palace of Ajrapur. Many levels form the palace beyond its gates, mirroring the platforms and steep stairs of the city. The palace was crafted as sister to the glimmering Ajrapur: a colourless sibling to that city of artists.

A fluttering in her chest makes Rahat take a deep breath at looking up at her ancestral home. She hesitates to dismount when they reach the closed gates. Either side, guards stand at the ready. They do not miss a moment as they rake their eyes over their company, and open the gates without a word.

Iliyah glances at Hazel, who stares right back. Qadira shares their uneasy look, but Rahat dismounts Prakaash and leads him through the gates by the reins before she can protest. Qadira's almost surprised when she spots Rahat's grin. She had thought the girl trepidatious over returning. Apparently not.

When the gates close behind them, the guards of the other side blow on their trumpets an elaborate tune. 'THE *RAJKUMARI* HAS RETURNED!' they cry, as if their spectacle in the city had not been enough of a herald.

Trumpet still in hand, one of the guards gestures for the *rajkumari* and her company to enter the palace gardens. From the courtyard runs a messenger, out of breath and red in the face. The young boy pauses long enough only to bow before requesting they follow.

As Iliyah and Hazel dismount, an unnoticed servant steps forward to take the *lindélofs'* reins. The Asthori almost whimpers at handing over Bijalee's rein. She gives the beast one last kiss goodbye on the muzzle before traipsing off after her cousin and Iliyah. Qadira, it seems, took the moment of brief distraction to transform herself into shadow. Where she might have gone, Hazel isn't sure, though she has a feeling she won't see her until the time comes.

Because, inevitably, the time *will* come, as it always does.

The messenger guides them through the gardens, the outer houses, and through the palace, until finally they come to a stop outside the audience chamber. Those they pass stop to stare, having thought their *rajkumari* dead or never to return. Only, it is not Rahat who steals their attention, but Iliyah.

'She lives,' they whisper.

'But no one survives dead magic,' others murmur in dark corners.

The *shehzadi* does her best to ignore them, but it soon becomes overwhelming. Only once they come to stop outside the intimidating rosewood doors does she turn to Rahat. 'I don't think I can do this,' she says, speaking so fast she trips over her words. 'Let's run away while we still have the chance.' She steps back, turning, but Rahat pulls her to her chest.

'Trust me,' she says, but Iliyah shakes her head adamantly. 'Trust me as I trusted you to save my life.' Placing their conjoined hands over her heart, she stares up into Iliyah's eyes. At least a head taller than her, it's a fair distance. 'They won't harm you,' she says. 'Promise.'

Hazel behind them says nothing. The messenger with his hands at the door remains silent, though his ears go red. He's waiting for their word.

From inside, they can hear the council shouting. Strong voices, all booming and echoing off the domed ceiling of the audience chamber. Deep voices are met with lyrical tones, snide and quick. This may be more difficult than they thought.

Catching Iliyah's look, Rahat raises a brow. 'What's the worst that can happen?' Behind them, Hazel drops her head to whisper, 'Don't answer that.'

The *shehzadi* frowns when they share a look. Then, slowly, she turns to the messenger, his hands shaking at the bronze door-handles. A soft nod, and the boy pushes them open.

Inside the chamber the argument continues, only growing in volume. As the door opens, a man throws himself from his seat to yell, only to be interrupted. The young man waves a hand, dismissing his interrupter to roar, 'We must give them *time!* It has been but six days; have *faith!*' He yells so loud spittle matts his cropped beard. The bells at his ears jangle as as he shakes his head, staring down a woman who dares argue.

'We do not know this—they might be—'

And as the Maharaja Ram Brijesh's eyes rest upon his daughter at the open door, he raises a silencing hand. The room around him goes still as someone pulls the yelling man and arguing woman back down into their seats. Confusion flows around the room as each and every one of them turns toward the door. They go still, frozen. But it is Tahir whose eyes Rahat finds first.

18

Twenty dignitaries and rulers seated about the table, and all of them with their eyes on three young women. *Holy hells.* Hazel feels fit to leap out of her skin. Just like the time she almost tore a priceless tapestry—only worse.

Tahir is the first to shake off the stupor, his eyes locked on Rahat as he pushes back from the table. The yelling man at his side watches openly as the Praitosí makes his way slowly around the table with all eyes on him.

'Rahat,' breathes the Maharaja, hardly believing his eyes. His daughter, home. Alive. He laughs a disbelieving laugh. 'Are you well?' he asks, unsure of what else to say.

A quick bow of her head, and a shared smile. 'Yes, *Abba*. And you?'

The Maharaja nods, unable to find his words.

The room is still, all but a few afraid to move. Officials sit forward in their seats, their hands plastered to the dark wood of the table as they watch, unable to keep themselves from doing so. Moments ago they had been arguing over the fate of Delorran, over whether Rahat might return. Only to find her returned, and with the thought-lost *shehzadi* in tow.

Iliyah locks eyes with her brother as he stands, Zehran almost throwing himself over the table to reach his sister's side. He reaches her first, wrapping his arms around her as he buries his face in her hair. 'I'm sorry,' he sobs. The boy's shaking. Iliyah runs a hand over his mussed hair, but does not relinquish Rahat's hold on her other hand. Their fingers entwine, even tighter than before. 'I failed you,' sobs Zehran, shaking uncontrollably, 'I'm so sorry.'

Reaching his side, Tahir places a silent hand at his brother's shoulder.

'You did that something stupid,' is all Tahir says to his bride, without sparing her a glance.

The words make Zehran go rigid. The *rajkumari* withers under their gaze until Zehran untangles himself from his sister to rest his hands on Rahat's shoulders. Eyes glued to his, she swallows hard.

'Thank you,' he says with a deep exhale. 'You saved my sister when I could not. I should have believed you.' The tears gleaming at his cheeks make her heart sink. When she nods, he sniffs and returns to his sister's side, to where Tahir stands cupping Iliyah's cheeks. 'You're safe?' he says. His hands traipse quickly down his sister's arms, checking for injuries until at last he stands before her, hands outstretched. His sister holds onto Rahat's hand like a life-line. He doesn't miss the gesture, nor the meaning of it. Giving a slight bow of his head to his betrothed, he flashes a resigned smile and turns to her father.

Her father, still in disbelief at the head of the council table.

Behind them all, in the corner of the room, a darkness starts to form like ink in water. A moment later Qadira forms herself in her swathes of black cloth from the shadows, to bow her head to those gathered. 'The queens are on their way,' she announces, and it's the first time Rahat realises that her mother and Iliyah's second mother aren't present.

Seated beside Rahat's father, Iliyah's parents stare at her with wide eyes. Her mother, the sweet Mahala, covers her mouth with a hand to keep the sobs from escaping. Silent tears stream down her flushed face. She'd thought Iliyah dead. At her side, the Emperor Bashshar laces an arm around her shoulders to pull her close. Neither has moved from their seat for fear this may be one of Iliyah's dreams.

Yet at the Maharaja's other side, Ashrit and Karnan have their heads bent together in whispering which even Qadira cannot make out. The two brothers, dressed head-to-toe in mourner's black, keep their eyes on their sister. As if she might disappear at any moment. Ashrit gives a nod to his brother. He flashes that brow-crinkling smile at his sister as Karnan removes himself from the table.

He's at her side in seconds, pressing a light kiss to her cheek as he runs a thumb over where her *tilak* would normally be. A sign of missing, of deep love. She returns the gesture as he leans in close. But he's much too pale for her liking, his skin ashen with exhaustion. His tired grin brings her back to the present.

'We're with you, if you want to make an announcement,' he whispers in her ear, and her thumb goes still at his hairline. He flashes the boyish grin that's always infuriated her. But there's something missing in his eyes. The *rajkumar* gives Iliyah a look as if she might understand. 'Marry my sister,' Karnan tells her.

Iliyah's blush deepens when she drops her eyes to their conjoined hands. Beside her, Tahir stands closest. With a look to his brother Zehran, the Praitosí *shehzadas* nod their agreement, albeit begrudging.

'This match is better suited than ours ever was,' Tahir tells his bride slowly, unable to hide the disdain in his voice. She's choosing his sister over him; he'd always known this day would come. Wetting his lips, he turns to his family, still seated and staring in disbelief at their returned child. 'I release the *Rajkumari* Rahat Brijesh from any agreements of marriage. At least, where I, *Shehzada* Tahir al Hiraj, am concerned.'

Iliyah squeezes Rahat's hand tighter, burying their joined hands in the folds of her *salwar* where they cannot be seen. The hair at the back of Rahat's neck stands on end in anticipation. A prickling sensation sits in her chest.

Tahir rests his eyes back on his would-be bride. 'But I never want to see your face again.'

Stilling her breath, Rahat feels the cold sinking in her chest. After a moment, she nods once, and the *shehzada* turns away from her.

The Praitosí Emperor gapes at his children, his mouth opening and closing like a dumfounded fish. Today was meant to be unremarkable. Today he had thought that they would release Delorran as they had always planned with an agreement to work together, though unfortunately without a wedding. And now...

Staring at his daughter, at the way she looks at Rahat, it suddenly seems all so clear. The way Iliyah had pestered him every time he set to ride to Ajrapur, how she always sent letters with him when possible. How she had asked, that one year, to live here amongst the Delorrene. How had he never seen it before?

'This is a grave insult.' He says the words before he fully comprehends them, watching Iliyah as her shoulders pull taut. 'To desert your betrothed—though for which, I will forever be grateful—and then refuse to marry him upon your return. You have put the fate of your country in a precarious position, Rahat.'

'I know.' She takes a step forward, tugging Iliyah's hand behind her and turning herself into a human shield. As if that might combat anything else her father has to say. The Maharaja simply sits with a hand resting at his turban, frustration scrawled across his chiselled features. This was not the turn of events he expected.

'Your Majesty, I understand that what I have done is betrayal, and I understand the danger I have placed upon my country,' she says, defying all odds and keeping her voice even. 'But I have done what I have done out of deep love for your daughter, and respect for the

Praitosí Empire. I ask that you try to understand what I thought was right.'

The Emperor furrows his brow, his sight switching between the woman petitioning before him and his daughter clutching her hand. 'Go on,' he bids.

Slowly, almost hesitant, Rahat brings Iliyah forward before their brothers. To stand together, hands clasped before them. A deep breath. 'I ask that you might... consider allowing me to marry Iliyah, instead. Allow our bond of peace not to flow between Tahir and I, but Iliyah and myself.'

The moment the words leave her mouth, she feels that heaviness lift from her chest. She no longer carries this world of guilt, this suffering that had plagued her for years. For no longer must she feel the need to hide.

At her husband's side, Mahala's eyes go wide. The Empress climbs to her feet, pushing back her chair which screeches against the polished floor. When she lifts her hand from her mouth, she's nodding. Chin quivering, eyes tearful, but she's nodding. 'Will this make you happy?' she asks her own daughter, in a voice thick with tears.

At seeing her mother so, Iliyah dissolves to tears. All she can muster is a nod. 'More than anything,' she says, gulping back her sounds of relief. 'I've wanted this more than anything,' she says again.

But the Emperor is shaking his head. 'A priestess cannot marry a princess for political gain. A priestess *cannot* take the mantle of her country. This is not the peace we agreed upon and—'

Silencing her husband, Mahala rests a hand at his shoulder with a radiant, tear-soaked smile. 'Let it be so,' she declares, making her husband balk, but she only shakes her head as she ignores him. 'You may marry when you wish.' Her tears turn to laughter, her joy over-flowing.

From the corner of the room, Qadira watches closely as the two princesses fall back against each other. Their faces speak of nothing more than happiness. Relief. But Qadira feels a crispness in the air. She wets her lips; this might be it.

The door behind the Maharaja's chair slams open, to reveal the Maharanee and the second Empress Safia Hiraj standing at the threshold. Rahat's mother Odelia hurls herself into the room for her daughter—but pulls herself up short.

It's the moment that Rahat kisses Iliyah's cheek that has the Maharanee stilled.

'Darling,' says the Maharaja from his seat, calling his wife over. The fear in his eyes makes her approach slow. Something here isn't right. 'Darling, Rahat's getting married,' he says, sniffing back the tears which threaten to fall.

'Yes,' says the Asthori Maharanee, with an obvious look.

'No.' Ram shakes his head and gives a small laugh. 'No, my love. To Iliyah.'

The silence starts to hum. The world about them freezes. Rahat feels a sharp pain in her chest as her mother turns her eyes on her, on them. On Iliyah.

But Safia strides through the room with her arms outstretched for her children. The happiness on her face glows as she takes Rahat and Iliyah and her sons into her arms. 'Thank you for bringing her home safe.' The Empress presses a gentle kiss to Rahat's forehead, as if she were a child. 'You have given us everything in the world.' The woman turns to her sons, flashing Tahir that same grin of his. 'Looks like you've another sister now,' she jokes, but the *shehzada's* only response is a begrudging smile. He had thought he would take Delorran. Now it is not so. Tahir gives his mother a look but she only shakes her head with a whispered, 'We'll find you a nice girl, win you the lands of Tehrar.'

That seems to keep him happy. He plants that indulgent smile on his face, so like Saadi's triumphant smirk. He'd never cared for her, not really. She'd always known.

'We can settle the matter of land later,' says Mahala.

Yet when Rahat looks up at her parents, her mother is still frozen to the bone. Pure rage colours her face a seething red. 'No,' she growls. 'No daughter of mine will be *that way*,' she says, drawing everyone's mortified attention. 'Men can't help themselves with their horseplay. But you? *No.*'

Before Karnan can hold her back, Rahat breaks away from those gathered. A gentle graze of her brother's hand down her back is all she feels as she steps forward. At the table, Ashrit shakes his head with a desperate look to his sister. *Don't do it*, he wills her, his hands white-knuckled on the table.

'You told me you loved me no matter what,' spits Rahat at her mother. She's had enough with this foolish judgement. Of what she insinuated of her brother. *And that he can be so resigned to it!* 'Are you even happy I came back?' she demands.

The Maharanee clenches her jaw. 'You were going to save your people.'

'Actually,' interrupts Emperor Bashshar, raising a hand without facing the Maharanee. He settles his bird-like gaze on his children. 'The agreement still stands...' A side-long look to his wife Mahala, who nods. 'Even though Iliyah cannot take a throne of her own. We have discovered we no longer find a need for *all* the lands of Delorran.' He nods. 'We find ourselves only asking for an agreement of trade, to increase your contribution to the Empire until our crops are replenished. The monsoons destroyed much; with work, we will again be self-sufficient.'

The Maharaja's mouth drops open in an 'O'.

'The Empire releases Delorran and wishes it peace,' says Bashshar, with a flick of his hand. 'We will no longer interfere with your matters unless you need aid. For now, we are at truce. *If* our ask is agreeable. If not we can always proceed with war.'

From his chair, the Maharaja nods his agreement.

'Which,' beams Safia, nodding to the Delorrene rulers, 'perfectly frees Rahat and Iliyah to marry, if they so wish.'

Deep down, Rahat thinks the woman too happy that the marriage is called off.

But Iliyah gives a shy nod, her hopeful eyes glued to Rahat's flushed cheeks. Looks like she's ignoring her second mother's grin.

'We do,' purrs the *shehzadi*, as the *rajkumari* flashes that nervous smile.

Yet the Maharanee strides forward. At her first movement, Ashrit throws himself from his seat to stand in her way. His features are set. His eyes gleam like flame. 'What is it that so repels you about *love*, Ma?' he demands, adding with a frustrated sigh: 'Leave them be.'

Behind them, Ram clears his throat. Drumming his fingers at the arms of his chair, he refuses to let this get out of hand. When at last his wife turns to him, he shakes his head. 'These girls have faced death together, my love,' he tells her, in a voice so gentle he might be whispering it between sheets. 'They have fought so much. And if this makes them happy, then so be it.'

Odelia goes taut. 'But—'

'THEY HAVE BEEN THROUGH ENOUGH!' roars Ram, at last getting to his feet.

The room goes silent in the ricochets of his voice. The domed ceiling captures all sound. The light gracing them through the stained glass feels too gentle, somehow. Those who watch, unable to do anything, sit uncomfortably.

In the corner by the open doors, Qadira rests back on the latticed screen leaning against the marbled walls. Shadows roll off of her in waves, softening the sounds of the echoes. 'They have fought for their lives,' she purrs. 'It would be cruel to make them fight for this too.'

A small smile plays at Ashrit's lips. 'Agreed,' he says, for the first time in his life agreeing with the desert faerie.

And slowly, those seated about the room find themselves nodding. Advisors and officials—all of whom had been debating not minutes ago over the fate of their country—they all nod, murmuring their agreement. For peace.

'No,' still says Odelia. Her voice is strained with pain. 'I refuse to accept this. It is not in my understanding. Rahat—' Her throat catches. It seems even now, she cannot say those words. And yet they bubble up her throat. '—I will never accept this.'

Finally, Rahat looks her in the eye. That deep sea green stares back at her, so foreign and out of place. Her flushed cheeks burn red against her alabaster skin. 'I know,' she says slowly, unable to stomach the disgust in her mother's eyes. 'But I don't care. I'm done with trying to make you happy.'

The queen grits her teeth. 'I am your *mother*,' she reminds her.

'And yet you refuse to accept me!' Rahat throws out her arms as if that might make her understand. None of this makes sense. 'How is that the way of a mother? How can I treat you as family if you will not do the same for me?'

Rahat stops herself before her tears can betray her. At her back, she feels a gentle touch of a hand—Iliyah, pressing her palm to the small of her back. Her brother joins her, placing a hand at her shoulder. They will stand with her.

Odelia opens her mouth to speak, but Ram slams a hand down on the table with a *thwap*, making the council flinch. 'We almost lost her forever!' he yells at his queen. 'Are you so ready to lose her again?'

Ignoring the fear in her husband's eyes, Odelia turns on Iliyah instead. '*You*,' she snarls, her pointed hand like a claw. 'You corrupted her.'

Confusion ripples across Iliyah's brow. Beside Rahat, she steps forward, doing her best not to laugh under such an accusation. Her voice remains smooth, calm, as she stares at the mother-in-law she'd never expected. 'I'm sorry you think so, Your Majesty. I'm sorry you can't see her still as your daughter.' A deep breath as she looks the Maharanee in the eye. 'But I will never apologise for loving her.'

The Maharanee Odelia Feiersinger has nothing to say. Not a single word will pass her lips. Of all the thoughts running through her mind, none seem to make their way to her tongue. Beside her, the Maharaja looks to his daughter with pained eyes.

'This...' mutters the Maharaja, cradling his head in his hands, his elbows on the table. 'This could have gone so much better.'

Everyone falls into quiet. Karnan frowns at his parents, disbelief written across his face. Hazel still stands by the doors; tears streak her cheeks. Never in her wildest dreams had she thought it might play out this way. Yet by the far doors, Qadira rests with her back against the wall. Slowly, as if she is the fading sun, the *kehrasa* dissolves into darkness. And the darkness disappears, nowhere to be seen as the Praitosí children huddle.

In the silence, Mahala takes a step back from the table. Draping her *dupatta* gracefully over her shoulder, she bids her husband rise as well. It's time to leave.

'I want you two to come with us to Praitos,' Mahala says firmly. Pulling her shoulders back and refusing to wipe the tears from her eyes, she commands the attention of the room. An Empress in her own right. 'Iliyah, Rahat, if you care not to live in Rahala, then I gift you the northern palace in Naares. It was once a gift to me, but is now yours. Now,' she stretches out her hand, 'will you join us?'

Zehran and Tahir take a step aside as the *rajkumari* reaches for Iliyah's mother's hand. Her hand is so warm it's as if she feels the glowing joy that shines in her eyes.

Rahat looks up at her father, but her mother has already left—stolen a moment in the silence to slip out the back door. Heart-wrenching sobs echo from down the outer hall, but Rahat pushes her guilt down. If she thinks about it, she might rush after her and give in. But Iliyah grasps her hand tight; no longer will she put her wants on hold. No longer will she give in and be something she's not.

'*Abba?*' Rahat asks, her voice breaking.

Her father does not move from his seat, though Ashrit places a hand at his broad shoulders. Father and son stand as one as he looks up to his daughter. His eyes graze over the Praitosí company standing with his daughter and Karnan. The words come from his mouth before he truly considers them, but he doesn't feel this is time for delay. 'You have my blessing to leave Delorran and make your place in the world together,' he says, meaning every word. 'If you need my aid, need only ask it. I am *disappointed* to see you leave, but I understand why you must. Know that you are welcome home.'

Ashrit's hand at his shoulder tightens as a silent sob rocks through his chest.

His voice is quiet now as he fights the grief threatening to tear him apart. 'I only want you to find your happiness, my darling.'

The way he sounds, the look on his face, it tears at her. Rahat breaks away from Iliyah and Mahala to reach her father's side. Ashrit murmurs a short 'good luck' as he brushes her forehead and presses a kiss to her cheek.

'*Abba,*' whispers Rahat, pressing her forehead to his.

Her father takes her face in his hands, his thumbs rubbing circles against her cheeks despite how he shakes. His breathing quivers, his cheeks damp with tears. His nose brushes hers before they pull back.

'Thank you,' she says softly, trailing a hand down his arm.

He shakes his head; he doesn't need her thanks. 'I just want you to be happy,' he tells her, gesturing back to Iliyah. 'Go.'

EPILOGUE

Ornate lattice-work casts shadows across the marbled steps leading into the palace gardens. Resting back over the steps, Qadira spreads out as she stares up at the Delorrene sky. The palace towers overhead, silent. All this silence since the news broke. What the final agreement was, who can know. The *kehrasa* left before it could be settled. But it looked like Feiersinger was losing.

The fresh icy waters of the fountain spark against her bare feet like spindrift waves. Against the red ink of her skin, it's heavenly. There was nothing like this in the jungle; she never wants to see a jungle again, if she can help it.

Nisha had manipulated her. The pain sits in her stomach at knowing that. And all for a sister... *I'll find her*, she thinks. Adilah has to be alive. She just has to.

Footsteps on the marble inside makes her sigh. It's Tahir; his sandalwood scent is stronger than ever before a journey, though she doubts he's realised such a small quirk. The *shehzada* stands motionless for a while beside her, simply staring at the fountain sprinkling icy kisses over her feet.

It's the fountain that most haunts her. In its centre stands a rearing Naj. The likeness is so true to reality that it makes her flesh crawl. Nightmarish claws. That whip-like tail. Though the ones Nisha controlled were a pine green and mottled brown. This one is alabaster, spouting water from its mouth.

The *shehzada*'s sigh is so deep that she looks up at him. 'What is the Asthori doing?' she asks him, curiosity hanging about her like a halo.

'She has no reason to stay,' he says, leaning against the pillar of the steps and keeping his sight out over the garden. 'She'll go with Rahat and Iliyah to Naares.'

Qadira's satisfied chuckle soon fades out to silent. 'And now your sister has all she ever wanted,' she says, feeling a grin pulling at her lips. 'But I want to know how *you* feel.' Knowing how her sight unnerves him, she turns her eyes back onto the fountain, that dreadful white Naj's teeth like talons.

If Tahir didn't know her, he might think her smug with that smirk. He shrugs, burying his chin in his chest. 'I guess it doesn't matter how I feel,' he says.

The *kehrasa* shakes her head. 'You think that,' she purrs, 'but it's not true. You may have lost a bride, you may have lost a kingdom, but now you've freedom to choose something of your own.'

He ignores her, falling silent until the trickling of the fountain becomes all but unbearable. The faerie at his feet flicks her tail, fur shining in the light. It's the satisfied sway of a happy kitty. The *shehzada* holds his breath, daring to speak it. 'You're not coming with us, are you?'

The faerie shakes her head.

'Where will you go?' he asks, watching her brow furrow.

'Rehmayan,' she says, tapping her toes against the garden grounds. She throws her head back to look at her master. 'Wings or no, I feel it is time to find her.'

He nods, finally understanding. 'Your sister,' he says.

She answers his nod with one of her own, resting her head back in the quiet to bathe in the sun. They sit silent for so long that Tahir isn't sure when she at last disappears, fading into shadow.

*

It's taken weeks, but they're finally here. Naares, the city of dreams.

The city itself stands in balcony-formation along a short cliff, its structures suspended above the opalescent river. All man-made hundreds of years ago. Walking through the city that morning had felt unlike anything Rahat has ever known. Iliyah never knew such beauty existed within the Empire—that there might be people who believe their purpose in life is solely to be happy.

After seeing this city, she now believes it. Earlier the sun had played its way across the sky as they explored the vast rooms of their new home. This is more than they ever could have imagined. And it's all theirs. This incredible place, this home of the first dream weavers.

Taking Rahat by the hand, Iliyah leads her through the rosewood doors at the end of the hall from their bedchamber. At the edge of one of the protruding balconies, they catch the gleaming of the lake before they enter the room. Its reflection shines across the ceiling forged of glass.

Rahat's breath catches as she stares up into the sky, the stars glittering just beyond their reach. In the centre of the room lay blankets and cushions, more than she can count. The smile on Iliyah's face tells her everything.

'I love this city,' Rahat says breathlessly.

A blush plumes at Iliyah's cheeks as she agrees. 'I've never been here before,' she says, twirling and pulling Rahat with her, 'but it already feels like home.'

A laugh bubbles up Rahat's throat, and she kisses her, overwhelmed to see that smile on her lover's face. Iliyah's lips are so soft she doesn't think she'll ever get used to them. When she pulls back, Iliyah's lashes are fluttering. Breathless. 'Maybe it's because this is the first time we can truly be ourselves,' she suggests, her words caressing the dream weaver's cheeks.

In response, Iliyah drags Rahat down onto the cushions. The princesses sink into the plush silks and velvets. They're so soft to the touch, she can't stop herself from laughing. 'I don't think I've ever been so happy.'

Iliyah hoists herself up onto her elbows to look at her. The moonlight shines like jewels in her hair. The stars glimmer in her eyes. 'No?' she asks. 'How about...' She leans in close, brushing a delicate kiss over Rahat's bottom lip. '...now?'

Rahat grins, her hands finding themselves at Iliyah's hips. The exposed skin beneath her fingertips feels like magic, like sparking flame. A deep rumble in the back of her throat makes excitement dance in Iliyah's gaze. 'You're getting there,' she says, with a voice like honey.

Cocky, Iliyah arches a brow and climbs atop her. She drags her tongue up Rahat's jaw, sending a shiver through her. 'Now?' she asks innocently, her fingers teasing at the hem of Rahat's blouse. 'Or...' Pressing a lingering kiss to the *rajkumari*'s lips, she finds herself smiling. She doesn't get a chance to finish her sentence. She's not sure she wants to, with how Rahat holds her.

Heat floods through them with each desperate kiss while, outside, the lights of Naares spark to life. Lanterns dance, strung up between homes spanning over the river. Above them, the dark world blossoms with colour as they spy the dancing lights to the north. This is home. And as they tangle themselves beneath the stars, the outside world is forgotten.

**

TURN THE PAGE FOR MORE QADIRA

ON LIGHT WINGS

Death comes on light wings.

With a prophecy like this trailing her, Tsarin has always thought her demise would come at the hands of her dragon. But as Johari tosses their wings and cries into the skies, she could never trust a creature more. The ice-blue water-dragon bows their head to their rider. Tsarin places a hand at her steed's nose, feeling the steam against her midnight skin. The scars across her arms glimmer in the dawn light. Travelling across the Rehmayan deserts has taken years. She's learnt things she never could have imagined. There are so many faerie species across these lands, so many of them which she'd never heard of.

But there is one tribe that Tsarin will never return to: the *u'óthi*. Half *u'óthi* herself—her mother had fallen for a northern dragon rider—she never felt safe about the southern tribe and their talent for necromancy.

But Nadeem is already waiting with the reins to a camel. The creature stands taller than she might have anticipated; the creatures almost feel larger down here, away from the furthest reaches of the world where the dragons roam. The gem-wrought isles have never felt so different from this land of sand and wavering horizons.

While the camel grunts at hearing her move close, she glances at Nadeem. The man barely spares her a glance. She had sent word ahead upon the back of a skitterdrack—a dragon the size of a canary and colour of the sands.

The vermillion markings over his chest mark him as a mute. Hesitant, he gestures for Tsarin to climb into the camel's saddle. A worn leather, it's soft against her thighs. But there are only two handholds. Sighing, Tsarin doesn't protest as one pair of her hands takes ahold of the handles, and the other pair loop over the bones curled about her neck in elaborate knots. The beads and seashells at her wrists jangle against the bone jewellery keeping her billowing gown anchored at her shoulders.

The desert wings are a gentle breeze over her freshly-shaved head.

Only when Nadeem turns to lead the camel does Tsarin notice his wings—or rather, his lack of. Poking out from beneath his shawl of faded red are stems from wings which could be nothing more than ripped from his spine. That explains the markings, the muteness. Tsarin would bet he has no tongue. He once betrayed his tribe; and has been stripped of what makes him *kehrasa*.

For the *kehrasa* peoples are nothing without their wings of darkest ebony or sunset hues. They are the flying death: assassins hired from all across the deserts to keep the people of their world safe. But there is one thing which makes the *kehrasa* even more dangerous. With their enchanted tongues, a *kehrasa* can steal the magic of whomever they slay.

Watching Nadeem closely, there doesn't seem to be anything specific about him. If he had managed to steal any magical talents from his victims, they would be marked on him as a warning to those who encounter him. But from what she can see of his chest and neck, there are no such talents to be wary of.

Even if there were, she doubts he would want to face an *u'óthi*, no matter her having only a small talent as a necromancer.

Behind them, Johari throws out their wings, stirring up the desert and casting them beneath the swiftest of storms. When the sands finally still, Tsarin and Nadeem are alone on the dunes. It won't take long until she reaches the most remote *kehrasa* tribe. She's only heard stories of them. To be wary is the main warning. Watch your back. And never reveal that dragon riders have more than two arms.

With water dragons, the dragon riders do not venture into the deserts. Their beasts lead them deep into the oceans, even to explore what lies beneath the ocean floor.

Not once does Nadeem look back at her, but she doesn't neglect to hide her third and fourth arms. Even perched at her collar bones, they remain invisible. If the *kehrasa* people think her two-armed, she will be dismissed as *u'óthi* and remain unchallenged. For if they see that she does not possess the six arms of her *numabi* dragon-riding sisters, then she may be in danger.

She is both, and yet neither.

People fear what is out of their knowledge.

And she was sent here to find something very certain.

'How much further?' she asks, forgetting for a moment her guide is mute.

A few minutes more, echoes a voice in her head. It's Nadeem, and it sends a spark of fear down her spine. Nowhere upon his ebony skin is he marked telepathic.

She sits upright in the saddle. 'Have you been listening in?'

I possess no more that power than I do of speech. The man looks back at her then. His eyes glimmer; at his mouth rests a smirk. *But you should know that your marks give you away.*

Her brow quirks. 'Which ones?'

Your scars, he says in her mind. *Only the u'óthi tribes are known for scarification across the face. I believe yours mark you as beautiful?*

He doesn't comment on the white skin over her cheeks and scattered over her arms. Perhaps he has seen others like her before.

A little hesitant, she nods.

Then you should not be nervous to meet the elders of my tribe.

Again, she nods. There's a tightness in her chest, unlike anything she's ever known. Of all the tribes she's met over the past twenty years, the *kehrasa* might finally be the ones to see through her illusion.

Perhaps that's what the prophecy always meant.

Before long, they're standing before the *kehrasa* elders on the outskirts of the tribelands. Their wings resting against their backs, they look like entirely different creatures from Nadeem. The guide bows his head and backs away once Tsarin dismounts. With the camel's rein in hand, he disappears from sight within moments. Not that the elders acknowledge him.

They're too busy staring at Tsarin. A line of scars runs up her cheekbones, drawing all attention to her onyx eyes. A stroke of red pigment over her nose and cheeks marks her rank amongst the dragon riders. She's a trusted member of their people, but what is she doing here?

The elders speak amongst themselves in a tongue Tsarin does not know. Their long hair is braided and spun into weighted ropes down their backs to rest between their wings. Fur peeks out from one of the women's faces as she looks Tsarin over. Fur—Tsarin remembers being told of this peculiarity. The *kehrasa* are the only faeries able to hide their truest features: naturally, their skin is the speckled fur of the cheetah.

Across the dunes, Tsarin spies a younger child resting on their back, wings brought up to obscure the wavering suns above. Their fur gleams in the light of the three orbs; their black-ended tail flicks contentedly.

The woman rolls her shoulders. Her wings a-flutter and she scrunches her nose, which morphs back into that of a mortal appearance. She lifts her red-stained fingertips to catch Tsarin's attention.

But Tsarin's eyes have alighted on a *kehrasa* girl peeking out from an underground tunnel. The girl's dug her hands into the side of the low retaining wall; and though she may think herself hidden, her raven black wings poking up from the ground. Thickly braided hair is swept back from her face, unlike some of the women who wear it draped in loops over their foreheads.

The girl's eyes shine like carnelian, like sunstone. Dozens of rings shine at her pointed ears—more pointed than the others', as if she may be of another tribe. But with the fur pushing up from under her skin, she is undeniably *kehrasa*.

Something inside the girl calls to Tsarin. She doesn't know who she might be, can hardly see more than half of her face, but there's something about her.

Without realising, she takes a step toward her, and the girl disappears for a moment. Her eyes are drawn to something beneath her—someone talking to her. Annoyance creases the girl's brow as she returns to spying.

Tsarin tips her head.

The girl's eyes go wide.

Then the elder trying to catch Tsarin's attention whistles. 'After your journey, you must be tired,' she says, quirking a brow when the dragon rider finally turns to her. The woman's eyes are dark as coal; they narrow. 'Everything is in place for tonight's celebrations for the equinox. Will you be feasting with us?'

The man beside her nods, keeping his hands clasped before him. A smile crinkles his kind face. 'We do not know what the *numabi* celebrate,' he says, making Tsarin's eyes shoot high. 'We saw your dragon,' he says by way of explanation, holding out those hands placatingly. 'We do not know... Do your people consume meat? Who is your patron?'

'We eat our grown reserves, and leave living flesh for our dragons,' she says slowly, casting her eyes over those gathered. Out the corner of her eyes, she's still aware of the girl who'd disappeared into the underground. 'And our patron is Ilori, the third sun.' She neglects to mentions that the third sun is a dragon rider herself.

She doesn't remember much more fo their interaction. She'd been too focussed on the girl who'd been dismally spying on her. The girl could simply not be an assassin. But her ears were looped with dozens of rings; one ring per every ten lives taken. So waif, so *young*. Could this be the bringer of death foretold?

From outside the tent, she can hear the drumming. Voices rise into the night that stretches on. And, as per *numabi* tradition, Tsarin only joins the celebrations of the equinox once the moon has reached her peak. Through the tent canvas, she watches the flickering orange light of the bonfire. It's built tall, the men rejoicing and bounding over the flames in single bounds.

The fresh pigment under Tsarin's eyes is cool against her skin. A bright red, it makes her dark eyes gleam. And she hopes the girl notices.

She takes a moment to still her nervous hands. As she runs two over the stiff canvas of the tent, the others go to the swath of cloth wrapped around her waist. Her yellow dress is the shade of sunset; the bones looped around her neck and trailing down her torso are carved from her first dragon, who'd perished in a battle with the u'óthi.

Running a hand over her head, she stills her nerves, and emerges from the tent. She's met by the cool sand underfoot. Before her, though her tent lays away from the underground homes surrounding the centre, she can see the size of the bonfire. Sparks ascend into the darkness. The crackle of the fire is gentle to the ear, the burning wood is heady, and she can almost taste the banquet's spices.

Dozens of voices rise as one, all working in harmony as she approaches the festivities. The song of their wings is louder than the crack and pop of the bonfire. Their midnight skin glints in the wavering orange light.

But even with all the distractions, even with all the darkness, Tsarin thinks she just might have found the girl. It's the rings at her ears that give her away. Thick braids trail down her back between her wings which don't seem to want to keep still. As if, though she does not dance, she wants nothing more than to move as one with the beat.

Just beyond the girl, younger faeries sway and leap, moving together about the flames. Their wings are ebony dark, glimmering onyx in the black—but some gleam with colour, hues jumping from their bodies like auras. There are some who bear no rings of victims; a curious thing, for a race of assassins. Then there are some like the girl, who cannot be missed with how the flames spark at the gold on their ears.

At their very centre dances a *kehrasa* Tsarin cannot place. An envy faerie twirls in the flames, their skin immune to the burns of the heat. Wild wings fan out, embracing the sparking light that follows their movements. Tsarin's never seen anything like it.

Slinking behind the backs of tents, she runs her hands over the stiff canvas. Tents which have stood here for years are softer to the touch, their canvas sun-bleached and worn smooth. The sand underfoot is soundless. The cries of the revellers are infectious. Tsarin knows the equinox marks a night without end: they will celebrate until the suns break. She knows her own people will be diving from the cliffs with their dragons at the northern-most isle of Rehmayan, the golden coasts of Ba'atu in sight. A smile lingers at her lips at the thought as she rounds the last tent.

The *kehrasa* girl leans forward on her knees, shovelling fruit into her face in a way that's somehow endearing. Her curious wide eyes are pinned on another woman about the fire. The other woman—younger than the girl, by the rings around her forearm—spins about her betrothed; their necklaces declare them as one. It must be a sister.

Still, the girl claps her hands in time with the beat of the drums. Her wings expand, shimmering in the light. And still, she wishes she could dance.

Catching a space about the bonfire, Tsarin leaps, tapping her feet and falling into groove with the dancers that reach for her. They grin, their mouths wide with joy. In the firelight, she hopes her lower arms remain invisible.

Spotting her turns, Tsarin catches sight of the girl. The girl who's now paused in her meal. She wipes her hands at her blouse, her biceps rippling. Tsarin wonders what they would feel like beneath her hands. *Stop it—* She shakes herself out of her mind as she kicks up her legs, finding the heat of the fire oh so close.

The girl's watching her still. Those eyes of gold glow, their slit pupils intoxicating. Before she can stop herself, Tsarin can feel her body drifting closer. Arms raised above her head, she watches as a pained look passes over the girl's face.

Her lower arms shimmer—the magic falls over her, soft and itchy as sand on the skin. Can this girl see through the illusion?

With the rings at her ears, she's killed hundreds. There is also the possibility she possesses hundreds of magical talents. The Sight could be one of those.

But still Tsarin moves to the drumbeats and wild calls. Her hips swaying, gyrating, her grin growing as she watches those about her celebrating. With her. There are so many bodies, so many dancers all moving as one. The flaming faerie in the centre of the bonfire rises into the night, their wings sparking with burning life. The cries of their people fill the darkness, alighting the night like the stars.

A gentle feeling builds in Tsarin's chest. She might never want to leave.

In the sand at her feet, the girl pushes up onto her knees. Tsarin crosses the space between them, only stopping when she stands before her, hand extended. 'Dance with me,' she purrs.

The *kehrasa* swallows, staring at her blankly.

Tsarin leans in close, so close she feels the girl's breath at her clavicle. 'Dance with me,' she says again, as the girl gingerly places her hand in hers.

In a second she's pulled to her feet, the girl stumbling into Tsarin's arms. Her wings rustle, feathers splaying as she catches her balance—her chest rubbing against the dragon rider's. Feathers brush Tsarin's fingertips. The girl in her arms flushes with warmth as Tsarin brings her in close. Those wings toss, stirring the sand at their feet, before the girl spins out of her grasp.

'Tsarin,' says she, the name falling from her lips.

The girl's eyes glitter black in the light. 'Qadira,' she says.

The name is soft on her tongue.

Bodies entwined and swaying, she lifts the girl—Qadira—off her feet. Swept from the sands, Qadira's raven wings catch the breeze. She throws out her arms and laughs, truly *laughs*. The way the joy beams in her features makes Tsarin catch her breath.

So it comes all too soon that Qadira's feet are back on the ground and she's moving away. Her eyes keep drifting over Tsarin's shoulder; Tsarin follows the look to find her staring at the woman with her betrothed. The woman is smiling, gesturing at the stranger amongst them. She only stops when she catches Tsarin watching. *The sister*, she reminds herself, shaking away what she might think was jealousy.

Again, Tsarin reaches a hand for the girl's waist.

But she keeps pulling away. A look Tsarin can't name crosses her face as she shakes her head. Those braids clatter over her shoulders, falling like cascades. The heat of her skin starts to feel like no more than a memory, a fleeting moment of bliss. Her touch is gone. And Qadira is turning away.

'I'm sorry,' she mumbles, brushing a hand back over her ears. Tsarin doesn't miss it when the girl drops her eyes to her arms—all four of them showing, in their patterns of black and white—reaching for her. 'I can't—I—' She shakes her head, and before Tsarin can speak, Qadira shadow-sings. Her form swirls before her in the space above the dunes, a flickering mass of shadow and sand that disappears into the night.

Tsarin's hands go cold. She won't forget the last look on Qadira's face, or that she was the cause of it. Does the girl think her a monster like everyone else?

Suddenly the celebrations feel all too much. The dancing flames, the swaying bodies, the leaping faeries who shoot into the sky on dark wings. Tsarin doesn't belong here.

And yet Qadira had made her want to stay.

*

In the early hours of the morn, Johari's cries reverberate across the dunes, shifting the sands. Tsarin had left the *kehrasa* tribe who celebrate on and on. Their music is so different to the dragon riders of the north.

The sands are cool as her feet sink into the dunes. The stars above wink in the dark swirling canvas of the abyss. The metallic sounds of Johari are growing closer. Yet her dragon is obedient; they have not moved from where Tsarin left that morn.

Date palm trees emerge from over the dunes in the distance. The slick dark green looks like oil under the moonlight. In the far-reaches of her hearing, Tsarin hears another pair of feet moving through the sands.

The magic spreads over her lower arms in seconds, concealing them from sight. It's itchy. Her sisters had warned her about that; she hasn't had to hide them much before, until her travels. She's still not used to it.

The white pigments of her skin glow in the moon's caressing light.

There's a cool breeze being swept from across the sea. It guides her toward the palm trees, and whether they're truly there, she can't be sure. When she had left Johari this morning, there hadn't been water nearby. If there had been, the water dragon would have found it. They would have sensed it.

But the desert is known for its shifting oases—and not in the way one might think. Mortals cannot access the plane in which these oases exist. To those few lucky mortals, this plane can be glimpsed, but like all magic it leads to their downfall. Faeries are lucky if they can approach an oasis without climbing over the bones of mortals who have fallen in the heat.

The scent of the pool wraps itself in her nostrils. She can already feel the wetness against her skin.

'Of course,' she hears someone grumble from a little ways behind her.

Tsarin glances back as she folds into he invisible planes. The magic spreads over her skin with a burning sensation; it tickles a moment before it becomes uncomfortable. Yet she sees the bones poking out from the sands which have shifted in the wings. A femur lays scattered from the rest of its skeleton—directly in the way of the approaching faerie's path. It's a *kehrasa*. Their wings cast deep shadows across their lands. Long braids sway with each step, but it could be anyone.

The bones skitter out of her way as the faerie moves closer. Tsarin is careful with her feet as she approaches the oasis. Anyone would panic at seeing footsteps appear in the sands of their own accord.

Yet the possibility of the *kehrasa* going to the oasis like Tsarin is small. The oases move; they might not know of its existence so close. But the bones could give it away.

When she reaches the top of the dune, she stares down into the oasis waiting. The shallow pool is hedged by low-standing pomegranate trees bowing with fruit.

Their rich red skin is smooth, glinting in the light reflected by the dark pool. It looks like a paradise, like home. The north of Rehmayan and Ba'atu are scattered with oases, with paradises across the coast full of crystal and glass.

Invisible to the creature, Tsarin feels their shadow fall over her. Yet when she glances back, their face is hidden in darkness. The winged faerie kicks up sand when they stretch their wings—and looks down at the same moment as Tsarin.

They sigh. 'I know you're there,' says the girl. It's Qadira. She reaches a hand for where Tsarin stands, finding her shadow is unable to reach the ground. Her fingers graze the exposed skin of Tsarin's back, sending shivers down her spine and turning her visible.

'Hi,' says Tsarin, hoping the girl won't drop her hand.

She smiles in an odd way. 'Hi.' The flickering life in her eyes tells Tsarin the girl hasn't slept with the celebrations still raging on. A frown crosses her brow. 'You have vitiligo.' She states the fact with an odd sound to her voice. 'I wasn't sure in the firelight if it was something else.'

No one's ever felt the need to comment on it before. She's not sure if she likes it. Tsarin wraps her arms around herself against the breeze and takes her first steps toward the oasis' pool.

'It's beautiful.'

She pauses mid-step. 'You think I'm beautiful?'

'You're...' Qadira closes the distance between them, reaching for her hand. 'Different. And I like that.' And before her eyes, Tsarin reveals her lower arms. The girl doesn't even blink. 'See?' She muses. 'Brilliant.'

Brilliant. The word echoes in her mind like it's some kind of magic. There's that draw to her again—a deep pull in her chest that stretches down to her stomach.

'You're different too,' she says, leading her down to the oasis with its crystal-still waters. 'You wear those rings in your ears where many in your tribe do not...' She lifts her eyes to Qadira's to find them staring back at her. They're full of curiosity and want.

'I like leaving this place, where others do not,' she explains. Qadira und a hand over Tsaein's shoulder, tracing where the white pigments of skin meet deep melanin.

'How many have you killed?'

The *kehrasa* drops her hand; her fingertips graze down her arm, scattering goose-bumps. Tsarin's never wanted someone's touch so much in her life.

When the girl doesn't answer, Tsarin disappears under the waters of the pool. The fresh water laps at her skin, washing away the paint over her shaved head.

Droplets catch in her lashes when she resurfaces, to find Qadira merely a breath away in the pool.

'Death comes on light wings,' she quotes, watching as Qadira's face changes.

Fur pokes through her water-soaked skin. The stretch of black below her eyes devours the dark hours of the morning. Her eyes gleam in the scattered light of the stars. 'Do you think I'll kill you?' Pulling her wings in tight to her back, she makes herself seem small. But there's no denying she can feel the draw between them.

Tsarin watches her a while. When she finally speaks, she makes Qadira jump. 'No,' she says, with a tone not all together sure. The girl before her is an assassin who kills to escape her world, after all.

'Two hundred and eleven,' Qadira says, drawing her eyes up to the stairs. 'Two hundred and eleven kills. Only thirteen gifts stolen, and not many of them useful.'

The dragon rider nods slowly. She lifts her shoulders out of the water. The bones of her jewellery sing, their hollow sound like music. Her dress sticks to her skin, exposing her taut form. A muffled sound sits at Qadira's lips as Tsarin moves closer, stopping only a breath from her mouth.

'Then I wonder what becomes my undoing,' she purrs, and before she knows it, Qadira reaches for the dragon rider to pull her closer. Her lips taste like pomegranate juice. They're soft, warm, intoxicating. Qadira shakes her Tsarin's arms; her wings envelop them, hiding them from the stars watching.

And when she pulls away, Tsarin is breathless. Qadira's lashes flutter. She bites her lip when they press their foreheads together to share breath between lungs.

Tsarin can't stop the smile that makes her lips twitch. 'Come with me to the sea,' she says, running a hand over Qadira's shoulders to rest between the crest of her wings. The soft feathers caress her fingertips. Her lips were so soft, she wants to kiss her again.

The breeze dries the water at Qadira's face. The fur peeking through caresses Tsarin's nose, making her want to laugh. Qadira breathes deep, and nods. 'I've never seen the ocean.'

The way Johari flies feels like the night is forming itself about them, swirling and becoming something new that only they will ever see. The wind in Qadira's wings makes her want to fly—to soar across the desert, at one with her land.

The deserts below feel suddenly so small. Qadira's never flown this high before; her wings aren't strong enough against these winds.

But sitting before her in the dragon's saddle is Tsarin, and Tsarin never wants to forget the feeling of Qadira's arms around her.

The closer they come to the coast, the fresher the air becomes. The salt from the sea becomes all they can smell. And Johari beneath them glitters like crystal, their scales hard as titanium. They radiate the arctic, though Johari exhales boiling water instead of fire. The water dragon grows faster, faster, faster. They bullet through the sky, slithering like a salamander.

The coast stretches out before them as the suns climb the sky. Hues of brilliant ruby and amber streak across the canvas of Abrecan. Johari ducks, sweeping down into the bite of the cliffs. Qadira screams in exhilaration, gripping Tsarin tight. They pull up seconds before they hit the water.

Qadira's wings fan out the same moment as Johari's. Only Tsarin's hands on Qadira's keep her upon the dragon's back.

Johari weaves through the standing rock formations at high-speed. The red sunlight dances off the ocean's surface as it crashes against the rocks. It glows, full of magic and the creatures of the deep. It's unlike anything Qadira's ever imagined.

Magic spark soft the water. The salty sea air feels trapped in Qadira's braids, filling her chest with calm.

Before her, Tsarin leans back and raises her arms. Her cries of freedom echo off the rock walls.

They cry out together.

This is different. Tsarin has felt free before, but always alone.

As she brings down her arms, she pulls Qadira's arms tighter around her middle. The *kehrasa*'s laughing. She leans into Tsarin's shoulder as the dragon rider looks back at the land disappearing behind them. Qadira's eyes swim as if drunk.

Her wings cry out to fly, to soar above the waters she's never before known. The desert is all she knows. But it is not all there is.

There is more out there in the world. And she wants to see it all.

***

ACKNOWLEDGEMENTS

I have to start by thanking my parents, who always believed in me more than I did. Thank you for instilling in me a love for musical theatre, epic fantasy, and reading. To Mum, for always letting me vent about imposter syndrome, no matter how it drove you insane —and to Dad, who kept me strong when I couldn't myself. Your bear hugs were never needed more than through this journey.

To my sister, who shows me what strength is every day.

To my closest friends, Darcy Foster and Cassandra Schilling, I owe so much to you. Thank you for the archery dates, the unnecessary fries just for the sake of fries, and all the Dungeons and Dragons. I love you two with my whole heart; may I be there every step along the way as you achieve your dreams, as you always have for me.

To the first readers and cheerleaders, you absolute *champions*, who kept my passion strong for this project —Hira Chaudhary, Romane Nguyen, Ash Pietersma, Ellan F., Regan Aarons, Amelia Hughes, Sanuja Fernando, Carrie Wee, Karina Ward, and Gioia

Rodriguez. Your feedback, friendship, and motivation has meant so much to me. Your constant questions about Abrecan kept me exploring this land I'd built. I could not thank you enough; without all your love for my world, this book may not exist.

To my incredible cover designer and illustrator, Sylvia Bi. You have done so much to bring my vision to life. I can't explain how I cried when I saw your work of Abrecan and my characters. Thank you.

And to the most important of all: my future wife Salsabil Hafiz. To say this book would not exist without you is no exaggeration. We have been through a lot these last few years, and we are so much the stronger for it. You have lost so much. But I promise you: we will make our own family, together. Thank you for the midnights debating plot holes over hot chocolates or chai, the carb-heavy breakfasts to keep me working, and always understanding my needs when writing. This book is for you.

ABOUT THE AUTHOR

Kerrie Koop

J. R. Koop is Jasmine Rose Koop, a demisexual lesbian who wears hearing aids. She started writing at twelve; the first dream of Abrecan came at fourteen. Since, she has written over nine books set in this world. She holds a BA in Creative Writing from Flinders University in Adelaide, South Australia, where she lives with her fiancée and their ever-growing library. This is her debut novel.

You can find her on social media and at her website writtenbyjrkoop.blog.

Illustrations are by Sylvia Bi (sylviabiart.com).